AMERICAN WIDOW

by

Ketty W. Johnson

©1983 Lingonberry Press
Printed in the United States of America
Published by Lingonberry Press
622 Locust Road
Sausalito, California 94965

ISBN 0-9611666-0-6
Library of Congress card number 83-90409

*This book is dedicated
to my father and mother,*

*Erik Oskar Wangman and
Anna Lisa Skomars Wangman*

who made the book live.

* * * * *

*And to Betty Dinneen,
without whom it
could not have been
published.*

Appreciation

I would like to thank Violeta Autumn for the lovely drawing of Ketty, Mary Alexander Walker for the design for the
book jacket, the Marin Writers' Group, the San Francisco
Writers' Group and all Ketty's friends for their support and
encouragement which made this book possible.

                                          Elmer E. Johnson

April, 1983

American Widow

Contents

Sweden

The sun warmed the earth in northern Sweden. It searched out the red boards of a group of one-story, two room *stugas* beneath the green boughs of pine trees. It dappled the paths leading from the houses to a clearing at a community pump. The shadow of a sawmill touched the wide lane that led from the pump to a mud road skirting the lumber yard.

It was an hour into the twelve-hour work day that began at six o'clock. Yet the sawmill was deserted. The river behind it ran empty of its usual rich burden of logs from the headwaters. It flowed free, spilling its freshness into the Gulf of Bothnia. The shouts of men out on the booms poling logs on the rippled surface were gone. Abandoned logs on land lay crisscrossed on the run up from the river. No man positioned one into the eager whine of a saw. The clear air was innocent of the pitch-pine smell of logs being ripped into long slabs. Thin smoke, rising through the trees from each *stuga* chimmey, added a sense of tranquility.

In all of Sweden, that day in August of 1909, this quiet was repeated. Everyone knew that the many lockouts and scattered strikes of the past months had ended. A new kind of peace reigned in the land. All working men everywhere were staying at home and there was no one to take their place. A general strike had begun and was now into its third day.

Lisa Veldman stood in the open door of the bedroom of the third *stuga* in the rough semi-circle of buildings. As she looked out through the main room and short vestibule to the community pump she saw three of her daughters. Marta, the five-year-old, stood near her, naked after a bath. Maria, working at polishing a pair of old brown shoes, sat on the top step of the two that led into the house. Beyond her, at the pump, Emilia staggered as she lifted the copper bathing tub she had rinsed to carry it upside down on her head. About to object, Lisa stopped as Maria turned suddenly and spoke to Marta.

"Shame on you," she cried, "standing there for everyone to see. Is that the way you are going to behave when you live at the Palmers? Get back out of the doorway."

Maria shook the shoe off her arm into the steps and disappeared in a flash of long skirts and bare feet. She was off to the toilet house again, Lisa realized, to hide her feelings. At the age of nine it was hard to accept the realities of life. Emilia dropped the tub. Lisa shook her head. She would speak to her, but not this morning. A child had to be strong and well fed to lift such a heavy thing so high. The arms and back of a half-starved eight-year-old should not be put to such pressure. It was enough that Marta's bones were weak and that her body showed so plainly the result of meager meals.

Emilia strained her way up the steps and into the *stuga*. She set the tub down, her face as red as her hair, then stormed over to her small sister. "Didn't you hear what Maria said?" she demanded. With a jerk she pulled Marta away from the door, then flung herself into the big rocking chair to sit and glare at her naked sister.

"Marta," Lisa called. The child ran quickly back onto the bathing blanket spread over the rag rugs. She hung her head, waiting to be scolded, and rubbed her hands over the washboard bumps of her ribs. Lisa sat down and drew her gently toward her.

"Aiy, yaiy, my little boney one," she said. Marta grinned, first at her sister in the rocking chair, then at another one who worked at the end of the long table near the stove. Paulina, Emilia's twin, was Lisa's "best worker" and had been given the hardest job to do. Marta watched her step down off the small stool and go to the stove, exchange one iron for another, then return to step back up and smooth it over the pinafore stretched flat on thick cloths spread over the table.

"Did you do the bottom yet?" she called. Lisa knew she was anxious about the embroidery there.

"It's going to be so pretty," Paulina answered, looking up with a smile. Marta wriggled.

"It doesn't happen to many little girls, Marta, like it is happening to you," Lisa said, and spoke with the voice she used when speaking of the New Kingdom. "Palmers are very fine people, asking us to let you come to live with them during the strike. They will help you in many wonderful ways."

Marta leaned against her knees to listen and stepped into the underpants held out in front of her. Lisa wondered how much she understood. She knew the child had been puzzled to have a bath in the morning, and that neither her sisters, her brother, nor even the baby, had bathed in the same water before it had been thrown out of the big copper tub. "Dear God," she prayed quietly. "Let it not be too late to strengthen the child's bones."

"Can *Tant* Palmer bake *knäkebröd?* Marta asked, twisting to look up, where wheels of that hard bread hung under the ceiling, on the pole that pierced their large center holes.

"Ack," Lisa answered, turning the child around to fasten the front of the pants to the button waist. "I'm sure she can, but she has people in her house who do these things for her. They make coffee bread with sugar on top, thick soups with egg dumplings, meatballs, gravy and potatoes. Remember you must eat whatever is set before you."

Marta sat down to pull on the red ribbed stockings Lisa had handed her. Emilia began to swing wildly in the rocking chair. Her feet were pressed tightly against the cross piece that connected the extra long curved rockers in front. She slammed herself backward to make the chair rock far up onto similar long rockers in back. Marta watched, her face betraying that she longed to be there with Emilia.

"Is *farbror* Palmer Pappa's brother like Evert?" she asked suddenly.

"Nay. You must know that, Marta. A child calls a grown up man, *farbror,* as though he was father's brother, if he is a friend of the family; just like a woman friend must be called *tant* by children."

Marta was silent, then suggested, "Let's ask *tant* and *farbror* Palmer to come here to live."

Emilia did not given Lisa time to answer. She stopped the rocker, set both feet on the floor, and holding the chair over her in an arc, called, "Hoo, hoo, Marta, where would they sleep?"

Marta stood up, hands on her hips. "With Mamma and Pappa," she stated.

With another hoot her sister flung herself backward into the rocker, her bare legs and skirt swinging wildly.

"Did you hear that?" she demanded, laughter almost swallowing the words.

"She's still little, she doesn't know," Paulina began, holding the iron poised over the pinafore, but got no further before her individual laugh, nyeh, nyeh, nyeh, joined Emilia's peals.

"That will do," Lisa silenced them. "Is the pinafore ready?"

"Nay, Mamma," came the hurried answer, "there is just a little more to do."

"Come," Lisa ordered the rocking chair rider. "Braid Marta's hair." She stood up and watched Paulina iron. She reached for the small straw whisk that lay in a bowl of water on the table.

"Wait a little," she ordered Paulina. "This edge has become too dry." She shook the whisk over the bowl. Then, with long strokes, brushed the edge of the pinafore. "Now, if you get a fresh iron, it will finish up very nicely." She moved on to the open door. "Yah so. Maria!" she called.

Bare feet pounded alongside the house and on to the step. Maria entered the room, the two shoes swept up into her hands. She held them up for Lisa's inspection. Her small sensitive face asked for approval.

"Pappa mended the holes," she said, "but, no matter how much I rub or spit, the tops still look worn."

"Ack! You did very well, and thanks you shall have," Lisa answered. She sighed and shook her head. "If only they don't hurt her. It is a long walk to Palmers. Give them to her. No, wait. Find a good pair of wool stockings for her too."

"But, Mamma, this is summer," Maria protested.

"I know, but heavier stockings over the ones she has on might make the shoes fit more comfortably."

Maria held the shoes at arm's length, one in each hand, twirled in circles across the room to a round top trunk under a window, and dropped gracefully in front of it to search in it for the stockings.

Lisa went outside, her head down to avoid seeing any neighbor who might be out this early. She made her way around the *stuga,* and found a spot where she could lean unseen against the back of the house. Fists clenched beside her hips she beat the boards of the building behind her, eyes shut, whipping her head from side to side. She stopped. Her soft round chin beneath her hollow cheeks and tightly shut mouth lifted in inner pain to the overhanging boughs of pine. She pushed herself tight against the house, the rough vertical boards catching at her hair like punishment. On other days her hair was strictly parted and slicked back smoothly into a tight bun. Out of his love for her Oscar found golden glints in it, but she always denied this, calling her hair an everyday brown. This morning it was uncombed and showed the restlessness of a sleepless night. It betrayed she had not taken time to undo the nighttime braid, but had pinned it into a loose knot at the back of her head. There had been no time for brush or comb before Oscar left to walk to the village to get the latest news of the strike.

Too thin for her thirty-eight years, she was engulfed by her dark skirt that served her everyday, even through the times of her pregnancies. The cord threaded through its top was pulled tight, the many folds of the skirt thickening her waist.

As she let her thoughts flow red spots appeared on her high cheek bones. How she would like to explode. Scream her feelings up into those branches. But she had to be calm, for the children's sake, and Oscar's. She would think instead how grateful they all had to be to God that a local strike had never taken place at this sawmill. Was she being disloyal to Oscar in thinking this? Oscar, chosen as spokesman by the sawmill workers, was never given the opportunity to go to Director Elwig to announce the unanimous strike vote taken by the workers in late spring; it had become evident Elwig had his source of information. Before Oscar could walk from the *stuga* to the sawmill, the morning following that secret meeting, Elwig had begun the lockout. It had been simply done. The big iron key, never used all the years it hung on its nail outside the main sawmill door, had disappeared. The tightly locked door announced to Oscar and the men who had all walked with him that they were locked out. The shrill of the sawmill whistle that called them to work had not sounded again since that day.

It had almost made her wish for the resurrection and the coming of the New Kingdom. Ah, but that was useless thinking. It was in God's own good time that the horn would be blown. Yet, how grateful she was that strife had not come to the sawmill as it had in other places, or to Oscar. Through the summer there had always been hope each morning that the key would be back on its hook. The general strike proclamation, announced in Stockholm three days ago, had ended that hope.

How long, dear God, would it last? Marta must have better and more food. The other children too. Children everywhere were growing bent with soft bones. Fathers needed more pay.

"Dear God, it is too hard to send her away. Do I sin in wishing the strike over and done with, no matter the outcome?"

Her hands slapped the boards behind her and stayed splayed out against the wood, her eyes wide, mouth pursed up in distaste at her thought.

"Nay, I must not even think of such a thing. It is a sin against my own family, against Oscar. The strike must go on until it is won."

But why was it that one of God's laws was understood by her, and by Oscar, but not by the Palmers? On one point their church interpreted God's will as they did. She knew that well. She had been raised in that church. Yet the Palmers, who could afford many, had but one child. As old as her eldest, Elvira, he was, and off to Stockholm to get higher schooling. Was there a law saying those who had so little must have many children, and those who could afford them could choose the number?

The anger that had stiffened her subsided.

"Forgive me, Lord, I do not mean my eight are not dear to me, nor that I no longer mourn the two we lost. Each one was as dear as life as soon as they were conceived. But why one for Palmers and ten for me?"

She began to pace back and forth. "No wonder Herr Palmer could come offering to take one child for the duration of the strike from any family with the most children. The Fredericksons wouldn't let one of theirs go, and Frida Gabrielson clutched hers around her as if the Devil himself had made the invitation. What a shame it is to have so many you can't care for them. Is that part of God's will? I blaspheme, I know I do, but I want no more. Is it wrong to wish for no more?"

Tears ran. She jerked a rag out of the pocket of her skirt and pushed it roughly across her face.

"I stand here sniveling like Alli," she muttered. "That's no help to Marta. Maria is not alone, it seems, in the need to face reality."
She hurried back into the house. As she stepped up the stairs she heard the girls' voices raised in angry argument.

"So they exploded too," she marveled. As she entered, all movement and voices ceased. The children stared at her. Emilia clung to Marta's braid, the blue yarn that was to fasten it in her other hand. Maria, alongside, had a face as red as Emilia's. Their mouths had only just closed over the shouts of anger. Marta, one hand reached back to jerk her braid from Emilia's grasp, was twisted around. In front of the three stood four-year-old Alli, the brown shoes clasped tightly to her chest. Beside her, on the floor, was a large green knitted bag Lisa had sent her to fetch some time past.

"What goes on here?" Lisa demanded, and received so many answers she had to shush them all. "Alli," she said. "Why are you holding the shoes like that?"

"Mine," Alli answered, her large blue eyes thick with tears.

"Yaw, we said they were to be yours," Lisa answered, "but last night Pappa decided Marta should wear them to Palmers."

Alli's eyes overflowed and her lower lip thrust forward ready for a full cry.

Her voice gentle, Maria said, "See, didn't I tell you?"

"But, Mamma," Marta began, "the black ones are mine."

"Come, both of you."

Marta yanked her braid free and ran to burrow her face against Lisa's skirt. Alli, still carrying the shoes, ran to hide herself alongside.

"Shh, shh," Lisa encouraged, as they pressed against her. She took each child by the shoulder and led them to the long bench at the table where she had them sit. "You both know that when winter comes those who are old enough to wear shoes must take the ones that fit them best. This year we thought you two might start to use the twins' old shoes we've been saving. We said Emilia's black ones were to be yours, Marta, but Paulina's are smaller and not so worn. Alli, won't you let her take the brown ones today? It would help her to have smaller ones to walk that long distance. I will stuff the toes of the black ones and you can start weaaring them as soon as you like...Help Mamma and Pappa, won't you?"

After a moment Alli nodded.

"Marta?" Lisa asked.

Marta took the shoes from her sister's yielding hands. Lisa smiled. "Now I have two more big girls," she said, and gave them each a soft spank as they got down from the bench. "Go and ask your sister, nicely, to finish braiding your hair. Alli, go set a bowl on the table, that's my fine girl."

She left them to go into the bedroom. When she returned she carried the baby on her hip. Johan trailed behind her to stumble sleepily out into the center of the room. He seemed tall for being only three years old but it was because he was so thin. His handed-down underwear hung loose except across his enlarged stomach. One hand clutched at his penis, the other further disordered the straight sticks of his dark blonde hair as he scratched his head.

"Paulina, take Johan out to the toilet. I can see he needs to go right away. Go, child. Paulina will wash and dress you when you come back."

In quick decision she went to the cupboard and reached for a small wooden *firken* that stood at the very top. Sitting down, she held it slightly tilted in her lap while she beat the yogurt in it into a smooth thickness, using a large wooden spoon. Marta drew close, as did the others. Lisa knew they understood that food was only for mealtimes, but they dared to hope. She stood up, pulled the one bowl up on the table toward her and poured several thick splashes into it, cutting off the flow with a quick scrape of the spoon.

"Go get your spoon," she told Marta, "and stand right here to eat this."

Marta hurried to an upright beam against the wall where short diagonal slots held the hand-carved wooden spoons of the family. Hers was third from the bottom. After each meal she licked her spoon clean, like everyone else did, and placed it back in the slot. Oscar's was highest; baby Carl's the lowest.

"Tie a towel in front of her, somebody." A towel was draped in front of Marta and tied with a big knot at the back of her neck. She ladled the yogurt into her mouth rapidly. Even when Lisa took the yellow mugs banded with black and white checks froom the cupboard and measured a small amount into each one, Marta did not stop. When the *firken* was empty except for a starter for the next batch, the mugs were tipped high into the hungry mouths of the four sisters and one brother. Maria alternated between drinking from her mug and tipping it into the eager mouth of the baby.

"It's so good of Herr Palmer to send us milk, isn't it, Mamma?" Paulina remarked as she watched Lisa fill the *firken* again with a thick flow from a large tin container.

"Don't sound like an idiot," Emilia flared, her upper lip still laced with yogurt. "He sends it to everybody here at our sawmill, not just to us."

Maria added, "Ever since the beginning of the lockout he's done it, hasn't he, Mamma?"

"And will until the strike is won, he tells your Pappa," Lisa answered.

"His store must make him rich," Maria marveled.

"Agda said his mamma has very much money." this came from Marta who had been sent to sit on a stool to keep herself neat.

"His mamma?" both twins whirled around to ask.

Emilia continued with scorn. "He doesn't have a mamma. He only has a wife. She's going to be your Tant Palmer."

"Agda Swanson doesn't know anything," Emilia insisted, spit flying from the corners of her mouth. "Agda's not much older than you are."

"Never mind," Lisa interrupted. "Small ears are not alone in not understanding what they hear." She stirred the milk to make sure the starter was well distributed, then lifted the *firken* up on top of the cupboard. "It's true *Fru* Palmer brought money into that marriage," she told the children, "but it is their money now. Just like Pappa's money, when the sawmill is working becomes our money when he brings it home."

"*Fru* Palmer probably wants us to win the strike too," Paulina commented, "then she can send Marta home and we can buy our own milk the way Pappa wants to. Isn't that so, Mamma?"

Her back to the children, Lisa frowned as she nodded in answer. Was it so? Did that fine lady understand the strike the way her husband did? She banged the milk container down into its corner, the exaggerated effort givng her some ease from her thoughts.

Why was it taking so long for Oscar to come back this morning? Had the railroad vote gone wrong? She went to the window. A few men had gathered near the sawmill, but the road to the village was empty.

She shooed the older girls to go make the beds. Thinning out yesterday's oatmeal with a scoop of water from the water barrel she set it to heat against Oscar's return. Already reheated this morning for the children's breakfast it was more soup than cereal now. It would have to do. Stirring it, she thought of Paulina's remarks. Oscar had learned nothing about *Fru* Palmer. Herr Palmer had never spoken of his wife to him. Neither Oscar nor Lisa had ever seen her, although it was impossible not to have heard that she was from Stockholm's fine folk, a family of large wealth. As for Palmer, Lisa felt she knew him first because they had bought shoes from his shop, and second from Oscar's reports. Throughout the summer Palmer had often come from town to be among the men who had taken to congregating alongside the sawmill ever since the first day of the lockout. From the distance through her window, or when she went to the pump, she had observed him. His well-dressed form was easily recognized among the other men. Sometimes he sat with them for hours in the grass that had grown so tall around the sawmill. How Oscar loved the debates that took place then. Full of talk when he came home, he brought a renewed spirit too. The other men accepted Palmer also, at first not sure how to talk with an employer in their midst. There was laughter, and sometimes shouts when the discussion reached some heated point. No one disturbed them, except an occasional wanderer.

Lisa's thoughts turned to the many hundreds of unemployed men who wandered all over Sweden. They hed been out of work since long before either lockout or strike. If the times were hard for those who had been working until the lockout, it was even worse for these men and their families, she knew. Yet no man walked through the group to knock on the sawmill door seeking an absent Herr Elwig. During the lockout they had known no boss was hiring. Now, as the strike closed down every industry, their numbers were not enough to set them all operating efficiently again. Oscar had pointed this out to her. The bosses made no effort to hire them. The silence of factories, mines and sawmills, guarded by sunning strikers, kept them away, or drew them to sit and talk in their midst.

Lisa drew comfort from what Oscar said.

"The only way there will be more jobs is when all working men get more pay. Then they can buy the things they need. Someone will have to make those things. That's where jobs will come from. Making clothes, shoes, books, furniture, even bicycles."

Lisa smiled. Oscar and his dream of having a bicycle. Maybe he would, some day. Only good could come out of winning this strike, she told herself. That they had come to know Palmer was part of that good.

Again she went to the window. Oscar was there. Men were hurrying from the *stugas* to join the group. What had he learned? She could not understand the reaction to what Oscar seemed to have to retell many times. Had the railroad vote gone wrong? The men seemed to be puzzled at what Oscar said. It couldn't be bad because some of them were smiling. She went to the door and stepped out. Greta Swanson was standing outside on her own stoop, straining her eyes and ears toward the men.

"What do you suppose happened?" she asked. "It had to be either a yaw or a nay vote."

"I wonder," Lisa answered. "Here they come. I've got to get back to watch the coffee. I put it on to heat. Girls," she called as she re-entered the house. "Pappa is here. Bring that other pair of underwear I made smaller for Marta and the other things I had laid out on one of the beds. Alli, go pick the knittting bag off the floor. The idea, leaving it there all this time. Marta has to carry her things in it."

Oscar came in, hung his cap on a wooden peg by the door and came to sit in his chair at the end of the table.

"Evert, Gus and I agree about one thing," he began as he picked up the steaming mug of coffee Lisa set before him. He drew a quick swallow through a lump of sugar he had put into his mouth, wiped his hand across his newly-clipped moustache and began again. "We agreed this must be the first time in the history of the world that a whole nation of workers has gone out on strike."

Surprised, Lisa said, "I can't believe you three forgot the national strike six or seven years ago."

"Nay. That was political. A strike to get the vote,and it lasted only three days. We mean this one. When it ends we hope there will be better pay for every worker in the land."

As if his answer told her what she wanted to know, she said, "So the railroad workers voted to join?"

"Yaw and nay," Oscar answered, and flung the last of the coffee into his mouth, draining the mug.

"What do you mean?" Lisa asked, and added automatically, "you shouldn't drink your coffee down while it's so hot."

He ignored her familiar remark. "I mean the railroad workers voted to go on working..." Lisa gasped. "...and instead will give a percentage of their pay to support the strike."

"They're going to do what? Give some of their money? How?" Lisa asked.

Maria, standing next to Oscar with Carl in her arms, asked, "Are they going to give you money, Pappa?"

"Nay, not money. Food."

"What's that? They are going to give food?" Lisa's voice was sharp. She thrust her way past the children, who had all gathered around Oscar, to look more directly at him. "For everybody? For us too?"

"Of course. They voted to use the funds to buy food for every striker's family. Figured the food had to come from somewhere, we were told, and they would benefit the strike more this way."

"Why, how wonderful, Oscar," Lisa sat down on the bench near him, and began to smile. She stopped. "Why do you look like that? Can't you see what this means to us?"

He shook his head. "You are like Evert, Lisa. You don't see what it really means. Gus saw it. With that vote we think the strike has been lost."

"Nay, what are you saying Oscar? Nay! How can that be?"

Oscar could no longer sit still. He got up and paced a few steps back and forth, scattering the children to hurry to find seats on the benches, or the day bed, out of the way. Frowning deeply, sometimes worrying his hair with one hand or the other, he continued. "The bosses have stockpiles of lumber, iron ore, every product they ship. They can go right on sending it off, making as much money as before. They'll feel no pinch at all. They've seen this coming for a long time with all the smaller strikes in other places and took care to be ready. Nay, that vote was wrong." He flashed long angry glances at her each time he turned on his heel.

For a while Lisa could find nothing to say. Then getting up to fill a bowl with cereal and urge him to sit and eat, she said, "Your brother Evert sees things pretty clearly most times. Couldn't it be he might be right? You and Gus Swanson might be too pessimistic. If we have plenty to eat we can last until we win."

"Not as long as the bosses can. Their money will never run out," he answered, waving his arms as if all the money were stacked right there in plain sight.

"Well, it is for you to say, but in the meantime we will have more food here in this house. That's my concern and happiness. Marta can stay home."

This brought him to stand still , staring at her. He stepped over to face her. "You think a few more potatoes, several scoops of oatmeal, and a few more herring are going to do for the girl what the cream, butter and fresh fruit of the Palmers will do? Nay, Lisa, the girl must go. Is she ready?"

Blindly setting the cereal pot back onto the stove, Lisa stared around at the children as if seeking help from them. Then she turned and hurried into the bedroom. She heard Oscar tell the older girls to watch the younger ones, and the sounds of steps told her he was following her.

There was little space for them to stand in the second room of the *stuga.* Three large beds, a floor-to-ceiling white tile stove, and a large wardrobe filled it, for the room was no larger than the first. Of necessity they stood close together, face to face.

"You don't even give it a second thought," Lisa accused, trying to speak so that her words would not go beyond the closed door. "You, who are so concerned about sending her into a home that preaches the gospel of the church and the catechism, instead of God's word as we read it directly from the Bible. You should be eager to keep her home now. Wait a little," she added more calmly, as he was about to speak. "We don't know how much food will come, I agree, but maybe enough. Let's wait and see."

"Lisa, stop and think."

Eyes closed, she lifted her face angrily toward the ceiling. From between her teeth she murmured, "Dear God, help me keep my child at home."

"Do not take God's name in vain, or pray in anger," Oscar demanded.

"In vain?" she spat, glaring at him. "It is a prayer I have been saying, uselessly, a hundred times a day."

"Nay, Lisa, you go too far. No prayer is lost. Remember this is not of God's doing, but of man's."

She dug into her pocket for a rag and held it up to her eyes with both hands. Oscar pulled her to him and waited until she relaxed against him. Their touchstone was the Bible, but he still had to be patient with her after all these years. It had taken her longer to unlearn the teachings of the established church.

"You are right, dear Lisa," he began, his voice a warm low rumble as he held her. "I have worried that our child will learn different values, but she won't be there long. I know that now. Besides, we have taught her well. She has heard the reading, the truth from the Bible here at home all her life. She's been present at every Ephriam's Messengers meeting we've attended ever since she was born, just like the others. I have faith she will take no harm, but trust instead she will get a better start toward health by leaving us for a while."

He waited.

"She is only five years old," Lisa argued, but in a whisper.

"You would deny her health?"

"Nay....nay." Her answer was almost lost as she nestled her head against him. He pressed it to him with one hand and tightened his other arm around her.

"Together we will do what needs to be done to help each of our children. This is a hard thing we do, but we do it because we must."

He lifted her chin and kissed her softly. She raised a hand and touched his moustache with gentle fingers.

"I'll be glad when it grows out again," she murmured. "It prickles. But I know *Fru* Palmer will be impressed. You look handsome."

He grinned and pulled her to him again. They kissed once more before she stepped away and went to the wardrobe to take his Sunday hat from on top of it. "Will you want your cane too?" she asked.

"Nay," he answered, although he had never worn the formal hat without carrying the cane, the one luxury he had allowed himself in all the years. "Remember, Lisa," he said, stepping over to place his hands on her shoulders. "If the strike lasts too long I will find work somehow, even if I have to go far to find it. Then Marta shall come home immediately."

"Nay!" she cried, "I could not bear it if you left us. You cannot mean you would go to America?"

"Lisa! I had no such thought."

"Where else could you go to find work? Not here in Sweden. You, with only one year of schooling, what could you find to do other than the sawmill work you've always done?"

"True, although I feel I could learn anything to do with machinery. I know I could. But this is useless talk right now. All I want is for you to know I will do anything that is right in the eyes of God to take of you and the children."

This time she reached to pull his head down for a kiss.

"I know that so well," she told him, and smiled into his eyes. "Let's say no more." Her hand bumped his side pocket. "Nay, you are not to take this book with you. You will start reading as you walk, like you always do, and forget that Marta is with you."

"You know me so well?" he laughed.

"I know you so well," she answered, and nodded toward the door. He reached for the handle, but she stopped him with, "Wait. Are my eyes red?"

He bent to peer into them and said, "A little, but not too much."

"The children must be wondering," she said, as she stepped toward the open door.

*

It was as Lisa thought. The anxious children faced the bedroom door. There was much she needed to say to reassure them, but instead she found herself on her knees in front of Marta, Oscar's hat on the floor.

"You are to go with Pappa now," she said. "He will take you to *Tant* and *Farbror* Palmer. Remember you must always be a good girl and do just as they say." She pulled at the hem of Marta's long skirt and straightened out the collar around her neck. "When there is work at the sawmill again, you will come back home. Remember that always, Marta."

Marta nodded. Lisa looked at her a long time. She picked up the hat, held onto the table and pulled herself up. She took a clothes brush that hung on the wall, and brushed the hat. "Where is the bag with her things?" she asked, and handed the hat to Oscar. She took Marta by the hand and led her to the door. Oscar stepped through first, and the rest hurried after him. They gathered in a clump before the step. Alli came last to lift the knitted bag high, reaching it up to Oscar. Lisa stooped as she tied a kerchief over Marta's hair.

"Eat what they set before you, and don't forget to say thank you." she told the girl softly, then said, "Go now."

Marta walked over to Oscar. Maria thrust the baby into the arms of the dark-haired twin and took Marta by the shoulder.

"Here," she said, "you can have this." She extended a small piece of lace. Before Marta could say, "For me?" Maria was gone, running toward a big pine tree beyond the house, where she had a playhouse under the dark branches that hugged the ground, forbidden to anyone else unless invited. Lisa placed a hand over her mouth. Maria's gesture was as moving to her as to the child who stood studying the bit of lace, so prized by her older sister.

Oscar cupped the back of the child's head with his hand and urged her forward. She stepped along, the lace clutched tightly as she turned to call "Goodbye."

Paulina, the twin holding the baby, stood bent to one side. Carl's weight was almost more than she could manage. Emilia had climbed on top of the big stone along the pathway, her red hair bright in the midmorning sun.

Alli had walked part way down the path and stood waving one hand high above her. Johan sat on the step eating a piece of *knäckbröd* someone had given him.

Lisa saw them all, yet the child walking away from her filled her whole being. The shoes, the toes already curled upward because there was emptiness in them, were like an accusation. She felt numb, could not take her hand away from her mouth for fear she would call, "Come back! Oscar, bring her back!" She moaned inwardly as Marta turned around when they reached the pump, her large smile telling her sisters and brothers, "Look, I'm walking with Pappa. I'm going to Palmers."

Emilia, still up on the rock, cupped her hands and shouted, "Be sure you get to sit on the seat that has running water when you peepee."

Oscar turned at that. Emilia jumped down quickly, and flew home, her bare heels flinging her skirt high.

Up to the quiet sawmill and down the mud road the two continued. Marta hopped a few skipping steps. The skirt of her dark blue serge dress, below the pinafore, hit the tops of her button shoes. The bright' yellow scarf was like a dot of sunshine against the dark of Oscar's back. Lisa could see her look down at his feet that kicked the dust as he walked. Now Marta looked up, perhaps to see his hard round hat so black against the blue sky.

A movement in a window, Hanssons', made Lisa aware that in every window in the circle of *stugas* critical eyes watched this separation of her family.

"So, you are really letting her go," a voice called. Lisa swung to face Greta Swanson. The sorrow of her face was repeated in that of Gus, behind her. Their five children crowded in the doorway of their *stuga*. "I know how you must be feeling," Greta continued. "Come in and have coffee with us."

At this Lisa could no longer hold back her tears. Unable to answer, she stumbled up the steps into her own house. Emilia was again swinging in the rocking chair, but stopped its plunging as Lisa ran past to seek the comfort of the bedroom.

The hushed murmur of the children finally made her dry her eyes to go face them and the day. It was hard to find enough work to fill the time of Oscar's absence. Yet she went from one task to another, never finishing any. At last she gave up, took her knitting and seated herself on a stool near the open door. The children stayed close — sometimes seated on the steps, other times coming to stand beside her. She could not speak. Instead she kept the needles busy, the stocking growing rapidly, although her eyes were constantly on the road.

When she saw him she became contrary. She hurried to put her knitting in the small square table that held the Bible, busied herself wiping the long dining table that had already been wiped several times. The children's eyes asked him what had happened, but she held up one hand, palm out.

"Don't tell me Marta cried," she pleaded. "I don't want to hear it."

Rebuffed, Oscar's face showed anger. "Then I won't," he said shortly, "but can I say *Fru* Palmer seems a most capable woman?" He went past her into the bedroom to put his hat back on top of the wardrobe. He returned to stand looking at his silent family. "Ya so, are we to spend our time mourning something that will help Marta?" he asked. "Lisa, pack some food and let us all go pick lingon. Perhaps there'll be a few mushrooms, too."

"Hurrah!" Emilia shouted. The girls dashed around. The baby was changed. Small wooden buckets and one large one were found for the berries. The length of bright patterned hand-loomed wool that covered Lisa and Oscar's bed was whisked off to go along for Lisa to sit on. Without comment she took her knitting and packed it with the food she had for their noon meal into a cloth and tied the ends together.

Oscar locked the door and hung the big key on its nail, high up on the doorjamb. The line of Veldmans, shortened today by Marta and their oldest girl, Elivra, who worked full time in a home in the village, curled around the end of the house and was soon deep in the woods. After half a kilometer they reached their favorite forest meadow.

The length of weaving was spread on the sunniest spot where Lisa could set up housekeeping. The older children urged Pappa to come. They knew where the most and best lingon were. But he urged them off, not to wait for him. He stood in front of Lisa.

"Are you all right?" he asked.

"Yaw, Oscar. Forgive me. I know I seem difficult. Let me sit here while you go into the woods. The sun will give me strength to hear about Marta. Go, the children want you with them."

He kissed her softly, and went off, scooping up the largest wooden bucket the girls had left behind. Lisa was left with the baby on the blanket. Alli and Johan looked for berries close by. They brought them to her, in triumph, in their hands, a few at a time.

She lay back next to the baby, letting the sun reach in to the sadness of her thoughts. Sun and rest, here in the beautiful forest, would help her to listen, when she could ask Oscar to tell her about Marta and *Fru* Palmer. He too would be helped to have this time to roam among the trees.

Alli and Johan, tired of berry picking, came to play next to her. They pushed sticks into the ground to make fences and set small pebbles inside, calling them cows and pigs. She dozed, tension easing as the time passed. The sun reached its highest point and far beyond before the berry pickers returned. Hungry girls opened the cloth and parceled out cold potatoes, cooked in their jackets, and pickled herring.

"Tell us of Marta," Lisa asked at last, picking up her knitting.

Oscar hesitated. He needed to spare her, yet speak truthfully. "She curtsied very nicely, but I did have to remind her to do it. I think it will please you to know she showed *Fru* Palmer her pinafore. As soon as we got there. She held up the part with the pretty sewing, and told *Fru* Palmer that "Mamma has sewed." Paulina, proud of her ironing, smiled around at everyone.

"Did she?" Lisa exclaimed. "You should have told us that sooner."

"Sooner?" Oscar began in indignation, but quickly continued in a more quiet tone. "When *Fru* Palmer invited us in, Marta...Marta cried out. Clung to that knitted bag of yours I was holding and called 'Mamma, Mamma' against it."

Lisa flung herself up onto her feet, the ball of yarn unraveling behind her as she went to stand at the edge of the clearing. Oscar followed immediately, scooping up the ball of yarn.

"She was all right, Lisa, when I told her it would please you if she would go in and begin her visit to the Palmers."

She nodded as she took the ball of yarn and began to rewind it, pulling off the bits of pine needles that had become stuck to it.

"When I left," he went on, "she was eating an orange sitting at their big table looking with large eyes at the many gold-framed pictures on the wall."

"Ha! Pictures!" she laughed. "Already her world is changed. Imagine, our girl living where there is the sin of pictures hanging on the walls."

Oscar stepped closer and spoke softly. "How can I tell you the sorrow that fills me that our child has to be away from us? All I can say is, if I could spare her this by giving up everything I eat, I would gladly do so." Lisa saw his torture. She touched him in apology and murmured understanding. "Those pictures, Lisa, are no sin of Marta's. From our teachings out of the Bible she knows that we do not hold with imitating any living thing. When she comes home we will be gentle with her and take glory in teaching her the TRUTH once again."

Lisa kissed the tips of her fingers and placed them on his mouth. Together they walked back to the blanket.

"Go on, eat," she told the children, who sat watching them, neither chewing nor lifting their food to their mouth. "Pappa is right," she went on, "what I should have said was I am so glad that already Marta had an orange. Oscar, you must be hungry. You didn't eat the cereal I heated for you before you left with Marta. Tell us the rest of it."

He picked up the potato he had deserted and continued where he had left off.

"Marta went in with me, we sat for a few minutes in their huge living room, met the maid, Jerda, and the cook, Anna. *Herr* Palmer was not there just then, but Jerda was sent to telephone him that we had come."

"They have a telephone?" several of the girls asked in almost the same breath.

"Of course," Oscar answered. "He is a businessman."

"But Pappa," Maria demanded, "what was the house like inside? I know which one it is and it is so big."

"Who cares about the furniture," Lisa objected, "what is *Fru* Palmer like? What did she say? How do you feel she will be to Marta?"

"I feel that right about now *Fru* Palmer is feeding Marta humming-birds' tongues and sugar cakes," he answered.

She slapped the air with an impatient hand. "No nonsense, please. Tell me more about our girl."

"She is going to get good care, that is what I felt. There is nothing more I can tell you, Lisa," he insisted. "I was in the house for moments only. You must realize that by how quickly I was back home to you."

Lisa returned to her knitting. "I will think of her getting thick slices of good bread and plenty of butter." She looked around the circle of her children. "If you have finished eating go wash your hands in the stream."

The older girls took Alli and Johan with them to the brook that edged one side of the meadow.

'Surely there is more to tell," Lisa said, reaching to turn Carl onto his stomach, his bare bottom toward the sun.

"Truthfully, Lisa," Oscar answered, "she did offer me a cup of cof-fee, but I wanted out of there quickly. The sooner the better for Marta. Let me rest from it now."

"Yaw, but tell me this one more thing. Did she cry when you left?"

"Nay, but I think she did the minute the door closed behind me."

"Poor child. But someday she will thank us."

"We don't need thanks."

"You are right. Lie down here in the sun."

"Nay, not yet. Look, the children feel our sadness. They are too quiet. Let me run with them first." He jumped up. "Who's going to see if I can catch them today?"

Five startled faces turned at his call. In moments the children were pushing and shouting to arrange themselves for one of their favorite games as he walked toward them. Excited, Maria and Emilia went to crouch behind Paulina, Alli and Johan. Marta's absence, Lisa no-ticed, made it impossible to have a double line. Oscar took a stand in front of the group, his back to them.

"Last couple out," he shouted.

Maria and Emilia leaped forward. Their bare toes dug into the forest loam. They flashed past Oscar, one on each side of him. He leaped forward in chase. Emilia's small mouth was tight with the determination to outrun him. Maria, her long legs swinging in smooth strides, outdistanced her. They ran in hopes of joining hands before he could catch either one. All three disappeared into the forest, Oscar's boots crashing through the low growth of lingon bushes. It was long moments before the shouts at the conclusion of the race reached Lisa. Redfaced and sweating the three returned, the two girls hand in hand. Oscar had lost. His arms spread wide, he pretended despair toward Lisa as he took his place again in front of the short line.

Lisa found herself shouting along with the others, "Run, run, don't laugh," as Paulina took a turn with Emilia. It did not help. Paulina's laughter, "Nyeh, nyeh, nyeh," slowed her legs and Oscar caught her quickly.

The older girls coached Alli and Johan for the next race. In spite of their encouraging shouts, and running along with the two, the race was over almost before it had begun. Johan ran directly to Oscar, capturing him by one leg with joyful arms. Alli skimmed over the grass in sudden and different directions, calling, "Watch me, Mamma, watch me," with no thought of anyone trying to catch her.

Johan lifted to his shoulder, Oscar came to Lisa. Laughing with her, he sent Johan back to the others with a gentle swat on his behind. He sank down next to Lisa.

"Ahh," he breathed, "that helped me as much as the children. As I was running, Lisa, I was glad Marta wasn't here. She would have wanted to run too."

"Tell me, did you hold her hand on the way over there?"

"I carried her part way. Her strength was too little for that long walk."

"Good. I thought perhaps you would have to do that. It was right that we sent her." There was silence as peace came to them. Lisa smiled down at him. He lay with an arm across his eyes, the sun glinting on his moustache. Perspiration glistened on his forehead and up into his thick curly hair.

"Right now I feel young," he marveled, and turned on his side, propping his head up with one hand to look at her. "You know, Lisa, because of the lockout, and now the strike, this has been my most wonderful summer."

"How can you say that, Oscar?"

"Because it's true. Do you realize this is the first time in our life that we have had time to be together on other days besides Sunday? Here in the woods and at home. I've come to know the children."

"True. It is also true that the children know you better. But hasn't it been a terrible summer, too? Too little to eat, sending Marta away, and the uncertainty about how the strike will end?"

"What is new about having too little to eat, Lisa? It isn't only these weeks of the lockout that has made our Marta sickly." He sat up, his elbows on his upraised knees as he watched the children. They had gone to wade in the stream. "Look at Paulina out there in the water, her skirts pulled up to her waist. Her legs look like she has had a pillow in between them too long. They should be straight. That didn't happen just this summer."

With a teasing smile she said, "You have to admit it was a very small pillow. They're not very curved."

He slapped her thigh with the back of his hand. "That's because you sacrifice your own food. How many times have I seen you lift portions from your plate to one or two of the children's and yet wouldn't let me give them some of mine?"

"You need to keep strong for all of us. The little I gave hasn't helped Maria or Johan. Look at them. She's so thin you can almost see through her out there. And Johan, he's all ribs and big belly. Look, the girls are going to give him a bath in the stream. Wash him good all over," she called.

"Young Carl here, " Oscar grinned, turning to point his chin at the naked baby, "he stays almost too fat."

In spite of his five months Carl still had difficulty in turning over on his own. He squirmed. Lisa lifted him up and held him over the grass. As if on order he wetted. She wrapped his diaper around him again and settled him in her lap. She found his bottle of milk and placed the nipple in his mouth. To her enormous regret she had never produced milk for any of her children since the firstborn, except for a few days. She hesitated, then made a decision.

"Oscar," she began hesitantly, "I have never told you this before, but I have felt so guilty to have birthed Carl weighing twelve pounds."

Oscar stared at her. "Guilty? Why should that make you feel guilty? This I don't understand."

"Maybe because you are a man. Did I eat too much of the food before he was born? I must have or he wouldn't have been so fat."

Oscar scrambled around until he was on his knees sitting on his heels in front of her. "What a foolish thing to think. Of course you needed more food with the young one growing inside you. We had the wrong kind of food for you. Of this I am certain. Potatoes, rice, knäckbröd, does not make for thin babies. Nay, Lisa, erase that guilt out of your mind, right now."

'And then, " she went on, as if he had not broken into what she needed to say, "when the birth was so hard and I had to stay in bed for a whole month afterward with milk leg, it meant that Elvira had to leave school once again. This is almost more than I can ever forgive myself."

"Forgive yourself? For what? That children are born? If there is any guilt to this then I am guilty too. But it is God's will. Are we to go against his plan?"

Eyes closed, she lifted her face to the sun. "If only His plan for us was already fulfilled. How I would rejoice."

He stared at her, the wide nostrils of his nose flaring as he drew a deep breath.

"What is it you ask of me?" he demanded. "To stop loving you? To be less than a man? You ask too much. Man's seed is not to be cast upon the ground."

"Quiet yourself, Oscar," she said, and wiped her eyes with quick palms, the water in them perhaps caused by the bright sun. "All I ask is God's help."

He begged forgiveness. "I am humble before you."

She shivered. She would pray that the next child would be small.

"You are not to be humble before anyone but God," she corrected him, and gave him a push with her foot to send him over sideways into the grass.

Relieved, he jumped up and went to get the bucket with its contents of lingon berries. His fingers inserted through the heart-shaped holes in the two longest wooden staves, he swung it to and fro in front of her. The sun rippled on the shining red berrries.

"Didn't we do well this morning, the children and I?" he asked. "Next time we'll find mushrooms. God in his good wisdom put these wonderful foods in the woods for us."

"Yaw, and man with his good intelligence picks them," she answered lifting Carl to his shoulder to burp him. "Call the children to come help pack up. It is time we go home. You'll be off to the Temperance Society meeting tonight, and gone until midnight. Don't wake me," and ignored his quick look of suspicious inquiry. "Gather up everything, children," she directed as they came toward her. "I'll cook that oatmeal into soup with milk for tonight."

"With raisins?" Emilia asked.

"Raisins?" Lisa exclaimed. "I am amazed you remember raisins, it is so long since we have had any."

Oscar led the way, cradling Carl in his arms. Lisa stepped behind him, leading Johan by the hand. Her feet were as bare as those of her children, although her left leg was wound around by a long strip of cotton from ankle to knee. It had become a daily necessity to control the varicose veins following the months of phlebitis. The twins came next carrying the small empty buckets. Alli and Maria were last, Maria's arms tight around the big bucket with its cargo of red berries. Alli, in front of her, cradled the red weaving in her arms rolled up like a long headless doll.

Usually Oscar led the family in song whenever they marched home from a picnic. The words to his favorite, "We wander through the forest on a high summer day," were in Lisa's mind, but she knew he had no more heart for singing than she did. There was an empty space in the line of children.

*

"Your words were prophetic," Lisa had to admit to Oscar early in September. On the sixth day of that month the strike was lost. The railroad workers had been unable to keep up with the monies needed to feed so many. "What will Elwig do? Will he take everybody back? Will he take you?"

Lisa had asked knowing that elsewhere spokesmen, leaders, men like Oscar, were already being fired, told they need not show up, cap in hand. The news traveled fast among the soulsick men.

Unbelievably, no one was fired by Herr Elwig. The sawmill resumed operation and soon it was as if there had been no strike. The weeks became months.

"Elwig has always said you were the best saw-setter in the land," Lisa reasoned again one day in March. "He has told you he admired that you can take care of anything that goes wrong with the machinery. Maybe that's why you are still there."

"I don't know, nor will I guess," Oscar had answered, "but that Ivar Bengson, Elwig's other ears, is mighty thick with the boss these days. He doesn't fart unless Elwig tells him...NOW!" Lisa shook her head in criticism, but Oscar continued. "I'm never comfortable because those two seem to be together all the time."

The old routines had been resumed, and the talk of the quiet days of summer put behind them. Winter winds had voices of witches as they shrieked around the corner of the *stuga*, accompanied by the sound of the sawmill working at full force.

Snow was high, reaching halfway up the windows. The single electric light bulb hanging from the ceiling did little to lighten the room. In the dimness beyond the long table Lisa sat in the big rocker, with Carl in her lap, using the smallest wooden spoon to feed him. She lifted the food from a bowl into her own mouth to chew it thoroughly before spooning it into his. At the table the older girls were finishing their homework. Solemn-eyed Johan watched Alli push a small reading stick Oscar had carved for her across the pages of an old almanac in imitation of her sisters' reading sticks that skimmed quickly across their open books.

"Finished," Emilia announced, slapping her book closed and lifting her arms as if in surrender.

"Me too," both Paulina and Maria declared, with Paulina adding, "Let's play something."

"Trip to Palmers," Emilia decided without consultation with her sisters and immediately climbed up to stand on the bench where she had been sitting.

"You must have another slice of meat, my dear child."

"Do let me give you another helping of potatoes."

"A taste of pudding, yaw? With a bit of cream?"

In mock tones of culture, Emilia, Paulina and Maria vied with each other to make the suggestions and ask the questions. Once more the game they never tired of was begun. They relived the family's visit to the Palmers the first Sunday following the Christmas season. Lisa remembered it well. The invitation had been for Christmas day in order that Marta would have her family with her. How hard it had been for Oscar to make *Herr* Palmer understand why they did not celebrate Christmas. According to their study of the Bible, Christ was not born on that day. To observe it was to celebrate the birth of a pagan prince.

"I would like some pudding," Alli joined in the game, and lifted a plate from the center of the table.

Maria whirled up from Oscar's chair. She hesitated at the side cupboard and went through the motions of filling a nonexistent dish from a nonexistent bowl. Face pulled into a grimace to help her keep level the dish that seemed to be between her outstretched hands, she minced over to the table. With a flourish she set the imaginary pudding down before her youngest sister.

"Why, you did that real good," Emilia approved, then sat down to pillow her head on her arm stretched out on the table. She pointed. "Look! Look! Alli thinks there really is something there. Look at her face!"

"I don't care,"Alli pouted, "I do want some pudding."

"Pick up your spoon and pretend to eat," Paulina suggested. "Maybe you could really remember the taste."

Lisa sighed. Marta had not come home. *Herr* Palmer had been quick to arrive, the moment he had heard the strike had ended, to plead that Marta be allowed to stay longer. She was filling out but she needed more time to be with them to reach full health. For two nights, Lisa and Oscar went over the reawakened arguments. Finally, knowing all the while they would, they agreed she must stay. There she still was, neither one willing to demand she come home to fare that was as bad as before the lockout and strike, and sometimes even worse. No wonder the children loved this game best, always beginning it with the food.

Emilia got up to stand on the bench again to make herself as tall as *Herr* Palmer. With a turn of her head she positioned her body. Alternately placing her hands as if she had them in pants pockets, or flinging them around, she mimicked that gentleman.

"Children," she announced, "if you have eaten plenty we shall now play games. What shall it be? Hide the thimble? Blindman's buff? Or do you have one that you play at home, that Marta knows and would like to play again?"

"Blindman, blindman," Johan piped.

"Nay," Alli protested, "we haven't done the part where Johan peepees on the velvet chair."

"Just a minute." Lisa's voice stopped them all where they were. "I have warned that if you mention that accident you would never play this game again. Do you hear me, Alli?"

"Yaw, Mamma," Alli murmured, eyes filling and lips beginning to tremble.

"Never mind now. Go on," Lisa urged, reluctant to end their fun.

"There won't be time for more," Paulina cautioned. "Pappa will be here soon, then we have to be quiet."

"The hour is late," Emilia announced, resuming the stance and voice of *Herr* Palmer. "There has never been a year without our guests dancing around the tree before plundering it of all its trimmings. Veldman. *Fru* Veldman. You must let the children do that now. It isn't the Twelfth Night so it must be all right for them to do it."

Yaw, Lisa told herself, *Herr* Palmer had outwitted them by keeping the Christmas tree beyond Twelfth Night, the usual time for its plundering. How her five had stood staring when they saw the decorated tree, its top branch touching the ceiling of the large beautiful room. It had been difficult to get them to hear when she told them to take off their coats and to mind Carl, who crowed and bellowed because he wanted someone to take him closer to all that beauty.

How she had feared Marta would suffer by their coming to Palmers, only to leave without her. It was not good to pull the child in two directions. Yet it had been she who had been close to tears when they left, because Marta had seemed to take it for granted she was not to go with them. What had made it even harder for Lisa was what she had seen when she returned from a trip down the long hallway from the fine large room to go scold her older girls.

She had been sitting visiting with *Fru* Palmer as best she could, for that lady was too much like the one she had worked for when she first came from Finland.

Emilia had interrupted.

"Johan has to peepee," she had whispered.

"You are not to whisper in company," Lisa had corrected her, then asked if Marta could show Emilia where the toilet room was. "You had all better go," she added, and to *Fru* Palmer, "They have talked so much about seeing that seat with running water I guess they had better get it done."

The children left. The stilted conversation continued until the racket from the toilet room became so loud it could be heard where Lisa sat in the living room. She hurried down the long hall.

"What do you mean making so much noise," she had demanded when she had flung open the door to the narrow room that held a toilet at its furthest end. Except for Carl crying in neglect on the floor, and for Johan who came stumbling out from behind the door, apparently frightened by the noise of the rushing water, the children were milling around the toilet. Arms flailing at each other, they yelled their determination to be next to pull the long chain that hung from a wooden box near the ceiling, or pushed each other aside to hang over the toilet to see the paper they had crumpled swirl down and away through the funnel-shaped tin bowl.

"So this is the way to behave?" she demanded. "You have had all the time you are going to have to see or use this toilet. Get out. Right now, and shame on you girls. Go back into the living room and sit quietly on those velvet chairs you admired so much. Let's see if you can behave like decent people instead of idiots."

They had scurried out of the room taking Johan with them, never mentioning he had not had a turn on the toilet. Lisa picked up Carl, wiped his face with the palm of her hand, and walked back to the big room. On her way she noticed a door slightly open. Without meaning to she looked in, and stopped. It could be none other than where Marta slept. Dolls were everyehere. In doll beds, on chairs, on shelves, and even a cradle holding several of them. Lisa gasped. Pictures were sin enough, but here were imitations of human beings. Never had they allowed a child of theirs to have a doll. She grasped the handle of the door and pulled it shut. Mouth pinched together, she was determined the girl was to come home. Oscar would agree.

But again Marta's health determined their decision. She was still at Palmer's even to this stormy day in March. It was for Lisa to sit here and wonder about her, and to remember the sting of embarrassment when she had found that Johan had wet the pale blue velvet of the chair where he sat. With no effort, Lisa heard again *Fru* Palmer's frantic directions to the maid, Jerda, to hurry the chair out into the kitchen and wipe it immediately with cloths dipped in warm water. She met again the glares of disapproval from a face suddenly thick with anger, as *Fru* Palmer refused Lisa's offer to help. No one had remembered to tell Lisa the boy had been too frightened of the rushing water to go anywhere near the toilet.

"Ach," Lisa told herself, "these thoughts I have to put aside. It is better to watch the children continue their game."

Emilia had jumped down from the bench and was directing her brother and sisters to join hands. In moments the five were circling Lisa and Carl in the rocking chair. Although the older ones knew Christmas songs, learned in school, they were careful to choose another tune as they skipped and hummed. It was Lisa who began singing "The Squirrel Sat in a Pine Tree," as she helped Carl to stand up in her lap.

One of the sisters called, "Now we plunder the tree." The children dropped hands, and began to pluck at Lisa's dress, sometimes even at Carl's blankets.

"I have an orange," declared one.

"Mine is a big red apple," shouted another.

"A yellow wrapped candy, a green one, and look, a blue one," yelled the first sister again.

"Look at Johan and Alli," Maria called, "they have all the gingerbread bakings."

Their shouts and tramping of feet blotted out the sound of the outer door being opened and shut. It wasn't until the inner door swung into the room that the pretended plundering stopped.

"Elvira!" Lisa cried, getting up out of the rocking chair to hand Carl to Paulina, who happned to be closest. "What are you doing here, and so late in the day?"

Elvira hurried to unwind the big wool scarf that hid most of her face. It was wound around her neck, up over her knitted cap, then down across her chest. The children crowded around their oldest sister, all of them talking at once.

"Take her coat, Maria," Lisa ordered, then scolded, "you didn't take off your boots before coming in, Elvira."

"I don't have time, Mamma, but I did sweep the snow from them," she answered. "I had to deliver a baby's coffin not far from here, so I stopped at the post office." She removed a mitten to dig into a coat pocket with a redddened chapped hand. "There was a letter there. From *Moster* Katarina in Finland." She handed the letter to Lisa who stood looking at it.

"I don't understand," she murmured. "My sister answered my last letter earlier this month. I wonder if..."

"Stop it," Elvira interrupted as she pulled her coat sleeve away from Maria. "I said I can't stay. I have to get right back. I'll be late as it is."

Lisa laid the letter unopened on the table.

"You will take it off, and right now," she said. "If those two women, who dress the dead and decorate funerals, can't let you stop long enough to have a good hot cup of coffee, and a rusk, on such a day I will go down there myself and tell them they can get another housekeeper and errand girl."

Elvira let her sister take her coat.

"Sit here, where I can see and talk to you," Lisa urged, touching Oscar's chair. She hurried to take the coffeepot from the back of the stove, and placed it where it would heat quickly. From the cupboard she took a few rusks, and put them on the dish at Oscar's place. She let the children talk as they flocked around their sister. One by one they settled on the benches near her.

No wonder they are excited whenever Elvira comes home, she thought. She is their second mother. How I miss her help. Elvira never complained all the years she couldn't be a child herself but had to work as hard as I did. Harder, for she was too young each time a new child came. Will she ever have time to play? With effort she put a feeling of guilt aside as the coffee steamed. Elvira held the mug up for the hot brew.

"Whose baby died?" Lisa asked, as she placed sugar and milk on the table.

"Fisherman Jacobsson's," Elvira answered. She plumped several lumps of sugar into the mug. "Do you know them?"

"Nay, but no doubt Pappa does. What sadness... It is a terrible thing to have a child die...how old was it?"

"Newborn."

Lisa lifted her hand to cover her mouth, breathing an anguished "Aiy yaiy," against its palm. After a long moment she sighed heavily as she wiped each eye with the back of her wrist.

Alli called to her from where she sat between the twins on the other side of the table.

"Mamma, we didn't die," she consoled.

"Hush!" Paulina demanded, swinging Carl over to the other side of her lap to bring her face close to Alli's. In a loud whisper she told her, "Mamma has had two babies die long before you were born."

"Paulina, never mind," Lisa admonished kindly. "Thank you, Alli. I'm very glad you are all alive." She turned back to Elvira.

"And you had to carry that coffin all this long way? Wasn't it heavy?"

"Not very. It was awkward, and my hands got so cold. I walked across the river on the ice. Didn't have to go all the way down to the bridge." She soaked a rusk in the coffee, and bit off the dampened end. "This is good," she commented.

"Thank you," Lisa answered. "Thanks to your help we can buy white flour again. I can bake coffeebread, even enough to make rusks too. But, tell me, how is it with you?"

Elvira shrugged her shoulders. "Nothing different," she answered. "*Fröken* Alma finds more work for me to do, and *Fröken* Ingeborg wants me to do it two times over."

"Don't you do it well enough the first time?"

"I do, Mamma, but that's the way she is. *Fröken* Alma says she thinks her sister even dresses the bodies twice over when she goes to the hospital or to people's houses when someone has died."

Emilia did an exaggerated shiver for everyone's benefit. Lisa paid no attention.

"Does *Fröken* Alma make you help with the wreaths she makes? I told you I don't want you to have anything to do with them."

"Nay, Mamma, there is so much cleaning, cooking, and running errands I don't have time to make artificial flowers."

"That's good, but I'm sorry you are so tired. Try to get some rest when you can. Do they give you enough to eat?"

"Oh, yaw, but almost always the same thing, herring and potatoes, potatoes and herring."

"Well, that is good food, and if there is plenty don't complain."

Elvira finished a third rusk, and tipped the mug to get the last of the coffee.

"It is so good to be here," she breathed, as she looked around the room. She stood up. "I have to go now, Mamma."

"Yaw, yaw, I suppose so, although we didn't really have time to talk. Here, let me help you with your coat."

When Elvira was bundled up again and putting on her mittens, Lisa reached for one of the reddened hands.

"Do you wipe your hands dry, really dry, when you have had them in water?"

"I try, but they are wet so many times and I am in and out all day long," Elviraa answered, her voice muffled behind the scarf that covered her mouth.

"You must do that. You aren't thirteen years old anymore. It is time to learn to take care of yourself. Do you do as Pappa says, urinate on them the last thing before you go to bed?"

"That burns so, Mamma, and it doesn't seem to make them better."

"Well, next time you are paid, take some of the money before you bring it home, and go to the chemist. Have him sell you some good cream to heal those hands. Will you do that?"

"Yaw, thanks. I will. Goodbye. Goodbye, everybody."

"Don't forget, pull the scarf up over your nose as soon as you get outside," Lisa coached, as the door began to close behind her eldest child.

The door swung open again. Elvira stuck her head back in, one mittened hand pulling the scarf down from her mouth. "Mamma," she pleaded, "do you suppose you could make some rice pudding for the next time I have a day at home?"

Lisa clapped her hands together. "I will make it, and somehow with plenty of sugar and cinnamon. Even butter."

"When are you coming?" several of the children called.

"A week from Sunday," she answered, before she banged the door shut.

Lisa turned quickly from the door. She set the children to work. Carl was put into his cradle with his bottle, potatoes put on to cook, the mug Elvira had used was washed and dried. With one corner of her apron Lisa wiped the few crumbs from the plate.

"Johan, go get Pappa a fresh pair of stockings. His might be damp. I hear him coming right now."

There was thumping and stamping in the vestibule.

"Paulina, get Pappa's water ready in the basin on the wash bench. Let Maria help you pour hot water from the stove to warm it a bit."

"Mamma," Maria said, turning her head to look over her shoulder. "You haven't opened your letter."

"I know," Lisa answered. She picked it up and puzzled over it again. "We will read it now that Pappa is here."

Oscar entered. Icicles dotted his moustache; his nose was red above it. As he pulled his fur cap from his head to slap it against his knee to remove the snow, Lisa looked up from the envelope. With a quick intake of breath she hurried to him, dropping the letter on the table without looking to see where it fell. His face was gray, drawn, the lines deep. His eyes had lost their blue, looking at her with dullness. They did not convey a sense of physical sickness, but a message of something wrong. She reached to help him off with his coat, but he shook his head. With a hunching of his shoulders he removed it and hung it on the highest peg, above the children's coats on the lower pegs on the wall.

"Was that Elvira I saw running roward the river?" he asked in a tight voice, as he took a long time to push his cap into the pocket of his coat.

"Yaw," Lisa answered quietly. She tried to see his face.

"What was she here for?" he asked, sounding more normal, yet he avoided looking at her. "She had a day off some days ago."

"She brought us a letter. It's from sister Katarina."

He turned, his face less gray. "All the way here just for that?" he asked.

"Nay, she had an errand to run up this way for the ladies. I'll tell you about it later."

"Yaw, we must talk later," he agreed. "Let us hear Katarina's letter. But didn't she send one already this month?"

"She did," Lisa answered, and understood he would tell her something, when the children were in bed. "Wash up and have some hot coffee first. Katarina's letter worries me."

"Open it and end your worry," he suggested. "It could be she wants to come for a visit."

"Pooh, not Katarina. She'll never leave Finland."

As Oscar wished, Lisa went to the cupboard to take out the circle of sausage. How glad she was that today she had managed to have meat on the table. Oscar needed it this night.

*

What could have happened at the sawmill, Lisa wondered as Oscar washed up and combed his hair. Hadn't Oscar hardened himself to Bengson's and Elwig's plotting, whatever it was? She directed the girls to set the plates on the table and get the mugs from the cupboard. How good those yellow mugs with their band of white and black checks looked standing next to the blue-enameled tin plates. It gave her ease to notice them again. If there had to be another child they would have to buy yet another plate and mug. She hoped Herr Palmer would still have them in his shop.

Oscar was almost ready for his coffee. Johan stood waiting, his pappa's dry stockings hanging over one arm.

"Yaw, haw," Oscar said, but did not give Johan the customary gentle slap on his rear as he thanked the boy and pulled the dry stockings on.

"Let us hear that letter now, the second one this month," he suggested, and took a gulp of coffee from the mug Lisa had filled for him.

The letter held in front of her, Lisa made her way to her chair at the other end of the table. The children rushed to their places on the two benches, excited by this unexplained second letter. Lisa tore it open with a hairpin from her bun. "Oh, it isn't very long," she said, as she removed and unfolded a thin sheet of paper.

"We can see it is short," Oscar said impatiently. "If you would go ahead and read we would soon know why."

"Yaw, I'll read." She settled her elbows on the table and leaned forward to get the light on the paper. She began:

"'Dear Lisa and Oscar,

'We are all well and there is much snow here...' Oh, I'm so glad," she interrupted herself. "That they are well, I mean. I was worried."

"Yaw, yaw, but go on," Oscar snapped. She returned to the letter.

"'I wrote you yesterday...'" Again Lisa interrupted herself. "Why, this letter must have lain in the post office a week or more."

"Never mind, go on," Oscar urged.

"'I wrote you yesterday, but something has come up that I must tell you. The foreman of the new sawmill here is leaving for America. His name is Ingvar Petersson. You remember Evar Petersson, his father? This is his eldest son. Sigurd told me about it this morning. I said right away, that's where Oscar should be working. You told us in one of your letters how terrible those men are at Oscar's sawmill trying to push him out, maybe. We talked it over. Sigurd said I should write, but first he went to see Petersson to ask him to talk to the owner of the mill about Oscar.'"

"Nay!" Oscar exploded. "Sigurd did that?"

They stared at each other across the length of the table. Lisa's mouth worked.

"Katarina, dear Katarina," she managed. "But, she should forget this dream of hers to get me to come home to Finland."

"Go on," Oscar hurried her.

"'Mangnuson, that's the owner's name, came to see us right away...'"

"Can you believe it!" Oscar exclaimed.

"'We sent him out to Emile Mackela's farm. Remember him? The Finn who worked with Oscar over there for two years?'"

Oscar nodded. "Yes, a good worker. Go on."

"'Mangnuson came back near supper time and said he wants Oscar to come work for him.'"

Oscar jumped up from his chair to stand behind it. His back to his family, he rubbed his hands through his hair, making a tangle of it. Lisa's breath left her as she sagged back into her chair. The hand holding the letter slumped into her lap. Abruptly Oscar sat down again.

"There is more?" he asked, his face hidden as he leaned his forehead on his hands, his elbows on the table.

Lisa sat up, and slowly began reading again.

"'Please come. It is not good that sisters should live so far apart. All ten of our brothers are gone, either dead or in America. Sigurd says to tell Oscar too that Mangnuson has had many supervisors in the four years the mill has been here. Finns and Swede-Finns. Sigurd thinks he wants to try someone from Sweden now. It might as well be Oscar. I pray that you will come. My eyes trouble me, so I write no more. Heartfelt greetings to you both, and all the children. Your sister, Katarina.'"

There was silence when she finished. Oscar didn't move. She looked back at the letter.

"Oh, she has something written here on the side," she said, then read aloud, "'I forgot to say you have to be here by the first of May.'"

It was then Oscar moved. He took his hands from his face and slid down, until he was resting his head on the top of the chair's back. He laughed. Lisa sat staring. His laughter grew, his moustache quivering above his wide open mouth. Uncertainly the children began to laugh with him, until they looked at Lisa. She was angry. True, Katarina had taken too much on herself this time, she thought, and she would have to write her once again to try to convince her that Sweden was their home. But Oscar need not react like that to Katarina's effort.

"What is there to laugh at?" she demanded. As if she had clapped her hand over his mouth, he stopped. He straightened up, got out his handkerchief and blew his nose.

"Forgive me," he began, "Finland..."

Lisa didn't let him get any further. "And what's so laughable about my homeland?" she demanded, her chin lowered, a deep frown between her eyes.

"Nothing, Lisa," he answered, "what I was going to say, if you had let me, was that Finland is God's answer."

"How did you suddenly decide that?" she asked. Then, more kindly, added, "I don't understand."

"I know. Let me see the letter."

It traveled from child to child until it reached him. Lisa sat holding herself, her arms across her breasts. She watched him read and reread the letter. Now and then his head shook with the refusal to believe what he read.

In the silence, the sputter of water bubbling over onto the stove and the rattle of the lid on the pot of potatoes startled her. She jumped up to lift the lid and move the pot to a cooler area. She slid the sausage from its dish on top of the potatoes. At last Oscar laid the letter down.

"So?" she asked. When he didn't answer she continued. "I'll write again and say our thanks. Is there more you want me to say?" He shook his head.

"We will decide what to say later, Lisa," he told her, with a quick look around at the listening children.

"Ya so," she said, and turned from him. "Quick, children, it is time to eat. Go wash your hands."

Oscar sat with his head bent, looking at his hands clasped together in his lap, as if he were praying. She found her eyes smarting, and turned away quickly to separate the children who were having a tug-of-war with the one towel. Disturbed about Oscar, she kept her back turned toward him.

"Did you know Fisherman Jacobsson?" she asked suddenly.

"Jacobsson who lives at the mouth of the river? Yaw, that I certainly do."

"So that's where Elvira had to go," she marveled. "She had to deliver a casket there today. It was for their baby. Newborn."

"Aiy!"

At his exclamation she turned and saw that he experienced the same painful memories she had had earlier. It united them again. She knew whatever he had to tell her would be easier for him now.

"Sit, everybody," she called, in a happier voice. "Let us all thank God for the food."

"Take the younger ones with you into the bedroom," Lisa told her older girls as the evening meal was over and the dishes done. "Tell them stories or play a game with them. There is plenty of wood to keep the tile stove hot in there. Pappa and I have something we need to talk about."

Although supper had been unusually plentiful, for Lisa had taken extra rounds of *knäkebröd* from the pole overhead, she was glad when it was over. Every unguarded gulp or appreciative smack of the lips from the children had brought Oscar's quick disapproval. Lisa had eaten very little herself. Oscar sat with his head lowered, pushing the food into his mouth as if it were something only to be swallowed. Even the sausage. When a child said anything he raised his head with a look that cut their words off in the middle.

"Here, take this with you," Lisa said, and dipped water from the water barrel into a mug and held it out to the girls. Maria took it and followed the rest of the children, each of them giving a side glance at their silent pappa as they went out of the room.

As soon as the door closed Lisa turned to Oscar. He had gone to the stove. Poling the fire with a piece of wood, he dropped it into the flames and set the stove lid back in place. She waited until he faced her. His face was unbearably sad. She went to him.

"Lisa," he said, quietly, "today I was laid off."

Involuntarily Lisa's hands jerked upward to cover her mouth, but instead she grasped Oscar's arms.

"What did you say...? Nay! That can't be. It just can't be!" Her voice rose. She shook him, then released him. They stared at each other, her eyes asking that it not be true.

He nodded. The effort, slow and heavy, removed the color from his face.

"Elweg didn't have the courage to do it," he said. "His handy hench-man, Bengson, did it, and gladly."

Shaking her head she tried to refuse the truth, but stopped as she saw his humiliation, raw and exposed.

"Tell me all of it. Let us sit here." She took his hand and led him to the nearest bench at the table. They sat, facing each other. "Did you go see Elwig?" she asked.

"Yaw, that I tried to do. But he was nowhere. Gone from the mill."

She straightened up to take a deep breath. "How could they do it?" she asked. "They still haven't found fault with your work. That I know."

"Nay, that they didn't," he agreed, "but they found something else."

"In God's name, tell me," she demanded.

He studied her before he answered. "It was because I get the *Bethlehem Star.*"

"What? Our religious paper? How can that be?"

"He said it was a Socialist paper."

"Socialist? Has he ever read it? Does he know it quotes the Bible throughout its every page, in almost every line?"

Oscar's voice was scornful as he said, "I often wonder if Bengson can read. But, Lisa, The *Bethlehem Star* is not far different from the Socialist paper. After all, it champions the cause of the working peo-ple, as Christ did. Later Bengson said I had been seen reading the Socialist paper."

"Who doesn't at the sawmill? Everybody but Bengson, I think. It goes from hand to hand here. Has for more years than I can recall."

"Yaw, of course. I wonder too, but wouldn't it be worth your going to see.."

Oscar got up to stand before her. "Are you going to suggest I go begging to the owners? Isn't it bad enough to be kicked out by that stinking weasel?" His nostrils flared as he snorted his disgust.

"Quiet! Shh!" she begged, with a quick look toward the bedroom door. Her voice became a hoarse whisper. "I'm not asking you to do anything, just thinking out loud. Sit down."

He sat again, leaned forward, hands clasped between his knees, his eyes studying the floor.

"You should have seen Bengson," he began, his voice so low Lisa had to bend to hear him. "He couldn't keep the grin off his face. Yet he looked frightened, as if he thought I would hit him. Hit him, ha! As if I would dirty my hands. I haven't hit anybody since I was a boy. Since I came into God's TRUTH I haven't even wanted to, nor would

I. But such anger, Lisa, such red hot anger was inside of me I felt I needed to go break the saw blade in two. Yaw, Bengson could see my anger."

"What did the other men say?" she asked, as he sat nodding to himself.

"The other men? They had all gone home. I thought I told you."

"Your brother too?"

"Yaw, Evert left when Bengson asked me to stay. There was something he wanted to talk to me about, Bengson said. We didn't do much talking. He said his piece, and I asked him for more reasons. He gabbled about the *Bethlehem Star*. Yaw, and he gave me my last pay." He sat up and from his pocket took out the money, and laid it in her lap. "That's what we have now, Lisa, between us and starvation."

She made a sound deep in her throat, a smothered groan, gathered the few coins in one hand, and rubbed the largest one between thumb and finger. They jingled as she dropped them in her apron pocket.

"There are other sawmills, Oscar."

"Not here where I have worked all my life."

"Then we will go elsewhere." He didn't answer. "I know it will be hard for you to leave here." He still remained silent. "I had to leave my home village in Finland to find work, Oscar."

At this he answered her. "It is more serious than that, Lisa." He leaned back against the table. "Where in Sweden do you think there is a sawmill owner who would let me be hired now? They have their own kind of union. You can be sure the word will be passed around... 'Oscar Veldman reads Socialist papers and was spokesman during the strike.' Nay, from now on my skill is not wanted at any sawmill."

She had no answer. She got up to poke at the fire inside the stove. The heat from the hot coals on her face helped to calm the anxiety that threatened to pull her to pieces. Carefully she laid another chunk of wood on the fire and watched it begin to burn. She could not look at him. Instead she remembered his drawn face when he had come home. She should have gone to him then, pulled all of this out of him to ease his pain, instead of letting him hold it inside himself until now. But there had been Katarina's worrisome letter. She clattered the stove lid back into place and whirled around.

"Oscar! Oscar! Katarina's letter!" She flew across the space separating them, knelt in front of him. Her hands clutched his knees as she looked up into his face. "So that's why you laughed. This time you took Katarina's letter seriously. It couldn't have come at a more perfect time. Yaw!" She dropped her head onto his lap. He lifted it up between his hands, and smiled at her. He moved his thumbs to arrest the tears that spilled in relief. She turned her head to kiss the palm of one of his hands, before she got up to sit on the bench next to him again.

"You remember that last week in February when we went to Finland so my *mor* could deliver our firstborn? You still had that patch over your eye. From that sliver of wood. I guess now we know that was the only good thing that came out of that accident. That you could go with me to Finland." She could not stop herself talking. "My brothers, they all liked you. Katarina, too. *Mor* also. It's a pity she is gone. Pappa too. I mean, how happy they would have been to have us close to them. Oh, it will be so good to see Katarina." She looked off to her native village where she could see Katarina welcoming them.

"Then you have decided we are to go?" Oscar asked quietly.

Startled back into the present she turned a serious face toward him. "Is there something else we can do?" she asked.

"Nay, nay, a workingman must work where they let him."

"You won't feel badly about moving to Finland?"

"Feel badly? Even if I should, what other choice do I have? What concerns me most, Lisa, is what the workers at the sawmill there would think of me. It is likely they will resent me because I'm Swedish."

She pushed herself away from him on the bench the better to see him. "Nay, Oscar," she protested, "of course they won't. Why do you say that?"

"Do you realize, Lisa, it is seldom anyone from Sweden goes to work in Finland these days? Hundreds come over here every year, but not the other way around. It will make a rarity of me. The Swede-Finns too will resent me for being a Swede."

"Ah, you are worried and too much has happened this day. You are talking foolishness. My family will welcome you, of that you can be certain."

"Even your cousin Segerson? He had plenty to say about my being a 'pure Swede' when we were there before."

"That was years ago. He's grown up, married, and has children of his own. No doubt he is a bit smarter by now. Don't make him the example of the rest of my family, or of the country. You'll see, they'll all come to know you for what you are."

She placed a reassuring hand on his arm. As he turned to answer her there was a sound of stamping in the vestibule. Someone pushed the door open. Oscar got up to welcome whoever it was.

"Evert, you here?" he exclaimed, as the visitor pulled off his fur hat, and unwound the scarf around his neck. "You have heard?"

"I have heard," came the answer in a deep growling voice. "You didn't think Bengson was going to keep that triumph to himself, did you?"

"Nay, but not so soon. Here, let me help you."

Evert motioned him away, to go sit in Oscar's chair, unbuttoning his coat. "Tell me about it," he said.

Oscar seated himself on the bench, while Lisa put the coffee on to reheat and set two mugs out on the table. She listened as he retold the firing. She heard the bedroom door squeak. It moved an inch as she watched, but when she started toward it the door shut and there was the thumping of bare feet. Her hand held out to open it, she turned away. Instead she went to Carl, in his cradle, to make sure Emilia had wrapped him well in his swaddling blankets. Looking at him she realized he would soon be too big for such blankets and for the cradle. In spite of herself she smiled, thinking of the small ears pressed to the back of the bedroom door. Well, they needed to know too. She would not scold. She returned to the table just in time to hear Evert.

"Damn him!" he cried.

Oscar held up a cautioning hand. "Nay, not even Bengson," he corrected. "He will earn his own reward at the coming of the New Kingdom. You need not condemn him, not here in my house."

Evert waved an impatient hand. "Let me say it my own way. That imbecile will have a hard time from the other men from now on. You can be sure of that. As for me, I'll not work there any longer. If they can do that to my brother, I am through."

"Nay, you must not do that!"

"Nay, Evert, do not do that!"

Lisa and Oscar had spoken at the same time. Oscar slapped his hand on the table. "Don't do anything in anger, Evert. You have a family to think of."

"Oscar," Evert reasoned, "put yourself in my place. If I were laid off what would you do? I know you would do the same."

"I can't deny that, that's true, but here we sit and talk calmly about what it means to leave a job. Where would you go?"

"I would have no trouble. I don't get that paper. I wasn't spokesman, although I would have been willing. There is something more, Oscar. I don't think this would have happened, really, if you had been a member of the Church."

Oscar guffawed, shaking his head. "So even now you try to get me back into the fold." He reached out to punch his brother's shoulder playfully. "I think it is you who has been reading my paper. If you understand that much you should begin to subscribe. There now, it was my turn to propagandize you for a change," he finished, as his brother sat shaking his head, but smiling.

"Annamaria has been at me for years, as you know," Evert said, "to leave here for a bigger town. Brother Johan, off there in Solefteo, will be able to help me into a new mill up that way. Let's not wory about that now. What is more important, what are you going to do?"

Oscar looked at Lisa. She went to the cupboard and brought the letter she had placed there before supper. She handed it to Evert without saying anything. There was only the sound of the fire crackling in the stove, the tick of the clock, then the pouring of the coffee into the two mugs as he read.

"My dear God in heaven," Evert exclaimed, "when did this come?"

"Today," Oscar answered.

"I don't believe it."

"It is true. God moves in mysterious ways. Finland is God's answer."

Lisa and Oscar exchanged glances. A smile grew on each face.

"That's when you decided," Lisa accused. He nodded. She hurried around Evert to the other side of the table, where Oscar sat. Full on the mouth she kissed him. Bending over, she laid her head on top of his, and encricled him with both arms.

"'Such a daring woman I have," he laughed, then lifted his coffee in a toast to her. Evert, matching him, lifted his mug to clink it against his brother's. They drank until the mugs were empty.

"Have another drop?" Lisa asked, leaving Oscar to get the coffeepot.

"Nay, thanks. That is all," Evert answered. " We will talk about Finland more tomorrow. I must get back to Annamaria. I think she is sitting at home crying. She was so upset when Anders Sjöblom came to tell us."

"So it was Sjöblom. Wonder who told him? No matter," Oscar said. He stood up to put his arm around Evert's shoulders as they walked toward the door together. "I can't say thank you enough for coming over. We know we are not alone. As for your leaving the sawmill...what can I say? Thanks seem so little. They will hate to lose you." They stood shaking hands, pumping them up and down many times.

"Whatever I can do to help, I will, Oscar," Evert assured his brother. "Know that. Annamaria will be happy to hear of Finland, but to have you so far away." He shook his head. "That is sad. Well, perhaps it must be. I'll go over and tell our *mor* about it, before she hears it from someone else.

"Nay," Oscar protested, "leave that to me. I'll go myself. She should hear it from me."

"Well, if that's the way you want it, all right. Goodnight. Goodnight, Lisa."

As Oscar struggled into his coat Evert left.

"You'll take the *spark*, won't you?" Lisa asked, knowing that without anyone sitting on the sled he would make a fast journey standing on the long runners behind the empty seat.

"Yaw, it shouldn't take me more than an hour there and back."

When he had gone Lisa went in to check on the children. Paulina and Maria were sill awake.

"Is everything all right, Mamma?" Maria whispered, her eyes as large and inquiring in the dim light as Paulina's.

"Yaw, sleep, dear children. Pappa is taking care of everything. He has gone to tell *farmor* something."

Back in the other room she decided to sacrifice some of the white flour, two eggs, and some milk. Quickly she mixed a batter, then cooked several stacks of thin pancakes in the black iron pan with its seven round depressions for frying. Thankfully she threw out the last of the many times diluted and reheated coffee. With a knitted shawl thrown over her shoulders she stepped out into the vestibule, carrying the square wooden coffee grinder. The door pulled to behind her, to deaden the sound for the children, she ground enough of the treasured pound of coffee Oscar had bought from his first pay after the strike had ended. Recklessly she ground enough for a full strong pot.

When Oscar returned they feasted, alternating syrup with the tart, but sweet, lingon sauce on butter-rich pancakes, accompanied by cup after cup of fresh coffee.

They talked late into the night. There were endless problems to be solved. How to raise the fare for the family across the Gulf of Bothnia chief among them. They would borrow some from Oscar's brothers, this they knew, and for the rest they would have to sell their furniture. Lisa's relatives would loan them enough, they were sure, until they could build or buy their own. What to do about Marta was the hardest to agree on. It was apparent to both of them that she must stay yet a while with the Palmers. That the child would be eager to stay with them was what worrried Lisa the most. But it had to be.

At last they pulled the sofa out and made their bed. Between them they carried Carl in his crib into the bedroom. The two girls, who had been awake earlier, were sound asleep, lulled back into security long since by the calm murmur of their parents' voices.

Back in the main room again, they undressed in the dark, said their prayers before they got into bed, then sought reassurance in each other's arms. Fear of another pregnancy thrust aside, Lisa met his need as well as her own.

Finland

"My mind has been like a big wheel revolving in opposite ways these last days," Lisa remarked. "One day it spins towards Sweden and the two I leave behind, the other toward Finland and Katarina."

"Mine too," Oscar agreed. "It is hard to leave. How will it go in Finland?" They stood at the afterrail of the boat, steadying themselves against the lift and plunge of the sea. Sweden was a green line on the horizon. The children, except for Carl who slept on a bench in the lounge behind them safely wedged in by their many bundles, staggered back and forth along the deck testing their sea-legs in this their first time aboard a ship. Their laughter spilled into the wind as the boat lifted and fell.

"I think every bone in me aches from the work of the last days," Lisa went on, "and my mind wants to go blank."

Oscar nodded, and put his arm around her. They watched the horizon, each of them silently reviewing the final days in Sweden.

The family's visit to Oscar's *mor,* the children's *farmor,* the visit taking the better part of a day; Marta's unsatisfactory visit home. The child had been foreign to her sisters in her ways and dress. Marta had been uncertain of her place among them. Lisa had explained many times there was not enough money to take her along now. She was to come later with Elvira. It would be soon, she was sure. The last night, spent sleeping with the neighbors; the Swanssons giving up their bed to crowd in with their children so Lisa and Oscar could use it. Carl slept between them, Johan on a pallet on the floor. The girls had been parceled out to bed down with other girls in various *stugas* around the sawmill. The sale had brought in so little money, the purchasers as poor as themselves. Then the farewell, the few members of Ephraim's Messengers there to say goodbye also. It had been painful, the sooner done the better. The train trip, almost over before it began, an agony of moving bundles and children between train and boat. Lisa closed her eyes and let herself drift, wishing for rest.

Without really listening she heard one of the girls say, "She should teach us Swede-Finn now, while we are on our way, before we dock in Kaskö."

Oscar's arm dropped from her waist, and his voice brought her eyes open, her mind alert again.

"You will learn nothing of the sort," he told Paulina, who had made the remark.

The four girls and Johan were clustered close to them, holding tight to the rail.

Emilia argued, "But, Pappa, how are we going to understand and talk to people if we don't know it?"

Maria hurried to add, "Mamma could teach us. She talked Swede-Finn when she was growing up, she told us."

"You will speak Swedish," Oscar insisted. "That other is not a written language. You are not to learn it."

"But, Pappa ..." two of the girls began.

"It is for Pappa to say," Lisa hushed them, a stern look around at the circle of inquiring faces. "The schools in my part of Finland teach only in Swedish. I have told you that many times. That the people have their own dialect outside the schools is true. We spoke real Swedish in my home, because like Pappa here, my parents insisted. But, like everyone else, we used the dialect when we had to. You will understand it soon enough, and everybody will understand you."

"What if people speak to us in Finnish?" Maria asked.

"I doubt you will hear one word of Finnish," Oscar answered with impatience. "You should know by now, you older ones, that the Russians have tried for almost a hundred years now, since they took Finland away from Sweden, to make the Finns adopt their language.

Your Mamma has told you. Yaw, Lisa?" She nodded as he continued. "For the seven hundred years Sweden ruled Finland we tried to make them speak Swedish, but the plucky Finns stuck to their own tongue in their own land. Which was right. It's only those with Swedish ancestors who still use our language. They call themselves Swedes, we call them Swede-Finns, like your Mamma here. How foolish your people were, Lisa, not to learn the language of the country. I hope to learn Finnish in time."

About to answer, Lisa was silenced by another eager question from one of the girls.

"We will hear Russian, won't we? After all, Russia still rules Finland."

"Russian? Nay. Most of the Tzar's representatives are either Finnish or Swedish, depending on what part of the land. If they are Russian they speak the language of the region. Along the coast it is Swedish."

Before the children dashed away, satisfied that at least one part of their life would not change, Lisa warned them, "No giggling or snickering now when the Segersons begin to talk. Ask me if you don't understand."

Again the two at the afterrail rested against each other, content with their own thoughts. Lisa wondered how they would fit into Cousin Segerson's *stuga* that night in Kaskö, but knew they would manage. How she wished the journey was over.

Late the next day it was. She stood in front of her sister, their hands grasped together tightly as if to let go would mean separation again. The wagon that had brought them and their goods circled their belongings now piled in the farmyard. The two horses stepped up their gait as the driver encouraged them back on the road to Kaskö. He yelled over his shoulder in perfectly understandable Swedish, "By the Devil's own horns, we get Swedes now to run our mills. Hear that, you fart-roaring, good-for-nothing Swede-Finn spawn? Get going before Satan decides to make you his darlings too!"

Lisa did not hear, but Oscar did and it seared deed into his memory. Lisa was too busy seeing herself in Katarina. They had always looked alike, although in her mind it was only Katarina who was beautiful. The same rounded but small pointed chin, high cheekbones with the glowing darker skin of some long ago Laplander, perhaps. Lisa searched the dark blue deep set eyes so like her own. They sparkled with welcome and happiness. There was no sign of any sickness in them that Katarina wrote about so often in her letters. Or was there? Was it the tears of joy that made their rims so bright a pink? Katarina was sturdy. She had more weight than Lisa remembered. She stood straight and tall. But then her birthing years had been short. The boys, the first two, right after Lisa had gone to Sweden; the last one, Eva, so many years later she was only the twins' age.

No time to wonder about that now. There was only need to sit and pour out her anguish at having to leave her two girls behind. To spill out the accumulated feelings about the firing, the pain at leaving what had been home for so long, and the joy of coming to Katarina. Faces almost touching they sat, their hands strained to hold together yet tighter. With short glances and even shorter nods, they sent the children out to see the animals, the men already out in the barns.

Katarina reassured her sister that what she had done was right. What else could she have done? As for Oscar, he had brought them all here, a job waited for him, and that was all she needed to say. Their talk was far from spent when Katarina said suddenly, "Come, I want to take you out to the barn too. Sigurd has something there to show you."

"I am ashamed I have paid so little attention to Sigurd, or your two boys and small Eva. My eyes seem to see only you," Lisa admitted, as they walked to the barn, Katarina carrying Carl.

"And I you. Your six are fine children, I can see," her sister responded.

The men and the children of both families were in the barn. A sheep stood in their midst being admired.

"This sheep belongs to your children now," Sigurd told Lisa and Oscar, after a nod from Katarina, his kind face happy with a large smile.

"For you and I to spin the wool and weave cloth for their clothes when there is enough," Katarina hurried to add before the two could respond. "We will keep it here, but it is theirs."

"Nay!" both Lisa and Oscar responded. Lisa continued. "You are too kind, Katarina, you have five to clothe. You need the wool yourself."

"Look," Sigurd said, and swung a small door in the back of the barn open. A sea of woolly backs was revealed. "We have plenty for us, and to sell."

There was much handshaking, hugging, and backpounding before the whole group made their way around the small farm exclaiming over the three cows, Sigurd's old horse and the few chickens in the chickenyard.

Preparation of supper, that night had joy in its every movement, the two women stirring, mixing and setting it out onto the table for the happy group that was their combined families. No one hushed the din. Not even Oscar.

For three days the two sisters had time to talk together. Oscar went early the first morning to report at the sawmill. After that he and the children were with Sigurd out in the barns. The following Monday he was to start work. That would give Lisa time to go with her girls to clean the two-room apartment where they were to live. It was close to the sawmill, Oscar told her. What was more, there was another apartment connected to theirs, another family living in it. It was a doubtful pleasure to Lisa to hear this. Had Oscar met the family? What were they like?

"Nay, they did not come out although I went in to the empty rooms that are ours. The two rooms are so much like our *stuga* in Sweden, Lisa, you will feel at home right away."

"With ears on the other side of the wall? I doubt that." Katarina knew of the family but made no comment other than, "The Qvists keep to themselves."

There was a windfall for the Veldmans stored in Sigurd's biggest barn. Bedsteads, tables, benches and stools from Lisa's own childhood home. Furniture too much for Katarina's use and no longer needed by any brother. Four dead at sea, two at one time. Four in the Narpes cemetery and two living in America, one of whom no one knew exactly where.

Sigurd, kind and with smiling eyes, always alert to other people's needs, unearthed them and with Oscar's help transported them to the new home. It took several trips, for Sigurd would not load the wagon too heavily in concern for his ancient beloved horse.

The Sunday before Oscar was to begin work, the two families made the trip together, taking the rest of the things brought from Sweden, and Katarina's gift of the family trunk. Lisa knew it well, the date 1839 carved into its bottom plank, 1840 in fanciful but not expert figures painted on its rounded wooden top. The front and sides were decorated with bright floral designs. She was not going to let Oscar have them painted out. Unlike any flowers she had ever seen, they had been put there by some unknown relative. They were to stay. But she felt she must object to the meaningful gift.

Katarina insisted. "We have the one from Sigurd's family. It is enough."

As Oscar began work, Lisa settled into the new home. She stood often in the doorway, engulfed by the sound of the saws so close to the double house. When she went to the stream below it for water she searched for some evidence of other buildings, other houses. But the fields and forests were the only neighbors in sight. Most of the workers came by bicycle from the village, or from farms long distances away. The two boys from next door were often on the steps next to hers when she went out. It was not until the fourth day she met *Fru* Qvist, and realized there were two more children inside. An older girl, Elvira's age, and a young boy, Johan's, and he seemed not quite right in the head. She had never seen either one leave the house. Already she had realized the woman had some kind of problem, for the boys looked neglected, unwashed, and in clothes that needed mending. Her girls reported that the boys never talked to them, only listened with open mouths. They wondered if they understood what they said.

"Good day, *Fru* Qvist." Lisa stood with brimming pail of water on her own stoop. One look and she realized *Fru* Qvist's problem was drinking. Her face was puffed, blood vessels broken on her nose and cheekbones, although Lisa estimated the woman was younger than herself.

"Yaw, good day," *Fru* Qvist barked, nodded, then scurried around the house on her way to the toilet.

Lisa sighed. So distant from Katarina they had to live, share a house with such sad people, and be so far from the village.

The three older girls started school. At home again the first day, they reported that indeed the Qvist boys could talk and understood what was said. The teacher was pleased that the Veldman girls spoke pure Swedish, as he did. Lars and Helmar Qvist certainly understood the teacher. They talked to them now, but always in Swede-Finn. The girls began to understand it.

Lisa was home alone except for the three youngest ones. Oscar was wrapped up in his work, talked only of it when he was home for midmorning breakfast, midday meal, at supper and in the evenings.

"I feel the resentment of the Swede-Finns," he admitted, "but so far there has been nothing I can put my finger on. I think it is because I am foreman. Well, I show them a good day's work every day so maybe they will soon accept me."

The sawmill had provided only the one double building for its foreman, and its watchman-handyman, Qvist. Lisa longed for visitors. The few times friends came to see her, and welcome her back to Finland, she found they had come more because they had not seen her and her family attending church in Narpes.

"Even if we had some way to travel that long distance, we do not belong to the church."

She said it deliberately each time. The sooner they knew, the sooner they would accept and, perhaps, listen to Oscar when he explained the TRUTH to them from the Bible. Anger, astonishment, and only once faint praise were the responses. Only a few came after that. Sometimes they came in the evening, mostly to get a glimpse of the heretic Swede she had married. Her loneliness grew.

The day came when Elvira was to pick up Marta and begin the journey to Finland. Lisa walked to a distant field, Carl on her hip, the other children running in happy chase. Beyond the two windmills, at the far end of the long open space, she saw the shimmer of the Gulf. It eased her to know the waters were calm, and she hoped they would stay that way for the girls' crossing. She tried to visualize Elvira's arrival at Palmers. It would not take them long to pack a few things to send with Marta. Only enough to fill the knitted bag. Two days later she found out how wrong she had been.

*

With deep content Lisa repeated, "It's so good to have you home again," and saw Elvira flinch a second time.

Why did the girl do that? She pushed the question aside and resettled herself to the joy of hearing more news of family and friends back in Sweden. There was so much to ask about, even though both she and Oscar had sat up until almost morning absorbed in the news of "home". It would be days before every kernel would be gleaned, the whole story of Elvira and Marta's trip across the Gulf told. Throughout every moment Lisa could glory that her two girls were back, the family complete again.

Elvira spoke with a new confidence, she noticed. The girl had matured. It was not only that her hair no longer hung in a braid but was pinned up. Should she tell the girl she had become ... handsome? Nay, one does not tell children such things. It would given them false pride. What a pity Marta had given Elvira such a difficult time after they had left Palmers. Maybe that was what still bothered her. She had admitted pulling Marta's forelock several times, the girl behaving not at all like a Veldman. That she had had to demand obedience need not continue to bother Elvira, Lisa told her, if she had spoken gently to the child right afterwards. Was Elvira mature enough to realize what Marta was going through? Perhaps not.

"... and Greta Swanson will have another baby in January, she told me," Elvira was saying, looking down into her coffee instead of at Lisa.

The lowered eyes suddenly brought to Lisa's mind the arrival of the two girls in the middle of the night. The moment Elvira had stepped back after the welcoming embrace her smile had vanished and her eyes had dropped down to Lisa's extended stomach. Even this morning, although Elvira talked with animation, her eyes avoided Lisa's. They were instruments of judgment, and she knew all at once that the girl read more than was intended each time she told her it was good to have her home.

"It is not so you can care for me before and after childbirth, my dear eldest one," she wanted to say. "It is only that I love you and am so happy to have you with us again. If only I could manage after the baby is born without taking yet another one of the girls out of school, I would insist you enter school again. Pappa would too, even more. You know yourself how important he feels an education is. It was why he went to the schoolmaster, back in Sweden, and asked that you be allowed to continue your study when you had to go to work to help us. He went and talked to those two ladies too, to give you time to study, and he came to listen to you recite, many times. You wrote and said you took your exams and headed the whole class. How proud we are." But all she could bring herself to say was, "Dear child, we cannot apologize to you for what God has decreed. Some day you will understand and I pray I will have the courage to talk to you about it before you have your own babies."

"I think I hear Marta!"

Begun as a shout, Paulina's words trailed down into a whisper, the warning to be quiet suddenly remembered. The girls, trailed by Alli and Johan, rushed toward the bedroom doorway.

"She's sitting up!" Emilia announced on tiptoe to see past Maria and Pauline. With a quick look back at Lisa she asked hoarsely, "Can we sing to her now?"

"As soon as the tray is ready," Lisa answered, and got up to help Elvira set it.

In a group, stumbling on each other's heels, the younger five entered the bedroom first. They were dressed in costumes, crowns of daisies on the girls' heads, except for Emilia, garlands of flowers around their necks, including Johan's. Emilia pushed past Maria. She was dressed in Oscar's Sunday suitcoat, his round hard black hat setting far back on her red curls, his cane under her arm. Above her small upper lip a mustache, drawn in black soot, curled. Maria was elegant, wearing two long red-striped linen towels, one in back, the other in front, the pins holding them together on her shoulders gay with daisies thrust through them. Paulina wore what could be nothing other than Lisa's nightgown, lifted up by a bright blue string of yarn around her middle and with another belt made of daisies.

Alli worked her way close to the bed and stood staring at her sister. The straw bonnet she wore was covered with daisies, their bright yellow centers echoing the curls they almost hid. Johan had to be pushed forward. Oscar's fur hat rested on his head but slid down over his eyes no matter how often he pushed it up.

"Good morning, Marta, welcome home," Lisa said, Carl in her arms. Elvira preceded her, bearing the tray set with a familiar yellow mug with a band of black and white checks holding bobbing daisies, another with steam rising from it, and a dish of freshly cut coffee bread. Lisa continued, "Since you had a birthday a few days ago, your brother and sisters want to welcome you with a regular Swedish birthday celebration. Start the song, girls."

"Now she shall live,
    Now she shall live,"

they sang, the birthday song quavering at first until they got help from Elvira and Lisa.

"Now she shall live
    Out to a hundred years,"

they continued.

Alli leaned forward to bring her face close to the girl on the bed. "Marta?" she asked.

"Alli," Marta answered, her eyes on the bonnet, not her sister.

Johan squeezed in next to Alli. Sweat trickled down his face from under the fur hat. "My name is Johan," he announced solemnly.

"Welcome home, birthday girl," Lisa said and grasped Marta's toes, blanket and all, to shake them. She had been so sure this Swedish birthday custom would make a bridge to bring her children together again.

"Mamma," Marta exclaimed.

"Yaw, that is me, and here I am. Did you forget you saw me last night? It was going on one o'clock and you were more asleep than awake."

"Look, I'm getting tired holding this tray," Elvira complained, "let me put it on her lap."

Marta glanced at its contents, then up at Lisa. "*Tant* and *Farbror* Palmer had sweet cakes for me on my real birthday, and a fiddler, and many singers, all dressed up in Swedish costumes. They woke me up with their music. Out at the country house."

"Pooh! They were all strangers, I bet. Our costumes are better, I think," Emilia exclaimed. "We made them up!"

"Maybe we shouldn't sing. We aren't good enough for her," Maria said in a hurt tone.

"Yaw, we should," Paulina insisted. "Pappa says we sing better than any church choir. Besides, our house is in the country, isn't it?"

Elvira laughed. "It sure is. Nothing but a sawmill and space here."

"And besides that," Emilia sputtered, spit flying, "we don't have any fiddler. Oh, lah de day! Want me to play on a comb, Marta? I could do it real fancy."

"That's enough," Lisa ordered. "To spoil this reunion by being cross with each other? Instead, let us sing one of our own songs. 'Welcome Our Heavenly Father.' It has just the right chorus, 'Long have we waited,' and that's what we have done, Marta."

Silenced by Lisa's obvious unhappiness, the older girls gathered together and sang, Lisa joining in from where she had seated herself and Carl on the foot of the bed. Marta listened but did not sing. Alli sang, her voice soaring sweetly. Johan leaned against the bed facing his returned sister, his head tipped back, the fur cap thrust away from his eyes.

In the quiet that followed, Emilia snatched the cap and placed it on her own head, the black hard hat held high in her other hand.

"Pappa said I was to wear it!" Johan shouted, and stamped after her as she strutted, tapping the cap with the cane.

"Don't tease," Lisa laughed, relieved that the humor of Emilia's antics had changed the feeling in the room. "Give him the cap. That's it. Johan, bring it to me. It is time we stopped playing, there is work to do." She stood up and unpinned the top of her skirt over the bulge that drew the front of it up high, then reached for Carl after repinning the skirt.

"Nay, Mamma, let me take Carl. You shouldn't be carrying him at all." Maria stepped in front of her to pull Carl to the edge of the bed, then set him down on the floor.

"You are right. Anna Strom, the midwife, warned me, Elvira, not to carry him more than necessary. Maria, fold the towels when you put them back in the trunk. Emilia, don't crush the flowers against

Pappa's coat. They will leave a stain. Take it outside and brush it, before you put it and his cane back in the wardrobe. Paulina, I'm sure my nightgown has become soiled around the bottom. Take it off and use a little soap and water along the edge than lay it on the grass to dry."

Talking to each one in this way, she made her way to the wardrobe to put Oscar's cap and hat away.

Marta called, "Who is going to help me dress?"

Lisa stood in the doorway.

"There are your clothes on that stool," she told her as she pointed. "You could dress yourself before you left us, I'm sure you can still do so." She turned and went into the main room.

"She needs help?" Maria marveled.

"Is she sick?" asked Emilia.

"Aren't you six years old now?" Paulina inquired.

"Wait," Elvira told them, bent over to take Carl's hands to encourage him to take some steps, "you haven't seen anything yet."

Marta came carrying her dress, her head high as she called to Lisa.

"I wore this for two days," she complained. "I need a fresh one from my basket."

Swiftly Lisa came back to her. "Is it dirty?" she asked. She took the dress to examine it. "Nay, it isn't. We will open the basket shortly, but this dress will do until fall when we go down to the river to do laundry. Unless there is a more practical one in the basket. We shall see later. Wear it now. Comb your hair and, if you can't braid it, ask someone to do it for you."

"I don't wear it braided anymore," Marta protested.

"You will now," Lisa told her, "like the others.."

"Alli's isn't braided," Marta complained.

"You are to do as I say," Lisa said testily. "Alli's curls don't need braiding. Your straight hair does."

The child walked slowly toward the bedroom, a pout on her lips. Lisa watched and could not scold or place blame on her. Where did the blame lie? On herself and Oscar? Perhaps, but would they have felt blameless if today the child was crippled? *Herr* Palmer? Nay. He had acted out of concern and kindness. *Fru* Palmer? It would be easy to say, go ahead, blame her. But I can't. The strike? Nay. Always there had been too little food. That was it. A man's work should pay enough to feed properly the children the Lord sends him. There were too many young in Sweden who paid in twisted bones, even up to this day. May the Lord give the men courage to try again and win to a better pay soon.

So she had to be patient with the child. Patience. Patience with the others too, and teach them where the fault really sits.

Screeches roared out of the bedroom. Lisa spun around and ran, but reached the doorway behind her girls. She pushed them further in and found Alli, her mouth agape, one hand lifted to hold her head, the other pointing at Marta.

"What happened?" Lisa demanded.,

"It's mine," Marta answered, her hands behind her back.

"Her bonnet," Elvira decided immediately. "She must have ripped it off Alli's head."

Marta edged backwards, a glare directed at Elvira, defiance making her mouth a tight downward curve.

"Let me have it." Lisa's quiet command changed Marta's face. Mouth quivering, she brought the bonnet to her.

"I didn't mean to pull her hair," she explained in a low voice.

"Alli," Lisa said, "go with Elvira and the others into the other room. I'll talk to you later."

She led Marta over to a bed, seated herself and drew the girl in front of her. "I know it is hard for you to get used to our ways again, Marta," she began, "but you are going to have to learn to do it."

"I didn't mean to pull her hair," Marta repeated.

"I'm sure you didn't," Lisa agreed.

"The hat is mine," Marta insisted.

"So it is. Did Alli ruin it by wearing it for your birthday celebration?"

"Nay, I don't think so," Marta said with embarrassment, twisting her head to look at the bonnet. All the flowers had dropped off and the ribbons trailed down over the top of the wardrobe, where Lisa had placed it next to Oscar's hat.

Lisa pulled Marta closer and put both arms around her, lacing her fingers together in the small of Marta's back.

"Remember this, dear child," she continued, "we are many and you are one of us. It is not right for anyone to have more than the others. Remember that always. When you are troubled, come to me or to Pappa. We will help you find your way again with all of us. Yaw?"

Marta nodded and leaned forward to nestle her head in the hollow of Lisa's neck. Her hands pushed hard against the roundness of the enlarged stomach. Abruptly Lisa thrust her away, then stood up to hold her close again for a few moments.

"Go tell Alli you are sorry. You'll feel better right away. Go." She raised her hand and brushed a sudden film of sweat from her forehead.

Peace was restored. Elvira and Maria set to work to make the beds. They called to the twins to take the night jars out to the toilet to be emptied and washed. When the two came back they were met at the door with rag rugs to shake, while the older two swept the floor.

Lisa busied herself again. She took time to smile encouragement at Marta when she came out of the inner room fully dressed, followed by Alli, who had needed no more than a hug and to be told she must help make Marta one of them again. But, mentally, Lisa shook her head. Marta looked like a guest. The fine material of her dress set her apart against the harsh serviceable cloth of the other dresses.

"Come," she called to her, "let me braid your hair this morning."

She found a piece of orange yarn on a wooden peg, and plaited it into two braids.

"Take Marta outside," she told Alli when she finished. "Johan is waiting on the steps for you. Come in and eat when Pappa comes home for second breakfast."

For the hundredth time she remembered the sharp disappointment of last spring when they reached this new home to find Cousin Ebba Sorenson's clay-daubed fireplace in Koskö, where they had spent their first night in Finland those months ago, was repeated here and in the same corner. How she missed her stove in Sweden, its black bulk becoming a treasured memory of convenience and warmth. Even in August the mornings were cold here, the fire in the fireplace doing little to warm the chill. And the electric light. When would Finland have electricity? She missed that too. She refused to think of the dark and bitter winter ahead. Thank goodness this morning was sunny. With effort she straightened up, one hand pushing against the hood over the fireplace. Again she unpinned her skirt and drew in deep breaths before she repinned it. With the rag she used to handle the pot on the hearth, she wiped her perspiring face.

"I am too tired," she murmured.

After the midday meal, when Oscar had gone back to work, Elvira and Paulina carried the large square yellow basket that had come from Palmers with Marta over to the table where Lisa had settled down. It held whatever the Palmers had sent along with the girl.

"Set it right here in front of me," she told them. Elvira had to use a hammer to get the stick out of the loop that held the lid down tight. Everyone crowded around as Lisa lifted the lid.

"Oh, my," she exclaimed as she smoothed her hand over a rose-colored wool blanket that was on top. "How soft it is." She lifted part of it, and rubbed it against her face. "This will be good for the new baby. How thoughtful of them to send it."

"But that's ..." Marta began, but stopped as Elvira poked her angrily.

Lisa looked at her. "Don't you think this will be good for the new baby, Marta?"

"The baby isn't new," Marta protested with a glance at Carl. The boy was seated on the floor crawling from one spot to the next in his own way, moving his buttocks forward, first one side than the other.

"Not Carl," Lisa laughed and avoided looking at Elvira. "There will be a new baby soon. This blanket came just in time."

Elvira tried to look unconcerned. The three other girls nudged each other, and pulled their mouths down, in silent judgment of uninformed Marta.

Alli had climbed up onto a stool. "Oh!" she exclaimed and pointed down into the basket. Everyone craned to see. A tangle of dolls lay exposed as Lisa drew the last of the blanket into her lap. There was a general intake of breath as the sisters all looked at Lisa.

"Oh! All my dolls!" Marta cried. She pushed in closer to the basket, but stopped suddenly, stepped back and looked at Lisa.

Lisa, her mouth tight, reached down and took out the first doll.

"Ohh!" gasped the girls as the doll, in Swedish Dalarna costume, came into view. Lisa's shoulders sagged as she held it out in front of her. The hand holding it fell into her lap. Bent over the basket, she sighed, "Oh, my."

"May I see it?" Paulina asked hesitantly.

"Well," Lisa mused, "I suppose you had all better have a look at them since they are here. Why would they do this when Pappa had explained our belief? Here, take it."

She passed the doll to Paulina before she lifted the next one. The dolls were handed around the circle, Marta aside, her hands behind her back. Petticoats, dresses, tiny sandals, artificial and natural hair were exclaimed over. Most marveled at were the ones with eyes that opened and shut.

"They look alive," Emilia decided.

"Especially this one," Maria agreed. "Looks like a real baby."

"This one has yellow braids," Alli exclaimed.

"She's from Holland," Marta managed, as she crowded in among them.

"What on earth is this one?" someone asked. It was Elvira who reached into the basket and pulled out a gold colored box with a small figure standing on one toe, a skirt of fluffy lace above her long legs.

"Give it to me," Marta demanded, "I'll show you." She took the box and wound it with a key on the bottom. The flat of her hand extended with the box on it, the doll began to turn as tiny bells of music came from the box. There were startled exclamations at first, then it became so quiet it was as if no one breathed. When the music stopped, Maria asked, "What kind of doll is that?"

"A ballerina on a music box," Marta answered, and placed it on Lisa's outstretched hand.

"What's a ballerina?" Emilia asked.

"A dancer, can't you see?" Marta answered.

"The music. Show me," Johan asked, pushing in to get closer to Lisa. She held the music box out toward him, turned it upside down to let him see her wind it, then turned it over to let the dancer pirouette once again.

"I never," she murmured. She let the performing figure travel from hand to hand around the circle of her children. She looked down to find that someone had placed a curly-headed copy of a girl on her lap. Lost in admiration of the handwork on the doll she forgot herself. "I really think these clothes were made by a tailor. Can you believe that? Look, Elvira, have you seen any finer sewing anywhere?"

"It's beautiful, Mamma," Elvira agreed, bending over to see better. "Wish I could have a coat like that."

"Yaw," Lisa answered and came back to reality. "Nay, this is enough now. We have seen them all. Put them on the table."

"Mamma," Marta said, twisting her hands together, "Everybody can play with my dolls. It's all right."

Lisa smiled and patted her cheek. "Thank you, but didn't Pappa explain about dolls to you last night? He told me he had to make you leave one behind at Cousin Segerson's."

Marta nodded, her eyes filling with tears at the memory. "It was my favorite. She was a Japanese doll."

"You should have heard how she bawled and carried on, Mamma," Elvira butted in. "Cousin Segerson acted like Pappa had gone crazy because he wouldn't let her keep the doll. Said their Bible didn't say any such thing about its being a sin. Their girl ran off with the doll into the bedroom."

"Never mind, Elvira. Pappa was proud of Marta that she did what he explained to her she must. It will be hard at first, my child, but you will have sisters and brothers to play with. They are much better than any dolls for they are real, not imitations."

Marta nodded, her eyes going to the dolls that lay side by side on the table. All the children looked at them, the wonder in their eyes matching the yearning in Marta's.

Loudly Lisa said, "Let's see what else is in the basket." It was an hour before it was emptied. Dresses had been held up to themselves by various sisters. Hems were studied for lengthening or shortening. Seams were explored. Underwear agreed to be large enough for the twins, and small enough for Alli as well as Marta. A new coat and leggings were lifted out. Maria took them, saying, "Why, look, they are big enough for me."

Lisa saw Marta's contorted face, protest held back by expected criticism. "Nay," she said, "they are Marta's to grow into. No one else is to wear them."

Marta jerked them from her sister and went to sit on the round topped trunk, hugging them to herself.

The last items were lifted out, shoes enough for both Alli and Marta. Faces were flushed, including Lisa's, at the riches strewn around.

"Put everything back except the dolls," she told them. "I will decide what to do with them later. Marta, you can hang your coat and leggings in the bedroom cupboard. All of you go out now. I need to rest. Take Marta and show her the windmills. I'm sure she didn't see them in the dark last night. But, I don't want to hear that any of you tried to catch hold of the windmill arms to ride them up before dropping off. Hear?"

Laughing, nodding, talking with excitement about the things taken from the yellow basket, they went out together in front of the stoop. Marta trailed slowly behind with a long look over her shoulder at the dolls.

Lisa heard Emilia greet her with, "Didn't *Herr* Palmer know it was a sin to have dolls?" She did not hear Marta's response for Emilia almost immediately exclaimed, "It *was* a sin no matter what *Herr* Palmer said."

"I didn't see any dolls when we went over there," Paulina joined in.

"He hid them, that's what he did," Emilia told her. "Afraid Mamma and Pappa would see them."

"He did not!" Marta yelled. "They were in my room all the time."

"Your room?" Maria asked. "You had a room just for the dolls?"

"Nay, silly, the room where I slept."

"All alone?"

"Yaw, all alone, in the room next to *tant* and *farbror*."

"They slept in the big room where the Christmas tree was?" Paulina wanted to know.

"Nay, in their own bedroom."

"My," Maria marveled, "we didn't see all those rooms."

"Yaw, you had Christmas with a tree and presents and everything. The Palmers were sinful people and that's that," Emilia stated with their hands on her hips.

Lisa stepped out onto the stoop. "That will do. The Palmers are good people and believe, in their own way. You will leave such talk to Pappa. Now, go."

Emilia grasped one of Marta's hands as she shouted to Maria to grab the other. Marta between them, they ran away from the house, yanked her over the ditch as they leaped it, and did not look back to see if the others followed. Lisa watched them all disappear, Paulina far behind, holding Alli and Johan by the hand, running only as fast as they could.

She went back in and spoke to Elvira, who had poured herself a cup of coffee and stood drinking it, looking at the dolls. "You will have to help me. Pappa will want to burn them at the sawmill. I want you to take them over there."

When the children came home the dolls were gone. Lisa said nothing about them, nor did anyone ask. She could see Marta's eyes exploring everywhere looking for them. But on the table lay the clothes the dolls had been wearing. "These you may keep, Marta," she told the girl. "Perhaps you and Alli would like to play with them. Here, Elvira and I made these for you and Alli."

She handed them each a rag doll with faint indication of a head but with neither arms nor legs.

"Show them to Pappa when he comes and perhaps he will let you keep them for a while."

Late that night before going to bed she went to see if Marta slept. She had not cried when Oscar had explained again, carefully and long, why the dolls had to be taken away. But now, asleep between Johan and Alli, her face was still wet with long weeping. On Alli's pillow lay one of the rag dolls dressed in the small coat Elvira had admired. Lisa looked for the other doll but did not see it anywhere near Marta. As she turned to leave she saw the white blob of it in the furthest corner of the room. It could only have gotten there from having been thrown with force. It was as innocent of clothes as when she handed it to Marta. She picked it up and stood shaking her head over it. "Learning to believe," she told herself, "is sometimes made too hard for a little one."

"The child hurts inside. A hurt we have to remove, and soon," Lisa reasoned as she and Oscar sat together for the the first coffee of the day.

"I will explain to her again," he promised. "I hesitate to tell her they are burned, even though she needs to stop wondering where they are."

Lisa shook her head. "Nay! Nay! That would only hurt her further. It will have to wait until she can read the Bible for herself. Then she'll understand. The hurt is not only for the dolls. It is much bigger, Oscar. She feels apart, not yet one of us."

"The others seem to include her, I notice."

"Only because I keep after them. Emilia is too quick with her words. Although the others are less critical, they follow her lead."

They sat silent. Oscar poured his coffee into a saucer.

"Time will heal them all," he said.

"Of course, but it is right now we need to do something more for Marta."

"What? What more can we do?"

She studied her hands circling her coffee mug. "I don't know. I try to give her extra attention but that doesn't sit well with the others." She gave a short laugh. "It seems I'm so tired these days I can't even think."

He went to her. "You are to let the girls do the work. Rest, Lisa. Elvira is willing. Let her do the cooking too."

Here was another problem they needed to talk about, but at this moment she could not bring herself to start. It would have to wait. A wave of weakness made her shiver. She took his hand to hold it against her face.

"Yaw, I have to do that. We will talk further tonight."

Oscar bent and kissed her forehead, found his work cap and left.

For days the noise at the sawmill could not drive Lisa's words from Oscar's mind. At his usual pace, from one end of the mill to the other, inside and out, almost at a run, he fulfilled his work and responsibilities. From the first day the boss-owner of the sawmill had realized that this new man was willing to work at any task. More important, he had ability and accuracy in mathematics. He used Veldman for this as well as at more manual tasks, besides his duties as foremen. Today he called him in to refigure the board feet of a stack of lumber that had been sold.

A sinful pride swelled up within Oscar as his pencil hurried expertly over a scrap of wood serving as paper.

"Here is the total I get," he announced, as he handed it to the boss.

"Nay, Veldman," Mangusson said, after he studied the result. "My figures are much higher."

"Let me do it once again," Oscar suggested, afaird that his one year of schooling had betrayed him. He took another chip of wood, and once more leaned over the plank that served as a desk to write the total. "It comes out the same." he announced when he finished.

Magnusson took the second scrap of wood and looked at it. "Well then, you must be right. Thank you, Veldman."

As though the happiness of working with figures had released his mind he suddenly knew what he could do to help reunite the children. It would even make Marta forget the dolls, he was certain. He did not notice that both wooden pieces of wood he had written on lay discarded in the sawdust. Nor did he see that Magnusson was making out the bill at his own higher figure.

That evening he pushed his bicycle out to the road over the plank across the ditch, flung his leg over it, and with a strong thrust on the topmost pedal spun it into a swift ride away from the sawmill area. He was on his way to join a Temperance Society meeting, Lisa believed, but he did not stop when passed the meeting place three kilometers from home. Instead he continued to a fork in the road, turned left, and rode another kilometer before he braked. He jumped off, lifted the bicycle over another ditch to set it down on a pathway. It was a shortcut to Berta Lund's who had loaned him the horse and wagon.

Less than an hour later he was back on the road. The large straw basket attached to the handlebar had been empty on his way over. It was now full with something that wiggled and grunted inside a large coarse sack. Rope was laced over the top of the basket so that no matter how the living thing inside it complained it had no way to fall out. Now and then Oscar patted the top of the bag to try to calm the noise and wriggling, but that made them both worse, so he stopped it.

He slowed down at the meeting place to tell a man going in that soon he would come to the meetings too. He rode off without looking back, so did not see the man spit scornfully into the dust, nor hear his, "Damned heretic Swede!"

All the children, except Johan and Carl, were still up when he rode the bicycle up to the house.

"Marta," he called, "go tell Mamma to come see what I have brought you and your sisters."

Eyes big, as they gathered to watch the wriggling bag in the basket, the children asked questions he would not answer.

"Come, Mamma," Marta called into the open door of the house, "Pappa has something alive in his basket." She hurried back to join the others that now included the Qvist boys too.

"What is it?" several voices repeated, but Oscar would not do anything more than remove the rope that held the animal safe. Lisa came slowly down the few steps of the house over to him.

"You didn't join the meeting?" she asked, then, "what do you have there?"

As Oscar lifted the sack out of the basket someone said, "It sounds like..." then finished with, "... it is! It's a little pig!" as he rolled the animal gently out on to the ground.

The pig struggled to stand up, looking around at the forest of feet and legs, then sagged down on its rump and shook its head.

"Is it mine?" Marta asked, no more able to take her eyes from it than any of the other children.

"Yours, and your sisers' and your brothers'. It is for all of you to take good care of," Oscar told her.

Everyone spoke at once. "We will, Pappa. It's so pink! Can I name it? Will it stay little like this?"

"Here *nasse,* here *nasse,* " someone called, and therewith gave the small creature, sitting in resignation in front of them, its name.

It was Lisa's loud angry words that put an end to all the exclamations. "You bring *pork* to our house, Oscar?"

Neighbor Qvist, who had arrived, turned to her in amazement, his aqvavit flushed face astonished. "Why do you ask him such a thing?" he wondered.

Lisa ignored him. She continued to stare at Oscar. The pig got up suddenly and charged right through the legs in front of it. The children, shouting to each other, streamed off in chase. Oscar and Lisa were left standing with Elvira and Qvist.

Oscar picked up the bag and rope to wind them together and put them in the bicycle basket.

"We can return it when it is full grown," he said, without looking at Lisa. "I thought right now it will give the children something to care for. Bring them together like you said. Berta Lund would not let me pay for it. Said it was the runt. Glad to give it to the children."

"Where are they going to keep it?" she asked, glancing at Qvist and wishing he would take his alcoholic breath back in to his wife, who probably was too busy drinking herself to even come to the door, where Dagmar and the youngest stood. She had no intention of discussing forbidden pork in front of Qvist.

"I'll build a pen, right over there," Oscar answered her, pointing to a grassy stretch some distance from the house. "The children will have to keep it clean and care for it."

"Couldn't you have come with a cat?" she asked.

He shook his head. "Nay, cats are too independent, Lisa. It had to be something that would depend on the children's collective care. Perhaps we can get a cat too. I would like that." He turned to Qvist. "How about it, want to help me build that pen?"

"It isn't my kids' pig," he answered and backed away.

"Ah!" Oscar returned, "look at them. Already they are beginning to enjoy it along with mine."

The children ran in the distance like a group gone mad with laughter, and blown by a strong variable wind. The pig darted in front or ran skittering among them creating collisions and tumbles as his many pursuers had to change course. Oscar watched smiling, and hoped that Qvist would work with him on the pig pen. Maybe it would keep him from swilling so much for a few nights. He set himself the task right then to get Qvist to go with him to join the Temperance Society. Maybe building the pen would be a way to start.

Lisa made another protest. "It's going to smell up the whole area."

"Nay, Mamma," Elvira countered, "when I went to Berta Lund's pig farm, on Pappa's bicycle the other day, for cabbages and beets, I saw how clean the pigs and the pig house was. There wasn't any smell at all."

Paulina came with the pig in her arms, the glory of holding a small animal shining in her face. Earnestly she looked at her parents. "I will keep the pen clean, and make sure he is taken care of. I will, I really will."

Lisa said no more, nor did she respond to other cries from the rest of the new pig owners, when they added their promises to Paulina's. She went back into the house to Carl, whom she had left sitting on the floor. The Bible would be open to Leviticus, Chapter 11, when Oscar came in, and she would show him the verses. How could he put behind him the word of God? What was happening to him? The law was clearly stated, as Oscar himself had pointed out to her. Neither to eat nor to touch the flesh of the non-cud chewing beast. In her childhood home here in Finland the meat of pigs had been part of life and no one had thought further about it. But Oscar had made a large issue of it one day early in their marriage. How well she remembered it. She had prepared pork, crisp and golden, and set it before him at supper the day after he brought his first pay home to her.

"What is this?" he asked, his head low over his plate as he studied its contents.

"Bacon," she answered proudly, "with a good gravy on the potatoes from the drippings."

He grunted his disbelief, then marched to the stove to scrape all of it into the fire. She watched horrified. He brought the Bible, set it before her on the table and with a finger underlined each word as he read out loud verses seven and eight. There was no way she could ever forget that, nor their message. But now this.

She started to fetch the Bible, but a crippling wave of weakness overcame her. Strength drained out of her. One hand reached out toward a chair but she did not have the strength to go to it. Instead she lay down on the floor where she was and dimly knew that Carl wriggled on his buttocks to come sit next to her. She lay still, letting strength gather again. It was almost as if she slept. Carl bumped his head against her in some clumsy movement. Aroused, she raised a lax hand and fondled his curls, but lay still a long while. At least there was energy enough to sit. She encouraged Carl to stand alongside, one hand holding him steady as she rocked herself back and forth. Weakly at first, then with catches of hysteria as she laughed. With effort she made herself stop, lifted the other hand to her forehead. It was cool. With a bark of laughter she reassured Carl, as if he understood, "It was nothing, just that I am so tired."

Her thoughts went back to Oscar. She asked Carl, "We've got to admit, don't we, that the pig might work?" She chuckled. "But, we've also got to say that when Oscar decides to sin to help his family, he does so in the most ingenious way."

She knew there would be no further talk about the pig.

Qvist did not help with the building of the pen although he was full of suggestions. He sat on a nearby hump of earth and with generous waves of his hands directed Oscar as he struggled with uprights and crisscross sticks of wood. Oscar was not handy with hammer and nails. He worked too swiftly. His nervous energy drove nails into horseshoe bends, and broke sticks by forcing them into place. Whenever he stopped to rest he tried to talk Qvist into taking part. Each time he was soon talking to himself for Qvist hurried away, back into his own house. There he would stay, fortifying himself with a drink, until Oscar's hammer announced it was safe to come out again.

The children, five of Veldman's and the two Qvist boys, ran errands in clusters. They brought Oscar's Finnish *puukko,* that sharp knife in its reindeer scabbard that had been given him by Sigurd, Katarina's husband, the day they had arrived at their farm. Oscar refused to wear it on his belt, as did all the men of that area, but kept it in the house. The children fetched him other tools, brought dippers of water, and held boards as he nailed or sawed. In between times they petted the pig. It was passed from lap to lap, talked to and stroked, sometimes becoming for a moment the center of a tug-of-war until Oscar put a stop to that.

Neither Lisa nor *Fru* Qvist came out to watch the building. Lisa found the journey out to the toilet was as much extra energy as she could spare each day. *Fru* Qvist, who seldom crossed the threshold of her own doorway, stood just within it looking past the Veldman section of the building to the site of the pen. One hand pushing up into her untidy hair, she muttered to herself, "They say that Swede is smart? He thinks a pig is a pet!"

When her eldest daughter tried to see out from behind her she elbowed her back sharply, snapping, "Those dishes done?"

The pen was completed. The big straw-lined box where the pig had slept for two nights was lifted in. It had worried the children that the board covering the box and weighed down with a big rock would not keep the pig from getting out. The first night, after late whispered consultations in the bedroom, the twins had been elected to creep out and make sure the pig was still there. They did not get past their parent's bed in the main room.

"Nay," Came Oscars voice. "Get back to bed. The pig is there. You don't have to go see."

There would be no need to worry anymore. The box, placed inside the pen and tipped over on its side to face the house, was easy to see through both the front windows and one of the windows in the bedroom. The box provided shade from the sun and shelter from the rain.

Lisa made the effort to come out to see Nasse enter its new home. The two Qvists swarmed inside helping the Veldman girls and Johan spread straw. They ran alongside each other to bring fresh water from the river in the wooden bucket Lisa had reluctantly allowed to be commandeered for the animal.

All of a sudden Lisa gasped. She felt as if a terrible weight was thrusting itself down through her body, and warm liquid gushed down her legs. She swayed as she stepped back to see a red spot on the ground where she had been standing. Without raising her voice she turned to Elvira who stood next to her, Carl on her hip.

"Don't say anything," she told her, "but something wrong is happening to me. Walk with me back to the house. Quick."

Elvira called, "Maria, look after Carl," as she put the boy down on the ground.

"Shh, shh," Lisa urged, her face drawn and white with a film of sweat glistening on it.

Lisa's fingers dug into Elvira's arm as she forced her to turn with her. Once her back was toward the others, she released her to grasp her skirt into a thick bunch and push it between her legs.

"Hurry," she pleaded, even as her steps slowed, making it necessary for Elvira to pull as well as push her forward, one arm across Lisa's back.

It didn't take long for Oscar to realize Lisa was missing. He hurried into the house to find her stretched out on their bed in the main room.

"I'm bleeding," she told him, as he bent over her. "Get Anna Strom."

"The baby is coming?" he gasped.

She shook her head weakly. "It's too soon ... two more months. Hurry."

He whirled about, but she half lifted herself to call him back.

"Katarina," she whispered, when he came, "get her...too." Tears ran from the corners of her eyes. She made no effort to wipe them away.

"I'll do that. Shall I send two of the girls to help out over there while she is here?"

Her eyes closed, Lisa nodded. "Maria..." she agreed, then, after taking a deep breath, added, "... and Paulina."

Oscar nodded, then asked Elvira, "Did you put something up against the flow?"

"Yaw, she had me put many of Carl's diapers there."

"Good. Go get one of the winter furs. Fold the bianket many times and put it under her legs." He bent over Lisa again. "Keep your legs raised up on the fur blanket," he told her, "untill the midwife gets here."

She made no sign she had heard. He turned back to Elvira. "You stay here with her. I'll tell Emilia and Marta to take care of the little ones."

Lisa's voice rasped in its urgency as she roused herself to plead, "Hurry!"

It was a quiet family that sat around the table when Anna Strom, the midwife, came. Oscar arrived shortly afterward.

He had whirled over the roads on his bicycle, first in one direction then another. Maria and Paulina had been sent to walk the distance between the two homes, cautioned to hurry, but to stay on the road, not take the shortcut through the woods. Elvira and Emilia helped the midwife remove Lisa's long skirts without getting her up or moving her too much. Since she owned no other underwear than petticoats, the inner one had become stained.

"You haven't lost much blood yet," Anna Strom told her, "and I think we can put a stop to it. Here, girl," she said, handing Elvira the soiled petticoat, "put this to soak in cold water."

The rattle of the farm wagon announced Katarina's arrival. She entered and went directly to the bed, not even untying her kerchief as she knelt on one knee next to it. With both arms encircling Lisa, she drew her gently toward her. Lisa roused and nestled into her neck like a sick child. "You came. How good that you came," she murmured.

Sigurd came in quietly, only long enough to set down a large *kontti,* a Finnish basket handwoven out of inch-wide birch bark strips and furnished with shoulder straps. He gave a quick nod as he looked in Lisa's direction, then left.

Between moans and slipping off into half-consciousness, Lisa asked about the two who had gone to the Olofssons. Katarina and Sigurd had met them on the road, and Oscar had waited at the farm until they turned in toward the house. Then he had sprinted on the bicycle, passing Sigurd's ancient horse pulling the farm wagon.

"You, children. Go in the other room or outside, "Anna Strom ordered from the fireplace where she poured water from the kettle ito a basin.

"Yaw," Oscar quickly agreed. "You have done well, all of you," indicating them with a swing of his hand. "It is better now that you do as she says."

Because the two boys and Alli were asleep in the bedroom, Elvira led the way outdoors and over to Nasse's pen. The three girls sat down with their backs against the fence. Although it was still light enough to see Nasse they did not turn around when it came snuffling up behind them asking for attention.

Emilia tucked her crossed feet in against herself and put her elbows on her knees to support her head in her hands. One leg rested warmly against Marta's outstretched ones. On the other side Elvira sat with her knees up, her skirt pulled down into a tent covering her legs. One hand fell into Marta's lap and lay there. Sitting sandwiched between her sisters, Marta felt snug and accepted. Carefully she slipped a hand into Elvira's and placed the other gently on Emilia's knee. Together they looked toward the house, each of them frightened into silence.

After a long while Elvira began to say, "It would be good if..." but didn't continue. She picked at the grass with her free hand and tightened the one around Marta's. Her chin lowered to her knees, she began again. "If Mamma loses the baby..." then was silent. She drew a deep shuddering breath, lifted her head up toward the sky. "Is it so bad to want to go to school?" she asked, her eyes pleading.

Lisa kept the baby. It would take many days of lying perfectly still, and getting up only to use the chamber pot. Anna Strom did what she could that night, most of which was to give advice, after packing cloths tightly to stop the bleeding.

"She needs food ," she told Oscar severely. "Good, rich food to help her hold onto the child until the right time." He listened carefully as she enumerated what the foods should be.

"I'll get them," he promised.

"I brought some with me," Katarina interrupted, and went to the *kontti* Sigurd had carried in. She took out containers of cream, chunks of cheese including a square of the sweet goat variety. Butter. Dark loaves of bread called *surkaka,* still in cloths that had been wrapped around them damp when they first came out of the *kakalugn.* That huge oven was part of Katarina's fireplace, similar to the ovens in all the houses in Finland, including the much smaller one here in the Veldman's home.

The children gathered close, their mouths watering in anticipation of the delicious bread tasting of malt that they had first experienced in Katarina's house. Spread with her good butter there was no better bread in all the world, they knew.

Anna Strom stood nodding over the display on the table. "Yaw, that's it. Meat and fish too, of course," she repeated several times. Then to Lisa. "Don't get up for at least a week, and only then if you feel strong enough. And when you go out, don't go jumping over any ditches. If you have to walk anywhere let the children carry a board along to bridge the ditches for you." With that she tied on her kerchief and left.

The food strengthened Lisa, although she could eat little of it at first. But what healed her most was having Katarina to talk to. Words spilled out endlessly as soon as Oscar was off to work. Katarina was reduced to, "Yaw haw," "Ya so," or an astounded, "Nay!" now and then. In between times Lisa slipped into sleep. By the third day she had slept enough and talked herself into peace.

Laughter began.

"Katarina, do you remember Olof Pearsson?" Lisa asked.

"Do I remember?" she exclaimed, lifting her hands from the bowl of cooked potatoes and rutabagas she was blending together with a wooden masher. "He was the one couldn't decide which one of us he was courting."

"And wanted us to bundle with him at the same time," Lisa cried, laughing so hard she feared the flowing would start again.

Katarina circled the table to come stand near her sister's bed. "So, we did one time, remember? Both of us on the other side of the bundling divider," she exclaimed. "And we cured him that night, didn't we?" She stood pointing the wooden masher at Lisa.

"With the help of some of our brothers," Lisa agreed, between gasps of delight. "Four of them were in the other beds across the room and kept giving Olof crazy advice."

"That's right. It was Eric who told Oldof he'd get a nosebleed if he climbed over that high divider, wasn't it?

"Yaw," Lisa laughed, "although the divider was just some blankets folded between him and us."

"And maybe it was Gideon who called out, 'You get between those two girls and you'll end up just a fat spot on the mattress. They're man eaters!' "

It took some while before Katarina could calm herself enough to say, as she wiped her eyes with her apron, "He sat up to bang those big feet of his down so hard his shoes made a noise like the end of the world had come. He was mad through and through. Left without a word, he did. Never came back either, did he?"

"Nay, and no wonder," Lisa sputtered, wiping her eyes with her fingers. "We told him crazy things too. You said he'd have to marry both of us and the boys too because we were all in the same room when he was courting. Remember?"

"Did I? Well, even though Olof was so big and handsome we knew he was silly in the head, and shouldn't have teased him so, or egged him on to bundle with the two of us."

"How young and foolish we were then, Katarina. Besides, it wasn't easy for any man to court us with our ten brothers to reckon with."

"Ha! We gave them some bad times too," Katarina recalled. "Especially the time Sigfrid was bundling with farmer Janssen's girl. The one we didn't like?" Katarina's lifted eyebrows asked if Lisa remembered.

Lisa nodded, smiling with guilt. "That was one Saturday night when we went over there. Sneaked in close to the house and began throwing grass and twigs in through the open window. And meowed like cats."

"Worse," Katarina corrected, "we had made mud balls when we crossed the ditch on the way over there, and we threw those in too."

Like young girls they shrieked with laughter. Katatina had to sit down on the edge of the bed. Lisa captured her sister's free hand as together they finished laughing.

Lisa began again. "Yaw, if we hadn't started running almost right away, Sigfrid would have caught us before we got home. I can almost feel right now how he would have yanked all the hair out of our heads."

"Me too," Katarina giggled, "I think he exploded out of that window after us." A knowing look on her face, she nodded wisely to add, "He didn't marry her though."

This time the laughter had triumph in it.

"Will I bundle with some boy some day?"

Startled, the two women turned to look at Elvira. They had forgotten that she sat on a stool altering one of Marta's dresses. Katarina got up quickly and returned to her work on the table. Lisa twisted slightly on the bed to face her daughter.

"Nay, Elvira, it isn't done much anymore. Those were in the old days when we were young. Besides, Pappa wouldn't allow it."

"Why not, it sounds like so much fun."

"So it was, sometimes, but it is better to sit up in a room with other people around than to lie fully clothed on a bed in a dark bedroom."

"Yaw, there is much that happened during bundling days gone by that shouldn't have," Katarina agreed, with a quick look at her sister as she smashed the vegetables with a firm beat. "Remember Svea Dahlstrom, Lisa?"

"Svea," Lisa murmured. "Yaw, she was the one...I will tell you about her someday, Elvira."

"Tell me now," Elvira begged.

The sisters exchanged a serious look. Katarina nodded slightly.

"She had a baby," Lisa said quickly. "The young man who was pappa to it was shipped off to America by his prosperous family. This was a long time ago before it was so popular for men to leave our homeland for that country."

"Did he send for her?" Elvira asked.

Lisa shook her head. "Nay, they weren't married.""Oh," Elvira breathed, then asked, "what happened to her?"

Lisa turned back to her sister. Katarina set the bowl aside.

"She's still at home on her parents' farm. They work her like a slave, her boy too. Dahlstrom is a hard man, an elder in the church and takes religion seriously."

The only sound in the room was that of the boys, Johan and Carl, playing in a corner with their blocks of wood Oscar had brought them from the sawmill. Elvira's thoughts turned somehow to the sailor who had helped her in Kaskö and who had asked her if she were going to the dance. She found herself wondering what it would be like to lie on a bed with him. Heat rose into her face. Embarrassment flooded her. She got up.

"I'll go meet the girls. They must be on their way home from school," she called over her shoulder as she went outside.

Katarina spoke first as the door closed. "She has to learn."

"She knows," Lisa said in return. "She's been a woman for some time, I think. She is already wearing an extra petticoat. It must have started while she was still in Sweden."

"It gives her no trouble?"

Lisa shook her head. "She has said nothing to me about it, nor asked." As if rehearsed, they both sighed deeply.

For a while there was silence between the sisters. About to speak Lisa hesitated. Katarina saw and lifted her eye brows again in question. Lisa took courage. "You were more fortunate than the Dahlstrom girl."

Katarina did not express surprise. Hands clasped together on the table, she said, "I always figured you knew."

"Of course."

"I didn't write it to you."

"You didn't have to. You were just beginning to go with Sigurd when I left Finland. Less than nine months later you let me know you were not only married but had your firstborn, Axel."

Katarina sat nodding. "That's the danger. Young love, strong feelings."

Lisa nodded also, and again hesitated. This time Katarina asked, "What were you going to say?"

"You had your first two so close together, then some years before Eva came. Since then no babies at all. Why is this?"

"After Olaf, the second boy, I wouldn't let Sigured near me. Then one night I couldn't help it, so there is Eva. After that I told him, it is either leave me alone or go sleep in the barn."

"Katarina! How can you do that? And to Sigurd who is so kind and good? What about you? Aren't those same feelings in you? Katarina, I...I..."

"It is either that or more children. Like you. Anything else is a sin to Sigurd, as well as to me."

"Of course. But...does Sigurd still sleep with you, in the same bed there in your big room?"

"He does, and we...don't."

"Ohh! Katarina! What a wonderful man Sigurd is. but, I do feel for him. For you too."

"Ach," her sister protested, waving her hands in front of her. "you get used to it. Try it."

"Aiy yaiy yaiy, Oscar would never be able to do that. I could never ask him to."

Katarina shrugged, got up and went back to her cooking. "What would Oscar do if Elvira came home in such a fix?"

Lisa closed her eyes against the thought, but answered, "He would be hurt, as I would be. But you know something?" She opened her eyes to look at Katarina, "Oscar can understand the weakness of the flesh, but he has often said he would never understand if any of his children became a strike breaker. Isn't he remarkable?"

"Strange, that's what I call it," Katarina stated flatly.

"That's because you live on a farm and can be independent, as long as people have money to buy what you raise. Just think, if the railroad union in Sweden had had enough money to keep the strike going it might have won."

"All I know if you are here, and that is God's wish, and mine. I'm glad I live on a farm, glad you're here, and that you are not going to lose the baby. That is enough for me. I don't want to hear any more such talk."

She turned away but suddenly hurried around the table and came to stand close to Lisa again, her face soft, her voice apologetic.

"Let's hope Elvira finds a good man and marries right off," she said quickly.

Lisa lay nodding in agreement. "If only she could go back to school. We were the two eldest, Katarina. You must remember how it was to always be raising the ones who came later. Didn't you mind?"

"Mind?" Katarina gave it some thought. "Yaw, I suppose I did, but in those days no one thought there was any other thing a girl should do. We went to school a few years. Elvira is a modern girl. Wants more schooling, and no wonder, her pappa is reading all the time. I've never seen so many books in a house. Where does he get them?"

"I wonder too, but he finds them. Borrows and buys when and wherever he can. Elvira reads them all too, almost faster than he does.

but I worry about her, Katarina. She is so all alone here. No one her age, except that poor Dagmar next door. There seems to be nothing I can do but feel bad about her."

Katarina returned to the fireplace, poured two mugs of coffee, spilled cream liberally into both, and came to give one to her sister and hand her a lump of sugar. She settled herself on the stool Elvira had deserted, and pulled it up close to the bed.

"Elvira will find her way. Don't worry about that," she began, then asked, "do you remember the time we tied that fellow's shoelaces together and he didn't know it until he got up?"

Lisa snorted with sudden laughter, and had to hold her coffee mug high to avoid spilling it with her giggles. "Of course. It was Per from over near Nornas." Gratefully she joined Katarina in another journey into memories. Peace and contentment grew as their voices mingled, and their laughter brought lightness once again into the room.

The newborn was small, gave no trouble. Lisa's strength grew as the good food continued, although now it was the girls who shopped. Lisa told them exactly what, and how much to buy.

It had been three weeks after the birth that she argued with Oscar one early morning, holding his arm to keep him from leaving for work.

"It won't hurt them to miss one day," she repeated. "You said the schoolmaster himself had told you how well they are doing."

"All right," he yielded finally and resettled his work cap on his head, "but let this be the only time. They are not to think school is a now and then thing."

"There's little chance of that," Lisa answered, and reached around to open the door for him.

"Three days!" the older girls exclaimed, when told that on Friday evening of that week the whole family would go to Olofsson's to bake the winter *knäkebröd.*

"But there's school on Monday," Paulina said, her sisters nodding in worried agreement.

Balanced on one leg, and about to push the raised one into the long stocking she held in front of her, Maria asked, "How can we stay through Monday?"

"Pappa is going to stop by and talk to the schoolmaster after work tonight." Lisa shushed the gasps, adding, "You are not to say anything to the schoolmaster, hear? That is for Pappa to do. Finish dressing, hurry up, there's no more to be said about it."

"I've never been to *Tant* Olofsson's," Marta reminded everybody as she sat on the floor buttoning a shoe.

"Not *Tant* Olofsson," Emilia corrected her. "She is Mamma's sister. You call her *Moster* Katarina, and Sigured is *morbror* because he is *Moster* Katarina's husband, just like you would if he was Mamma's brother."

"I know, I know. I just forgot," Marta responded, while she buttoned the other shoe. She abandoned the buttoning altogether as she noticed the older girls had clustered to whisper to each other. Maria was speaking as she pushed her head in among them.

"...and maybe *moster* will bake a big oven pancake too, like she did when we came from Sweden." They glanced quickly at Lisa. They knew if she heard what they were saying, something that sounded as if they were asking for food, someone would have her hair tugged in punishment.

But Lisa, busy with the younger children, paid no attention.

"If you need an army to bake *knäkebröd,* you've sure got one," Emilia called, as she trooped out the door with the other three schoolgirls. Lisa looked up to laugh, and wave a hand in thanks.

Marta poked her head back in. "It's about time we do something besides just stay at home."

"That Marta!," Elvira began, and took a step toward the door, then it slammed shut. She gathered the dishes into a rattling pile. "She thinks we should be like rich people's children, off on a country visit every few days." She dumped the dishes into the washpan with something like hate.

"Elvira," Lisa said to her eldest, who never spoke about hurts or disappointments. "I've heard there is to be a dance in the village at the end of next week. Would you like to go?"

Elvira swung around, water dripping from the straw dishwashing brush in her hand.

Her face was a mixture of hope and confusion.

"You don't mean... Would Pappa let me go?"

"Pappa and I met at a dance."

With a grunt of surprise Elvira strode over to seat herself near Lisa who spoonfed the baby. "You never told me Pappa danced."

"He didn't. Never could. He played a horn at the dance."

"Pappa played music? You never told me that either."

"I know. He had to sell the horn long before you could remember. It's too hard to talk about."

"But, Mamma, Pappa says dancing is a sin. When you show us dance steps at home it was always when he was off at one of the

Temperance meetings, or talking to someone, somewhere, about the Bible. Never, when he was around."

"That's true," Lisa hesitated. "Maybe that is because I needed a little fun myself. Perhaps I should be ashamed. Of course we couldn't do it when Pappa is here and make all that noise. You girls stomped pretty hard when you dance. It is only right Pappa should have quiet when he is home, the sawmill noise is enough in his ears for one day."

Stunned at Lisa's revelation, Elvira was moved to make a first admission of her own. Cheeks flushed, she said, "Oh, Mamma, how I've wanted to go. You know what I used to do in Sweden?" Lisa shook her head. "I used to stop and look at the dances in town on the nights the two *frökens* sent me on errands that went past the dancehall. Sometimes I even danced outside the window, all by myself. That accordian music, it was so beautiful. Will they have accordian music here too, Mamma?"

"They will. The same tunes too, I'm sure. Even my favorite." She hummed the beginning of the Blue Danube Waltz. Elvira jumped up and invited her to dance. "Nay," Lisa laughed, "it's too soon after the birth. Another time I will."

Elvira waltzed over to the dishpan but returned to Lisa, serious again. "Pappa will never let me go."

"Leave that to me." Lisa settled the baby in a new positon, and scapped the final bit of oatmeal from the bowl, chewed it herself, then spooned it into the eager mouth of the child. "One thing you will have to do," she told Elvira, "is ask Dagmar to go with you."

"Dagmar!" Elvira stepped back in surprise.

"Yaw, Dagmar. She needs it as much as you do. Not only that, but also because I will not let you go alone."

"But Mamma, Dagmar never gets to go anywhere, worse than me. How can I get *Fru* Qvist to let her go?"

"I'll help you there. We won't ask her until the day of the dance, then she won't have time to think up some reason for keeping Dagmar home. I'll work it for you. But, remember Elvira, it is for Pappa to say. If he can't see it my way you cannot go."

"Oh, Mamma! When will you ask him?"

"Tonight. I will walk with him a way when he goes out with his Bible."

Elvira set to with a will at the dishpan, and the house was tidied and cleaned better than any other day since she had taken over all those duties. She sang as she worked. Sometimes Lisa joined in.

"Oscar," she said later, her hand tucked into the crook of his arm as they walked together that evening. He wheeled his bicycle alongside. "I have something to suggest concerning Elvira. I want you to listen before you answer me."

"I always listen to you, my dear wife," he teased.

"Nay, I mean it. I want you to let Elvira go to the dance Saturday night."

The man and the bicycle came to a full sudden stop. "What!" he began, but Lisa shook his arm and raised her voice, drowning out his.

"That girl is working day and night for us, and has no time or place to meet anyone her age, as she should be doing. For her there is no chance for further schooling. All three of us know that. You and I know it is because she has to be our constant help. If not because of me and a new child, then because we need the money she can get out and earn. I am going to insist she be given the right to go to dances, and meet other young people."

"I have no chance to say anything in this?" he demanded, trying to begin his usual pacing back and forth but hampered by the bicycle. "She has Dagmar. I see her teaching that girl how to read. That should give her fun and satisfaction."

"That brings up another point. Dagmar has no freedom. None. Our girl has not much more, Oscar. Someday both of them may well go off to find a kind of freedom we would not like. Think of that. Do you want that to happen with Elvira? Of course not. I am going to make sure Dagmar goes along with Elvira, at least the first time."

"So you plan to have our daughter take part in sin over and over again?" he shouted.

Lisa waited. letting silence grow heavy between them, then she used what she had hoped she would not have to. "When you blew your horn for others to sin at dancing did that not make you a sinner also?"

He gasped. He turned away from her, faced her again, then flung his leg over his bicycle and wheeled away. She took a few running steps after him, cupped her hands to her mouth and called, "It is for you to say, Oscar."

He stayed away longer than on any other night. Lisa hoped it meant he had made a convert. It would ease things if so. Elvira undressed, but sat reading, lifting her head each time there was a sound. When they did hear him, Lisa motioned her to go into the bedroom. One glance told Lisa there had been no convert.

Oscar went to place the Bible on the small table and asked, "Elvira is sleeping?" Elvira came back into the room slowly, her nightgown white against the dark bedroom door.

"You understand the Bible says dancing leads to harm and dissipation?" he asked the girl.

"Yaw, Pappa. It also says it was used in celebration and victory," she answered.

"But not men and women together, like today," he returned.

Elvira stood silent.

Lisa put her sewing aside, but kept silent also. Oscar picked up the Bible only to put it down again.

"You may go, but take Dagmar with you."

Elvira rushed over to him, made a short curtsey and said, "Thank you, Pappa, thank you." She ran to Lisa and gently smoothed her hand against one of her cheeks. Lisa smiled up at her, and said, "The coffee is hot, let's all have some."

*

"We're all ready," Paulina announced on Friday evening. Supper dishes had been washed, the fire banked, and everyone had rushed around gatherng things needed for the stay at Katarina's. Paulina peered over the blankets piled on top of her two outstretched arms.

'Give some of those to Emilia," Lisa ordered. "It's too long a way for you to carry so many."

"Let me have one," Oscar suggested. "I'll take it out and use it on the bicycle seat for Johan."

"Take one for the basket too," Lisa added, "or will it fill it too high for Carl to sit in?"

"I'll see," he answered, and held his hand out for another blanket.

Oscar was to walk with them to Olofsson's farm. He had fitted a new fat candle into the glass and wood toilet house lantern. It hung in readiness over the bicycle handlebar. He would light it when they reached the woods this night that had no moonlight to show them the way.

At last they started. Oscar walked in the lead, Carl snug in the basket of the bicycle, a blanket wrapped around him. Johan straddled the softened seat, and leaned forward at an impossible angle to grasp the handlebars. The smile on his face knew no end. Oscar's arm held him steady as the laden bicycle was trundled over the frozen bumps of the road and woodland pathway. A birchbark *knotti* on Oscar's back was filled with sausages, salted herring well wrapped in layers of

paper, and the rye flour and yeast for the baking of the *knäkebröd*.
Elivra and Maria took turns carrying Alli piggyback to rest her short
legs. Lisa carried an apple cake, slices of the precious fruit baked in a
circle on its crust to beautify her special recipe. It would make
Katarina's eyes shine. With her other hand she lifted the lantern high
overhead as they entered the woods. Joy spilled around inside her,
walking here with her family. The pine trees of her homeland were
friendly guardians, their rough bark and reaching branches as familiar
as the faces of her children. "These are my children, all nine," she
wanted to say, and nod back at a swaying branch. But instead found
herself mouthing silently, nine are enough. As if Oscar could see her,
even in this timbered darkness she pressed her lips tightly together.

"You're here at last," Katarina greeted them, as they pushed open
the door of the farmhouse, *"Välkommen, välkommen,"* she added.
"Here, let me have the little one. Come in out of the cold, all of you.
Quickly. Coffee is ready. There'll be hot milk for the younger ones
soon. Eva, put some milk in a pan and set it near the fire."

Sigurd came to help. He took Carl from Oscar, who had carried
him in under one arm, Johan under the other. Cousins Axel and Olof
came to hang up coats, scarves, and knitted caps.

It was late before everyone had their fill of drinks and the
smörgasbord of sliced meats, pickled beets, and cheeses. Cardamon
coffee bread and small bakings too, of course. Oscar left directly after
the children, who except for Elvira, were bedded down on the floor.
He had to care for Nasse as well as go to work. Paulina lifted her
head, from where she lay betweeen her two sisters, to give him instruc-
tions, once again, how to care for the pet.

Saturday was a day of glory for Lisa. To be here with Katarina at
the long baking table was like being girls together again. They took
turns to mix the dough, to roll it out thin, and to cut it into flat rounds
for Elvira to dimple with the wire baking brush. Sometimes Elvira had
to remove the center the floured cutter had left intact. That empty circle was for the pole that would go through each crisp round to lift it
into storage under the ceiling at home.

Each time Lisa scooped up another thin circle onto the long-
handled wooden bread-spade to toss it expertly onto the hot bricks of
the oven, she reveled in the blistering heat of the hot coals that had
been raked out into the deep brick trough in front of the oven. Deftly
she slid the bread-spade under a round, fully baked, and tipped it
carefully among the other rounds stacking up at the end of the table.
Talk between the two sisters was never ending. Absorbed in their

work, and each other, they gave little notice to their older children, and only enough that was necessary to the younger ones.

Early Sunday morning Oscar arrived, gathered his family to him at the end of the big room and asked the Olofssons to join them in worship. Katarina, as if indeed she was going to church, went to the bedroom and came back wearing her Sunday shawl and carrying her hymn book. Sigurd, for all his kindness, would not join them.

He explained, "Forgive me Oscar. It is good that you read from the Bible but you are not ordained."

"Ack, Sigurd," Katarina scolded, but gently, "it is only two times a year at most we make the long journey to church. It won't hurt us to listen to Oscar."

"I will not go against my church," he answered.

"Nor will I," she said, "but this is my sister and her husband I listen to."

"You can do as you like, but I will sit over here. If the boys want to listen they can."

The boys went outdoors. Eva came to stand next to the twins, her plump blondness a contrast to their slenderness.

Sigurd, his hands idle because it was Sunday, seemed far away, for the room was twice as long as theirs at the sawmill, and half again as wide.

"We shall read," Oscar announced, standing in front of the furthest window, "of the feeding of the multitude. Elvira, you begin."

He handed her the open Bible, and she read swiftly and clearly. At Oscar's nod she passed the book on to Maria, who continued the reading. One by one, those who were old enough read from the Bible, at whatever speed and ability they had. Help on the bigger words was quick and from many sources. Lisa and Oscar took turns to finish the chapter, Oscar last. Heads bowed, hands clasped, they prayed.

"God bless these dear relatives who give us the opportunity to bake the bread that will feed our hunger until spring," Oscar finished.

"Amen," the family said with him, as well as Katarina and Eva. "Let us sing 'The Future of God's People,'" he suggested. "You will not find it in your hymn book, Katarina, it is one of our own.Humming, he set the first note, then with arms waving led his family into the music. Elvira harmonized with him.

Their combined voices filled the large room with joyful sound.

"That was wonderful!" Katarina admitted, as the last note died. "If only you were singing it in the rightful church of the Lord."

"What do I need to be doing to help you this day?" Oscar asked, to cover Katarina's momentary embarrassment.

"The fire needs building in the *kakelugn*," Lisa told him."It had better get started right away."

"We'll show you where the wood is," the five younger girls shouted together.

"Quiet!" he frowned at them, "one at a time is enough."

"We three," Maria said, indicating Paulina and Emilia, "Brought the wood in a wheelbarrow yesterday. The woodpile is way out alongside the small barn."

"I helped too," Marta protested.

"Me too," Alli joined in.

"As you should," Oscar said. "You are here to help. I'm glad to know you did."

"It's hard to carry all those logs in here. The *kakelugn* uses up so many of them to make the floor of the oven hot enough for baking."

"Then let's get started. Go get your coats," he told them. "Before we start I have something to tell Elvira. I heard Svennson is looking for a girl to help in his store. I rode over to see him and told him about you. He said he knows you and thinks you would do just fine."

Elvira had been folding the blankets they had slept in, but dropped them back onto the floor as she hurried over to her parents.

"You can start on Tuesday morning," Oscar told her as she stopped in front of him.

She glanced anxiously at Lisa, then back to Oscar. "Must I start so soon?" she asked.

"You have two days before you need to go," he answered.

'Am I to live there too?"

"Yaw, they have a small room up above where you can sleep with their oldest girl."

Her hands pressed to her chest, Elvira turned a worried face to Lisa. "That means I can't go to the dance?"

"That's up to Svensson," Oscar told her.

"Nay, wait a little," Lisa intervened, "it won't hurt him to be another week without a helper. You go see him on Tuesday and tell him you'll start working on the Monday following."

Oscar snorted and flung his hands upward then slapped them against his legs. "Let's hope the job is still hers by next week."

"No need to worry," Lisa told him as Elvia looked at her with a radiant face, "No one else has been around to ask for it, nor will be. He has needed someone in that store for a long time but counts his *öre* too close to hire anyone before this. Is he going to pay her a good sum?"

"Yaw, yaw, I saw to that, never fear. I wouldn't have any of mine working for nothing," he answered. "All we have to sell is the work of our hands."

"Of course, Oscar, I should have known you would do that," Lisa soothed him. "You go see Svensson Tuesday morning early," she told Elvira, "and tell him I need you the rest of this week."

"Thank you, Mamma. All right, Pappa?"

"Hmph! What can I say? I'm overruled all the time." He turned on his heel and went out, followed by the five younger girls.

That evening Elvira trapped cousin Axel out in the barn. Maria, the twins and cousin Olof were along too.

"You're going to the dance Saturday night, aren't you?" she asked Axel.

"Ya," he answered.

"Then dance with me now."

"Here? Are you crazy?"

"Nay, really. I've never been to a dance and I need to dance with a man."

It was the last word that melted him. Up and down the center of the barn they danced, cows' tails now and then slapping them as they dashed past. Maria, envious, but unable to convince the younger Olof to dance, raised her arms above her head and dipped and swayed herself.

"You are all crazy," Emilia scorned, slapping the air with disgust. Olof echoed her, when his laughter was controlled enough so that he could do other than hold his stomach. Paulina added her giggles while she petted the cows.

In the house Lisa admired the silk shawl Katarina had worn to the prayer meeting.

"It's our *mor's*. Do you remember it?" Katarina asked. Lisa nodded. "There is hardly a bead missing." Katarina's hands stroked the taffeta that hung in two points in front of her, the shawl once more across her shoulders. She cupped the beads dangling from each point, pooling them in her palms for a moment. "If I go before you it is to be yours."

"Nay, Katarina!" Lisa protested. "It must be Eva's."

Katarina shook her head. "It will be yours," she said, and removed it to encircle Lisa's shoulders with it.

"Thank you," Lisa said, and pressed the cool silk against herself.

On Monday afternoon Sigurd took the family home. The bread was in the wagon carefully guarded by boards placed so that nothing could bump or crush the crisp rounds. Carl and Johan were aboard too, seated on the folded blankets, the baby between them. Lisa sat up on the driver's seat. Sigurd walked alongside holding the reins as he drove the horse. At the very back of the wagon there stood a tall rocking chair. It rose high above the bed of the wagon. Sigurd had made it as a surprise for Lisa. It had been kept a secret out in the barn, covered over. Not even the prying eyes of the Veldman girls had discovered it. Only when the bread had been carefully placed and covered had he come down carrying the chair. Lisa had cried, for it was almost a duplicate of the one sold in Sweden.

"I'll take the reins," she offered.

"I know how to drive a horse," Marta called, from where she walked. "*Farbror* Palmer showed me."

Lisa realized it had been some time since Marta had mentioned the Palmers. But she had to raise a scolding finger to silence Elvira and Emilia, who called to Marta, "That's what you say," and, "Bet he never did."

"That will do," she warned Marta, who ran forward shouting, "He did! He did!"

Sigurd patted the rump of the horse, and refused Lisa. "Jonas here would know it wasn't me. No one else has ever driven him." He gave a soft toss to settle the reins more comfortably on Jonas' back.

As they neared home the girls raced ahead to see Nasse, Paulina in the lead. Nasse petted, they helped carry in the bread, and struggled together to find exactly the right place for the chair Sigurd brought in before leaving. Many hands made quick work of threading the *knäkebröd* onto the pole, Maria and Elvira up on the bench to lift them up into place just before Oscar got home.

The house was a clatter of voices when he came, many fingers pointing to the abundance of bread that filled the pole from end to end under the ceiling.

Oscar laughed as he congratulated them. "There's enough to last well into spring and beyond. What's this?" he demanded, as many hands pulled him toward the new rocking chair.

"Sigurd made it," Lisa told him.

"And we said you were to be first one to rock in it," someone cried. "Get in, Pappa," called several others.

"It's for Mamma to rock the youngest ones," Elvira explained.

"Then she should be first," he told them.

"Nay," Lisa upheld the children. "It was agreed you are to be first."

Oscar allowed himself to be pushed into the chair. He sent it swinging to the very ends of its long rockers, front and back.

"It's a good chair, isn't it?" Maria asked, as he sat back, his feet comfortable on the crosspiece far out in front connecting the two curved rockers. The chair slowed down.

"It's a wonderful chair," he answered, then got out to look at it. "Sigurd is too kind, Lisa. How can we ever repay that good man?" He rubbed his head with one hand, and puffed his lips out as he stood thinking. "Well, then, Lisa is next," he said, and motioned her to come be seated. He handed her in as though she were getting into a beautiful coach. She swung back and forth.

"Bring me the little one," she said. Elvira laid the child in her lap. Lisa rocked gently.

"Stay there," Elvira told her. "I'll take care of getting supper on the table."

"Nay, this is enough," she answered. "Everyone must take a turn."

She got out, put the baby in the cradle, and hurried to the fireplace. The children took their turns, Elvira last. Each of the younger ones called Lisa to watch them rock. Later, when all but Elvira had gone to bed, Lisa sat in it, Oscar alongside on a stool. One hand on the arm of the chair, he controlled its swing.

"I feel the home we had in Sweden is right here with us now," she said, and laid her hand on top of his.

*

"You! Is there something the matter with our pig?" Lisa called from the open door early one morning soon after the children had gone to school. She had seen, through the window, a man inside the pen scratching Nasse's back.

He looked up. "Nay. I find her healthy and bigger than I thought she would be." The voice puzzled her. It didn't sound right. "I'll be in for a cup of coffee, Lisa," the voice continued.

Startled, Lisa stepped back to shut the door, but watched the intruder close the pen gate, and walk toward her. It was a woman dressed in man's clothing. Instantly she knew it was Berta Lund, the pig-farm owner. How well she remembered her astonishment when Oscar told her the farm was owned and run by a woman, Berta Lund. More than that, she had been appalled to hear the woman dressed herself in men's clothes, all the time.

"Come in," she invited, as Berta Lund stepped up the stairs and reached out her hand. She shook it saying, "I'll have to wash out a coffee mug. The breakfast dishes aren't done."

"Let me," her visitor suggested. She stood just inside the door to remove her coat. She was a big woman, close to Lisa's age, her face dark with exposure to all weather. Tall, the tassel on top of her knitted cap made her seem even taller. The legs of her pants were stuffed into the tops of Russian leather boots, wrinkled at the ankles but smooth up to her knees. They shone with polish, except where mud had spattered. Without invitation she sat down on a stool, and with strong pulls removed the boots and set them near the door. In stocking feet she went to the fireplace, picked up the kettle of hot water and took it to the washbench. She poured water into the small basin and washed her hands thoroughly. Lisa stood rooted near the table. She had never had a guest who made herself so at home, or called her by her given name without asking permission to do so.

"I've been meaning to get over here to meet you, Lisa, but my work keeps me close to the farm," Berta Lund told her, as she lathered her hands, then rinsed. "I hear many good things about you."

Berta Lunda laughed. "The people who tell me about you think they are bad things, but to me they are good."

"Ya so?"

"Yaw," the visitor answered, eyes friendly, mouth smiling broadly. She picked up the kettle again, and poured water into the pan where the morning dishes were stacked. Even though Lisa protested that one mug would be enough, she proceeded to do them all. "You won't miss one turn of washing dishes, I'm sure," she said, then returned to her earlier remark. "I've heard that the nonsense of baptism isn't for you, nor is occupying the senseless seat in the state church one of your failings."

Lisa dropped down onto a bench too stunned to find words. For the first time in memory she had met someone who approved their religious practices right off. Yet, even as she marveled, she noticed that the long overblouse of her guest was immaculate. About to get up and assume her rightful role as hostess, she was further immobilized when Berta Lund stepped to the hearth and poured coffee into two of the newly washed mugs. She took the coffee as it was handed to her as though she was the guest in the house. Unable to comment on what Berta Lund had said, she did notice that the hand that offered the coffee had fingernails that were trimmed, rounded, and very clean. It was easy to believe, now, that the scientific pig farm was as spotless as Oscar and the girls who had gone there to buy vegetables had told her it was.

"I came to see your newborn as well as to meet you," her guest offered. She seated herself at the table with her mug of coffee. "The child isn't very new anymore, I know, since it's almost Christmas, but it's the first I could get over this way." She nodded at Alli, who to Lisa's amazement, had come to stand smiling at Berta Lund with no sign of her usual shyness. "This one I know," Berta said, and fondled Alli's curls. "I've seen her often on the roads with her sisters. But who is this?" she asked, and leaned to peer around Alli.

"Tell *Tant* Berta your name, Johan," Lisa urged, amazed to find herself using the familiar *Tant* Berta instead of *Fröken* Lund to the boy. "I must go get Carl," she excused herself. "I have left him too long on the pottie in the other room."

"Carl!" she exclaimed, shaking her head in disappointment as she helped him off the pottie. She squatted to bring her face down to his level. "Bad boy! You didn't do anything. How is it that you have become more the little one than the newborn? Always waiting to do it in your diapers," she scolded, as she dressed him, giving herself time to adjust to the woman in the other room. "Nay, hold both my hands and walk," she told the boy. "It is time you learn. Maybe that will help things."

The visitor, along with Alli and Johan, was bending over the cradle when she re-entered the main room.

"It looks healthy," Berta commented. "At least as much as I can see of it in its swaddling cocoon. It's a girl?" As Lisa nodded she asked, "I expect she is to be your last child?"

"What do you mean?" Lisa asked, shocked. "How...can I know that? I...I'm a married woman."

"No reason to have more. You have how many now?"

Too taken aback to answer, she herded the three children into the warm corner near the fireplace. "Take care of your brothers," she told Alli, and handed her several small balls of yarn out of her knitting bag. "Roll these between you on the floor, don't throw them." At the table, she lifted her coffee and took a deep swallow, without looking at the woman who sat across from her.

"Forgive me," she heard Berta say. "I speak too openly about matters you feel are none of my concern."

"You startled me," she admitted, looking into Berta's worried eyes. "No one has spoken of such a thing to me. Nay, I correct myself. My sister did, but only once."

"When she came to care of you when you almost lost this one?" Berta asked, nodding in the direction of the cradle.

"You know about that?"

"Of course. Such news does not stay within four walls. Katarina Oloffson was right. You are fortunate to be here to raise this new one."

"I know," Lisa agreed, "but you see I was run down. Too much had happened while I carried her. That's all. I'm getting very strong now."

"Are you? You look forward to the next one?"

Lisa flinched, pushing away the thought of yet another childbirth. She forced herself to look calmly at her guest. *"Fröken* Lund," she said, using the formal address, "since you speak so easily of not having children, forgive me...you are not married...yet you have two..."

"Bastards?" Berta asked.

Lisa gasped. "I didn't.. I meant to say..."

Berta cut her off. "Mine are not bastards, Lisa. Nay, don't be disturbed," she urged, as Lisa tried to apologize. "It's just a word. I wonder who thought it up? Whoever did, that word should apply to him only. Nay, Lisa, every child is the honest fruit of man and woman."

"But Moses gave us the law to live by."

"He did, in Deuteronomy. Told the Israelites a bastard shall not enter the congregation of the Lord even unto the tenth generation."

"That's right," Lisa agreed, "but forgive me again if I point out, it was to prevent children from being born out of wedlock."

"Prevent!" Berta stormed. "Better he should have outlawed barns, haystacks, or spelled out that young folks should couple only under the noses of their parents."

Aghast, Lisa could say nothing.

"I'm right, you have to give me that," Berta continued. "You were in Sweden when I came here from Vasa to buy the farm and start my piggery. But you grew up here, a Swede-Finn like myself. Didn't you know there were a few around even then who suffered the title of bastard?"

"I knew, of course," Lisa admitted, bending her head to pull out a hairpin and re-insert it.

"Since you've come back you've heard of others?" Berta asked. "More than my two, I mean?"

"Yaw, I know it hasn't worked entirely." Lisa rounded her shoulders as if to guard against revealing her sister's too early pregnancy, more than sixteen years ago. Relief surged up again, and she praised God silently, once more, that Sigurd had married

Katarina. "But it's better than no law at all," she offered.

Berta heaved a sigh, sat back and pushed both hands up under her knitted cap as if to cool her head.

"Better?" she asked. "For whom then?"

"Don't misunderstand me, Berta," Lisa pleaded. She turned her empty coffee mug around in a circle, concentrating on it rather than her visitor. "It has always worried me that it is the children who must bear the stigma. But, Moses said that it would always be so for the children of such unions."

"My two carry no such thing," Berta protested. "I tell them they are as legal as any other child just by being born. Never mind what other people say or how they behave." The air seemed to crackle with the intensity of her words.

"They are fortunate in you," Lisa told her, looking up. They sat silent. Lisa drew a deep breath. "Berta, why didn't you marry?"

"For many reasons. Mostly because I want to run my own life."

"The father of the children agreed?"

"Fathers," Berta corrected her. "The children have different ones."

Unable to respond to this astounding information so freely given, Lisa sat silent. A guilt grew, pushing a warmth up into her face. She twisted around to look at the children, and felt the need to get up and look into the cradle. The child slept peacefully. How could it be, she asked herself, that she listened and talked of such things to a stranger? One who seemed to be more man than woman with her attitudes and clothing. It wasn't that she had never heard or taken part in womanly talk. In Sweden, especially at the fall and spring baking at the bakehouse provided by the sawmill, she had heard plenty from other wives. But never anything like this. The women there had left her pretty much alone once they knew she had taken Oscar's religion. Even her friends among them had regarded her with disfavor when she stopped having her children baptized, beginning with the twins. It had taken Oscar that long to bring her around to that.

"Gossip has reached you," Berta was saying, "that I'm a loose woman?"

Lisa shook her head. "Oscar says you are a hard worker and honest. He tells me your pig house is unbelievably clean, and very scientific."

"He's a good man, your husband. Does his own thinking. I'm glad he thinks well of me."

Lisa struggled against saying it but heard herself ask, "Why two men? One man is more than enough."

"When I was ready to want my second child the first man was married."

Embarrassed, Lisa murmured, "I don't know what to say."

"What would you say to this, then," Berta asked. "When it got around that I was with child many men came to the farm for other reasons than to buy pigs. They soon learned there was nothing there for them other than pigs."

"Shameful," Lisa whispered. Then more loudly, "But young men are like that."

"So they are," Berta said, "but I can count on the fingers of more than one hand the married men who came also. I soon told them their duties were in their own beds."

Lisa sat shaking her head.

Berta continued. "Their women almost spit at me when we met on the roads. Church goers, all of them. Their men too. Occupy a seat in a pew every Sunday, right next to their wives."

"The women, at least, are honest," Lisa countered. "They believe in the Word."

"Do they?" Berta wondered. "They want no truck with me, but willingly come to the farm to haggle the price of my pigs down until I wouldn't be able to make a living. But I get even."

Startled, Lisa asked, "How's that?."

"I go to church too. As many Sundays as I can get away from the farm. Put on my skirt, and off I go."

"But I thought you..."

"That's right, you did hear me congratulate you on not sitting in the senseless seat of the state church. But, you see, I'm a business woman. I need to show up so those same ladies will remember my pigs are for sale."

"Nay," Lisa drew the word out long making it a criticism, "now it is you who is shameful." She got up and busied herself buttering *knäckebröd* to give to the children.

"Think so?" Berta asked, coming to stand nearby. "I do what the other business people do, with a difference. I know that's why I go there. They pretend to themselves that it isn't the reason they're there."

"Even so," Lisa answered, "it is wrong."

"Perhaps," Berta, admitted, taking the coffee pot and refilling the two mugs.

Her back to Berta, Lisa said, "When you first came in you made me think you didn't believe."

"Believe what?" Berta asked.

"The Bible. Yet you quote Moses accurately. But now I'm wondering again. You make me think you don't believe."

"I believe all right," Berta answered. "It's a history book. I know it well."

"Then how can you talk of a married woman not having children?"

"For the same reason I have my two. It's for you and me to decide. No one else."

"Nay! Nay!" Lisa objected. "It cannot be so. In the book of..."

"I know. I can quote it, Lisa, throughout the books. Just remember, I believe, in my own way. Tell me this, have you read any of the papers put out by women's organizations?"

"Of course I have. Not here yet, but in Sweden," she answered, glad for the change in conversation. "I did read translations of Finland's Minna Canth before I left here. She was such a strong writer about women's lot in this country. And my own Alli there, is named after Alli Trighelenius."

"Marvelous," Berta exclaimed. "Our own Swedish suffragette in Finland." She turned to smile at Alli. "You can be proud to be named after the woman who worked so hard to give us the vote," she told her.

Alli came to stand next to Berta who stroked her hair back off her forehead fondly, then told her to go back and keep the two boys busy.

"She was born that year, 1906," Lisa told Berta. "You know, don't you, that neither of those two women, nor the women's papers, concerned themselves with what we are talking about? They do not go against the teachings of the Bible."

"That's right," Berta agreed, and reached out to grasp one of Lisa's hands. "But someday women will choose openly how many children they will give birth to."

Lisa was silent.

"You went to some of the meetings in Sweden before you came here?" Berta asked.

Lisa placed her other hand over Berta's. "When could I have done that? I have eleven children, nine of whom are living."

"So, there you are. Don't you think that's enough?" Berta demanded. Lisa pulled away.

"It's God's law. There is no other way," she exclaimed.

"There is, and it's no sin," Berta said quietly.

Suddenly Lisa felt she was being a traitor to Oscar. "Berta! I must not listen to such talk," she cried. "I will not." She got up and marched over to the hearth to push the coffee pot closer to the hot embers.

Berta threw her hands up in the air. "Shall we talk about the Panama Canal then, and wonder if it will ever be built?" She boomed with laughter, bringing the children over to look at her, Carl tipping his head upward from where he had scooted to sit in front of her. Berta twisted to follow Lisa's return around the end of the table. "Or maybe you want to talk about that Norwegian's search for the South Pole, if he isn't already just another lump of ice on that white landscape underneath the world? You choose, so we won't step on each other's tender toes any more."

"Ack, neither your toes nor mine are that tender," Lisa objected. "We need not go that far afield to find subjects that are not personal. For instance, what is more worrisome than what is happening in Germany, and where will it lead?"

"Now there you have something serious."

"As Oscar sees it, they are reaching out to take all the markets of the world. It can only mean trouble, I think."

"Ya so! I hear you read the papers thoroughly."

"Nay, Oscar reads them to me at night, sometimes. I find no time to read."

"That's another thing that has to change. Time for you to read. My house is full of books. Your Oscar has borrowed many of them already."

" My Elvira also. There you have a reading woman. And not only her, but all my girls read."

"Signs of the future," Berta beamed across the table. "I met your four girls this morning on their way to school. That's another reason I came. They asked what to do about their pig out there. I told them I would take it back for the winter, if you agreed. My pigs are inside all year round, perhaps you know, and she will be well cared for and warm."

"Oscar and I think you should take Nasse back now. She needs to be with other pigs. Besides, she is getting too big for the girls to handle."

"Good, but why not let me slaughter it? You will have meat for the whole winter."

"Nay, thank you," Lisa exclaimed, one hand lifted swiftly in protest. "Forgive me, but we do not eat pork. It is forbidden."

"Berta nodded. "Ya so, that too," she said sadly. "Well, then I'll take her when I leave. The children can come and see her whenever they like, tell them. Today if they want to. I must get back, I've stayed too long."

"How old are your children?" Lisa asked, reluctant to have her guest leave.

"Gideon is seventeen, Naomi almost fifteen. The two were all I wanted. They are doing well at school in Åbo," she finished as she stamped her feet down into her boots. Her coat back on, she pulled her cap over her ears. "Will I be welcome to come again?" she asked.

"Soon, Berta," Lisa urged. "There is so much to talk about."

"Yaw, that there is," Berta agreed.

"When will you come again?"

"Perhaps in a week."

With a quick warm shake of Lisa's hand she was off to the pen. It seemed no effort for her to lift Nasse into the wagon she had brought to the gate by leading the horse to it. She half stepped, half jumped up into the bed of the wagon after the pig was on board, and went to stand behind the high seat, picking up the reins. From the open doorway Lisa heard her cluck to the horse, watched her wheel the wagon around toward the road. Nasse huddled close to her legs. She lifted one hand in farewell, and shouted against the noise of the sawmill, "I'll bring copies of the women's papers next time."

Lisa waved and nodded.

'Mamma," Alli called, "Carl's done it again. He smells bad."

"Why do you have to look so much like a angel?" Lisa sighed, and grasped him by both arms to trot him before her into the bedroom.

That evening she told Oscar of the pig-woman's visit, but never mentioned the disturbing question Berta had raised. At the end of a week she began to watch the road. On the day she saw the wagon coming she stirred up the fire to heat the coffee. Embarrassed that she had not offered her guest as much as a crumb of *knäckebröd* before, she set out generous slices of coffee bread baked in anticipation of the next visit. Berta should know she was welcome.

*

Emphatically Oscar told her once more. "He's dishonest, Lisa! I've caught him at it more times than I can tell you. He's known for a long time that I was on to it."

"So you have said many times tonight. All I can say is what I've been saying all evening. It is no reflection on you, Oscar."

"Isn't it?" he demanded. "I've known it for months yet never said a word to him. Or worse, I went on letting the customers be overcharged. Here it is well into May, and I caught him at the cheating way back in January. Everybody thinks I do all the figuring. He makes sure of that. Eventually someone is going to realize they are being overcharged. Who do you think is going to be blamed?"

He sat down on the edge of the bed to shuck his pants off. Lisa slipped her nightgown over her head, then took the pins out of her hair.

"It's past nignight, Oscar, and you keep going over the same things. We don't seem to be able to resolve it tonight. Let's get some sleep."

He rubbed his fingers over his underwear, scratching his body. "I've got to face him with it, that I know," he said.

She went to get hairbrush and comb. "Will that change him, do you think?" she asked.

He considered this a long moment, then shook his head. "Nay, I'd be a fool to think he would change with just a few words from me."

The sound of the brush sweeping downward through her hair seemed loud.

"I don't know what more I can say to help you," she said, as she began to braid her hair, "but I do know that we all need you to stay and work at the sawmill. What would we do if you lose this job?"

He nodded, and hung his pants on the back of the big rocker. "Maybe if I could do my figures in front of the customers I could announce the correct sum out loud. Then he wouldn't be able to change them upward."

He settled down into bed while Lisa went to blow out the kerosene lamp on the table.

She lay next to him and knew that in spite of his worry he had been so worn out he had gone to sleep as he was saying his prayers. His hands were still laced together on his chest. It had been a disturbing evening. Oscar had been unable to eat properly. Had paced back and forth, shushed the children into troubled silence until she urged them off to bed. For once he had not sat reading, nor did he take the Bible and go out. How Oscar could go on trying to bring God's TRUTH to unfriendly people she had to admire, even as it worried her. Infidel, crazy man, traitor, unbeliever were some of the words he brought back to tell her he had been called. Yet he never seemed discouraged. If people would not talk to him of the Bible, he talked temperance. There too he met vehement opposition, but seemed to thrive on all of it. Sometimes he was welcomed, but that was when the talk turned to Finland's need for independence from Russia. Then he came home replete with coffee and good baking, sure that next time he would be able to convince them of the TRUTH.

But tonight the worry of his dishonest boss had taken the spirit out of him. He had made several trips to the toilet until she asked if she needed to boil him some milk to tighten his bowels. He had shaken his head and gone to stand in a window looking out.

Her hands clasped tightly together under her chin, she prayed and asked that Oscar would keep his job. It had been a good winter. Elvira's face smiled at her. How the girl chattered now each rest day she came home from Svensson's store. Lisa gave thanks again that the first dance had been such a success. And Dagmar. It was good to see how she was standing up to *Fru* Qvist, at least to go to dances whenever Elvira sent word to come along. Even Oscar had to admit the new liveliness of the two owed much to the dances. Yaw, it had been a good winter. The usual colds among the children, but no severe problems, except for Marta.

The change from the rich food in Sweden to their simple fare had put sores on her head. They could not think of any other reason for them. None of the other children had been so afflicted. From oil, to a paste made out of potato flour, to the ointment Elvira had used on her chapped hands, Oscar tried to cure them. But they only grew larger and seeped. He made a trip by bicycle to the next village where there was an *apotek*. There the chemist told Oscar to cut off all the girl's hair right down to the scalp and then apply the medication he sold him.

It was not only Marta who wept as the hair fell to the floor. Maria hurriedly knit her a multicolored lightweight cap to wear, even in school, after the teacher had been told why.

Almost more tragic to Marta than the loss of her hair was that she alone of the sisters was not chosen to sing in the school play. Lisa tried to comfort her by saying it was probably because she would have had to wear the cap in the play and that would not do. The child wept bitterly, and reverted to the spoiled youngster of the Palmers, with the natural result the older girls once again taunted and excluded her from their circle. At last Lisa decided the child had to have a special treat. She would take her, and the youngest, to Katarina's for two days. Away from the others she could give her special attention.

At the farm Marta had deserted her to follow Sigurd in the furrows he plowed as he told her stories in his soft slow way. He drew the child's attention to the birds, named them, and all the growing things showing up in the rebirth of spring. On the way home Marta had showed off her new knowledge, darting from the pathway through the woods and fields to point out correctly each growing plant. The noisy welcome home included Marta, as much as it did Lisa herself and the youngest. For the next several evenings the older girls allowed Marta to tell them Sigurd's wonderful stories. She seemed to have memorized them completely. Lisa smiled to herself and wondered if perhaps the spoiled child was gone and instead they now had a great talker and a beginning naturalist.

*

The brothers in Sweden had been repaid. Elvira worked and brought home money to help. Berta Lund had become a close and dear friend, not only to Lisa, but to Oscar and the whole family. Her many books found eager readers in the house and her visits were welcomed, the children always asking about Nasse. When she and Berta were alone, except for the three youngest, their talks went into every field of life except one. Lisa would not let her talk about preventing conception. She could not go against God's word, or Oscar. Yaw, the winter had been good to them. Whispering, "Amen," she fell asleep.

A week later Marta and Alli came down with scarlet fever. Only a sore throat at first, then a burst into a fever that turned their skin into a burning flush. She pinned blankets over the two bedroom windows to keep them in darkness, and refused to let any of the other children into the room. Although all four of the older ones had been sick with the disease while in Sweden she feared they would get it again. She had Oscar carry mattresses and blankets into the main room for the twins, Maria, Johan, and Carl. The big rocking chair, and the baby's cradle, had to be stored temporarily in the vestibule each night to make room. The baby slept between her parents in the big bed.

Lisa cared for the two sick ones alone, urging them to drink water often, laying cool wet rags on their foreheads after rubbing them down with wet towels many times day and night.

On the third day of their illness, in mid-afternoon, she heard men shouting outdoors. A glance through the rain-streaked window showed her Oscar hurrying homeward, his face stricken. Behind him stalked the boss-owner Mangnusson, his arms waving in the air, his hands clenched into fists. She ran to the outer vestibule door and flung it open.

"Cheat! Behind the back operator! Sneaky Swede! Take your family and get out of here!" she heard him yell.

Oscar turned several times, bringing the two-man procession to a halt momentarily, but she could not hear what he said for Mangnusson shouted constantly. Oscar saw her, and raised his hands in a gesture of futility. She ran down the steps and over to him, to clutch his arm with both hands as he walked toward home. When they reached the steps he turned, put his hand on Mangnusson's chest and gave him a push backwards, startling him into silence.

"You listen to me, Mangnusson," he shouted, "you are the one who's been cheating. You know it, and I know it. Your anger is one proof of it..."

"You lie," Mangnusson yelled, throwing angry glances at Lisa. "I never cheated anyone in my whole life. You're the one. It's you who did it, and you cheated me today."

"Veldman cheat?" It was *Fru* Qvist who had come to stand in the open doorway of her vestibule, "That I can't believe."

"That's right, Ma," Dagmar said, her face showing up behind her.

"You keep out of this," the boss yelled, "or I'll kick your man out of the house too,"

Fru Qvist stepped back, pushing Dagmar as she closed the door with a bang.

"*Herr* Mangnusson," Lisa scolded, "you have no right to say that of Oscar. He has told me..."

Mangnusson roared, "This house belongs to me. I want you and your sick Swede brats out of here by tonight."

"That is impossible," Oscar answered. He grasped Lisa's arm tightly as she gasped and started to speak. "But, don't you worry," he continued, spitting the words into Mangnusson's face, "we'll be out of here by tomorrow night."

"Oscar, nay!" Lisa cried. "The girls are too sick. We can't move them."

"I won't stay in his house a minute longer than we need to, Lisa. Go back to your cheating, Mangnusson. I don't want anything more to do with you."

Mangnusson dug into his pocket and brought out some coins. He flung them on the ground in front of Oscar.

"Here's your last pay," he shouted. "There is more there than you have earned, but take it and start packing."

"I want only what is owing me," Oscar answered. "Take back what isn't mine."

Mangnusson turned on his heel and left without glancing down at the money. The Veldmans watched him go.

"Mamma? Pappa?" Marta and Alli stood in the doorway of the vestibule, their frightened red-speckled faces wrinkled up in the light. Johan and Carl's faces were thrust out to each side of them.

"Nay!" Lisa shouted. "Go back to bed this instant, you two. Get out of the light. Boys, get away from them. Hurry up."

"Did *Herr* Mangnusson hurt Pappa?" Marta asked, as Lisa rushed both girls back to bed, and ordered Johan and Carl to get up on the bed-sofa and stay there.

"Nobody is hurt," she assured the girls as she tucked the fur cover up to their chins. "It is just that Pappa will not be working at this sawmill anymore. Now you lie still. Close your eyes and keep quiet." She went back into the main room wiping her wet face with her apron.

Oscar came in, the money in his hand. He laid it down on the table, stepped over to the cupboard and picked up Marta's school slate and chalk. Before he sat down to figure he took out his handkerchief to wipe his face and hands, then began writing on the slate. Lisa went to stand near him. When he did not look up she gave his shoulder a sharp push.

"Leave that," she told him. "What happened?"

He dropped the chalk and placed his elbows on the table to grasp his hair in his two hands as he bend forward.

"Yaw, Lisa," he began. "I couldn't have done it any worse. I'm ashamed. I'm no diplomat. I just couldn't deceive." He sat shaking his head, his shoulders and head bent.

"Well, talk, don't just sit there like that."

"I'm trying to, Lisa, but I've got to think how to tell you."

"Just tell me!"

She pulled up a stool, her anxious face close to his.

"You see, it was like this. First thing this morning he told me he had to go to Vasa and wouldn't be back until afternoon. Wilhelm Andersson was coming in the morning to pick up his big order of lumber for a new barn and would pay cash. Together Mangnusson and I went through the mock business of figuring, but this time I didn't give him my chip of wood to throw away. I pretended to agree that his figures were correct. Oh, Lisa, you should have seen the knowing smile on his face, because he thought I was going along with his cheating."

He stopped, his face pale, sweat shining on his forehead.

"When I counted the money over to Mangnusson he knew what I had done. If the money didn't tell him my face did. He began swearing at me so loud I'm sure the men heard it over the buzz of the saws. Then he had the gall, Lisa, to ask me to hand over the rest of the money, as if I had kept the overcharge."

"Nay!" Lisa breathed in disbelief.

"He did," Oscar assured her. "Then you could have heard me all the way over here to this house. He knew he had gone too far. He threatened to punch me, then told me to get the devil off his property. He'd see me in hell before he'd have me work for him one more second. That's it. You saw and heard the rest."

"What a horrible man," she cried, "and now he wants to make you the guilty one."

"Exactly," Oxcar agreed. "'That Swede, who doesn't go to church, is the cheater,' he will say, lying to everyone." He picked up the chalk again. "I've got to figure out how much he overpaid me and go throw it down at his feet right away," he said, the chalk scratching against the slate.

"You'll do nothing of the sort," she responded, and placed her hand on the slate. "You're not to lower youself to his level, Oscar. Take it in to him, count it out as you put it on that plank of his, but take one of the other men with you to see and hear you do it."

He sat back in his chair. "You're right, Lisa," he agreed. "It won't be easy to go back, but I'll take Jon Juslin with me. Everyone trusts his word." He sat forward again and finished his calculations. "I owe Mangnusson two kröner and fifteen öre."

She watched him stride purposefully out into the steady rain across the distance that separated the house from the sawmill, jump the overflowing ditch, and disappear behind one of the stacks of lumber. Turning back into the room she took fresh water in the basin into the bedroom and bathed the two girls again. Her deep sighs evoked a question from Alli.

"Did Pappa made you sad, Mamma?"

"Nay, dear child," Lisa answered. "It was Mangnusson who made both Pappa and me sad. But if you two get well, then we will be happy again."

"We will," both of them promised, and lay very still with cold wet cloths on their forehead. But their worried eyes followed Lisa as she left the room.

*

"Lisa," Pappa called from in front of the house a short time later, "I'm off to find us a place to live."

He stooped to encircle his right trouser leg with a bicycle clamp, pulled his bicycle away from the house where the eaves gave it some shelter from the rain, and rode off. If he heard her hasty opening of the outer door, he did not turn around. Unerringly he found the plank over the ditch although the water had risen to cover it. Half standing he pumped the bicycle down the muddy road, building speed and distance.

Hours later he stood before the fireplace removing his soaked clothes. Lisa hurried back out of the bedroom, his other pair of long underwear in her hands. She elbowed the three older girls away from around him.

"Stop asking him question," she spit at them, "can't you see he is shaking? One of you warm up a towel at the fire. Fill the washbasin with hot water, somebody, and bring a cloth wrung out of it. Oscar, get out of that wet underwear right now. That's it. Take the hot cloth from Maria and rub your legs good. Johan, Pappa will talk to you soon, Emilia, take Johan and Carl to bed. Give Pappa the towel," she told Paulina, who stood holding it close to the fire.

It was a relief to be doing something more than running to look out the dark windows, or to open the outer vestibule door to see better through the heavy downpour if Oscar was anywhere in sight. When the children had come home from school she had told them he would no longer be working at the sawmill. After that she had said little else. Mouth clamped tight, her face grim, she had blocked them out as she strode from cupboard to fireplace. As the children ate she settled herself on a stool, her head bent over her knitting. The needles flashed rapidly as she gave them all her attention. It was strange for the children to see her so intent, she who seldom looked at her needles even when turning heels on stockings or knitting an intricate pattern. When asked a question she looked up blankly.

Maria tried once. "Why isn't he going to be..." She fell silent in mid-question as Lisa lifted her head to look at her with dull eyes of anguish. Maria went to settle on the floor close to the cradle, rocking it gently, hushing the fitful cries of the youngest who seemed to feel the unease. Emilia crouched close by and made shadow pictures on the wall to keep Johan and Carl quiet. The girls exchanged worried glances.

Questions tumbled over themselves within Lisa.

What now? Where to? What is he thinking? Where is there work for him?

She could not let herself respond to the children, nor go in to the two sick ones. In that dark room she knew she would lose control. The only thing to do was knit rapidly. Her fingers ached from holding the steel needles too tightly but she only gripped them harder.

He must not leave us. Is that what is in his mind? I won't listen. Where can we go? Who will hire him? In Finland? In Sweden? Then suddenly she thought...America? Her hands fell into her lap and she stared in frozen fear straight ahead. That foreign land. Years to live apart. Nay! Oscar, nay! She resumed her knitting but slowly. "Dear God," she prayed, "help us. Help us."

When he came to the door at last she jumped up so hastily the knitting fell to the floor and trailed behind her. Maria scooped it up and threw it onto the table, one needle falling unnoticed to the floor. Between them, Lisa and the girls had pulled Oscar into the room, his jacket cascading puddles down onto the floor, his boots thick with mud. Anxiously Lisa had told him, "Don't say a thing until you are warm and dry."

Oscar finished drying his legs. Lisa took the towel and rubbed his back. He struggled into the dry underwear and went to the washbasin. Bent over, he lifted hot water in his cupped hands onto his face and neck.

"Ahh, that feels so good," he sputtered, and took the towel from Lisa. Through its folds he began, "It's a big house, not like this one, Lisa. It's all by itself, no other house very near. No house attached to it either. You'll like that, I think." He nodded his head in the direction of the wall that separated their home from the Qvist's.

"Begin from the beginning," she said with impatience. "What did Mangnusson have to say when you went in with Jon Juslin?"

"That's right, I haven't told you that," he said, and shook his head as he hung the towel on its peg.

"Get Pappa his Sunday trousers," Lisa ordered over her shoulder at the girls. "Dry stockings too. Hurry up."

"But Mamma," Maria complained, "do you want us to go in there?"

"What am I thinking of," Lisa scolded herself as she rushed across the room, her hands lifted in disgust at herself. "Pour Pappa some coffee then while I get them." She returned in a moment to hand him the dry clothing.

"Everything that happened before I went off to find the house seems like years ago," Oscar said, stepping into the trousers and buttoning them before sitting down to put on the dry stockings. Lisa poured a generous stream of milk into his coffee mug as he reached for lumps of sugar. Lisa continued to stand, the tin milk container still in her hand.

"Go on," she urged.

"I have done so much and ridden so far since then," he told her after gulping several swallows of coffee. He frowned as he recalled the scene at the sawmill. "Mangnusson said nothing, only glared. When I set the money down on the board he got even more stiff-necked and red in the face. He began to stare at Jon. Jon had a hard time to look undisturbed. I hope Mangnusson won't hold it against him that he went in there with me."

"Let us hope he is not that evil. Did any of the other men say anything to you?"

"Nay, some of them had seen what happened earlier but could not have heard what either Mangnusson or I were talking about. They must have guessed because there were plenty of them twisting their heads around hoping to see what was going to happen next. Jon will get the truth to them, that we can be sure of."

Lisa agreed. "Where have you been all this time, and what house is it that you found?"

"Sit, Lisa, I can talk better if you sit. Maria, pour her some coffee too. Come girls, sit with us."

Lisa set the milk container on the table and sat down, but ignored the coffee Maria brought her. Maria settled next to her sisters. All faces turned to Oscar.

"Remember the house on the road to Narpes on the other side of the village?" he began. "The one that belongs to Elvira's boss, Svensson?"

Every nodded. Lisa asked, "You mean the one that was a bakery years ago?"

"Yaw, that is what he told me it had been once."

"But that is such a big place," she protested.

"So it is, but we need use only two rooms. The main room, much bigger than this one, and the small room next to it. But let me go on. It has been empty a long time so I went to see him about it. When he heard I wasn't to be at the sawmill anymore he didn't want to rent to me. I told him I would be in first thing in the morning with money, so he agreed. I rode over to Berta Lund's after that, then to Emile Mackela's. Both of them will come with their wagons tomorrow afternoon to move us. Last of all I rode over to Katarina and Sigurd's. Katarina cried when I told her what had happened."

"And no wonder," Lisa sighed, and felt guilt for she had not thought of her sister once since Oscar had been fired. "She will take it hard, I know, because she feels responsible for our coming here."

"Well, she will be here tomorrow."

"Isn't that like her?" Lisa broke a piece of *knäckebröd* and sat crumbling it onto the table. "Oscar," she asked as he drained the last of his coffee, "should we move the two girls tomorrow?"

"Mangnusson would be here to throw us out if we tried to stay even one day longer, I think. How do the girls look?" he asked.

"Their fevers are down, I think, but not broken yet."

"I'll go look at them," he said, and stepped around the mattresses on the floor where the two boys were already asleep on one of them.

"You've done a good job with your wet towels, Lisa," he said, as he came back from the bedroom. "Their bodies feel cooler. They are sleeping restfully. Don't worry. We will wrap them well and cover their faces. It will be late afternoon before we are ready to take them out and over to the new place."

"But to take them into a cold house in the rain, Oscar!"

"It won't be cold, Lisa. Elvira will be there. I asked that she be allowed to take her rest day tomorrow, and go over to get the house ready for us. She'll be there first thing in the morning to sweep and scrub it up. There's a shed some distance from the house. Behind it I saw a woodpile. She'll have both rooms warm long before we get there. I expect the rain to stop tonight. It was letting up before I got home."

Lisa swept the crumbs on the table in front of her into a small heap. "You've thought of everything, Oscar. Thank you. Maria, go dish up supper for him. Stir the pot good so you get plenty of turnips and potatoes, as well as the soup." She turned back to Oscar. "Poor Elvira who has to give up her free time. Yaw, I know," she added quickly as he started to object. "She didn't grumble, I'm sure, but agreed right away."

Oscar nodded as he began to eat, after saying a short silent prayer.

"Here's some soup for you, too," Maria told Lisa, and set a bowl of it in front of her, her wooden spoon alongside. "You didn't eat anything when we did."

Lisa waved it away, but seeing Oscar stop his spoon halfway to his mouth she lifted a small portion of the soup into her mouth. Swallowing quickly she set the spoon back in the bowl, where it stayed.

"Tell me," she began, "have you thought where you are to find work? We have only enough to pay rent once again, without depending on Elvira's earnings."

"I thought of little else, Lisa, as I rushed about. Sometimes," he told her, laying his spoon down, "I had to stop the bicycle and get off to walk in order to think about it. I had such a headache."

She stood up hastily. "You should have told me. I'll get a cold cloth for your forehead."

"Nay, Lisa, sit." He waved her down. "It's gone. I was able to walk the last few kilometers pushing the bicycle by thinking of your good hot meal waiting for me."

"You walked?"

"The wheels got so thick with mud I couldn't pedal anymore. But your good food is taking care of both my head and my tired muscles. I feel strong again." He ate some soup quickly, and looked around the table, including the girls along with Lisa as he began to smile. "I'll tell you what I've decided to do."

Lisa grasped the edge of the table, her knuckles white as she gripped hard.

"You remember I said there was a shed some distance from the house?" he asked. All heads nodded. He continued, the smile growing large, his eyes only for Lisa now. "What do you think of this? I'm going to set up a bicycle shop in it."

There was no sound from anyone. As if to make sure they had heard him correctly the girls examined each other's surprised faces. With one accord they slid down to the end of their bench. Emilia, furthest away, got up on her knees and leaned in over the table past her sisters to join in asking excited questions.

"You really are?"

"A real bicycle shop?"

"To sell bicycles?"

"Are you going to fix bicycles too?"

More questions overlapped each other. Oscar answered only by nodding continuously, his eyes intent on Lisa.

The look of surprise gradually left her face. A smile began. It turned into laughter. The laughter grew, became loud, and finally uncontrolled in volume. She slapped her hands over her mouth, agonized eyes still looking at Oscar. He jumped up and hurried to go sit next to her.

"You've been so worried. I know that," he told her, encircling her waist with his arm. Placing his forehead against hers he murmured something too low for the now quiet girls to hear. Maria got up and circled the table to stand close to them, while Emilia and Paulina slid back down the bench again to be directly across from their parents. Uncertain if they should laugh too, they did not begin, for Lisa's laughter stopped suddenly. Her arms crept around Oscar's neck for a moment. Suddenly she grasped both his ears and shook his head, smiling into his face.

"Thank you, Oscar, thank you," she said. "There is no one who can surprise a family more than you can. What do you say, girls?"

"You're glad we've going to have a bicycle shop?" Paulina asked, still uncertain what Lisa had meant with her odd laughter. The other two nodded in agreement with the question, eager to hear her answer.

"Glad?" Her voice quavered as she continued to search Oscar's eyes. With a final shake she let go of his ears, and told him, "Words can't tell you." Oscar grinned foolishly at her.

"We'll celebrate," she announced, getting up. "I'll make some hot chocolate. While I do, Oscar, don't you think you ought to tell the girls what happened at the sawmill? I haven't told them anything but that you will not be working there anymore." She went to the cupboard.

But Oscar, rejoicing that his news had brought her hope, could not speak of the firing. He lifted his legs over the bench to face the table. Maria placed his unfinished supper in front of him. He ladled several spoonfuls into his mouth. The broth, rich with fat and savory with herbs, made him feel warm. It was good to be surrounded by his three big girls, who looked at him with trust. The talk of Mangnusson could wait. Instead, mouth sometimes overladen with potatoes or turnips, he fantasized for them.

"We'll have a bicycle shop a mile long," he told them, "with a thousand bicycles. You three can each have one with a great big wheel in front, and a small wheel in back. How would you like that?"

"Pappa! No one but a circus clown can ride such a thing," Emilia protested, giggles making her sputter.

"And what do you know of circuses?" he demanded in mock surprise.

"Nyeh, nyeh, we've seen pictures of them," Paulina managed in support of her twin.

Emilia jumped up and hurried over to the rocking chair that had not yet been put out into the vestibule for the night. "Look," she cried, and straddled the arm of it facing the back. With the foot on the outside of the chair she pumped an imaginary bicycle pedal as she assumed the position of a rider. Her hands held imaginary handlebars as she exaggerated steering. "I can even turn corners sitting high up here on this great big wheel," she called. "Watch!"

Lisa, pouring hot water into the cocoa, sugar, and a bit of milk she had stirred into the mugs in front of her, laughed as appreciatively as the others when Emilia seemed to steer around successive sharp curves. She called, "That will do, you clown. Come, the hot chocolate is ready."

"Someday I'll take you to a circus," Oscar promised, "We'll all go, everyone of us on a bicycle."

"You'll have to get one with eleven seats all in a row then," Lisa suggested.

The girls laughed.

Maria announced, "I've seen pictures where there are two seats, one right behind the other. Isn't that right, Pappa?"

"Yaw, there are bicycles built for two," he agreed. "Maybe as soon as the twins can go earn their own money they can order one from me. I'd make good money on such a sale."

"We'll do it, Pappa," both girls exclaimed but were hushed hastily as Lisa pointed to the sleeping boys on the mattress behind them.

"It's very late, finish your drinks and get to bed. Oscar, tell them."

He hesitated, knowing what she wanted him to do. It was Maria who decided him.

"Why aren't you going to work at the sawmill anymore?" she asked.

The other two across from him sat stiff and silent, waiting for his answer.

"All I will tell you tonight," he said, "is that Mangnusson and I had a serious disagreement. Mangnusson is boss, so he fired me." The girls gasped. "Tomorrow morning when we are all rested I will tell you the whole thing. Let us pray together now, and get to bed."

He knelt by the table. The others hurried to do the same. Quietly he asked for guidance, and that no harm would come to the two sick ones by having to move them the next day.

It was a long time before the two parents made their way to bed, stepping over the five sleeping children on the floor. Together they had once more rubbed Marta and Alli with cool towels, given them water, and sat with them until they slept again.

*

"Sure," Lisa told Katarina over the fur covers she was bringing in from the bedroom, "Oscar never dreamed of having a shop of his own, and certainly he's got much to learn about running one. But, you do know he is a good mechanic."

"None better," Katarina agreed, taking more items from the food cupboard to place them in the big yellow basket that stood on one of the benches at the table for easier reach. "How long does he think it will take before there is enough money coming in?"

Lisa set her burden down on the sofa-bed where both Carl and the youngest sat up out of the way. Since other blankets were already piled around them they were lost to sight, except for their heads. Undisturbed, Carl continued to play contentedly with several small wooden cooking spoons, dropping them in and taking them out of a crock used for salting fish. The youngest one shouted in delight each time they rattled down or out of the crock.

Brushing her hair up off her forehead with her arm, Lisa went to stand at the table near her sister.

"We haven't talked about that," she admitted, lowering her voice as she glanced around at the twins. Paulina was washing a window, Emilia was taking up the rag rugs to shake outdoors, and roll them ready for carrying out to the wagons when they came. "I know he's as worried as I am," she continued, "but right now all we think about is moving. Somehow Oscar will manage. I've got to hang onto that."

Katarina nodded. "You've got a smart man, Lisa, but he's bullheaded in lots of ways. Many people here hold that against him."

"Bullheaded?" Lisa exclaimed loudly. "That's not what you mean. You mean he practices what he believes. I would not change that even if I could." She glared at her sister.

Katarina shrugged. "It has cost him plenty, two times already."

"So, what are you telling me?" Lisa asked angrily. "That I should tell him he has to bow, scrape, and be dishonest to keep a job? Give up what he believes in order to be accepted by other people?"

"Nay, nay," Katarina said softly, and placed a hand on Lisa's arm. "All I'm trying to tell you is that now that he isn't boss, foreman at the sawmill, you'll find that it'll be very hard for him to deal with the Swede-Finns. They accepted him somewhat before because of his job, but now they're the ones Oscar will have to look to for customers. I just want to prepare you, Lisa. There might be very few willing to come to him to have their bicycles fixed."

The urgency to get the work done was suddenly no help to Lisa. All morning she had used it to keep from revealing too much to her sister. She swung around to go hide her feelings in the bedroom, but as quickly turned back again, her mouth working.

"You know," she said, in almost a whisper, "I thought of nothing else all the night long?" Without looking to see where the bench was she collapsed suddenly on it, her eyes asking for help.

Katarina picked up the two mugs from the center of the table, filled them with coffee, then slid one across to Lisa.

She sat down next to the basket. Sipping frequently she encouraged her sister to talk. Quietly, keeping her voice low, Lisa poured out the worries of the previous afternoon and evening. Hunched over, their heads bent toward each other, Katarina listened.

There were no interruptions, for Oscar had left to pay the rent. He took Johan with him, after telling the children the full story of Mangnusson, the cheating and the firing. He had been pleased by their exclamations of anger, disbelief, and their loud statements of support. They turned willingly to the work. Emilia had been sent to run to school, first thing, to tell the schoolmaster the Veldmans would not be there that day. She was warned not to tell anything more than that they were moving. He would hear soon enough the bad news. Maria had been bundled off carrying a bucket, rags and a broom borrowed from the Qvists, to help Elvira clean the new place. Oscar was to stop off there also, to see if there was anything he needed to do to make the place livable. The twins continued their work but very quietly. They strained to hear what the two women were saying. Emilia skirted the table as closely as possible on each trip out and back with a rag rug.

At last Lisa sat back, sighing with gratitude. "What would I do if I couldn't see you at least once in a while, Katarina? I never want to be far from you again. One good thing about this house we're moving to, it's closer to you."

Katarina laughed. "In America you could hop into one of those horseless buggies and chug right over to see our brother, Sten, and his Blanche in Duluth." She said their sister-in-law's name carefully, making the "ch" a "k" and sounding the "e" at the end. "Such a name," she marveled, saying it once again, "Blunkeh."

Lisa nodded in agreement. "How could Sten have married someone who can't speak Swedish?" Without waiting for an answer she called, "Paulina, Emilia, come rest, and have some coffee and dunk. There's coffee bread on the table." When they reached for generous slices of the bread to soak in the pale brown liquid, she asked them, "How long do you think it would take you to learn to speak American?"

"Two days," Emilia said, lifting two fingers in the air.

"Nay," Paulina contradicted, "two years."

They all laughed together.

"Thank goodness that's one thing you won't have to worry about," Lisa told them. "We are staying right here in Finland." She selected a piece of coffee bread, broke it in two and dipped one end of both pieces into Paulina's coffee. She got up and took them to Carl and the youngest who reached eagerly for them. "I had better get back to work. Oscar will be here for midday meal, I'm sure. I want that bedroom done, except for Marta and Alli's bed, before he gets here."

"Don't push those heavy beds around in there when you sweep," Katarina warned her. "Let me come in and help."

Lisa waved a hand at her and went into the bedroom, calling over her shoulder, "You stay out. I'm no weakling."

Late in the afternoon the house was clean and everything ready to move. Oscar came back in early afternoon hungry, and reporting that the new place was warm and the girls working hard. Katarina left before the wagons arrived, anxious about her own family's supper. Emile Mackela and Berta Lund made quick work of loading the furniture and mattresses onto the wagons, along with Oscar's help. Last of all Oscar carried Marta, and Berta carried Alli, to lift them up onto the mattresses piled high in Berta's wagon.

"Don't sit up," Lisa warned them, "and don't take the blankets down from your face, or let the light get to your eyes."

"I'll watch that they don't," Berta assured her, and slapped the reins on the back of the horse as she climbed up to stand in front of the high seat.

Fru Qvist and her youngest stood in their doorway, the two boys seated on the steps to watch. Dagmar helped, flying in and out with the others to carry anything she was handed. Often she wiped her eyes and nose with the back of a hand, crying soundlessly.

"Tell Elvira," she whispered to Paulina, "that I'll see her at the next dance."

When Emile Mackela clucked to his horse, Lisa sat among the furniture on it with the two youngest. *Fru* Qvist raised a hesitant hand and called, "Come back and see us, won't you?"

List raised a hand in return and nodded, although she knew she never wanted to come back. She turned her head so she would not see the sawmill, or the men working near it. It was a relief when the sound of it was lost as the horse plodded down the muddy road.

"Hold tight," she called to Johan, who rode past sitting in front of Oscar on the bicycle. Then to Paulina and Emilia who trotted behind the wagon to keep up, "Walk, don't run. You'll wear yourselves out." They ran harder, Emilia reaching back to pull the slower Paulina along. They were eager to keep close to the wagon.

"Welcome home," Elvira and Maria called from the doorway as the wagons pulled up to the old bakery building. Lisa did not answer, too anxious to get down and hurry to the other wagon to get the sick ones into the house, and in bed. Rain had held off but now it came drizzling down. A man passing by on a bicycle got off and came running to give a hand at carrying in the mattresses and furniture. It was Peter Rudolfsson, the Baptist minister.

"Coffee is served," Elvira announced when the table, benches, and stools had been wiped dry and set in place. Except for the two scarlet fever victims, everyone gathered around the table.

"Yaw," Lisa said, after looking around the room with critical eyes while taking swallows of coffee, "you girls have done well. My thanks to you both. But, Oscar, you didn't tell me the roof leaks. I see the girls have had to set a bucket to catch rain in the bedroom."

"There will have to be more buckets," Maria reported, stepping swiftly over to one corner where water was beginning to ping against the floor. She pointed gracefully upward, pirouetting under her up-raised finger. "We're going to have running water like the Palmers, but not coming through pipes," she laughed.

Elvira stood aside nursing one hand with the other.

"I'll see with I can do to patch the holes," Oscar promised.

"Soon, I hope," Lisa told him. "Elvira, what's the matter with your hands?" She set her coffee on the table and went to her.

"Oscar!" she exclaimed, "come see this!"

"What has caused this?" he asked, turning Elvira's hands to examine both their backs and palms. Red, drying-looking scale covered them on the outside. Angry cracks between the fingers oozed into the palms.

"It's the lye, Pappa. It has to be so strong in the water when I scrub the floor each night at the store," she told him.

Lisa cried, "You put lye in the scrub water every night?"

"Yaw, the storekeeper wants the floor to stay white," Elvira explained.

Anger Lisa had buried through the night and day found release, hard and clean, against an employer.

"What insanity! Only an idiot would demand anyone put their hands in lye every day. Why haven't you come home to show us this?" she demanded. "Too busy going off to dances, but willing to sacrifice your hands just so people can clump their dirty boots on a white floor? Maybe you want only stumps at the end of your arms. I won't have it. You will not work there one more day. Oscar?"

"Slowly now, Lisa," he told her. "Let's find out for sure if that's what it is. Elvira, are you sure it was the lye water?"

"Of course it was," Lisa stormed. "You only have to feel the sting of lye once to know that's what did it."

"It probably is, Lisa," he answered quickly, "but do quiet yourself. I'll go to Svensson, and I'll certainly tell him she won't be back until her hands heal."

"She's to go back? Nay!" Lisa insisted, her face angry.

"Elvira interrupted. "But, Mamma, Pappa knows we need my money now more than ever before. Don't we?"

Lisa grasped Elvira by the wrists and lifted her sore hands towards Oscar's face. "Is the money more important than the girl?" she demanded, and dropped the hands to storm further. "If need be I'll find work. I could at least go and milk cows at some farm. I haven't forgotten how. We won't starve if she stays home until she can go work in some more humane place."

Oscar raised his hands in defeat. "All right, but let's not argue in front of our friends. I agree, she'll stay home."

"Good. Paulina, where is the salve packed? The same Elvira had when her hands were chapped in Sweden? Go find it. Put it on thick, Elvira, and wrap your hands in rags. You're not doing another thing until those hands are well again. You put me to shame that I set you to clean here today."

"Maria did all the scrubbing with the broom, Mamma," Elvira answered, taking the salve from Paulina.

"Thank you, Maria, that makes me feel a little better."

Berta Lund stepped in from the shadows where she had retired with Pastor Rudolfsson and Emile Mackela during the family discussion.

"I could use some help on my farm," she said. "Can any of your children drive a horse?"

"I could," Paulina cried, excited. "I never have but I know I can."

"I'm sure of that," Berta agreed. "I don't know who is better with animals than you are, Paulina, unless its your *Morbror* Sigurd. Your mamma told me it was you who took such good care of Nasse. But you might not want to do this. You're a neat young lady and this would be to drive the manure wagon."

"I wouldn't mind that," Paulina assured her.

"I'll need two people, another one to shovel the manure into the fields from the wagon."

"I could do that," Emilia shouted, elbowing her way in to stand next to her sister. "Paulina can drive, I'll shovel. I'm real strong." She bent one arm, her hand balled into a fist to show she could make a muscle.

Together the twins looked at their parents. They both nodded.

"I need a cowherder soon," Peter Rudolfsson announced, stepping forward. "I'm more farmer than preacher, you know. My boy can't handle them all alone in the fields. He has a lame foot from infantile paralysis, you know. Is there one of the children who could do that?"

Oscar looked from Rudolfsson to Berta. "Are you sure you are not just making jobs in order to help us? It is very kind if you are, but we would not want you to do that,"

"I hire one or two children to help in the spring," the pastor assured him, "and it might as well be one of yours."

"I do too," Berta said, "and if it isn't yours it will have to be someone else's young."

Emile Mackela interrupted to make an offer in his halting Swedish. Learned the year he worked in Sweden, it was ungrammatical, and strongly accented with Finnish, but was the Swedish spoken by the Veldmans, Pastor Rudolfsson and Berta. He did not speak in the dialect of the area.

"I maybe should ask for one girl come work my house? My wife she can't talk any but Finnish. My kids too."

Oscar walked over and shook his hand. "Thank you, Emile, that's kind of you. Elvira's hands have to heal, then we'll see."

"Pappa," Elvira protested, but quietly, "I can't speak Finnish."

"I could go, Pappa," Maria offered, "but I can't speak Finnish either."

"You I need here to help me," Lisa told her.

"Quiet, quiet," Oscar ordered everybody, and asked Lisa, "Do you think Marta could be a cow herder?"

"Why not?" she answered. "She's the same age as Pastor Rudolfsson's boy. They're both in the same grade at school. But, Pastor, would it be agreeable with you if Alli went along with Marta?"

"She is what? A year younger?" he asked.

"Yaw, but dependable."

"Why not? The more to keep those cows in my fields the better."

"We will do it!" two young voices called from the bedroom. Lisa hurried in to the two sick girls. In a few moments she came back to stand in the doorway, a broad smile on her face.

"Their fevers have broken," she announced.

*

Oscar went to Svensson's to tell them Elvira would not return to work there. Lisa was not satisfied with his report.

"I don't care if their's is the only store in the village. You didn't have to soften it for them. I know we have to buy there. Of course they feel bad at losing such a good worker. I'll go myself and tell them what I think of them."

"Lisa, Svensson was beside himself with anger. He yelled at his *fru*, right in front of me, accusing her of being the one to pour lye in the water."

"It doesn't matter which one did it. They are both criminal."

"It is done, Lisa. Let it be," he ordered.

Grumbling, she had to agree. "It is for you to say, Oscar."

But there was no rest for her. They needed kerosene. Alone, she went to the store, slammed the container onto the counter making Svensson jump back as if she had aimed it at his large stomach. *Fru* Svensson came hustling out of their living quarters, angry eyes narrowed, nostrils flared as she looked down her nose at Lisa.

"Your girl put the lye in herself," she shouted immediately. "Every time."

"Now I have heard the first big falsehood of this day," Lisa retorted, her own head lifted to glare back. "You should be whipped, Edla Svensson, for what you did to her hands. Get me kerosene and a spool of white thread. That's all I want from you."

She looked into one set of cold eyes, then the other, her hands fists on the counter in front of her. The door behind her opened, some other customer entering. She did not turn to see who it was. *Fru* Svensson poked an elbow into her husband.

"Get the kerosene, I'll get the thread."

Lisa slammed the coins for her purchases on the counter, took the container and thread, and turned to leave. Beede Gran, the village gossip, stood facing her. It had not been a customer. Lisa turned at the door.

"After this I will send my girls to buy what we need. I will tell them to listen so they can come home and tell me how badly you continue to twist the truth. Beeda will get the news around, won't you, Beeda?"

Lisa opened the door, stepped out, and closed it softly behind her without waiting for an answer. How good she felt to have had her say.

For some time the girls vied with each other to go to the store, to hear if *Fru* Svensson still lied, but because she seldom showed herself, and Svensson said very little, they soon lost interest.

To Lisa's relief Pastof Peter Rudolfsson became a frequent visitor at Oscar's shop that summer. Like Oscar he was shunned because he was a defector from the state church. He preached the gospel of John the Baptist. Native to the area, although educated in Sweden like Berta, he had a few supporters who made up the flock of his small church. Yet there was no one he enjoyed more than Oscar Veldman when it came to discussing the Bible and world affairs. Whenever he had time he rode over on his bicycle to visit. Sometimes discussions reached roaring pitch, neither man hearing the other's interpretation. Most times they talked quietly, each learning respect for the other, each getting moral support.

Oscar was severely in need of his new friend's visits, Lisa knew. Too often the few who came to have "that Swede" mend their bicycles left owing him, with a promise to pay soon. Often he had to go to their homes in search of the money. Through Jon Julsin the truth of what had happened at the sawmill got about, but it had not made things easier for Oscar. The attitude, as he came to know it through his girls coming home from school, the Segersons, and Pastor Rudolfsson, seemed to be he had been a fool to face Mangnusson with a fact that everyone already knew. He should have kept his mouth shut, let the ones buying from the sawmill protest if they felt they had been cheated. Why did Veldman think he could come over here to Finland and point a finger to correct things for them? Nothing had been changed except that he had lost his job. That was no skin off anyone's nose but that Swede's, who turned his back on the church, and did not let the children learn the catechism in school. If any of the sawmill workers felt he was the champion of honesty, they had not let him know. He thought he understood. They did not dare. Mangnusson would fire them if they showed sympathy.

To date Oscar had sold only one bicycle, and that to Elvira. He rebuilt it out of an old one, making it as good as new. Elvira, who had gone to work in the home of an attorney in Narpes as soon as her hands had healed, insisted on paying for it.

"Let me take ten *öre* out to Pappa," she insisted each time she brought her earnings home and turned them over to Lisa. "He needs to enter it separately into his books as part payment on my bicycle. It will help him know the shop is going to make money."

"You must keep some for yourself," Lisa told her.

"I do. I keep out enough for what I want to do," she answered.

"You buy tickets for dances, is that it?" Lisa asked, but without criticism.

"That's right," Elvira admitted. "I go to every one I can. The bicycle takes me, even if it's a long way there and back. You know, Mamma, once I went all the way to Kaskö? I didn't get back until five o'clock in the morning, it took so long to ride those kilometers."

"Nay, but Elvira, that is too much. What did your employers say to that?"

"Nothing. They didn't even know. I was back in plenty of time to make breakfast for them."

Lisa shook her head in disapproval, but did not seriously object. Elvira continued to turn over most of her pay.

Maria too left home to earn money to help out. Oscar agreed that it was to be for the summer only. In the fall she was to go back to school, not to miss out like Elvira had. He went with her the first day, when she went to live in the house of the chemist in the next village. There she was to care for their only child and to help in the house. Every other week, when she was expected home for a day of rest, eyes would search down the road for her.

"Here she comes," someone would call out happily, sometimes adding, "it's a big package this time."

It was Maria's special joy to buy meat for the family. For those months it was the only time there was meat for Lisa to cook. Whoever spied Maria first was always rewarded with an extra helping of it at the noonday meal.

"Thanks, a thousand thanks," Lisa told her gratefully, each time she took the package and the few coins Maria handed her, left over from the purchase. "Are you managing the child and the work all right?"

"I tell you, Mamma, the more I'm with that little boy the more I appreciate Johan and Carl. He doesn't want to eat anything. Can you imagine that? Oh, he's a good boy, all right, but spoiled. Always has to have his way. He cries everytime I leave. Isn't that something?"

"He must like you."

"Yaw, he does, and so much he won't let his mamma give me anything else to do. I have to play with him all the time."

"You like that, I suppose."

"I'll say. I'd rather play than dust furniture or sweep floors."

"Hmm, you'll get spoiled. Dusting and sweeping are a part of life too," Lisa scolded, but gently.

Emilia and Paulina finished spreading manure that spring, but continued to work for Berta on many days through the summer. First at planting her large vegetable garden, later weeding and hoeing it.

They harvested carrots and beets to bring to Lisa, like bouquets of flowers. Later they came like two trolls with sacks of potatoes, or cabbages, slung over their shoulders, bumping aginst their backs. The twins were happy working for Berta.

Oscar alone brought no foodstuff for Lisa's cupboard, and little more to her apron pocket. As fall frosts began the girls went back to school. Alli too, who started her first year. All but Elvira's monies ended. The flow of milk, vegetables, and meat came to a stop.

Oscar sat in the shop studying the few entries in his account book. Spirits low, he wondered how he could get more work brought in, when Peter Rudolfsson burst into the shop.

"Oscar!" he shouted, "the telephone company is looking for a home to put their central in. Why don't you apply for it? You'd have to do it right away. Today. In Vasa."

Oscar didn't need to think twice. Immediately excited he did not even take time to thank Peter but pushed him out ahead of him as he rushed to lock the shop door behind him.

"I'll go tell Lisa I'm off to get the train in Narpes right now," he said quickly. "There's time to catch it if I speed to the station on the bicycle."

Peter understood the urgency. He shouted after him as Oscar raced toward the house. "I'm going with you to be your character witness. You'll need one. All they need to know is that I'm a pastor. I don't have to tell them what church."

At this Oscar stopped and turned around. "Thank you, Peter, thank you. You give me the gift of hope."

Homeward bound that afternoon, swaying with the motion of the train, he sat with hands folded peacefully in his lap. Gratitude toward Peter on the seat next to him was so sharp he had difficulty finding a way to express it. He took his hand and shook it, hard and long, his smile matching the pastor's.

"Thank you, Peter. You realize how much you have helped me? I had no idea what to do next. I did think of going from door to door asking people to let me fix whatever they had that needed mending. But if I did that I wouldn't be at the shop when people brought their bicycles in. I tell you, this central makes all the difference. At least until my shop is really a paying business. Thank you. My hearty thank you. I can't say more than that."

He released his friend's hand with a final warm shake, sat back to take a deep contented breath and looked out the window. Hands together across his stomach his thumbs twirled around each other, as he urged the clacking wheels to go faster. He sent his good news ahead in the sound of the train whistle as it chugged around a small curve. Half listening to Peter he saw himself reflected in the window as a stream of black smoke, spewed from the chuffing smokestack, flew past. As if the sight of his own face was the unlocking key, he suddenly remembered something with such a strong sense of guilt that he closed his eyes and turned away quickly.

"Peter," he said, his hands clutched together in a tight knot, "let me tell you something I've done."

"Yaw?" Peter answered, although Oscar had interrupted him.

"Something I'm ashamed of."

"That so? What can that be?"

"I wrote to America without telling Lisa."

Peter laughed. "Is that so bad?" he asked, but seeing his friend's distressed face, added, "was Lisa supposed to know?"

"It was wrong of me to do it, but I told myself I didn't tell her because I didn't want to frighten her. Convinced myself I was writing only to get information out of curiosity. But I knew all the time I was asking if I could come to America."

"To America!" In his astonishment Peter turned sharply in his seat. "Are you thinking of going? Are you actually?"

"Nay," Oscar exploded, "but you see it had been over three weeks since anyone had brought me work to do. It looked so bad for the shop. I couldn't see myself going on living off the earnings of my children, as willing as they are to work. It was then I wrote to Lisa's brother in America." Silent, he studied the back of the seat in front of him. Peter waited. "Lisa fears my going away, and rightly so. It would mean years before we could be together again. I wouldn't like it either. More than that, she's heard so many of those tales going around about men who never send for their families, or disappear, for whatever reason, in that big country. I can understand her feelings, although she wouldn't have to worry about my doing any such thing."

"There are two American widows in my church," Peter interjected. "They tell me they had the same fears."

"I suppose they did," Oscar agreed. "Peter, I know now what it is to be a foreigner. Here, at least, I can understand what is said, even when it is in anger. Over there it would be a new language altogether. For me, and the children, it might be easy to learn. But, for Lisa, I don't know. Women are so much in the home. Where would she learn it? American ways must be very different from those of Sweden and Finland. But all that aside," he pounded one fist against a knee, "to think, that although I knew how Lisa felt about it, I could write that letter without telling her. How I wish I hadn't done it."

Peter comforted him. "There is still time to tell her, isn't there? The answer hasn't arrived yet, has it? She will understand."

Oscar shook his head. He felt a clutch of fear that perhaps on this day, when he was not home, the letter would have come. Nay, it was too soon. He calmed his worried thought. It couldn't arrive for several more weeks, at the earliest. The news of the telephone central, told to Lisa first, would help, as much as anything could, to minimize her anger at his deceit. Confidence returned as he thought of the good news. He pressed eagerly over to the window to see if Narpes station was in sight.

"A telephone central?" Lisa asked, when she could get a word in. The two men babbled at her when they rushed into the house. She searched Oscar's face, then Pastor Rudolfsson's. Slowly she understood. Her face began to reflect their smiles. "How wonderful," she beamed. "Sit down and tell it to me from the beginning again. We are to have a telephone central here?"

Both men removed their coats talking all the while, coats and caps crammed onto the bench where they took seats side by side. Lisa continued to stand to ask one more question.

"How did it ever come about?"

"It's thanks to Peter here," Oscar answered, rubbing his hands together between his knees in happiness. "The telephone people came to him, isn't that right?" He encouraged his friend to tell her.

"Yaw, they thought I might know who would be willing to have it put into their home."

"So he thought of us," Oscar interrupted, "and we are going to have it right here in this house."

"It's wonderful, Oscar, and thank you, Pastor. Your thoughtfulness knows no end." She sat down on the bench opposite them. "But you say I am to run it?" As they both nodded she tilted her head thoughtfully and examined her hands, slack on the table in front of her. She moved them together, and with her right hand twisted the two plain gold rings on her left ring finger around. "I don't know anything about running telephones. I've never even talked into one. You'll have to do it, Oscar."

"How could I? I have to be out in the shop if any work comes in."

"Put it out there then," she suggested.

"You would have to run out to answer it when I'm off trying to collect the money owing me," he explained. "Besides, people might want to have a call put through at night. We wouldn't hear it if it was out there."

"I'm sure I don't understand how that thing works," she said, "I'd do it wrong, and they would only come and take it away from us."

Oscar rapped the knuckles of one hand against the table and got up to stand looking at the ceiling as if help would come from it.

"*Fru* Veldman," Peter Rudolfsson said. "Oscar said right off when we came in that you'll get paid for running it."

"Yaw, I know, you both said it, and it makes me so glad I hurt inside. Who knows better than I do how desperately we need the money. But it is Oscar who is the mechanic, not me."

"You don't have to be a mechanic, Lisa," Oscar told her, coming back to place both hands flat on the table and leaning across to look at her. "You can learn to run it in a few minutes. They showed Peter, here, and me, how to do it this morning in Vasa. All you have to do is listen, then push plugs into the right holes and turn a crank until someone answers."

Lisa shook her head. "I'd have to see it to understand what you're telling me."

"You will, tomorrow," Oscar shouted happily, standing straight again. "They'll be here in the morning." Pastor Rudolfsson sat nodding.

"Well, let's leave it till then," Lisa told them. "We'll see. Pastor, you were satisfied with the cow herders?"

"Yaw, indeed," he laughed. "My boy had a good summer with the two girls. Your Marta was boss, from what he tells me, not only of the cows but also of my boy and Alli too."

Lisa chuckled. "Our Marta has to unlearn some things she learned during a year away from us. It's done her good to work this summer. She has to learn she's a working man's daughter."

Oscar called to them, his arms measuring a spot on the wall alongside the door. "It's about this big," he said. "We'll have them put it right here."

Lisa glanced over at him but turned back to the pastor.

"I guess it isn't only Marta who can learn new things. I can too. I can't say nay to the money, it's as simple as that. I hope I can run it well enough to keep it here."

"It's easy to run, *Fru* Veldman. Even the girls will be able to put the calls through in a short time," he assured her.

"So be it," Lisa told him. "But how is this? I haven't poured you any coffee. Forgive me." She hurried to set mugs brimming with the hot fluid on the table for them, and poured another for herself. Before she drank she said, "Thank you, Peter," and then again, "thank you."

He smiled without telling her she had called him by his given name.

"Aren't you girls ready yet to leave for school?" Lisa shouted the next morning. Oscar was moving the pegs from one wall to the other to make room for the telephone central. His hammer almost drowned out the questions the girls yelled at him as they dressed and ate. "I can't hear myself think this morning," Lisa complained. "You five have pestered him with the same questions a hundred times. Go to school."

Oscar stopped hammering. "Let them ask," he told her. "It isn't often such an exciting thing happens to us."

"Yaw, yaw, they've asked. They know enough about it by this time. It was the same last night too."

"We're going, we're going," several of the girls called to her, as they rushed around to find their coats that Oscar had dropped here and there while emptying the pegs for moving.

"We'll hurry right home after school so we can see it right away," Marta told them as she led the exodus out of the house. "I talked in the telephone at Palmers, many times. I can show the others how to do it."

"Who needs you to," Emilia snarled quietly, bringing her mouth close to the back of Marta's head as she tramped on her heels going out the door.

Maria filed out last. "Pooh," she cried, holding her nose high in the air, as she made a wide circle past Carl. He stood in the middle of the floor dedicated to what he was doing. "He's done it again," she shouted, and slammed the door behind her, as if to seal Carl's smell within the house.

"And no wonder," Lisa muttered, as she went to him, "nobody took time to give him any attention this morning." She took him into the bedroom. Oscar, laughing, went back to his pounding.

The pegs were in place when she returned, and Oscar was sitting in his chair at the end of the table. Urging Carl up onto a bench she set a dish of oatmeal in front of him. He grasped his spoon and ladled the food into his mouth rapidly. Lisa went to gather up the youngest, settled her on her hip, and returned to place a bowl on the edge of the hearth and fill it with oatmeal and milk. Remaining at the fireplace she bent and spooned up a generous helping of the cereal into her own mouth. Again she dipped into the bowl and fed the child.

"Don't eat standing over there," Oscar complained, a deep frown on his face. "You know I don't want you to eat away from the table like the other women do. Your place is here," he tapped the table with a strong finger, "where all women should eat."

Lisa made no comment but picked up the bowl and came to the table.

"Johan, if you're finished go out and play," Oscar told the older boy sitting with an empty bowl in front of him. Quickly he crammed his last piece of *knäkebröd* into his mouth, got up, found his coat and cap, and hurried outdoors.

Carl scraped the final bit of cereal out of his bowl, set his spoon down, and burped loudly.

"One says 'excuse me,'" Lisa told him with a quick look.

"S'cuse," Carl echoed, slid from the bench, crouched down and walked under the table bumping his head as he surfaced on the other side. One hand rubbing the spot among his yellow curls, he squeezed between the bench and the table until he was out at the end nearest the door.

"That one has his own way to get where he wants to be," Lisa commented.

"Go out," Carl told Oscar. Oscar found his coat and helped him into it, pulled his cap down over his ears and helped him open the door to let him hurry outside to join his big brother.

Oscar came back to the table, and sat down again.

"Coffee?" Lisa asked.

He shook his head. "Nay, thank you," he said, and settled more firmly in his chair. He cleared his throat several times, then said, "Lisa, I've got something I must tell you."

"Hmm?" she answered, busy scraping the oatmeal from around the child's mouth to spoon it back in between the eager lips.

"I...I wrote Sten in Duluth some weeks ago," he said, and braced himself, his hands pushing against the table to firm himself up against the chairback.

"I know," Lisa answered, still busy with the child.

"I've felt so guilty about deceiving..." he began, then lunged forward in his chair to shout, "You know? How could you know? Sten's answer couldn't have come yet."

"Of course it couldn't. It's just that you're not a very good thief, Oscar."

"What?"

She pointed with the spoon at the cupboard door where unanswered letters and writing material were kept. "The day you wrote to him you came into the house from the shop. It seemed to me it was for no reason at all. I took the opportunity to go out back to the toilet. When I came in the cupboard door was slightly open. Sten's letter, a new envelope, and you were gone. An hour later you left the shop to bicycle off to the village, again for no reason as far as I knew. Besides, that evening Sten's letter was back in the cupboard, I noticed." She neither smiled nor looked cross as her eyes met his.

"You're not angry that I didn't tell you?" he marveled.

"At first, but I knew almost right away why you didn't."

"Woman," Oscar cried, "you couldn't have known."

Lisa held the bowl to the child's mouth and let her drink the remaining milk before wiping her face with her hand and lifting her down to the floor. She set the bowl away, folded both arms on the table in front of her and leaned toward him.

"Listen to me, Oscar," she began, "ever since we left the sawmill I have watched you turn in a smaller and smaller circle. Nay, don't interrupt. I need to get all this out of me. I've been thinking about it too long." She wiped one hand across her mouth, undecided how to continue. Oscar sat upright, holding back comment with difficulty.

"Both here and in Sweden," she went on, laying one hand out on the table toward him as though to soften what she had to say, "you were off almost every evening either to discuss the Bible with someone, or to go to Temperance meetings." She gave a short huff of a laugh at a sudden thought. "I think here in Finland you went mostly to be a thorn in the side of the Swede-Finns."

Oscar did not smile. His mouth was tight beneath his mustache.

"When we moved into this place all that changed, Oscar," she continued, "you changed. You began to stay home evenings, at first more often than not. Now you are home every evening. I know it is because you were so hurt. It can't be easy for you to go out, only to have people either ignore you or smile with scorn at whatever you say. It has hurt me too, each time you tell me about them." Oscar's face reflected the sadness in hers. "But, that's no excuse to bedevil...yaw, I said bedevil," she repeated, raising her voice as he opened his mouth to say something, shaking his head. She did not care if it was to deny her the use of the word, or if it was resistance to what she was about to say. She began again. "To bedevil both me and the children. Mostly the children."

"Nay, now I must have my say to that," he interrupted angrily.

"Wait," she pleaded, both hands lifted, "hear me out. What I'm going say will help us, believe me. I understand the agony you've suffered since leaving the sawmill. The pain you feel, knowing that the shop isn't working out, is my pain too. I know your feelings each time our girls bring home their earnings, even though I know how much you appreciate and expect their help. You'd be a man of stone if you didn't feel lessened by it." She slid closer to him down the bench.

"In the weeks when no work was coming in to the shop, every day I expected you to come tell me you would have to consider going to America. When I saw that you had written to Sten, without discussing it first with me, I knew how hard pressed you were."

"That's it," Oscar exploded, no longer able to be silent. Eagerly he searched her face as he tugged his chair closer to her side of the table, "but that's not the only reason, Lisa."

"Shh," she held a palm out toward him as if he was one of the children. "Let me tell it, then you'll know I understood. You didn't want to frighten me."

"That, and more," he cried, relief so great he couldn't sit still.

"You hoped that before Sten's answer came," she went on, leaning even closer to him, "the shop would be doing better. Then you could tell me that you had written out of curiosity, but that there would be no need for you to go away."

He jumped up, both hands to his head as he rubbed his hair. Laughing, he leaned down toward her, his smile so broad she could not help but return it.

"To have you tell it to me in my own words," he marveled, "is more than I can grasp." Sitting again he gazed at her happily, his hands laced together over his stomach, his two thumbs twirling swiftly around each other. Tangled curls hung over onto his forehead.

She laughed. "We've lived together a long time, Oscar, and should know each other's thoughts. You should have known mine."

He shook his head, sighing. "Nay, you are always a surprise to me." He leaned forward again, his face more serious, but a teasing glint in his eyes. "Is it because I deceived you that you have insisted that the child be between us in bed every night these many weeks?"

"How's that?" she asked.

He smiled knowingly, bent forward so that his chest came close to the table, and turned his head slightly sideways to look up into her face. "Was it punishment for me because you knew I had written Sten?"

She straightened up, pulling away from him. "Nay, it was not for that reason."

He would not accept that as an answer. "I'll not deceive you again," he promised.

"Don't," she replied, "you are not good at that either."

He could not respond to that. "To think I have let our misfortunes lead me away from preaching the TRUTH. As for the Temperance meetings?" He shook his head. "I don't know about that. Yaw, I will go. That is where the people are. It might convince them to bring me work." He studied his own thoughts for a while, then lifting her hand smiled and asked, "Now, aren't you going to tell me why you keep the child between us?"

For a moment she considered giving him the true reason, but instead evaded, saying quickly, "She's too big for the cradle."

He straigntened up. "Ho, if that's all I'll get some lumber when the first money comes in from the telephone central, and make her a bed she can share with Carl. Maria has had the two boys sleeping with her long enough, I think. We could open up and use one of the other rooms. The first small one down the hall doesn't leak except in one place. Don't think I could squeeze another bed into the one they're all in now."

"Slowly, Oscar, the money has many places to go when it gets here. If the shop doesn't start paying we still won't be able to make it for long. You need to spend all your time figuring out how to get business out there."

At peace, Oscar went to lift her chin and kiss her. She patted the bench next to her. He sat, his back to the table, but turned to face her.

"What you say is true," he admitted, "all of it. I guess I was too wrapped up in my own misery to know I showed my feelings so badly. But things will be better now, including me," he finished. With one finger he traced around her lips gently.

She pushed playfully against him with her shoulder.

He continued. "I must go out with the Bible again, I agree."

"Good," she told him, "but I will miss you in the evenings. I have become used to having you at home."

He pinched a few hairs above her forehead between thumb and forefinger and rubbed them back and forth. "I couldn't have been that bedeviling," he grinned. "Besides, you can't have it both ways, you know."

She laughed, but changed the subject. "I wonder what Sten will say in his letter."

"Now, there we have something to look forward to. I figure it should get here in no more than another few weeks, if he has answered right away."

"What did you write in your letter?" she asked.

He told her the many questions he had asked. What monies it would take to get there? Where did most people get that money? Where did they live once they were there, and how long did it take to get work?

She nodded. They were the right questions to have asked. "I hope Sten writes more than just answers to your questions."

"Of course he will. Sten is a good letter writer."

Their talk turned to Lisa's brother and his family in Duluth. They sat comfortably together for a long while. They were still at it when Johan opened the door.

"There's a wagon with some men in it coming here," Johan announced.

"The telephone central!" Oscar exclaimed. He hurried outdoors to welcome them, ignoring Lisa's call to put his coat and cap on.

*

Three months later, on a night late in November, several young voices shouted, "Let me! Let me!" as the telephone switchboard sounded. For once Paulina got there first. Emilia and Maria breathed over her shoulder in frustration as they watched her expertly push the plugs and wind the crank to connect the caller to the party asked for.

Lisa stood across the room shaking her head at them. "If it wasn't that you're in school during the day I'd forget how to run that thing," she told them.

"It's such fun to do," Maria answered her.

"Fun? Hardly that," Lisa said, "but because of it Pappa will be here soon with the two new bicycles. It's almost time for Berta to get here bringing him and the bicycles from the train in Narpes. Go out and wait for them at the shop. He'll have his own bicycle and the new ones to lift out of the wagon. You could help him."

"We'll go too," Marta and Alli clamored, as the older girls began putting on their coats.

"Go, but don't pester Pappa for a ride on those bicycles. They are not his, they are to be sold."

When the new bicycles were safely delivered into the shop Berta drove off, refusing to stop for a cup of coffee. The whole family, Lisa included, with the youngest on her hip, gathered to admire them. Oscar kept busy wiping each spoke, each handlebar, making sure the chains were oiled, the seats firmly set. He would not let the children touch any part of them, although they offered to help shine.

"We're on our way, Lisa," he gloried, his mustache bristling from his broad smile. He paced around the two bicycles set in the middle of the floor. The children made a march out of it, following him to halt when he did, to bend and look with him as he worked on the "two beauties" as he called them.

"Oh, I have something else I'm going to sell," he announced, and took a large paper parcel out of his coat pocket and set it on the small counter that held his account books and papers.

"What's in it?" several of the children asked as they crowded around. He only smiled and worked at untying each knot of the string that held the paper together. Quickly he rolled the parcel open to reveal what it held.

"Ooh!" the girls cried, "candy!"

"Exactly," he agreed, "I will be selling candy as well as bicycles. See, I will lay them out here on this counter, and when people stop in they will buy one, or two, or many, and it will give us a little extra income."

"Can we have some?" Marta asked. "They're all so good. I had some every day when I was at Palmers."

"Oh, you and your Palmers."

"Alli! That's enough," Lisa scolded the girl, who stood, hands on her hips, scowling at her sister.

Oscar laughed. "Do you have an *öre* or two?" The girls all shook their heads.

"When I have sold both bicycles then I will let each of you choose any one candy you wish. But now I'm hungry."

Lisa hurried back to the house, the children streaming behind her, to set his supper on the table. Oscar stayed behind to lock the shop carefully, after many proud looks at the gleaming cycles and the candies arranged in display. There wasn't room for his own bicycle along with the other two, so he wheeled it up to the house and put it in the long hall that connected the main room to the unused rooms in back.

Too excited to sleep well that night he was up early and out to the shop. Lisa had not had time to remove her flannel nightgown when she heard him yelling. His tortured voice carried through the crisp cold air all the way into the house. Barefoot, she ran out, leaving both doors open behind her. Over the long frozen path she sped, her nightgown lifted in both hands to give room for her speeding legs. Cold wind brought tears to her frightened eyes searching ahead for some sign of Oscar. In one leap she cleared the two steps up to the shop unaware that her braid, lifted by the wind and her sudden stop, slapped her across the face.

"Oscar, what is it?" she called into the open door. "Are you hurt?"

He came to her, hands lifted above his head into fists. His mouth was wide open as if he was trying to get enough air to yell again. His eyes were wild. There was a sickly blue around his nose and under his eyes. Digging his fingers into her arm he pulled her inside.

"Look for yourself," he said, spitting the words at her from teeth suddenly ground tightly together.

At first she did not understand, then realized the two bicycles no longer stood there. Then she saw the window furthest from the house had been shattered, the glass strewn over the floor. The counter where the candies had lain was broken off the wall, the candies on the floor. Most of them had been ground by some hard heel into messy globs. Spare parts for the bicycles lay everywhere, twisted, broken, and even flung out through the window along with his papers and books.

A sound like an animal in pain kept coming from deep inside Oscar.

"Nay, Oscar! Who could have done such a thing?" Lisa cried. The words issued with difficulty out of her tightened throat. "Some crazy person?"

He reached out and jerked her backward as she started to walk further into the shop.

"The glass," he shouted, pointing at the floor. He gulped air, his voice raw and uncontrolled. "Crazy people," he corrected her. "It took more than one to wheel the bicycles away and wreck most of the spare parts."

He pointed to the empty pegs on the furthest wall that had held his collection of parts for mending bicycles. His boots crunched glass as he went to pick up pieces of a bicycle chain. It had been pried into many sections by his own screwdriver, his hammer lying alongside. The screwdriver was still tangled in one part, its handle broken. He flung the chain and screwdriver from him to slam against a wall. With his boot he pushed some of the other parts that littered the floor.

"But who?" Lisa moaned. "Why?" she asked, her head shaking in the attempt to deny what she saw.

"Infidel, they call me. That's why!" Oscar began. "Swede. That's why!" he continued, his voice rising. "Because I pointed out what they knew and did nothing about," he roared. "But mostly because I worship the Lord in my own way. That's why!" he finished, and whirled to go out and sit down on the step in front of the door. He lowered his head onto his folded arms resting on his knees. Lisa ran and stood in front of him.

"Oscar," she said, placing her hand gently on his bowed head, "you told me before we left Sweden that you feared you wouldn't be accepted here. I can only admit now that you were right. I'm so ashamed of my countrymen."

He reached out and flung his arms around her, pulling her to him so that she almost fell, his face thrust hard against her stomach. Slowly she settled into his lap and together they cried, their faces pressed tightly together, the pain of his sobs shaking them both.

"Nay, this will not do," he gasped, as he became more quiet. He stood up and set her on her feet. "You must get on into the house before you catch cold," he told her. "Why, you have nothing on your feet," he added as if he noticed only then how she was dressed.

She hesitated to leave him, and stood using the bottom of her nightgown to wipe her nose. The cold wind blew against her.

She dropped the nightgown and wrapped it more tightly against her with both hands, feeling the cold for the first time. He removed his fur cap, wiped his cheeks with it, then reached over to wipe her face too.

"You have no need to apologize, Lisa," he said quietly. "They might be countrymen of yours but they aren't your kind. Go in. I see the children crowding the door and windows. I'll come and call the sheriff in just a little while. Let me get hold of myself first."

"You won't stay long out here, will you?" she asked.

He shook his head. "There is nothing I can do here anymore," he answered.

"Get dressed," he told the children, before he went to the telephone switchboard. He put in the call to Narpes, cranking the handle hard and long. The children, who had been immobilized by what Lisa had told them, went quietly about finding their clothes, their attention concentrated on listening to Oscar talk to the sheriff. His voice was raised to an unnatural pitch.

"Can we go see the shop?" It was Emilia who dared to ask when he finished.

He shook his head. "There's plenty of time for that later. I want to talk to all of you first." He went to stand in front of the fireplace, feet apart, hands behind his back, his head bowed as though he studied the floor. Lisa tried to hand him a mug of coffee, but he didn't notice. She poured the coffee back into the pot.

"Perhaps it's best you children stay home today," he began, and looked at her. "What do you say?"

"I think it would help us both if they were here," she admitted.

"But, tomorrow they go," he said.

"Yaw," she agreed.

The children had drawn close, some sitting or kneeling on the benches, others standing nearby. Johan went to Oscar, Carl hurrying to go with him, and stood looking up at his Pappa.

"I want all of you to see what someone did out in the shop. Johan and Carl too," he told them looking from one to the other. "It's an evil thing that's been done." His voice broke. He rubbed his hand over his mouth and mustache before he could go on. Alli began to cry.

Lisa took her by the shoulder. "That will do," she said. "You aren't helping Pappa. Stop it!"

Alli lowered her head and moved over on the bench to put her face against Paulina, who encircled her with her arm.

Oscar spoke now as if to himself. "It is the ignorant who hate, who did this evil. Their punishment will be in remembering what they did here last night, and they will have to face the Lord on Judgment Day." He took a deep breath, and looked again at his family. "Yet, it isn't for us to bring judgment on the evildoers. What we must learn out of this is never to judge anyone by the language they speak, or what country they happen to be born in. Can you understand that?"

The older girls nodded first, the younger children joining in after a quick look around at their sisters.

"But, Pappa, they stole. Isn't that wrong?" Maria asked. "Aren't they to be punished for that?"

"They will be," Oscar answered, "according to the law of the land, if they are ever caught. But, it is not for us to do."

He strode away from the fireplace, all heads turning to follow him as he went to stand looking down at the youngest, still in her cradle.

"Her feet stick out the end when she's out flat," he commented, as if it was the most important thing he had to say. He turned on his heel and came back to the fireplace, all heads following him again. He continued as though he had not interrupted himself.

"Most of all I want you to remember," he told them, his voice stronger, "if someone worships differently from the way you do, measure them by their daily acts, nothing else."

He cleared his voice several times, then turned to cling to the iron corner post of the fireplace, gripping it with both hands. Head lifted, eyes closed, his lips moved.

"Pappa," Maria said, in deep sympathy, and moved forward to go to him.

"Nay, nay, nay," Lisa told her quietly and stepped in front of her. "Go get your coat on, and take all the others out to see for themselves.

Be careful, don't touch anything, don't let the boys pick up any of that candy. Alli, blow your nose."

When they were gone she poured a fresh steaming mug of coffee. "Come away from there, Oscar. Sit down and drink. It will help you."

He sat, but it was some time before he had interest enough to lift the mug to his lips.

"What did the sheriff say," she asked quietly, when he had taken a quick sip.

"He'll be here when he can," he answered, his voice calm although still hesitant. "I don't expect anything will come of it, but at least I've reported it."

"If only he'd find those two bicycles."

He nodded, took a larger sip, and sat silent, his face troubled. At last he looked at her.

"Lisa, I'm sorely tried to love my enemies this morning," he confessed, shaking his head in despair. "It's so easy to say, 'love thine enemies!' It makes sense when I read it in Matthew, but it's so hard to do when the enemy shows its face in such a terrible way."

"I understand," she agreed.

He got up hastily. He shouted, "I'm so sinful in my thoughts, Lisa," and pounded his fists against his sides.

"You are mortal man, Oscar, not the Son of God," she said, tears smarting behind her eyelids.

"But to fulfill God's Word is my life's guidance."

"Give yourself time, Oscar. The wound is fresh. Let it heal, and you'll find you can love again."

His face hardened. "I feel I don't want to find it, Lisa. Not now, and maybe never again." He began to pace back and forth. "My feelings frighten me."

"Stop talking like that," she forced herself to say, sympathy giving way to impatience. "You're beginning to feel sorry for yourself."

Unbelieving he looked at her, rubbed his face hard, then grasped the hair of his head in both fists.

"Can't you see what is happening?" he asked, dropping his arms to hold his hands palms open toward her. "I'm being tested, and have been found wanting."

"Leave off, Oscar," she snapped, her voice deepening as she spoke sternly. "Control yourself," she ordered. With the flat of her hand she poked his shoulder so hard he staggered backward.

He slumped down into his chair. Slowly he sat erect. Hardly moving his head he nodded.

"That's better," she said. "The children should be back any minute. Eat some cereal." She went to the fireplace and filled a bowl and set it on the table. "Eat, then you can face whatever needs to be done this day."

With a laugh that sounded like a groan, he echoed her, making it a question. "What is there to do this day? Cleaning up the mess," he answered himself. "What then?"

"Plenty," she said. "We are going to talk about America."

"What!" he exclaimed, and hurled himself out of his chair to stand in front of her. "You're giving up?"

"Giving up?" she repeated after him. "What is there to give up?"

"You do mean, I should go to America?"

"Exactly. I can understand very well when something is plain black and white. What is there for you here in Finland now? Or in Sweden? America has to be the answer, no matter how much I don't want it."

Without speaking they looked at each other.

"I can't see any other solution," he admitted, at last. "Can you?" She shook her head. He continued. "We agree, then, there's no way we can make it without the shop, or my finding some other place to work here in Finland?"

"That's right," she said, coming to sit on the end of the bench near him. "There's no point in wasting what little we have coming in from the telephone central for you to travel anywhere in this country looking for work. They won't hire you, that's certain."

He nodded in agreement. "Right now Finland has few jobs for their own Finns, Swede-Finns, or a stray Swede. Besides that, I have the wrong faith, wrong nationality, wrong principles it seems. My good woman," he added, attempting to joke, "you married the wrong man."

"Ack," she responded, wrinkling her nose, "what kind of bargain did you get?"

"Great," he smiled, and patted her arm. The smile faded as he sat back. "Yaw so, we've made a big decision," he said, "bigger than any in our life before. It has taken us just a few minutes."

"We didn't make it," Lisa corrected him, "it was made for us, last night out in the shop. Now I'm the one who's frightened."

"Don't be," he urged, leaning forward again to reassure her. "We'll work it out, with God's help. Wish we had Sten's letter, now, with all the answers to all those questions I sent him."

"We do."

"Nay, you burned it, remember, after we had read it? You said we didn't need that information since you had learned to run the telephone central very well, and knew it would stay right here in our house."

"The envelope, not the letter. I practiced a little deceit myself," she admitted, with no shame. "Even though I was sure we'd never use it I thought there might be others who could. So many leave for America these days."

"Good woman," he grinned at her, "let's see it."

"Not now, I hear the children coming back. We will talk of it tonight. Let's keep this to ourselves until we have discussed it much more."

As the children crowded together back into the room, Oscar nodded his head.

*

"Open it, Pappa," Maria pleaded. "We took turns carrying it very carefully all the way from the post office."

"See?" Emilia added, pointing to the printing on the package that instructed: HANDLE WITH CARE — BREAKABLE. "Hurry, open it."

"Nay," he answered, removing a few short nails from his lips. He had been about to point them into the new sole of a shoe threaded on-to an iron last in front of him. "We will take it up to the house so Mamma can be with us when I open it."

In the months since the shop had been broken into he had started to work there again. It was here, away from the noise of the household, that he wrote the letters to America, using a table and stool he had made from lumber Sigurd brought him. It was March before the final communications traveling to and from America had all been received and answered. There had been many to Sten in Duluth. Also to Ulf Mathiasson, a boyhood friend, who had gone to America where he had married and was raising his family in Waukegan, Illinois. The shop also became Oscar's reading place, mostly books about America, borrowed from Berta Lund and the schoolmaster. It was only lately that repairing shoes and boots had become a minor source of cash. He had learned a bitter lesson, and now demanded payment, from the few who brought him work, when they came to reclaim their mended footgear.

He set his tools d̶ ̶.̶.̶ and took the package, leading the way up to the house. The girls ra̶.̶.̶ alongside scuffing through the light fall of new snow on that early April afternoon.

"See here, Lisa," he shouted, before he had the second vestibule door fully open. "The package is here. The one my brothers wrote they were sending."

He set it on the table. "Ack, I didn't bring my *puukko* with me from the shop. Somebody get me a knife to cut the string."

Lisa handed him a scissors.

"It's not a very big package," Maria teased. "It couldn't be a new suit for your trip."

"Nyeh, nyeh, you're being silly," Paulina laughed. "It isn't even big enough to be a pair of shoes."

"You're right," Emilia backed her up, "but it could be a whole bunch of money, all in a big lump."

"You're crazy," Marta snapped, poking her, "money isn't breakable."

At last Oscar had all the wrappings off and the box inside open. Again there were more wrappings, but this time it was a soft length of white cloth he unwound from around the article deep within its folds.

Long appreciative oohs, and gasps of surprise, came from the family. Oscar sucked in a sudden breath when the gift lay in splendour in his hand. A gold chain rippled out between his finger to hang swinging back and forth.

"A watch," he said, so quietly it was hard to hear him. And again, "A gold watch and chain."

He looked from it to Lisa and back again. Chin moving erratically, he pushed his lower lip to control his mouth, and shook his head. "Haven't they done enough for me?" he murmured, lowering his head to study the watch from a distance. "I've always wanted a watch," he told himself out loud. Lips tight against each other he shook his head again.

"Wonderful men, your brothers," Lisa agreed, and came to look at it more closely, standing so that the youngest, in her arms, could not reach out and grasp the shining timepiece.

"Can we see it?" several of the girls asked.

He allowed the watch to travel from hand to hand, but gripped the chain firmly should it slip from a small hand holding it for a moment of wonder. Everyone held their breath as he wound it and held it to his ear.

"It works!" he marveled, looking around the smiling circle with a smile of triumph of his own. Again the watch had to make the rounds as he held it for each young ear to listen to its lively ticking. He offered to let Lisa hear too but she refused.

"I can hear it all the way over to here," she laughed.

"They should not have spent the extra money to send it to me," Oscar told them, although he could not keep the happiness out of his voice. "They could have kept it and given it to me when I stop off to see them on my way through Sweden. I'll be there in just another month."

"Then we wouldn't have seen it, Pappa," Paulina said.

"I think they wanted to send it here so Pappa wouldn't miss the boat," Emilia remarked. "Just think, you will always know exactly what time it is."

"No more looking up at the sun," Lisa laughed, "when you are away from a clock. Good thing, because maybe the sun is in a different place in America, and would fool you when you tried to tell time by it, as you do here."

"To think," Oscar whispered, head bent over the watch again, "it will go with me everywhere."

"Put it in your pocket, like *Farbror* Palmer's," Marta suggested. "The chain will look smart hanging in front of you."

"I would have to put my vest on," he replied.

"I'll get it," several voices cried, but it was Emilia who got into the bedroom first to yank his vest from the peg. Victoriously she bumped the other sisters aside as she rushed back to hand it to him.

They all stood in front of him as he put the vest on, then placed the watch in the right hand pocket. Carefully he threaded the chain through the second buttonhole up from the bottom, buttoned the vest, then fastened the other end of the chain to the left hand pocket. Slowly he turned from side to side, each member of the family exclaiming at the perfection of the arrangement. Many times he lifted the watch out and slid it back in to practice nonchalance.

Maria came to touch the chain gently with both hands, unable to say more than, "Ahh, it is so pretty."

"Somebody might snatch it," Emilia worried, reaching out to pull on it. Oscar clapped a hand over hers and with the other pushed her away.

"Don't fear," he assured her, "I will have it fastened good and proper, and keep my eyes open at all times. What time is it?"

Together they all swung around to study the clock on the wall. Everybody told him the time. Carefully he set the hands on the watch, and again had to show it around so they could all see that it said the same time as the big one. "Where shall I keep it, Lisa?" he asked.

"Why not up on that shelf," she suggested, raising her chin toward the open shelf holding a china platter. It had been given to her as a wedding gift by the family she worked for in Sweden. Its bright colors were the only decoration on the walls besides the two embroidered cloth strips of the tray holder that hung below the high shelf.

"Nay, it might fall off," he protested.

"In the cupboard then," she suggested, "where we keep the letters."

He shook his head. "Someone might set a dish on it by mistake."

"In the trunk," Paulina urged. "In the secret compartment."

"Yaw, that's the place," he agreed. "But I will have to remember to wind it every night."

In a body they went with him to the trunk. He lifted the rounded lid, pulled the piece of wood up alongside a small covered compartment at one end, and tucked the watch into the false bottom below it, where the money for his journey to America also lay hidden. He pushed the wood back down into place, and stood, head cocked, listening. He grinned at Lisa and commented, "Can't hear it now. How about coffee all around to celebrate the wonderful gift?"

Lisa and the girls busied themselves setting out mugs, milk and the sugar cone.

"I'll write to brothers Johan and Evert as soon as I get that shoe finished I'm working on. Then I have to go to Vasa and convince the telephone people to let you keep the central when you move."

"Time is getting short, Oscar. I'm not going to be able to manage, even with the money borrowed from Ulf, if I don't have the income from the central until you start sending me money from America."

"I know. Tomorrow I'll go get a place for you to live."

The talk turned back to the watch, then to the brothers in Sweden, and finally to the subject uppermost in their minds, his coming trip to America. They dunked the coffee bread rusks Lisa had set out, talked happily, continuously, interrupting each other, their mouths full.

Lisa knew that terrible day when the shop was destroyed was not forgotten, but a living coal that burned in their memory throughout all that came afterward. It had welded them together as they worked to eradicate its physical evidence. The girls helped her clean, Oscar repaired the window. Late that day Sigurd and Katarina had ridden up in their wagon, the only time Katarina could remember he had hurried the horse out of a walk. Strengthened by them and by the help of the family, Oscar had collected the salvageable bicycle parts and the next day had gone to Vasa to sell them back to the supplier for far less than their value.

But tonight their talk was of happier memories; Ulf Mathiasson's answer to Oscar's letter.

"Full of welcome it was," Oscar repeated once again. "Said the Steel and Wiremill Company of that town of his, with the difficult name, would have work for me he was sure. Invited me to stay with them in their flat. That means their home, you know. I could sleep on a cot they would set up in their main room until I found a room of my own."

"Do you suppose parents in America don't sleep in the main room like you do?" one of the girls asked.

"*Tant* and *Farbror* Palmer didn't," Marta said quickly. "Maybe in America they have many bedrooms like the Palmers do in Sweden."

"Ulf isn't rich like the Palmers, is he, Pappa?" another sister asked.

"I'm sure I don't know," he answered, "but since he offered to loan me the money, and it is actually here, he must have financial respect in that country. Couldn't ask for a better friend."

"Remember when Sten's letter came?" Lisa asked, smiling. "I saw you coming on the *spark,* over the snow, waving it over your head like a small flag."

"Do I remember? When I jumped off the *spark* kept on going until I thought it would end up in the woods. Ah, but your brother did a wonderful thing in that letter. Sent me the passage money without as much as asking how much I would need. You have good brothers too."

Lisa nodded, but remembered something she did not speak about. When Oscar had showed her the bank draft in that letter she had asked, "Is it money?"

"It is money," he had answered with a wide smile.

"Nay," she had breathed, the word hardly above a whisper as she studied the paper. Suddenly she had thrust it out toward Oscar, who took it from her in amazement, as she jumped up and went to a corner of the room where she stood, her apron lifted to her face. She remembered the sound she made, like a mewling kitten, her shoulders shaking as she began to cry. Oscar had stuffed the letter and bank draft under the sugar cone, out of reach of the two boys, hurried over to her and turned her around, pulling her tightly to him. At last she gained enough control of herself to reassure the younger ones who had come to cling to her.

"Mamma was surprised, that's all," she told them. Then to Oscar,

"All this time I have thought, maybe you would not really have to go," she had admitted. "This makes it so certain." She had rested her face against his neck and let the tears flow quietly.

With a sigh she returned to the celebrating family around the table. "What?" she asked, unable to say who had been asking her something.

It was Marta. "I asked you," she repeated with impatience, "do you suppose we'll all have watches when we get to America?"

"What kind of foolish talk is that?" Lisa answered. "Paying off the borrowed money will be the first thing we do."

Oscar added, "And it will take a long time, I'm afraid."

*

"I'm so grateful to be leaving this place," Lisa said, as she twisted the big key in the lock and hung it on its hook alongside the door-frame. "The new place is so small I don't know how we can all fit in, but I don't care. It's tight and warm, and the roof doesn't leak."

Oscar nodded as he helped the hired driver tie the last of the house-hold goods onto his wagon. "It is good you will be right among farmer Albertsson and his family. Good thing he had that hired man's quarters empty. His boys are old enough now, so he doesn't need to furnish a house for a hired man and family."

"I'm glad the house is way back by the big barn. We won't be right on top of him and his family."

The driver spit out a cud of tobacco and carved himself a new one with his *puukko,* swung up onto the driver's seat and slapped the reins against the back of the horse. As the horse strained to start Oscar pushed in back to help. The children came running from a last look in-to the windows of the empty shop. When the wagon reached the road the family walked behind it. Oscar carried the youngest on his shoulders, and Lisa knitted as she walked. Carl was last, walking between two of the girls, who held his hands, or made a seat of their four hands and carried him.

When the caravan passed the Svensson's store Lisa recalled the day of the last moving and Elvira's sore hands. She remembered too how she had gone there shortly after that. She had not been back since. Yet, there they were today, both Swenssons, waving at them with something like friendliness. Perhaps because they would no longer be their landlords. It was hard to say. Maria and Paulina smiled at them.

"Stop it," Emilia hissed, and yanked Maria's arm down as she was about to wave.

"Maybe they're sorry," the two tried to tell her.

"Hmph," Emilia snorted, and lifted her head high, stepping along faster.

The telephone men moved the central the same day. The telephone line had been strung up to the new place the day before. Inside the house the equipment board took up precious living space in the main room but its presence was a comfort. It would bring in steady income.

The loan from Ulf had helped Oscar buy a new suit and shoes, as well as paying for the moving. The rest was stored safely in the secret compartment of the trunk, with the watch, to be used only if needed. Although every home of the region had a handcrafted trunk identical in build with theirs, and a secret compartment in exactly the same place, they were not worried about their hidden wealth. Seldom had those primitive banks been looted or robbed.

Two weeks after the move it was time for Oscar to leave. The night before he was to take the train to Kaskö, and board the boat to Sweden on the first leg of his journey, Lisa worked late packing and repacking Elvira's suitcase with his things. Small as the suitcase was, it easily held all he was taking to the new country. A change of long underwear; the richness of a new pair of pants, the cloth a gift woven by Katarina, and cut out and sewed by Lisa; a shirt; five handkerchiefs made from the linen that had arrived with the watch, each one hemmed by a different daughter; his straight-edge razor and a bar of Lisa's soap; a comb; and old scissors, sharpened and a broken point reshaped on Sigurd's grindstone. He tested it by trimming his mustache before giving it to Lisa to pack. His fur hat and the Bible, with the address of Ulf in Waukegan, Illinois, carefully written below the date of his marriage to Lisa and the names, birthdates, and deaths of the children. Four pair of heavy long stockings and three pair of short ones, all of them knitted out of yarn Lisa had spun on Katarina's spinning wheel.

"You are to wear these when you get into the summer heat in America," she instructed, showing him the short ones knitted from the lightweight wool.

"It will be summer when I get there," Oscar commented. "From what I read, it is very hot near that big inland sea they call Michigan. I will think of you every time I put them on."

"Just remember how I told you to wash them," she replied, avoiding the caress he attempted to give her as he spoke. "You do it wrong, they'll all be so small you'll have to send them back for the youngest to wear."

"Don't worry, I'll manage."

His workday shoes were wrapped in paper and stuffed at each end of the suitcase. Writing paper and envelopes rolled into a tight cylinder had been thrust into one. A tightly corked bottle of ink and a pen, with a new nib, in the other. His wooden spoon lay on top of the clothes.

"I won't need to take that along," he objected. "That fellow I told you I met in Vasa, when I went to get my papers in order, told me everywhere you go to eat in America they give you fork, knife, and spoon to use. He should know, he just came back from there."

"Smart man to return," Lisa commented, then contradicted the unknown informant. "Never mind, you'll not be embarrassed if you get to some place where they expect you to have your own spoon to eat with."

On the round-topped wooden trunk lay the new suit, its dark wool cloth stiff and durable. A shirt and a clean pair of stockings lay on top of it. The underwear he was to wear first on the journey he had on, for they were his sleeping clothes as well. They had been washed and dried during the day while he wore the pair now packed in the suitcase. Below the trunk stood the new yellow leather shoes, the light from the kerosene lamp reflected like dots of gold in their pointed toes.

On the table lay another handkerchief, this one hemmed by Elvira, but also embroidered with his initials. Four books, with several copies of the religious paper, *The Prophetic Light,* were strapped together with a wooden handle attached for easier carrying. Two of the books were gifts from Berta Lund, the other two from Peter Rudolfsson. Close to them, shining as if light came from within its gold case, lay the watch, the chain a pool of gold next to it. Its ticking was loud, bringing the early morning departure closer. His cane he had presented to his dear friend, Peter Rudolfsson.

"Aren't you done with that suitcase yet?" Oscar demanded, as the clock struck eleven. "You've done it over so many times. Leave it be and come to bed."

It was the second time he had pleaded with her since the last of the children had gone to bed. It had been a noisy evening. The children, except for the two youngest, who slept peacefully in the bedroom, buzzed with last minute things to tell or ask him. The girls came to look into his face with eyes of excitement, but with their young brows creased with beginning worry. To get them to bed had been a long process, neither parent rushing them away, although anxious to have this last night to themselves. Johan fell asleep on Oscar's lap, and was carried in and placed alone in one of the three beds that crowded the small square room. Carl and the youngest slept in one of the other beds. Later they would be lifted to share the one with Johan, leaving two beds empty for the five others.

At last there was quiet, no further quick widening of the bedroom door to let yet another daughter out to say another remembered thought to Oscar. Lisa worked over the suitcase, leaving it only to help him fill the big copper tub for him to stand in as he bathed, to wash his back, and to pour clear water over his hair when he finished washing it. Each time she was near him, he attempted to give her loving pats or kisses, but she avoided them, hurrying back to the packing. Hair rubbed dry into a tangle of curls, then tugged by a comb into smooth waves, he put his underwear on and went to pull their sofa bed out, and to sit on its edge. He called to her again.

"Lisa, come to bed."

She let the lid of the suitcase drop, but stood where she was, her hands resting lightly on it. He got up to go to her, but she hurried over to the bedroom door, pushed it part way open and stood listening, head bent, before pulling it shut. Oscar met her halfway, her hands lifted to unbutton her dress.

"Let me," he smiled, and pushed her hands away to work at the buttons himself. She stood quietly as his fingers loosened them, his lips brushing her face with soft kisses. Suddenly she grasped both his wrists.

"Nay, Oscar, I can't," she cried, her face contorted with the effort to be quiet and yet declare herself violently.

Startled he stepped back. "What?" he demanded, one hand lifting again to the buttons on her dress. She slapped it down, and hurried to the other side of the room, away from the bedroom door, her hands on top of her head, her crossed arms covering her face. His bare feet made no sound as he strode across the rag rugs.

"You must," he urged, "this is our last night together."

She shook her head and dropped her arms. "I can't, Oscar," she repeated, mutely pleading with him to accept what she could not do.

Roughly he pulled her to him, locking his hands together behind her back.

"You can't expect me to go without loving you once more," he demanded hoarsely. He shook her, his eyes searching her face as she twisted and turned, trying not to look at him.

"I have to, Oscar. Let me go. Let...me...go!" She strained with both her hands against his binding arms.

He released her and stepped back, breathing hard. Stumbling, she sat down on the edge of the bed. He came and sat next to her, his arms around her again, but loosely, forcing himself to speak calmly.

"I understand your fears. You've expressed them often enough, ever since the youngest was born. Nay, nay," he quieted her as she made a sudden move, "you haven't said it in so many words, but the youngest one placed between us too often spoke loudly enough. But, Lisa, how can you let me go knowing it will be years before we are together again? You know you will always be my only love."

She pushed his arms away and faced him. "How can you ask this of me, Oscar, if you understand? You know, for certain, that I am not with child, because of my bleeding this past week. Are you asking me to take the chance of bearing one with you far away? Oh, Oscar, why do I have to put into words what hurts me to speak out loud to you?"

He swayed as if she had given him a blow, got up and walked away from her. For a while he stood looking straight ahead, then came and sat next to her again.

"You haven't become pregnant this past year, and the youngest is almost two."

"Two," she laughed. "How fortunate. Most times there has been less than two years between the births. This last one we almost lost before her time. Have you forgotten that? None of this cools your need, or makes you hesitate? Abstinence is not a sin."

He took a deep breath then exploded, "How can I leave you alone, lying next to you, this night of all the nights in our life?"

"I'll go get the youngest."

As she started up he pulled her back, "Nay, Lisa. You shame me. Leave her where she is. You must let me hold you. I can't leave without that at least."

She settled back down, but asked, "Will you stop at that?"

He nodded, his face strained. "I'll get up and go sleep in the rocking chair, if I can't leave you alone. I promise."

He held his hand out to her. She took it, and together they knelt to pray.

"Dear God, take care of this wonderful woman and my family," he pleaded. "Keep them safe until we are once again together."

Neither of them heard, or saw, that Maria had opened the bedroom door quietly and stood watching them.

"Dear Lord," Lisa added, "keep this good man from harm, and help us rejoin him soon." Together they said, "Amen," as the bedroom door closed softly.

She took off her shoes as he went to blow out the lamp. In bed he pulled her tightly up against his side, one hand smoothing her face. She kissed it each time it passed her lips. Quietly, they talked far into the morning. Once he gave a cry that was loneliness itself, turned to pull her close and took her lips in hard long kisses. As his passion became too strong, he flung himself out of bed and outdoors. She lay quiet, one fist crammed against her mouth, until he returned. Shivering, he settled next to her again, and she gathered him to her, cradling his head against her throat. Toward morning they slept, to wake at five o'clock.

Oscar got up first and reached a hand to help Lisa out of bed. They smiled at each other in uncertain victory. He dressed quickly. Lisa had no need to dress for she had slept fully clothed. Quietly, they went about getting him ready to leave. Next to each other on one bench at the table, they ate the leftover cinnamon-rice dessert from the farewell supper. They spoke in whispers. One by one, the older three girls drifted out of the bedroom to take seats across from them. Lisa went to the trunk and from the secret compartment took out the leather pouch Sigurd had fashioned for Oscar. Pulled tight by leather thongs, it could be flattened out, to show no evidence it was in the pants pocket of his new suit. Lisa had taken the extra precaution, also, of making the pocket deeper by ripping out the bottom and sewing an extra piece of cloth to it.

Once again he counted the money and checked the papers the pouch held. He pulled it shut, wrapped the thongs around it and pushed it deep into the pocket. He carried the closed suitcase, tied for further security by a piece of rope, out to Elvira's bicycle, and strapped it firmly in place. Two evenings before Elvira had ridden the bicycle home, so he could use it to catch the morning train in Narpes. His own bicycle had been sold long ago. The two stolen ones had never been recovered. At midnight he had given Elvira a ride back on the handlebars, pumping hard over the level road. This morning he would leave it with her, where she worked, then walk the rest of the way to the railroad station.

"Yaw," he said, and stood as if he wondered what had been left unsaid.

"Ya so, it is time," Lisa told him. She went to get the food she had wrapped in paper for him, to eat on the train, and the boat to Sweden. "Put your shoes on, girls, and come on out."

Oscar took the bundle of books, but turned and went into the bedroom. Everyone waited, standing where they were, until he came back. He brought his Sunday hat, put it on his head and hurried out of the house. They followed. One by one he kissed the girls' cheeks, their young arms grasping him around the neck. Maria held on the longest. He gathered Lisa to him, for what seemed forever to the girls, kissed her, picked up the books he had set on the ground, settled his hat firmly on his head, then flung himself onto the bicycle. He pushed off, the books dangling from one hand grasping the handlebar.

"Wait!" Lisa called, and held the package with his food high overhead. He circled back and took it from her, unashamed to let her see the tears in his eyes. He rode off, the bundles at each end of the handlebars balancing his outline, as he leaned forward to build up speed. Lisa held her hands to her throat and walked after him. The girls kept pace, to stop when she did, as he reached the curve in the road. He stopped, got off, set the books down and waved.

"I love you...all," he shouted, the words coming back to them thin and clear. Before they could answer he was gone, the road hidden by the trees.

Lisa stood silent. The girls turned to her, their eyes questioning, lips trembling. Still listening she paid no attention. At last she moved, but only to drop her hands. "He doesn't have to throw his leg over the seat each time. It's a girl's bicycle," she said.

Together the girls looked back down the road as if they could watch him remount. With a long reach of her arm she bunched them together. "Get inside," she told them, "it is time you got dressed." Reassured, by the everyday tone of her voice, they raced each other back into the house.

"You didn't wake me," Marta yelled, her face screwed up in anger when she came out of the bedroom.

Alli complained too, her face clouded, ready for tears. "He's gone?" she wailed.

"Yaw," Maria answered, "but he came and said goodbye to you while you will still sleeping."

Marta stamped her feet.

"That will do," Lisa told her, with no uncertainty and strode over to grasp the hair above her forehead. Giving it a small yank, she continued. "In this family we do not stamp our feet. We have told you, you were to leave that kind of behavior behind at Palmers. Remember that." As Alli began to whimper, she turned to her. "Both of you said goodbye to him many times last night. He was torn enough this morning to have four of us out there. Get dressed, it's soon time to go to school."

Lisa accomplished little that day. She ached to get out and walk until she was too tired to walk anymore. At noon she spread a cloth out on the grass, brought the leftover meatballs from Oscar's favorite supper dish she had prepared for last night's farewell meal and his traveling packet of food, and had a picnic with Johan, Carl, and the youngest.

As soon as supper was over that evening she told the older girls to mind the children and the telephone central, took her shawl and left the house. "Don't worry," she told them. "I'm going for a walk. I might be gone an hour or more, but I'll be back before you get your lessons done."

Undecided which direction she should go she circled the house, then hurried to the road leading to the sawmill. Head down, holding the shawl tightly about her, she walked as if there was too little time to get there. Halfway she stopped, looked around, shocked that she had planned to go to the sawmill. With a sound of disgust, she turned and wandered through a section of forest. Too soon she came to a long wide meadow out of the welcome darkness of the trees. Two windmills, a long distance apart, stood in the middle of the meadow. There were no people. She began to run, her shawl flapping behind her as she clutched it with one hand. At the first windmill she stopped, then sat down breathing hard. Her head sank forward, but at the sound of a squeak from the windmill she looked up. The arms were moving slowly. She jumped up and caught hold of the lowest crosspiece of one arm. Jerkily she was lifted a short distance upward before the arm came to a sudden stop. Screaming she let go, remembering to bend her knees the way she had done as a child when riding the forbidden windmill arms. She fell to the grass, rolled over and lay spread-eagled on the earth. Her mouth wide open to the sky, she yelled her inner agony out in painful bursts. Gradually she quieted, wept, and turned to press her face tight against the new green spring grass, her knees drawn up to her chest.

"No baby," she whispered, the grass tickling her lips, and surprised herself with a curt laugh.

Calm, she got up, found her shawl, wrapped it around her and began the journey home. She ran, feeling guilt that she had traveled so far, and only now worried that she had left the children alone on the first night of Oscar's absence. Near the house she stopped to let her breathing become quiet. With a corner of her shawl she wiped the perspiration from her forehead, then fanned her face with it until she felt cool. As she stepped up to the door she tucked loose ends of her hair into place.

"Mamma, may I sleep with you tonight," Marta came running to greet her with as she pushed the door open.

"Nay, me, me," Alli clamored.

"Starting tomorrow you can all begin taking turns sleeping with me," she replied as she hung up her shawl. "Not tonight."

Alone in the bed, much later, she lay awake, her eyes burning and feeling stretched too wide as she looked at the dark ceiling. In early dawn she saw a movement near her. It was Maria.

"Mamma? Are you all right?" she whispered.

"Yaw," Lisa whispered in report, and raised the blankets with one hand. "Get in," she said.

The warmth of the slender body, nestled to her, brought temporary peace. She slept.

*

Five minutes after the door had slammed it was being pushed open again. Lisa ran to the fireplace and grabbed the kettle of boiling water in her greasy hand. Frantically gathering up the skirt of her apron to protect her other hand, she put it against the bottom of the kettle.

The door swung wide. Berta Lund took a step in, then froze in place with a grunt of surprise.

"What on earth?" she gasped, stunned by Lisa's contorted face and threatening posture.

"It's you," Lisa moaned

"Yaw, it's me. Who did you think it was? The devil?"

Lisa shook her head and went to put the kettle back near the fire. "Come in. I was just greasing my hand. I burned it with boiling water a few minutes ago."

'How did you do that?" Berta asked, and went to bend over Lisa's extended hand. "It's certainly red. But, why the plan to scald me alive?"

"Not you. Alfred Ohlin.'

"Alfred? Has he been here?"

Lisa nodded. "You didn't see him skulking off somewhere?"

Berta shook her head. "What was he up to?"

"No good, that's what," Lisa answered, and rubbed butter on the burned skin.

"You should put your hand in cold water. that'll help it more than salty butter."

"This will do. I have to finish kneading the dough."

"Let me do it. You sit down and put your hand in this."

Berta dipped water from the water barrel into a small wooden bucket and set it on the table in front of Lisa's chair. She hung her jacket on a peg, then washed her hands. "What was Alfred here for?" she asked, as she began to knead the dough that lay in a swirl of flour in the center of the table.

A flush crawled up into Lisa's face. She bent to hide it by studying her hand in the water. "I'm not sure I should tell," but realizing Berta had stopped work to stand looking at her, she continued, running the words together, "he wanted me to go to bed with him."

"Nay!" Berta exploded. "That idiot!"

Lisa agreed, nodding her head, her mouth turned down in disgust.

"We were sweet on each other when we were in school, but I've never thought of him since. I've seen him two times, since I came back to Finland. Once in the store, and once when I went to a Temperance meeting with Oscar shortly before he left."

Berta's eyes bored into hers. "Tell me exactly what he did."

"He came in, like everybody does without knocking. I was surprised, but of course I welcomed him. He didn't want a cup of coffee."

"How noble of him," Berta snorted. Lisa smiled feebly.

"The three children were outside, like now, Johan tending Carl and the youngest, and I had just turned the dough out on the table. He asked me about Oscar. I was telling him, when he interrupted me. 'It's too many months for a woman to be without a man,' he said, and I answered, 'Yaw, I miss Oscar so much.' Then, can you believe this, Berta?" She hesitated, wiped her hand across her mouth, then lifted the burned one out of the water to grasp the edge of the table with both hands. "He said, 'You don't have to miss what you need. I can make up for those months for you right now. How about we go into the bedroom?'" Lisa bent low over the bucket of water, shame flushing her cheeks.

"That bastard!" Berta shouted. "I'll kill him!."

"I'm so embarassed that he would think I'd do such a sinful thing."

"You embarrassed? He's the one should be red from top to toe. He should be strung up on the highest spruce tree...So...then you picked up the kettle?"

"Yaw, he grabbed me by the shoulder, but I twisted away, and how I got to the kettle and threw water at him so fast I don't know, but he left in a hurry. I don't think I hit him, but it sure landed on my hand."

"Damn his soul!" Berta roared.

Head lifted, Lisa made no protest at Berta's blasphemy, except to say, "Nay, I fixed him. Oscar wouldn't have approved of the things I called Alfred as I threw that water, but I don't regret one syllable of it. He'll head for the deepest part of the forest should he ever meet me face to face again." Gathering courage from the growing approval on Berta's face, she added, "I won't care if all the world hears me, but he will. He'll never approach another American widow, at least."

To Berta's surprise Lisa began to laugh.

"You should have seen him," Lisa went on, "when I sloshed that water through the air. He jumped back like this." She got up, spread her arms like curved wings, pushed her rear way out behind her and jumped backward several times. "I think he was sure I was going to boil his most precious member." She stood in that position grinning at Berta, who burst into loud hoots, slapping her knees with floury hands.

"I hope you did," she whooped, and went to punch the dough as if Alfred himself lay on the table.

Interrupting each other they shouted punishments they dreamed up for him. Their laughter swelled and ebbed. Lisa wiped her eyes with her wrist, her laugh bubbling down until she was silent.

"Poor Anna Ohlin," she sighed. "I hope she never knows what her Alfred was up to."

"She knows," Berta stated in a matter-of-fact voice. "Has, for years. Long before he decided American widows were created especially for him. You're not the first one he's tried to bring his 'gift' to. Maybe you fixed him so it'll be a long time before he offers it to anyone again." Berta gave the dough a hard slap.

"Maybe I fixed him for good," Lisa hoped.

"Dreamer," Berta returned, "Anna, you know, like so many other women, can't leave her husband. There's too many children to feed. Eight of them. Who knows, maybe this is their way of keeping Anna from becoming pregnant again."

Shocked, Lisa said, "I don't want to believe that," and remembered the words she had breathed against the ground below the windmill. "It's a shame, no matter what the reason, but one thing I know, he won't come here again."

"Just keep your water boiling," Berta teased.

"Let me take over now," Lisa begged, throwing the water from the wooden bucket out the door as she went to check on the children. They played close by.

"I'll make the loaves," she said, as she closed the door. "How about you pouring coffee for us? Sorry the coffee bread isn't baked, so I could offer you some."

Berta waved an appreciative hand. "The cardamon smell is so good it makes me wish I could stay, but I can't. How goes it was Oscar?" She took her coffee and went to pinch a piece of the raw dough, and popped it into her mouth. She settled in the rocking chair but did not rock, for the space was too small in the crowded room. "Did you get a letter since I was here last?"

Lisa nodded. "He's moved to a boarding house run by a Swedish woman, a Sköning, and is busy in the Temperance Society over there. He has met many Swedish people. Finns too. He writes an American word in every letter now for all of us to learn. Puts the Swedish meaning right after it. The girls do very well, and I'm not so bad either, t'ank yew."

"Which means, *tak*?"

"Yaw, they have to use two words to say it," Lisa informed her.

"How is Oscar's work at the wiremill?"

"He still doesn't say much, but I can read between the lines. He doesn't like it. It is even noisier than the sawmill, for one thing, and some of it is dangerous. Let me finish up here, then I want to read you part of his last letter. I can't stop thinking about it."

The soft slap of the dough, as she quickly braided the lengths she had formed by rolling pieces against the table with the palms of her hands, was a quiet accompaniment to the ticking of the clock. They waited in companionable silence until she finished. The loaves placed in a baking pan and covered with a cloth for the final rising, Lisa went to the cupboard and got Oscar's letter.

"It's about Ulf," she said, as she scanned the pages to find what she wanted. "Here it is," and as though bracing herself began to read. "'I haven't written you this before because I thought it would upset you too much. But I have reasoned with myself that I must tell you so it won't come as a shock when you are finally here. Besides, you need to know about this man of God, Ulf. When he met me at the train I didn't know what to say, because he had only one arm. Yaw, it was lost in a terrible accident at the wiremill. Now, don't get all worried. I tell you right away I don't work in that same area where it happened. It is safer where I am. Think of this instead. The wiremill gave Ulf some money because he lost that arm, but not enough so that he can support his family on it very long. It was out of that money he made me the loan.'"

Lisa returned Berta's stunned look. "Wasn't that terrible? And to think he would loan Oscar that money."

"What a tragedy," Berta agreed. "He is more than a good friend."

"If there is anyone I am eager to meet it is that good man," Lisa said. She returned to the letter. "'All Ulf does now is sweep floors and wash windows. How he can do that I don't know, but he does so in the office building of the wiremill.'"

She looked up to find the sympathy she sought.

"Maybe in that country they have a mechanical broom for him to push around," Berta suggested, with doubt.

Equally doubtful Lisa said, "Perhaps." She folded the letter and put it back in its envelope. "Oscar goes on to tell me Ulf says there is much talk among the men, still, about that accident. They want to make the wiremill put controls on those machines. But Oscar thinks that will not happen, unless the men threaten strike."

"Are they going to?"

"He can't tell. Says he doesn't know enough American yet to talk to more than just the Swedes. They seem to think it won't happen, or if it does, not for a long time. Too many of the men are still deep in debt from getting there from all the different parts of Europe, Berta. They borrowed, the same as Oscar did, and have to save every *orë* they can to bring their families over, or have already brought them there on borrowed money. They need every payday, just like Oscar does."

"Doesn't sound like the land of gold-paved streets, does it?"

"Nor of milk and honey," Lisa added. Brow creased, her hands clasped tightly together, she said, "I thank God Oscar is not working where it is dangerous."

"Amen," Berta agreed.

Lisa went to the door and checked the children again. As she closed it she turned and said with a shy smile, "Oscar also said that in the next letter he can start sending me money."

Berta's reactions was most satisfying. "Hurrah! Hurrah! Hurrah!" she shouted, getting up out of the rocking chair to wave her empty mug on high.

Laughing Lisa got the coffee pot and filled both mugs. Their talk turned to the past months and the girls. The two younger girls had herded Rudolfsson's cows, Maria had cared for the chemist's boy again, and Elvira still worked in Narpes. Whenever Elvira came home,

Lisa told Berta, she would recite the recipes of the company meals she had cooked in that fancy home. Meals so rich, and with such unusual ingredients, Lisa could only gape, her mouth watering. There was pride in her voice as she talked of her eldest. "But tell me, Paulina is doing her work well for you?"

"That she is," Berta responded. "I can send her to give any number of pigs their daily scrubbing, and know they will be clean. The floor of the pig houses have to be washed twice a day and she's right out there. Works harder than my regular man, and looking mighty small in an old pair of my boots. I think the pigs know and like her. Perhaps because of Nasse, who still comes running whenever Paulina calls her. That pig, certainly no longer a runt, must have spread word that here is a friend."

They laughed together. Lisa remembered Nasse's huge size, when she had gone to the pig farm with all the children in midsummer, to see their old pet and her second litter.

"Yaw," Berta was saying, "Paulina is a good worker, but I miss having Emilia around."

"I do too," Lisa agreed. "Her spunk is an uplifter, but I have to admit that sometimes she is almost too much for me. But, I'm glad that at least one of the girls can have a holiday. I hope Ragnhild doesn't find her a problem."

"Bah!" Berta objected, "she'll enliven that house up there in the north."

"I hope so. It was good of Ragnhild to invite one of the children for the summer. I hardly remembered that she existed. Haven't heard from her, or even thought of her, since before I left for Sweden to work. We're distant cousins, but didn't know each other very well. How she heard Oscar had gone to America I don't know but she showed up here that day with her horse and carriage. Emilia was eager to go, when she offered to help me, by taking one of the girls for the summer. So I let her."

"You did right," Berta assured her, as she got up to leave. "I'd better get on. I'm back from delivering three pigs to a farmer near Kristinestad."

"So far away? Paulina said you were going somewhere today, but she did not say it was so long a trip."

"Yaw, I left around four this morning."

"Good of you to stop in. It is always a happy time for me when you do."

"For me too, even if you do greet me with boiling water." Berta grinned, and went for her jacket. There was the sound of voices and feet outside. She pulled the door wide. On the stoop stood Emilia. Her copper curls hung in front of her sweating face, her blouse was pulled out of her skirt and smudged with dirt. Her *pjäxor* were thick with dust. One hand was raised to grasp the door handle. Behind here were the other children, Johan straining as he carried the youngest.

"Emilia's home, Mamma. It's Emilia," both boys shouted.

"You here?" Lisa gasped, and searched the road leading to the house. "Where is Cousin Ragnhild?"

"Home where she belongs," Emilia answered, and stepped briskly past the two women to hurry to the food cupboard. "I'm hungry," she complained, and swung the door open to examine what was on the shelves.

"What? Wait," Lisa demanded, and went to pull her daughter around to face her. "How did you get here alone?"

"On the train, Mamma," Emilia answered.

"You traveled alone on the train? Why did Ragnhild send you alone? What have you done?"

"She didn't send me. I didn't do anything, it's what she did," Emilia returned, her mouth spitting, her eyes narrow slits of anger.

Lisa snapped, "Tell me. All of it. Begin."

Berta quietly took a seat on a stool near the door. She lifted the youngest from the floor, where Johan had set her, and settled the child in her lap. The two boys went to stand near Emilia.

"She didn't invite me for a holiday, Mamma," Emilia cried, her face red, her small mouth grim. "She wanted me there just to get someone to work for nothing."

"You expected pay for the little she asked you to do while you visited her?" Lisa cried.

"Little?" Emilia yelled. "I had to do everything. Then she wouldn't give me much to eat, except what was left over when they finished."

Lisa gasped. "You don't mean that."

Emilia nodded, tears threatening. "I told you, I'm hungry."

Lisa felt up and down her daughter's arm. "Yaw, you are thin," she said. "Here, I'll fix you a sandwich, but I want to hear more. Go on."

As she buttered pieces of *knäckebröd* and cut slices of goat cheese, she listened.

"Cousin Ragnhild never told anybody who came to the house that I was related. She always said I was the new hired girl. Hired! Hunh! She never paid me anything. If I got all the work done in the house by the middle of the afternoon, which wasn't very often, she sent me out to clean the stable. I never had time to play. I just worked." Emilia paused, aware of Berta's interest, and became uncertain if she should speak out loud what she needed to tell next. "Mamma," she began again, but waited until Lisa stopped to look at her. "I took enough money from the place where I knew she kept some hidden..."

Lisa dropped her knife and whirled to grasp Emilia by both shoulders. "You stole?" she cried, her face close to her daughter's.

"Nay, Mamma, nay," Emilia protested, patting Lisa's face with both hands. "I wrote a note and put it where she would find it right away, telling her you would send the money to her, as soon as I got home."

Lisa straightened up with a groan, gave Emilia a shake then released her. She handed her a sandwich and poured her a mug of milk.

"Go sit and eat," she said, as she dished out a bowl of fruit soup rich with prunes, dried pears, raisins, and thickened with sago. "Here you can use my spoon. When did you leave there?"

"On this morning's train. I wanted to come home long ago, almost the day after I got there, but I knew she wouldn't let me. Today she drove off somewhere with her horse and buggy, and I knew it was my chance." *Knäckebröd* crackled between her teeth as she chewed a generous bite. "Every day I listened for the train whistle, so I knew what time I had to get to the station. I knew the train went to Narpes and home wasn't far from there."

"How did you get here from Narpes?"

"I walked."

"Oiy, yoiy, yoiy," Lisa breathed, shaking her head. "It's too much to take in," she murmured, then more loudly, "Ragnhild, I remember, as being a very nice person."

Emilia chewed rapidly and gulped milk. "Oh, she's a good person, all right," she agreed, putting her sandwich and milk down. She got up and strolled back and forth in front of Lisa. Quickly tucking her blouse down into the belt of her shirt, she acquired the mature walk of an older woman, her hands moving in the mannerisms of Ragnhild, the inflection of her voice that of her cousin.

"How good of you to come for afternoon coffee, *Fru* Petersson. I regret Pastor Petersson could not come. You will have to excuse the clumsiness of my new maid, who is just learning how to pour coffee without spilling into the saucer. Yaw, the house glistens with cleanliness, but I have to keep after this uncivilized servant all the time."

"She didn't say those things," Lisa objected, "did she?"

"She did," Emilia insisted, "but maybe not all at the same time, or in exactly that way. She said even worse things to me."

"Like what?" Lisa blazed.

Emilia hesitated. "She used words we are forbidden to say, Mamma. Called me a slut because I'm not neat. Said I was a whelp sired by a heathen Swede. Oh, Mamma, she is mean."

Mouth stern, Lisa asked, "What did you answer when she said that?"

"I yelled, 'It takes a real heathen to call good religious people heathens!' She looked like she was going to slap me, but I raised my fist and went at her, like I was going to punch her in the stomach."

Berta interrupted, startling the two, as her feet lifted to crash down on the floor, her mouth wide as she roared with laughter.

"That's my girl," she shouted, and got up to set the youngest down. "You come back and work for me, with Paulina, in what's left of the summer. I'll pay you cash money so you can send it to that bitch." She raised a hand to Lisa. "This is one time that word needs to be heard in this house," Berta informed her, and wriggled her jacket more firmly onto her shoulders. At the door she called back, "I'll see you first thing tomorrow morning, Emilia. I'll tell Paulina. She'll be glad to have you back, the same as I am. Oscar would be proud of both of you, Lisa," she ended with a parting shot, and left.

In silence Lisa and Emilia waved farewell while the two boys hurried out to watch Berta drive off.

"Pappa would be proud, Mamma?" Emilia asked. "Of me?"

An arm tucked around the girl's shoulders Lisa answered. "I think so. Berta said it correctly, I'm almost sure," and smiled.

*

The poles for dipping water out of the well in the farmyard stood against the September sky like trees blazed clean by lightning. The silver-gray bottom pole stood tall next to the wooden platform of the well. The upper one, attached and balanced at a steep angle, lay in a crotch formed by a long-ago-severed limb. A sturdy rope dangled from it, an iron hook attached to its end.

It was a few minutes' walk for Lisa to the well, past the chicken house, around the woodshed, and over the packed dirt of the farmhouse yard.

Lisa was on her third trip to the well this morning. She had scrubbed the inside of the water barrel clean and was refilling it after sunning it for most of the day. The children, Carl and the youngest, followed her back and forth, but each time they arrived at the chicken house they stayed there to look at the flock behind the wire gate. At the well Lisa brought the balanced pole down, hooked the bucket into place, and pulling hand over hand on the rope sent it down to splash in the water below. The heavy butt end of the log brought the dripping bucket up when she let go. As it reached her level she grasped the rope again and tugged the log sideways until she could lower the bucket onto the ground and unhook it. Released, the log swung up into the air again.

About to pick up the water she saw the farmer and his wife drive into the yard in their wagon.

"Mail for you," he called. Jenny added, "From America."

She ran and took the letter and a bundle of papers with grateful words of thanks. Immediately, before they could trap her into visiting, she rushed back to pick up the bucket and collect the children.

"Run home," she told Carl, and thrust the letter into her apron pocket. She put the papers under one arm and picked up the bucket. With the other hand she grasped the youngest and ran, the child's toes touching the ground only now and then.

At the house she set the bucket down outside, seated herself on the stoop and slit the envelope with a hairpin. She waved the children away to play. Hunger for news of Oscar made her read rapidly. At one point she stopped to gasp out loud, "Elvira?" then read on to the end. A tender smile curved her lips as she finished. She reassembled the many pages and read again, this time slowly.

The third time through she stopped at the paragraph about Elvira, reread it twice, then sat staring at nothing. At last she got up, picked up the bucket and called to the children to stay close by. She missed Johan's help: he had started school only a few days ago.

After she emptied the water into the barrel she stood looking at the telephone central. Never had she used it to call Elvira on her job. It was not to be done. Should she do it now? She hesitated, her eyes on the switchboard. It buzzed. Startled, she went to plug in the call.

"Central," she said, and listened. "Yaw, I had to go get water, but came right back," she told the voice grating on her ear, and put the call through rapidly, turning the handle with angry vigor. The ear and mouthpiece back in place, she waited impatiently for the call to end. Quickly, she called the lawyer's home in Narpes.

"Good day," she said stiffly, when a voice answered, then relaxed.

"Oh, I'm so glad it's you, Elvira... Yaw, it is me...nothing is wrong... we are all well here... Just listen, and I will tell you. Pappa's letter just came... yaw, nay, no money... Don't talk, let me tell you why I called. He writes something you must read yourself. When are you coming home? Is that all right with your *fru*?... I see. Good, I do want you to read it before I tell the others. I'll have coffee ready...ride carefully."

"I can only stay ten minutes," Elvira told her a half hour later when she leaned her bicycle against the house.

"I've been watching for you," Lisa responded. "I poured your coffee as soon as I saw you so it would cool. Here, read the letter."

Elvira took it and went to settle down at the table. She made no comment as she hurried through the pages, but jerked her head up when she came to the paragraph about herself. She bent closer to the page and read with total concentration. Her hands dropped to the table, the letter between them.

"I should go to America now?" she asked.

Lisa nodded, "So he says."

"How can I do that? I haven't saved much money."

"Yaw, you have. Ever since Pappa started sending me the bank drafts I've been able to put what you give me away. I get many *kröner* for each dollar he sends. I manage on it, and have saved Ulf's money for the clothes the rest of us will need when we leave. The question is, do you want to go now?"

Elvira's mouth opened and closed before she could answer. "Of course I want to go, but I thought we were all to go together."

"We were, but as he says you can earn more over there than you can here. That's why it makes sense to me that you should go. Besides, I know how lonesome he is for us. It would help him to have you there."

"It's a long way to go by myself, Mamma."

"You came alone, bringing Marta, when you came here from Sweden."

"That was just overnight. It would be weeks before I'd get to Pappa. But I want to go," she added quickly.

"That settles it," Lisa said, and urged her to finish the letter and drink the coffee.

"I can't believe it. Am I really to go? Alone? It can't be."

"Read. You have to hurry back in a few minutes."

Elvira read, lifting her head to look at Lisa after each page. "How I wish I knew how to speak American," she exclaimed when she finished.

"You'll learn fast enough with all the reading you do. I must say if it takes reading to get into the New Kingdom you will be ushered in with haste, along with Pappa."

"Maybe I can go to school in America. To learn the language, if nothing else, Mamma. When will I go? Do I have to get some papers like Pappa did? I mean, a passport?"

"Of course. You will have to do all of that, and more, before you are ready. But I want you to sail before the winter storms start. We haven't time to talk today, girl. You will be home again, when?"

"Friday. Shall I tell my *fru* I'll be leaving for America?"

"Wait until we have a full day to talk about it together. You better get back. I don't want her to find you gone when she gets home."

"She won't mind. She knows I had to go buy meat and won't be surprised if I'm not there when she come back from Vasa."

Elvira gulped the cold coffee and got up. "I see Pappa sent you a new bundle of the Swedish-American newspapers. Can I take some of the old ones with me?"

"Of course, but bring them back. Berta will want them next time she comes this way." Lisa went to the tray holder on the wall. As she handed several issues to her daughter, she commented, "When you get time to read, I'm sure I don't know."

"I do it at night, in bed. Oh, Mamma, I can hardly wait for Friday so we can talk about America." She hurried out to her bicycle and rode off. The two young ones in the yard returned her wave. Lisa nodded from the doorway. "How I'm going to miss her too," she murmured.

Time telescoped once everyone knew Elvira was leaving for America. The lawyer and his *fru*, although sad to loose her, were instantly helpful. Papers were speeded up, steamship schedules studied, the date set, and the ticket purchased. Material for a dress to travel in was chosen, its purchase supervised by the *fru*, who spend a morning helping Elvira select it in Narpes. Lisa hired the local seamstress to make the dress, from a pattern Elvira had found in a copy of the Swedish-American newspaper.

"I still say you should have picked a pattern with a wider skirt," Lisa complained.

"Oh, Mamma, it is an American style. My *fru* chose a pattern from that paper too. Her skirt is even narrower."

"Such a style. Pappa will have something to say, I'm sure."

Dressed to leave, Elvira was the envy of her sisters. They declared her dress a heavenly midnight blue, the soft fabric like velvet to their envious hands. Her new shoes glistened so brightly, they encouraged the little ones to stoop to see their reflection in them. Lisa listened to their collective worldly wisdom as they agreed that the white centers of the long row of buttons, up the side of the shoes, had been made of real pearls. Her hat, the latest in fashion, they were not sure they liked. Narrow brim with a rainbow-colored silk ribbon wound around its crown, ending in a tailored bow, seemed too plain. Elvira confessed, when Lisa was not within hearing, that it had been her second choice. The one she yearned to buy, she knew, would never pass Lisa's inspection, for it carried three ruby-red artificial roses. No imitation of any living thing would she allow Elvira to carry on her head to greet Pappa in America.

To Lisa the girl dressed in the clothes of a modern woman was still a child. Too young to go off alone. Yet she saw the maturity Finland had given her. America would finish making her eldest into a splendid woman. If only she could be somewhere near in these next important years. Ah, well, it could not be. It was too bad there could not have been a new coat, too, but the money had not reached that far. Elvira's money was spent, and some of the telephone income, too. Even some of what Oscar had sent. Lisa regretted not an *orë* of it, but knew no more could be spent in safety.

Everyone hovered to watch Elvira pack her new suitcase, much larger than the one Oscar had taken to America. Face flushed, she glanced up at Lisa when Maria asked, "What are those?"

"My *fru* showed me how to make these, Mamma. I don't have to wear an extra petticoat anymore."

"Yah so," Lisa said, and held out a hand for one of the pads of cloth. "I see. But, how do you fasten it?"

With a quick glance at her sisters, Elvira held up the long strip of white cloth and said, "You tie this around your waist, then pin the ends of these other things to it."

"Ya haa," Lisa marveled. "Excellent. That will do," she exclaimed at Maria, Emilia and Paulina, who were poking each other with knowing elbows, and giggling behind their hands. "If you know what these are for, stop your nonsense and pay attention. The time isn't far off when each of you will need them too."

Lisa sent the whole family, except the youngest, to the train station in a wagon she spent a bit more of the telephone central money to hire. She shook hands with her eldest, then held her hard for a moment before the girl climbed up to sit next to the driver. He paid no attention to the excitement, but sat spitting tobacco in long arcs out onto the grass, to Johan's wonder.

"Write as soon as you get to Sweden, and again before you leave for America," she repeated once more, and picked up the weeping youngest, who wanted to join her brothers and sisters in the wagon. Again she repeated, "Greet Pappa for me, and tell him how much we all miss him." As the wagon moved off she called, "Don't let Carl get too close to that train."

"Goodbye, Mamma. Goodbye," Elvira called, and twisted herself around to wave until she could no longer see Lisa and the struggling child.

The telephone central buzzed in the house. Lisa made an angry, impatient face, shifted the youngest into a firmer hold, then turned on her heel to run into the house. She slammed the door behind her.

*

That winter Lisa was lonely but comfortable in spite of her diminished family, the small house and the bitter cold. Oscar's letters were cheerful. They came regularly, bank drafts enclosed. There was money to buy wood from farmer Albertsson to keep the cooking fireplace and the bedroom tile stove supplied. Alli complained a few times of a pain in her side. Then the two boys came down with whooping cough.

She sent a letter to the two in America. "Johan stands beside me as I write. He whoops so hard it seems impossible one small boy can make such a noise. He struggles so hard to get air back into his lungs, it seems he draws himself up and grows half again as tall as he really is. I hold him often at night, and give him tar on sugar lumps. I have them both steam over hot water, a towel on their heads, as long as I can keep them at it. For a while it eases them. The sickness should finish its run before long if it goes the way it has for the others in the past. I will write you as soon as it is over." Later she wrote again.

"Johan has become so thin it frightens me. Carl, thanks be, has lost some of his fat. Today Johan went back to school and Carl plays and cares for the youngest once more."

She did not mention Alli's pain. There was no need to worry Oscar with it. The girl continued to complain, but only now and then. Momentary in duration, the pain was gone almost as soon as mentioned. Yet, after each episode Lisa kept the girl quiet, for she had decided it was only that the child ran too much. Alli sat in the window, trying to see through the frost-etched panes, straining to watch her sisters and brother play in the snow. In those dark afternoons, Lisa's longing for Oscar became sharp. It was always he who had known what to do for the children's ailments. It was he who knew what leaves of grass to pick to make a poultice for an infected sore. What brew would coat a sore throat with soothing relief, and how to bind a twisted ankle or sprained finger. If there had been broken bones, she was certain, he would have known how to splint them for healing. Much of his wisdom had come from the books he read.

In early spring, before any thaw had taken place, Alli had nausea with a sharper attack of the pain. Since there was no chemist in their village Lisa sent Maria on skis to her summer employer, the chemist, to buy a packet of purge crystals. By the time she returned, Alli was without pain or nausea. Reluctant to put the child through a purge unnecessarily, Lisa put the fold of white paper, holding the crystals, up behind the colorful gift platter on its shelf. Should the nausea or pain return she would use it.

It was still there on a night early in summer as she sat reading the latest paper Berta had brought her, the twins at the other end of the table playing a game. A speech made by a German officer-of-state held her attention. He boasted that Germany had built a navy to rival Britain's. She gave the paper an angry shake, and felt as though, suddenly, the Baltic Sea had shrunk, and the landmass of Germany had been brought too close to Finland. She read on. Their army, the speaker exulted, was finer, larger, better trained and equipped than any other in the world. She shook her head, and remembered something Oscar had said. "No country builds up its might as a game. They do it to make war, because some other country has what it covets." She nodded in agreement and read further. "Germany's precision instruments and technology is of an excellence never before known. Our industry is foremost in the world."

"Yaw," he agreed silently, and laid the paper down, "that means they need material of all kinds, too. They'll go toward to get it. That's what he is saying. He is a disciple of the devil, that man. It is written in Revelations."

She went to get her copy of the Bible and looked up the verse she wanted. "For they are the spirits of devils, working miracles, which go forth unto the kings of the earth and the whole world, to gather them to the battle of that great day of God Almighty."

Armageddon, she told herself, and wondered what Berta thought of the speech. And Oscar? She would clip it and send it to him right now. She put the paper aside and went to get writing tablet, pen and ink.

Pen dipped in the bottle, she sat with it poised over the paper. Should she tell Oscar she wished she could find another place to live? Nay, to do that she would have to tell him why. Besides, she was not sure the telephone people would consent to another move. Oscar did not need to know that farmer Albertsson was a man split in two. More good than bad, but the bad was terrible. He was kind when sober, but the nights he drank he was cruel. Never to her, or her children, but to his wife and his two boys. But especially to his horse. Never when he was driving it and sober, but when drunk he would go into the barn and torture it. The screams of the horse and its stamping was a nightmare of evil to hear. The bedroom was closest to the barn, the screams of the horse so loud and terrifying the girls would have to pull the pillows over their heads to drown them out. The first time it happened Paulina had been so upset she had darted out of the bedroom in her nightgown and was almost out of the door, to go to the horse, when Lisa caught her by the arm.

"You stay here. I will go see what is making it scream and stamp so."

By the time she got her shawl and boots on and got to the barn door, to open it a crack, the screaming had stopped, although she could see the horse toss its head wildly, its frightened eyes glittering in the half light in the barn. It stamped crazily in its stall. Farmer Albertsson stood some distance away, a wild evil smile on his face, his shoulders hunched and shaking as he laughed. He did not see Lisa. Quietly she closed the door and realized the man was drunk. She had not dared to go in.

The next day she had gone to talk to his wife.

"Leave us alone," Jenny had pleaded. "He never remembers everything. Don't say a word to him. He'll take it out on you if you do, just like he does on us."

Nay, she would not write of that. Albertsson never came near her, and he was more than kind to the children at all times. When he was sober the horse seemed not to have any fear of him, strange as it seemed. Instead she wrote of Jenny.

"She comes to visit only when she happens to be nearby and hears the telephone bell. She likes to sit and watch while I run the switchboard. I encourage her to try, but she is like I was when I first started. Afraid. Remember?"

Noises came from the bedroom where only a short while ago, Marta and Alli had gone to bed. She made no move to go silence them, but learned over the table to watch Emilia and Paulina play, "shut in a sack." Their slate pencils scratched as they gave each other directions to draw lines connecting the numbers they had written on each slate. It looked to Lisa like Paulina was trapped for there was no way, for her to draw a line between two numbers Emilia named, without having to cross lines previously drawn connecting other numbers. She neglected the letter to see if Paulina could get out of the "sack."

Not yet accustomed to the light evenings after the long dark nights of winter, Marta and Alli were still awake and playing a game of their own.

"They're blue," Marta whispered too loudy.

"They're not! They're brown!" Alli scoffed.

"Blue!"

"Brown!"

"All right," Marta whispered, her lips tickling Alli's ear, "I'll make one and you look and see." She stood up on the bed and lifted the back of her nightgown. "It's the same color as its sounds, blue."

"Sounds don't have any color," Alli hissed, as she struggled to get up onto her knees and steadied herself by holding onto her sister's legs. She positioned her face close to Marta's buttocks.

"They do too," Marta twisted around to tell her, and warned, "watch close now." After a few moments of straining she produced a small exposion of gas.

"I didn't see anything," Alli whispered hoarsely.

"I didn't have enough," Marta returned, "so you'll have to make one for me to see."

They jockeyed around to change places. Marta lifted Alli's nightgown and let it drape over her head. "Go ahead," she ordered, almost too loudly from her temporary tent.

"I can't. I'm trying, but my side hurts," Alli complained.

"Stop talking about your side. That's all you do. Mamma told you it is because you run too much at school. Now, try again, and try harder."

Alli bent forward, almost losing her balance on the curved mattress. All of a sudden she produced a respectable sound. Immediately Marta flung herself backward, the nightgown caught on her head, pulling Alli to tumble on top of her.

"Phew!" Marta bellowed, "you smell terrible." Tangled together they forgot to be quiet. Separated at last, they lay laughing. Alli held her side with both hands.

"What color was it?" she asked, big eyes peering at Marta through yellow curls.

"You stank," Marta shrieked holding her nose as proof. "I couldn't look."

The bedroom door swung open. Lisa came in. "What's going on? she demanded. "Are you trying to wake the others?"

The two made haste to crawl to the head of the bed, where they grabbed wildly for the cover and slipped under. Wide-eyes, serious, they returned Lisa's stare.

"I'm sorry, we were just...playing a game," Marta answered. Alli nodded alongside.

"I've told you, a thousand times, bed is no place for games. If you make another sound, or another move, I will be in here with the birch switch. Do you hear?"

The girls nodded, not at all fearful of the birch switch. Its use had been promised them many times, but had never been applied to either one. They murmured they were sorry, and wriggled further under the covers. Alli pressed her hand against the pain in her side, but Marta lifted hers up from under the covers as soon as Lisa left and closed the door. She poked Alli with her elbow and bent the forefinger of the hand she held up in the air. Up and down, round and round, she wiggled it in defiance of Lisa's order. She did not notice that Alli had no smile for her daring, nor that a band of sweat had popped out along the hairline of yellow curls. When Alli moaned she poked her again, to whisper, "Be quiet!"

It was after the older girls were in bed and asleep that Alli gave a sudden loud cry, sat up in bed to cry out once more. Lisa came running in, leaving the letter she had been finishing.

"What is it?" she asked, pushing the door wide to see who called out.

"It hurts," Alli guavered. "My stomach hurts, Mamma."

"Let me see you. Come in the other room."

Alli started to obey but cried out more loudly and flung herself back on the pillow.

"Paulina," Lisa said, over her shoulder to the twin nearest in the bed. "Go get the lamp so I can see Alli better."

She pulled down the covers and placed her hand on Alli's stomach. "Did you eat something away from home today you shouldn't have?" Alli stook her head and moaned again.

Marta, half awake, pulled at the covers and told her sister to be quiet.

"Hush," Lisa said, "turn the other way and go to sleep." Paulina came with the lamp. In its light Alli's half closed eyes, dull with pain, were revealed. Sweat beaded her face. With a cloth from her pocket Lisa wiped away the sweat and asked, "Show me where it hurts." But Alli's two hands fastened around Lisa's wrist and she tried to settle her cheek in her mother's palm, in search of comfort.

Emilia lifted up on elbow in the next bed, asked, "What's the matter with her?"

"Shhh, shh," Lisa answered quietly, "let's not get everyone awake."

Alli sat up suddenly panting hard. "I'm going to vomit," she moaned.

"Quick, bring the potty," Lisa ordered.

They were no extra piece of furniture in the bedroom where Paulina could set the lamp, so she ran with it, quickly, into the other room; then hurried back to pick up the potty and bring it to Lisa. It was too late, Alli had learned over and vomited on the floor.

"Oiy!" Emilia groaned, her face pale. "I'm going to be sick too. It smells so bad."

"Stop it!" Lisa barked. "This is no time for you to have a queasy stomach. Hurry up! Do what I tell you."

Emilia hurdled the end of her bed, in order not to come anywhere near the smelly mess on the floor. When she returned she held the bucket and rags out to Lisa at arms length, then quickly ran out of the room. Lisa wet one of the smaller rags and laid it on Alli's forehead. The girl moaned constantly while Lisa mopped the floor. Paulina came to take the potty and rags outdoors, and carried fresh water out into the night to clean them further. The three younger ones in the third bed moved about restlessly, the youngest whimpering as the elbows and knees of her brothers pummeled her.

"Emilia," Lisa called in a loud whisper. Emilia stuck her head in around the door post. "Go pull my bed out and take Johan to it."

Johan, who lay in front of his younger sister and brother, heard her. He got up as if walking in his sleep and went into the other room.

"Mamma!" Alli screamed, and pulled herself into a small ball, pressing both hands to her stomach.

"I'm here, little friend," Lisa told her, and turned to call to Emilia. "Blow up the fire and put the kettle on to heat. Paulina, are you there?" As Paulina came in a hurry, she said, "Bring a fresh towel and fill the washbasin with hot water as soon as you can and bring it to me."

She turned back to Alli, wiped her face with the damp cloth, and put it back on her forehead as the child tossed from side to side. "You will be better as soon as I get a hot towel on your stomach," she assured the child. She lifted the girl's nightgown and looked again at her stomach. It seemed bloated, but she wasn't sure. She murmured words of encouragement, and held the child each time she sat up to retch. At last the hot water and towel were brought in. Lisa wrung the towel out in the water and placed its heat on the girl's stomach as warm as Alli would take it. For a few moments it quieted her. Lisa sat down on the bed. Alli breathed in quick pants through her mouth. Through the night Lisa applied the hot towel, Alli's moans sometimes lifting into stuttering wails. Lisa bent close, murmuring soothing words, and held the hands that clawed at the towel, when they were not flailing the air. Suddenly Alli screamed, pushed the blankets down with both hands as her body arched, her shoulders and feet alone touching the bed. She collapsed and was still, her moans tearing at her throat.

The three girls, who had been sleeping fitfully, sat up. Marta more asleep than awake, asked, "Why does she have to make so much noise? Make her be quiet."

Bent over the sick child Lisa did not answer. She studied Alli's face. It seemed to her it was not as tortured, although it dripped with sweat in spite of the damp cloth on her forehead.

"Whatever it was," she said at last, including two older girls who sat with worried faces, "I think it is over. The heat must have taken care of it. Go back to sleep, all of you. "Here," she told Marta, "I'll tuck you in. Alli will be quiet soon, I'm sure."

She stayed beside Alli, waiting.

As the early summer sun brightened the room she saw that Alli had changed. Her eyes, half closed, were still dull with whatever sickness it was that coursed within her. Her face seemed to have thinned, or was it the shadows that made it seem so? Moans still rasped in her throat, but they were not loud any longer, and less frequent. Each time the hot towel was replaced, her body struggled against it. At last she lay quiet.

When the wall clock in the other room struck five, it brought Lisa out of her doze on the edge of the bed. Quickly she turned to Alli again, and drew in a breath of terror. The child's face was like a skull, the eyes drawn into their sockets. Splotches discolored her fair skin. Her breathing barely moved the blanket. It lay as undisturbed and smooth as Lisa had made it the last time she had applied the towel. Her hands shook as she uncovered the girl, took the towel off and stood looking at her stomach. In sudden decision she covered her again and went running into the other room, dropping the towel on the floor as she ran.

The doctor in Narpes. She would have to call him. The kilometers to the town made him seem as far away as America in her anxious thoughts. In her haste to connect the call she fought against remembering the only other time a doctor had been sent for. It was not for the poor to call a doctor whenever a child had an ailment. She and Oscar had learned that long ago. But when their second boy, along with other children at the sawmill in Sweden, had come down with throats closed, stopping off the air into their lungs, Oscar had run all the way to town to bring the doctor. Diptheria, the doctor said it was, and went from *stuga* to *stuga* to treat others sick in the same way. She cranked the handle again, turning it twice as long as before, and remembered also with pain the death of their first boy, newly born. She strained to catch an answering sound in the earphone. Oh, where was that doctor? He could tell her what more she could do.

Betrayed by her childhood training and her desperate need, she bent her knee into a quick curtsey when she heard his voice at last. Without thought to tell him her name, or even to use the title of Doctor, she asked quickly, "Can you tell me what more I can do for my child's upset stomach?... All night...Yaw, she has screamed and vomited, It looks to me like her stomach is getting dark...the skin, I mean. Hot towels, as hot as she could stand... You say it sounds like the kind of stomach trouble that can't be cured?...Breathing? Yaw, except that now I can hardly see her do it. But her face, her face is so sunk in... Would you come? Too late?... Nay! Don't say that! She is not dead! That sickness goes quickly? Surely not that quickly. She became sick only early last night... Yaw, many times through the winter, but it always passed away... But tell me, what more can I do now? I see. I must go to her."

Weeping, she flung the ear and mouthpiece onto its hook without remembering to say thanks. Hand over her mouth, she ran back to the bedroom and bent over the child. Alli's breathing was now so light the blanket no longer lifted. Lisa turned to the sleeping girls, Paulina and Emilia, and wanted to wake them. To have someone tell her Alli would get well. Instead, she sat down again on the bed and took the child's hand in her own. It was cool. She reached over and smoothed the curls from her forehead, and found that cool too. The shallow breathing stopped altogether for a moment, then began again with a shuddering intake of air. Lisa opened her own mouth in an effort to help the child breathe. After a long moment Alli inhaled once more, but then stopped.

"Nay!" Lisa cried, her face bent close to watch for another breath.

"Alli! Alli!" she called, waking the older girls. "She can't be dead," she told them, and rubbed Alli's hands, her throat, her face. With a cry she ran to the telephone central, but stopped in front of it, the cloth she had used on Alli's forehead pressed against her mouth.

Emilia and Paulina hurried out of the bedroom.

"Alli looks terrible," Paulina said, tears in her voice.

"Is she dead?" Emilia asked in a whisper, and clung to Lisa's free hand.

Lisa shook her head, but spoke to herself. "It's no use. It is too far for him to come. He said he couldn't be here in time. That is what he said."

Suddenly, she whirled about and went back to Alli, telling the twins, "Get the mirror and bring it to me."

Emilia ran to climb up on the washbench and lifted the small mirror down, running with it into the bedroom. Lisa took it and held it gently over Alli's face. She forced herself to wait for several moments then lifted it and studied the glass. There was no mist, even when she ran a finger over it. She tried again, and when the answer was the same, sat slumped on the edge of the bed, the mirror dangling from her hand.

Paulina took it and laid it on the other bed. "Maybe you should call the doctor," she suggested hesitantly.

"It's too late," Lisa answered. "Alli is dead." She roused herself to lift the small hands, straightened the fingers, and placed them gently, one on top of the other on Alli's breast. As she reached to close the child's half open eyes, the twins began to cry. She put an arm around each one and drew them into the other room with her. Arms tight around each other, they all cried, Lisa's head resting sometimes on Paulina's, sometimes on Emilia's. She found herself thinking, "The girls will soon be as tall as I am."

There was the sound of birds outdoors in the awakening day, and she noticed the unfinished letter to Oscar lying on the table.

*

The wagon waited in front of the door with Alli's coffin resting on the straw in the back and the girls and two boys seated around it. Lisa climbed up onto the seat with the driver. Katarina handed the youngest to Lisa before she climbed up. The driver spat tobacco solemnly by leaning his head over the side and letting the juice slip quietly past his lips. The day was unusually warm, the journey to Narpes long, for he drove a funeral pace. Seldom did either of the women speak. The children were silent, except for the youngest, who prattled with the joy of a wagon ride. Now and then she reached up to grasp Lisa's chin, laughing and pointing to the swishing tail of the horse. Along with the rattle of the wagon and clop of the horses' hoofs, these were the only sounds.

Lisa, rested, grateful for the squirming warmth of the child in her lap. Occasionally she twisted around to look at Marta. Still vivid was the memory of the child's reaction to her sister's death. As if it were happening now, she saw Marta again when she awakened the day before.

Marta had stopped in the middle of the main room, both hands grasping folds of her nightgown as she rubbed her skin. She yawned, then looked at the clock.

"Mamma," she exclaimed, "it's late, and Alli isn't awake yet. We've got to take the cows to pasture. Alli," she called, and turned to go back into the bedroom.

"Marta, nay!" Lisa told her sharply. "Stay here. I didn't wake you earlier because your sleep was interrupted too many times last night. Emilia and Johan have gone to tend the cows."

"Johan! He's too little, and Emilia will twist a cow's tail to make it run fast, so she can hang onto it and get a fast run herself. You shouldn't have let them. I'm going to wake Alli."

Lisa had no heart to react to the strange bit of information she had just received. Instead she took Marta by the arm to stop her.

"Stay right here. I want to tell you something. Alli was very sick during the night."

"I know, I heard her. Is she still sick?"

"Nay, Alli will never be sick again, Marta. Early this morning she was so sick she could't live any more. Alli is dead."

Marta stood staring, watching Lisa reach for the cloth in her pocket and wipe her reddened eyes.

"You mean...Alli...died?"

Lisa nodded, as with her free hand she pushed the still too thin hair away from her daughter's forehead, a gesture she had done so many times during the night to the one who lay so still in the other room. As she looked with sympathy, the girl's hands clenched into fists. She brought them up to shake them in front of herself, her mouth opened wide, her eyes holes of darkness.

"I didn't mean to do it, Mamma," she cried, tears flooding her cheeks. "I didn't mean to make her die." She screamed through rending sobs. "I thought she hurt because she ran so much. She didn't want to do it, but I didn't know it would hurt her that hard."

Stunned, Lisa grasped the girl and talked to her. Nothing she said lessened the girl's anguish. It was too much for her. She put her hands to her face and standing there cried too.

Marta's sobs became quiet. Lisa felt her hand touch her.

"Don't, Mamma," Marta said, her breath catching.

Lisa wiped her eyes and nose. "Sit here with me," she coaxed, "and let me talk to you." Marta sat, wiping her cheeks with the backs of her hands.

"You see, Marta, it was something inside Alli that...couldn't come out. Dear God, what could it have been?...it couldn't come out! Nay, Marta, don't. We must not cry now while we talk...Listen to me. You and I have something good...to remember, don't we. She laughed last night. Remember? It was because of you she had a good time before she got sick. Do you see?"

"But...I made her...try...so hard."

"Try what?"

At this Marta began to cry again. Lisa encircled her shoulders tightly with an arm and urged her to hush. At last, between gulps, Marta told about their experiment the night before. Sure that Lisa would scold her at having done what must be a sinful thing, she wept wildly.

Lisa searched for words that would erase guilt from the child's mind.

"It is good to wonder about many things in this world. Even the color of a fart, Marta. You need not sorrow about that, little friend..."

"But, but..it hurt her side."

"Nay... I think that hurt started long ago, Marta. I want you to remember that I am glad you and Alli had fun doing it. Yaw...I am glad."

She wiped Marta's face. The hairbrush lay on the wash bench where someone left it. She picked it up and with smooth strokes brushed the girl's short hair. The scalp, healed long ago, still showed the scars through the thin short strands.

"You are like Pappa," she told her. "He wonders about everything in this world. That is why he reads so much. Remember?"

Marta nodded.

"Perhaps," Lisa continued, "someday you can read in a book what color they are. I think even that is written somewhere."

"I don't care what color they are any more," Marta quavered.

"Marta, listen to me. I should have called the doctor... long ago. When Alli had those first pains in winter... perhaps... perhaps this would not have happened." She fought tears.

"A doctor? Here to our house? Marta asked between hiccups. "Just like at Palmers'? A doctor came to look down my throat many times when I was living with them. Every time I had a cold."

Lisa felt the sting of guilt. "This time I called the doctor," she said.

"You did? Did he come while I was asleep?"

"Nay, he said it was too late, and it was. So, you see, it was not your fault, it was mine."

Marta thought about it. "But you did right, Mamma. You put hot towels on her."

"Yaw, I did that, and I hope that made things easier for her."

Marta pulled away as Lisa finished brushing. "I remember how good it felt once when I was sick and you did that to me."

"Do you? That's good to hear. Now, I must go ask the carpenter in the village to make a coffin, and to get Morgensson's Agda to come prepare Alli. Paulina has gone to tell *moster* Katarina. Later I will call Maria and tell her too."

That had been yesterday morning. Marta had been comforted, but so had she.

Narpes lay quiet in the heat of noon as they pulled up at the graveyard gateway. The two long rows of small red split-log houses, sitting low in the long grass near the church, were empty, theirs doors closed. Their peaked gray roofs stepped in corrugation toward the white of the church wall. The yellow bell tower to one side, and the church with its tall central steeple, where like guardian hosts to the small building, as well as to the brown square parsonage at their head. It had been many years since Lisa had been there.

She tried to crush the memory of happy times in her youth, winter and summer, when she had come for special services. Quick scenes flashed in her mind. Garlands of flowers at midsummer. Burning torches at Christmas, their flames sputtering against the dark sky of early morning. The clamor of the sleigh bells as the horse pulled the sled through the glitter of newly fallen snow. Past trees thick with hoar frost that the flames turned orange for a magic moment. Her family had stayed in one of those houses overnight, many times, because it had been too far to drive home again. Every small house had been occupied by other families, who had come long distances, too far for their horses to travel twice in one day. The stables, further from the church, were built of the same split logs and also painted red. She wondered quickly, in spite of her sorrow, if Katarina remembered how they would hurry out to the stables to tease whatever boys were their favorites at the time. To impress them with their presence, as the boys hitched up their family's wagons after services.

Guilty at not having been able to stem the memories, she glanced at her sister. it was obvious Katarina was not thinking of those days, for at that moment she said, "I'll go tell them we are here."

"Thank you. Take this with you," Lisa reached under the seat to lift the knitted bag and from it took her Bible. Out of it she pulled a paper. "Here, I have written Alli's full name and ours, where she was born, and when. The person I talked to at the church, when I telephoned, told me to bring it."

Katarina nodded, took the paper, and climbed down to hurry toward the parsonage. After a while she reappeared with the pastor. She walked rapidly, her black skirt whipping around her ankles to keep up with his fast pace.

"*Fru* Olofsson tells me you have been here in Finland for almost three years," the pastor went on" I have never seen you at church. Your name is not in the church books."

"Nay, Pastor, I was baptized here, the same as my sister and all my ten brothers, but I no longer belong to it, nor does my husband."

"No longer belong?" he exclaimed, and looked around. He saw and knew the driver, but searched further, ignoring the children.

"Your husband? Where is he?"

"In America."

"He was baptized?"

"Of course. He was born in Sweden, of Lutheran parents, but you see, we study the Bible at home...and..."

"The child, she was baptized?"

"Nay, it is not our belief to do so. The children and I will read from the Bible at Alli's grave."

"You will not! This is holy ground, and no one but an ordained pastor can do so in my churchyard. You will not bring that child in here."

"What?" Katarina and Lisa spoke simultaneously.

"What do you mean?" Katarina managed to ask. "The child must be buried here. This is where her grandparents, her uncles, and more are buried."

The girls searched the two women's faces, fear of the pastor sending them to cluster around Lisa. She stepped out in front of them.

"Alli, in that coffin, is without sin. She is a child of the Lord and knew the gospel of the Bible well, as taught to her by us. She has more right in that graveyard than those I know about who swindled, fornicated, or drank themselves to death although baptized before they were too young to choose it for themselves. I will not leave here untill she is admitted."

She locked eyes with the pastor, determination as strong on her face as on his. He glared at her, turned on his heel, and walked away. Over his shoulder he called, "You will have to wait."

Lisa consoled the girls before she noticed Katarina's dejection. She stood head bowed and shaking. She went to her.

"I'm sorry you had to be here for this. He is a hard man, that one. Upset, because Oscar and I have left the church. Perhaps I spoke too strongly. Katarina," she coaxed as her sister's head did not lift, "you will see, he will find that he must let her be buried here."

"I hope so," Katarina whispered, and dabbed at her eyes with a handkerchief edged in black lace she took from her black funeral purse. "The old pastor, in your time and mine, was an understanding man."

"That he was. I am sure in the hundreds of years of the church there have been many fine pastors serving the people. Today too."

"Yaw, indeed," Katarina answered with some spirit. "You must believe that, Lisa. Why we had to get this one I'll never understand. Perhaps someday we'll get one with more heart."

The driver had led the horse over to the shade where a large mountain ash stood. Lisa's dress was too warm. She let the two younger ones roam. They went to pick golden dandelions along the rock wall. It was a long time before the pastor returned.

"You cannot bring her in through the gate," he told the two women as he strode back to them. "You must lift the coffin up over the wall."

"What?" Lisa and Katarina exclaimed together, and this time exchanged horrified looks.

"Over the wall? Why?" Katarina demanded.

"Because she has not been baptized. First, you must pay for the tolling of the bells."

Lisa stepped up to him in anger. "Through the gate or over the wall makes no difference to that dead child, you can sleep on that, *Herr* Pastor, but I will not pay for any bell tolling. This child is not of your faith, not a member of this or any other church, and I will not have church bells tolled for her."

Katarina pulled Lisa around by the arm. "Lisa, you can't mean that!

The bells are tolled for everyone who dies."

"I do mean it. I am to write Oscar and tell him his child had to enter the graveyard over the wall, and yet I paid the church money to toll the bells for her? I will not. Pick up the coffin, girls, I will help you. Come, Katarina, you take the other end."

Their weeping made it hard for the girls to obey, but the effort needed to lift the coffin to the top of the wall quieted them somewhat. They held it there while Lisa and Katarina hurried to the other side. The driver came to help them lower it, and then the three of them carried it toward the graveyard. The children followed. As they rounded the corner of the church the gravedigger saw them and pointed to the location of a newly dug grave. As he lowered the coffin with the help of the driver, the family knelt to pray. The driver looked around to see if the minister was in sight, and since he was not, he too got down on one knee. Before she stood up Lisa gathered a handful of earth and let it fall as gently as possible on the lid of the coffin. Paulina took the crushed flowers from Carl and the youngest, bent down into the grave and laid them on it also.

The pastor was not in sight when they went back to the wagon. Lisa hurried, letting Katarina and Maria gather the children. There was silence except for weeping as the wagon started homeward. Troubled, the youngest looked from face to face. Lisa lifter her to press her face against the child's body as she cried.

The swish of the horse's tail went unnoticed as the wagon made its way through the town. There was no sound of church bell.

*

A package arrived from Elvira. Maria, home for a few hours, had brought it. It was flat, actually a large thick envelope. Lisa was the center of an excited group as the young crowded around her when she slit it open.

First to identify the contents was Marta. "It's the patterns for our clothes to go to America," she cried. Many hands reached to take the patterns to see the pictures. Lisa slapped them away.

"Don't grab like that. Wait. Let us see if there is a letter too. Maybe one from Pappa also."

She pushed the papers apart and with a happy exclamation found one from Elvira. "Is that all?" she asked no one in particular. Her search for one from Oscar was fruitless. She turned her disappointment against the absent Elvira. "She writes so seldom it makes me angry."

"Read it, Mamma, or shall I?" Paulina asked.

"You do it."

" 'Dear family: Here are the patterns, for your American clothes, you asked me to choose and send. They are the latest styles. Even for Johan and Carl. Is there enough wool yet from *moster* Katarina's sheep? I am fine. I have many friends, Mamma, and we go to dances every Thursday night at the Temperance Hall in Waukegan. There I see Pappa sometimes. The people I work for have many fancy dinner parties and I learn to cook more fine foods. I work hard but there are no children in the house. How much easier that makes it. They are grown up and live far away. When you see Dagmar tell her I hope she is still trying to read and will get to go to school someday. I am too old now, I know, but I don't mind any more, Mamma. I hope everyone is well. My warm greetings to all of you, to *moster* Katarina, *morbror* Sigurd, and their boys. Eva too. It will be a happy day for me when you are all here, but especially for Pappa. Your daughter, Elvira.' "

Although the girls' eyes turned expectantly toward the patterns on the table, Lisa continued to sit as if still listening. She reached out and took the letter.

"She does not say how Pappa is," she complained.

Maria turned away from the patterns with difficulty to say, "If he was sick she would have written it."

"Yaw, you are right. Let us hear the letter once more."

Maria took it and read rapidly. As soon as she finished the girls reached out to the patterns again.

"Look! This must be for the boys," Marta cried, picking one up. "See?"

Lisa took it, studied it, then said, "So it is. What does it say here?" and handed the pattern to Emilia.

"Boo-stair Broo-ven," she read, pronouncing the letters in Buster Brown.

"It is a very manly design, isn't it," Lisa asked, studying it again. "Look, it has a belt all the way around. See, Johan?"

He came to lean on her as he studied the picture.

"I will make it from Pappa's old suit. You will like that, won't you?" He nodded, then went off to sit in the big rocking chair.

"Here, Mamma, look at our patterns," Maria said, "aren't they wonderful?"

"Let me see."

The girls hunched over the table, their heads so close together Lisa had to push them back a bit so she could see too. There was no end to the gabbling, admiring, wondering about the pictures. Patterns were chosen, traded, chosen again, until finally Lisa made the decision.

"This for you, Maria. This one for the twins, and of course this one is for Marta."

"It is easy to decide that one is for you, Mamma," Maria told her, as Lisa sat studying solemnly, but with a growing smile, the pattern she had known immediately was hers.

An hour went by before the excitement calmed and the discussion dwindled.

"Perhaps Sunday," Lisa drew a satisfied breath to say, "we could all go to Katarina's and show her these. She has said it is time we start spinning thread from the wool of that sheep that they gave all of you. I wonder whose loom I could use for the weaving once the thread is spun and dyed?"

"Cousin Ebba has a loom," Marta offered.

"Ho, she is far off in Kaskö," Lisa answered, accompanied by a spluttering of Emilia's lips as she expressed her contempt for her sister's suggestion. "Nay," Lisa went on, "it has to be here somewhere. Katarina will set up her loom, I know, but I would like to get to one near here. I want to weave too. Well, I will talk to her about it," she finished, and gathered up the patterns to store them in front of the tray in the hanger on the wall.

Silently she wondered about Elvira's friends. Especially the young man Oscar had mentioned in letters, never Elvira. But, why had Oscar not written also as long as the package was being sent? There was such uncertainty in the world now, what with all that was happening in Austria-Hungary, perhaps his letter was still on its way.

The telephone board sounded and she went to it, shooing the eager girls away from it.

"Central," she said, and turned the handle to ring the telephone she had connected for the caller, and thought of the war between Austria-Hungary and Serbia. Concern and unease were running high in Finland, she knew. The Tzar's call, for general mobiliazation in Russia only two days ago when the war began, would reach deep into the minds of the people of Finland. Would he take the young men of this country too if Russia was attacked? She was grateful Elvira's young man, whoever he was, lived far off in America, not in Finland, to be included in war plans, possibly. At least Elvira had that. The board rang with a second call. She completed it without interruption to her thoughts.

Resistance would be great against serving the Tzar. Her own voice, although unheard except at home, had always been raised for independence, even though she was a Swedish citizen now because of her marriage to Oscar. So many others, women as well as men, had spoken and acted openly for it over the years. Oscar had been among those who spoke out for it too.

Again the board sounded. She asked herself as she turned the crank, would Finland rise like it had some years before? Yaw, in 1905 it was. Then the whole country had gone on strike for six days. For independence and an end to the Tzar's dictate to Russianize the country. A grim sound, almost a laugh, broke through her lips while she connected yet another call. The Tzar, Grand Duke of Finland, had saved his Finnish Grand Duchy for himself that time by granting more autonomy, and quickly.

Yet, recently, he had started pressure again for his Russianizing program. An excitement grew in her as she hoped that this time, should he call the young men to serve, resistance would lead to Finland being able to wrench itself from foreign rule.

Two more calls came for her to tend to. She worked at placing them and murmured to herself, "I have never seen this central so busy. I believe every person who has a telephone has either called someone or has been called. It is like they have all gone mad."

At last the board was free of calls and remained silent. Thinking of Finland's independence she understood what price it might cost to buy. She went back to the girls and tried to put the thought out of the mind.

"I expect Pappa's letter will be here any day," she consoled herself aloud. As the girls agreed and quickly put the patterns back in the tray hanger from where they had taken them for another session of admiration, they were all startled by a voice answering Lisa's comment.

"Maybe it won't." Berta Lund strode in, a stricken look on her face. "Haven't you heard? Today Germany declared war against Russia."

"Nay! You can't mean it!" Lisa gasped, and went to her. "It isn't true!"

"Too true," Berta answered, and slumped down onto the bench beside the door. "You didn't hear it on the telephone?"

"I don't listen in, and no one has offered to tell me."

As Lisa spoke the board rang again. "No wonder this central has gone crazy with calls suddenly." She went to it, connected the call and returned to interrupt the girls, who with frightened eyes, were asking Berta one question after the other.

"I was just wondering if the Tzar was calling up Finland's men too. Have you heard?"

Berta shook her head. "I don't think he'll dare."

"Why?"

"Afraid to give the rebellious Finns arms."

"Hah!" Lisa exclaimed. "Like the king of Egypt. Fearful to arm the peopole of Israel, he was. It's in second Moses. Get the Bible, one of you."

Marta ran and brought it. It took Lisa only moments to find the passage. She read it out loud.

" 'When there falleth out any war, they join also unto our enemy, and fight against us.' There is hope in the words, Berta. May Finland be spared the sin of any war, I pray to God."

"Amen," Berta agreed, shortly, then added, "we can't predict the future, Lisa. I'm wondering if you shouldn't get to Sweden right off."

"Right off? How could I do that? Oscar has to send the money first." She tried to joke, "Johan and Carl are in no danger of conscription for some years yet."

Berta did not smile, "I don't want to frighten you, but his money might come too late. If Finland becomes trapped into serving the Tzar you might not be allowed to leave."

"Ack, how could that be?" Lisa asked, and without waiting for an answer said, "in any case, I must wait for Oscar's letter, Berta. Tell me, what more have you heard?"

"Not only heard, but seen. The Tzar is sending Cossacks here to 'keep order,' " she almost shouted the last two words then added a sneering, "Damn him!"

"Berta!"

"Excuse me, Lisa, but I'd like to see every one of them, the Tzar too, packed off to Germany. We can rule ourselves. We don't need those black-caped, fur-hatted, horse-riding villains to keep Finland's order."

"You have seen them on horses?" Paulina asked.

Berta nodded. "Even in Narpes."

Everyone crowded closer , Johan almost under Berta's chin, as she continued.

"Resistance would grow rapidly to his stinking Russification plans of our country if he didn't send his watchdogs to nip whatever action they can manage to spy.' "

"Pappa said that one time, not many years ago," Maria recalled, "Finland collected a half million signatures to a petition to the Tzar, protesting new laws he made. The Tzar didn't know anything about it until it was handed to him in St. Petersburg."

Berta rubbed her hands with pleasure. "You're right. In 1899 it was. That's fifteen years ago. For a whole week people met secretly throughout Finland, discussed the petition, and signed it. Not one Russian official in the land heard a whisper about it until the news of the committee's return from St. Petersburg."

"Nothing changed, though, did it?" Emilia asked.

"Some, but not enough. That's why we still work at it."

"You signed it?" Marta asked.

Berta grunted. "Signed it? For all of that week my house was crowded with people late at night to discuss the petition. There wasn't a one who didn't sign it."

"It's no wonder the Cossacks have been sent here," Lisa interrupted. "We haven't felt much suppression in the Swedish sector of Finland. But, perhaps, there will be more of it now for us to feel and see."

"No doubt," Berta agreed, "just keep out of the way of the Cossacks. Should the war end I suppose they'll leave us again."

"How terrible it is, this war," Lisa moaned. "It is the work of Satan. All men must find the freedom to say nay to war."

Berta stayed for an hour to talk, to read to them from the newspaper, to discuss what it meant to all of them. The coffee mugs were refilled, the large oval enamel plate in the center of the table replenished with deep fried pastries. Marta reached out a finger dampened with a quick lick of her tongue to lift a last crumb to her mouth as she listened.

"They begin the march to Armaggedon," Lisa said, but not for the first time.

"Ack," Berta responded once again, "it will be over in a few weeks."

"But Berta, you said the war could continue to spread," Maria contradicted her. "It might even stop the boats on the Atlantic Ocean. That would mean we couldn't go to America."

"Read for yourself," Berta told her, and pushed the newspaper across the table. "I waited in Vasa to get it before I took the train back. You can see for yourself they think it will be over soon. I'm not ready to call it Armageddon like your Mamma here. But, Lisa, I hope Oscar can send for you soon."

Lisa nodded and wished again that Oscar's letter had been in the package. He must know she needed a bank draft soon. Perhaps tomorrow the letter would be here, arrived on the same boat as the package but delayed somehow.

"Well, the war is far away, somewhere beyond the Alps," she said, putting reassurance into her voice. "The ocean is not part of it and Armageddon takes time to build. We will be with Pappa long before it gets any bigger."

Maria smiled in relief, and got up. "It's time I get back to my job, but first can we show Berta our patterns?"

Again the family clustered around the table the pictures of the dresses and the Buster Brown suit spread out for study and admiration. Berta responded with enthusiasm. She discussed each pleat, fold, every collar and cuff, and was as vocal as everyone else in deciding what colors should be chosen for the materials yet to be woven.

"Emilia," she teased, "you are going to have to be a lady when you get into that beautiful dress trimmed with piping. Think you can?"

For answer Emilia ran to Lisa's sofa-bed, pulled the red hand-loomed cover from it, draped it over her shoulders and caught one trailing end up in a hand. Back and forth she swished past Berta, her other hand lifted to push her curls upward into a tippy resemblance of an adult hairstyle. Her hips swayed, her feet placed daintily, toe first.

Berta lifted her hands high to clap them in appreciation, laughing heartily with the others. "You'll be your Pappa's pride, I can see that. All of you." Still laughing she went out the door.

"I have to go too," Maria said. "My *fru* and her boy have gone visiting. They will be back soon after I get there."

Everyone went outdoors to wave Maria off in one direction on the bicycle that had been Elvira's, and to Berta in another, as she called, "Lisa, listen in on the telephone. Keep up with the news."

*

Farmer Albertsson stepped inside the door, snow thick on his fur hat.

"Your girls like to ride in my sled?" he said, without formal greeting. "I'm going to Kaskö. Would the older ones like to go along?"

Emilia flung herself in front of Lisa. "Yaw, yaw!" she yelled, and without waiting for an answer flew to jerk her coat and *damasker* from her peg on the wall. She sat down on a stool, an arm already thrust through one sleeve of her coat and began to wind a *damasker* around one leg. The hand-woven wool strip went around swiftly, from ankle to knee, as she made it tight, although uneven and crooked. The red and blue tassle at the top end she shoved under the top band to make sure the leggings would stay up and keep her legs warm and dry.

"Kaskö?" Lisa asked the farmer. "Such a long trip when a storm is beginning?"

"This is just a flurry from a cloud passing by. The sky is clearing. The morning star promises a day of sun. It's going to turn even colder. The crust on the snow is hard as rock. It will make for a fast trip there and back. I have only one stop to make in Kaskö then we'll turn right back and hurry home for supper."

"Please, Mamma," Emilia pleaded, halfway finished with the second legging.

Lisa hesitated. Except for school the girls had been confined indoors for weeks. It would do them good to get out, away from this small crowded room. Albertsson certainly was sober. When he drank it was always at home, and at night. She had never seen him drive the horse when he had been drinking.

"You're sure you'll be coming right back?" she asked.

"Certain. I left plenty of work for the boys to do, but Jenny's ailing so I need to come back to care for the chickens."

"Well..." Lisa began, and saw Paulina's dark eyes pleading also. She reasoned out loud. "It would be good for the girls to visit Cousin Sture and his *fru*. We haven't heard a thing from them in almost two years. Maria, would you want to go along?"

"Nay, I'll stay here where it is warm. Besides, I haven't finished my schoolwork."

"Can I go?" Marta asked.

"Only the older girls were invited, didn't you hear?" Lisa answered. "All right, you two, take the fur blanket off your bed with you. I'll fix food for them to take along," she told Albertsson, "if you can wait."

"I'll be out in the barn. The horse is already hitched up," he said and stamped out.

Two boiled pieces of sausage, cheese, and buttered *knäckeboöd*, Lisa gathered. A handful of dried fruit was added and tied in a small bundle for the girls to take along. "If only I had something to send Ebba," she wished.

Maria suggested, "That wool runner I just embroidered for the rocking chair. How about that?"

"You are willing?"

"Yaw, I will make another for us if you can let me have the yarn."

"That I will. Thank you, Maria. She will appreciate it." She turned to the twins. "Tell Ebba, Sture too, if he is home this day, the news of Pappa. Look at her weaving so you can tell me about it. She is very proud of it, and should be. Emil must be old enough to be married now, I think. And Anna Stina. I do hope she has grown up a little and overcome that bashfulness of hers."

Emilia buttoned her coat with impatience.

In sudden thought, Lisa said, "Your feet. Take your *pjäxor* off and put a second pair of stockings on."

Paulina lifted her head from winding her *damasker* smoothly and evenly around her leg. The tassels hung decoratively where they should although they were never to be seen by anyone under her long skirt. She complained, "Mamma, we already have our *damasker* on."

"No matter," Lisa responded, and went to bring two pairs of short wool socks, old ones of Oscar's that she had not sent with him because they were too darned. The twins groaned but stuck their feet out, their *pjäxor*, the Lap boots all the children wore ever since they had come to Finland, pushed off onto the floor. Lisa picked one up and looked down into the boot. It was roomy, the curled up toe lifted to a high point in the cream colored reindeer leather.

"When did you put fresh straw in them last?" she asked.

"Not long ago," both girls answered.

"Good, then your feet will be up off the cold ground and keep dry as well. These extra stockings will help."

When the sled disappeared into the dark morning Lisa waved from the doorway. The younger ones woke up. Busy with them, Lisa found she regretted she had let the girls go. Fear for them was growing, of what she would not admit to herself. She shook it off and told herself it was foolish to regret what could not be undone.

In the light of middle day she made a trip to the farmhouse to ask about Jenny's ailment.

"Ack, it's nothing," Jenny assured her, "only woman's complaint. I'll be fine before it's time to care for the chickens. Don't know why he told you he had to be back because of them. I always get out there, no matter how I feel."

Her answer strengthened Lisa's unease. "Is there something I should know that you aren't telling me?" she asked.

"Nothing," Jenny shrugged, but turned her back to busy herself at the hearth. "They'll get back. The horse will bring them no matter what."

Lisa went to pull her around to face her, "What do you mean, no matter what?"

Jenny raised her shoulders high, one hand pushing Lisa away. "Just that. Don't worry. They'll get here sooner or later."

Strong worry filled Lisa as she made her way back through the barnyard snow.

At suppertime the sled was not back. An hour later Lisa made a second trip to Jenny through the black and white night, the bitter cold sealing her nostrils together as she hurried over the slippery skin of the snow.

"Where do you think they are?" she asked, as soon as she got inside the farmhouse. "Maybe I could telephone someone."

Jenny shook her head with a look of guilt.

"If you suspect something, tell me," Lisa demanded.

Jenny answered with anger, her eyes darting at Lisa. "Ask my boys, maybe they can tell you."

The two sons, hunched over harness straps they mended, looked up from where they sat. The youngest spoke.

"Visiting someone, I guess," he said, with a sidelong glance at his brother. The older crippled brother grunted, but kept his head lowered over his work.

Lisa left, slamming the door behind her. They knew something but were not telling her. She did not want to guess at what it could be, but suspected. Her worry now was a torment.

The clock struck nine, and what seemed like two hours later it struck the half hour. Lisa stood in the doorway once more straining to hear the sound of the horse over the snow.

"Why did I let them go," she mourned for perhaps the tenth time. "I should have known better... Wait, do you hear something? Yaw! Here they come!"

She turned to push Maria and Marta back into the house. "Get the pot back onto the fire. Is there plenty of hot water? They'll be frozen. Their plates, put them out."

"They are, Mamma, have been for hours."

"Yaw, of course. I'll warm up their nightclothes. They'll want to get into them right away."

The sound of the two girls running to the house, then their stamping up the two steps, brought the three away from their tasks to stand facing the door. It was flung open. The twins, scarves twisted on their heads, eyes snapping, and anger written plainly on both their cold reddened faces, came storming up to Mamma.

"Never again will we go riding with that...man," Paulina shouted. Her dark eyes snapped with fury.

"He's an idiot, that's what he is, Mamma. You know what he did?" Emilia asked, outshouting her sister while clawing at her coat to get it off.

Lisa lifted both hands to her head, then clutched each girl by a shoulder. "You're all right?" she asked. "You haven't been hurt?"

"We're all right, Mamma, but farmer Albertsson sure isn't," Emilia answered, tossing her coat onto the peg on the wall and sitting down to unwind her damasker.

Lisa asked, "What's the matter with him?"

"He's unconscious, I guess."

"Unconscious? Where?"

"In the back of the sled," both girls answered.

"In the barn?"

"Nay, outside it," Emilia reported.

Paulina stood folding her scarf, but had not unbuttoned her coat. "I wanted to wait and put the horse in the barn, Mamma, but Emilia wouldn't let me, she was so mad. The horse needs to be rubbed down and ought to be in out of the cold."

"Of course," Lisa agreed, and asked, "didn't one of his boys come out to do that?"

The girls shook their heads. "We didn't see any light over there. Maybe they're not home."

"Of course they are home. Albertsson can't lie out there unconscious and sick. We've got to get him into his house."

"He's not sick, he's drunk," Emilia explained.

Lisa whirled to her. "Drunk," she repeated in a voice that sounded dead to her own ears. The unformed thought she had pushed away all day had been given substance. Guilt shook her. Her voice rose in anger. "Is that what you meant when you said Albertsson did something?"

The girls looked at each other. Emilia began. "He got so drunk he couldn't drive, so Paulina made him go lie down on the straw in back and she drove. I sat up on the seat next to her."

"All of a sudden he rose up and pulled Emilia down onto the straw back there with him, and..."

"And pulled my skirt up and tried to get hold of my pants to pull them down."

Lisa staggered toward Emilia both hands stretched out to her as she gasped in horror.

"He didn't, Mamma. He didn't get them down," Emilia cried quickly. "I grabbed a handful of straw and jammed it straight against his face and pushed as much as I could right into his mouth. That stopped him. And I yelled like a...a...lion for Paulina to help me."

"I did, Mamma, I did. I held the reins with one hand while I turned and beat him with the whip around his head every chance I could when Emilia was out of the way."

"She really hit him. I could hear the whacks and snap of the whip, I tell you. All of a sudden he fell down, like a big sack, and began to make a sound like a snore."

Lisa reached behind her to find a seat, sat and buried her face in her hands. Inwardly she cried, "Oscar, Oscar, what have I done? Why aren't you here?"

"Honest, Mamma, we're all right," the twins came to tell her, touching her.

"I know, I know," she agreed, and looked up, wringing her hands, then pounded one fist against her chest. "I can never forgive myself for letting you go. I should have known not to do it. Where did he get the whiskey?"

"I suppose in every one of the houses he stopped in on our way home," Paulina answered.

"What dishonesty! He said he was bringing you right back. Did you go into those places too?"

They both shook their heads.

Paulina corrected herself. "I did go into the last one, but just inside the door to yell at him we were too cold and wanted to get home. His friends helped him out, and shoved him up onto the seat."

"Yaw," Emilia agreed, "and I wanted to spit on them because they were just as wiggle-legged as he was. Besides, they kept saying things like, 'Look at that, will you? The girls of the foolish Swede are very pretty. Nicely grown too.'" The scorn in her voice put her mouth into a deep upside down curve as she aped them.

Lisa moaned.

"You know, Mamma," Paulina added, "those men handed him a bottle too, and he kept drinking as he drove. That's why he got so drunk he almost fell off the seat. And that's why Paulina had to drive after we stopped and make him get in the back. You know, Mamma, the horse was acting so wild when farmer Albertsson drove, but as soon as Paulina took the reins it quieted right down."

"The horse knows me," Paulina said, "and knows I wouldn't hurt it, ever."

Lisa closed her eyes for a moment, her face lifted heavenward, her lips moving. "All right," she said, after a moment, "I will hear the rest when we have that horse in the barn and the man into the house. Evil as he has been, we cannot let him lie there and freeze to death. Paulina, come with me, but first go see if the Albertsson boys haven't come to help him."

Paulina returned to report no one was there, the horse still outside the barn.

Lisa went to get her shawl talking all the while.

"You are always around that horse. Go unhitch it. Maria, maybe you could run to the house and see if you can get those boys out there. Marta, stir the pot so it won't burn." She tied a kerchief on her head, then noticed Emilia again.

The girl had gone to the table to sit on one of the benches. Her arms lay lax on the tabletop, her head face down between them. Lisa hurried to her.

"What is it? Are you all right?"

Emilia sat up slowly, her face sickly pale, her eyes half open.

"I guess it hit me in the stomach all of a sudden," she said. "I felt kind of sick for a minute."

Lisa hurried back to the fire, poured coffee into a mug, added many lumps of sugar, then just a touch of milk.

"Drink this down. It will settle your stomach."

She waited until Emilia drank half of it. When she saw the color return to the girl's face she patted her shoulder, then went to join Paulina.

It was midnight before man and horse had been cared for and the complete story of the trip had been told, including the visit to cousin Segerson's. Lisa touched the girls often during the telling, gave them oil to rub on their chapped faces, and sent them to bed after a joint prayer of thankfulness that they were safe and unhurt. As she settled into bed she knew what she had to do first thing in the morning. She stayed awake fighting waves of guilt, and ached to have Oscar lying next to her, although she was grateful it was Emilia who lay in the curve of her arm, unhurt and sleeping deeply.

The lantern out in the barn made an oblong shaft of light onto the snow through the partly opened door in the early morning. Lisa left the house quietly so as not to awaken the girls. She hurried toward the light through new snow. It was Albertsson in the barn, she knew immediately, for the horse was stamping and neighing in a frightened way. She heard him talk to the animal, his voice cruel. Lisa slid through the small opening, stepping over the new mound of snow that had been created when Albertsson had pulled the door outward. For a moment she had to stand still to quiet her fears for she realized the man was still under the effects of his drinking.

"You devil, you slimy spawn of Satan, how did you get so many oats in your bin you couldn't eat them all? Where is the damned arm of evil who wastes food on you, you blasted four-legged, hide-covered bag of dung. I'm going to knock the shit out of you."

There was the sound of something slammed with strength against the flesh of the horse. As the horse screamed and staggered in clattering stamps to one side of the pen, its head tossed high, eyes wild, Albertsson shot out behind it, leaping to get out of the way of the slashing hoofs. He dropped a metal bar he had been holding in one hand and staggered toward Lisa, his face in his hands, moaning loudly, "Oh, my head, ooh, my head."

"Albertsson." Lisa's voice was loud and harsh with anger. The warm air of the barn was thick with the smell of hay and manure.

"*Fru* Veldman!" he uttered, his arms swinging wildly, as he struggled to regain his balance. He had staggered back so far he was again within reach of the horse's hoofs still stamping in fear. He leaped sideways. "What brings you to the barn?" he asked, his face knotted with the effort to speak rationally.

Lisa walked over to him, keeping a distance from the horse also.

"Perhaps you had better go soak your head before I tell you what I have come to say. Can you understand what I am saying?"

"Yaw, yaw," he answered hurriedly, his eyes squinted at her.

"Then I will tell you, and you had better write it down, maybe big on the outside of the barn, so you will never forget it. I am here to tell you if you ever lay a hand on one of my girls again I will, myself, whip you to a small piece of flesh. You will scream louder than your horse has ever done. Do you hear me?"

"What? What?" He backed away from her, his hand brushing his forehead as if to clear it to hear better. "I touch your girls? Never!"

His eyes darted to the cow stalls, over to the hay bins, past Lisa's shoulders. She saw he knew what he had done. Lisa brought her face close to his and almost choked at the reek of alcohol. She made him look directly into her eyes.

"You remember, all right, that you tried to rape Emilia. Go look at your face where Paulina's whip has crisscrossed it."

He raised a hand to the welts that showed even through his morning beard. one finger traced them as he stared at Lisa.

"Oh, my God," he cried. "oh, my God." Suddenly his attutude changed. A crafty look narrowed his eyes. He pushed Lisa back a few steps.

"They lie!" he shouted. "Bring them here and I'll tell them to their faces they lie. I'll get the truth out of them."

"I've already heard the truth," Lisa answered, and grasped the front of his jacket in a hard fist. She shoved him backward. He staggered and stepped into manure in the trough behind him. "Oscar isn't here to defend us, but I am. Burn it into your brain, drunk or sober, what I told you I would do if ever again you touch one of my children. And leave the horse alone!"

She released him quickly and walked out of the barn. The distance to the house seemed endless, as with skirt lifted, she sped through the snow. Any second Albertsson's hand was going to grasp her from behind. She stumbled in through the two doors and ran to cling to the iron corner post of the fireplace, her head bent on her two hands that gripped it with fierce strength. How could she, who had never raised a hand to strike anyone, have threatened a man with such violence, with such words? A tug of her children's hair had been the most she had ever done to any living soul. Trembling began and shook her whole body. Panting, as though she were ill, she made her way to the rocking chair, hands slack at her sides. Strength drained from her. She got into the chair, her head leaning against the comfort of the tall head rest, and let herself whimper. It became a soft drone, like a song she sometimes hummed to put a sick child at rest. She rocked gently, the chair making a small accompanying sound against the floor. At last the rocking stopped, as did her humming. After a long while she raised her hand and with a corner of her shawl wiped her face, surprised it was wet.

As she got up out of the chair she cleared her throat, for it was sore as if she had been screaming. Her shawl hung on its hook; she went to the fire to stir it up. She shook her head. Women alone. Albertsson, sober or drunk, would not be a friend anymore, but she would have to live with it until they could leave for America. How she yearned to be with Oscar.

*

"Katarina? You here? Welcome, welcome, dear you." Lisa got up from the spinning wheel crowded somehow between the rocking chair and the sofa-bed. "There is nothing wrong at home?" she added quickly, as she went with outstretched hands to greet her sister.

"Nay," Katarina smiled, embracing Lisa. "See who is here with me?" Another woman stepped in through the open door to stand smiling alongside Katarina.

"*Fru* Rudolfsson!" Lisa exclaimed, and hurried to extend a welcoming hand.

"Agnes, I am called," *Fru* Rudolfsson corrected. "You have it cozy here," she added, removing her head scarf as she looked around.

"Crowded, I think would be the right word," Lisa laughed, "but I am so grateful to you for letting me use your spinning wheel. I have really finished with it except for a very small bit of wool. Have you come to fetch it back?"

"Nay, nay, there is no hurry with it at all."

"Oh, how good it is to see both of you. Let me put fresh coffee on. Come, come sit. Take your shawls off. Here, here, let me hang them up."

Lisa bustled back and forth, too excited to settle either to coffee making, or in taking her visitors' shawls.

Katarina laughed. "Go make the coffee, we can hang things up ourselves. You flutter like a headless chicken."

"It is so long since I have seen you, Katarina, and you... Agnes. You have never been to visit. What joy to have you both here."

Interrupting each other they settled down at the table to exchange news of children, of family doings, and finally caught up on news of Oscar and Elvira. At the third cup of coffee Katarina turned to Agnes and lifted her eyebrows in question. Agnes smiled and nodded.

"Lisa, we have come to give you some news."

"Yaw? What is it?"

In the basement of Pastor and *Fru* Rudolfsson's church there stand four looms ready to weave the cloth for your American clothes."

"What? You mean...? Four looms? Where...? Who? Did you two arrange this?"

The two women laughed and nodded at each other, delighted their surprise had been so well received.

Agnes continued the information. "The women of the church are ready to help you dye the thread and weave the material. Katarina has already brought what she has spun for you and we have come to pick up what you have here."

Lisa was too stunned to say anything but sat with both hands flopped onto the table next to her coffee cup. When she could find and control her voice again, she said, "Thank you, thank you, dear friends. How can I find anything more to say?"

"No need," Katarina answered, and pushed her cup away to ask, "Bring a slate, we have to figure how much of each color you are going to need and what patterns to weave."

It took a while for Lisa to be able to leave off her wonder enough so she could give her whole attention to the figuring. But it was finally done to everyone's satisfaction, although it took most of the afternoon. The yarn Lisa had spun was collected and stuffed into big bags Agnes had brought with her. Only then did Lisa wonder how they had come.

"Sigurd brought our loom in this morning and we set it up. He will come here to pick me up when he and the pastor have finished a job the pastor has asked him to help him with. I think I hear the wagon arriving now."

There was another round of coffee with Sigurd before the ladies left with him, the yarn on its way to the church, the date set for the beginning of the weaving. When the girls were home Lisa had difficulty letting them talk, for she was so full of thankfulness to her sister, to Agnes, and to the women of the church, as well as to its pastor, that she hardly heard their questions. At last Maria grasped her by one arm and shook her.

"Are you going to let us go to the church too, to watch the weaving?" she had to shout.

"Yaw, yaw. You can take turns because it will be in the evenings. It will take many nights, so you older ones can take turns coming. sure I will never get back home much before midnight, if then. Besides, I don't suppose there is much room in that basement with four looms in it and all the weavers. Can you imagine the women who have offered to weave, and the ones who loaned their looms."

Again she was off in her own world of wonder. She named the women she had been told would come. Women she knew only by having met them on the road or in the store. One, only one was an old school friend, and a Lutheran. She marveled aloud until everyone of the girls slept, then sat at the table writing rapidly to Oscar, and then to Elvira.

Yardage seemed to have exploded into the room. The weaving was done and had been brought home only moments before. The girls had carried them and now selected their own particular length to take in front of the small mirror, preening and crowding each other aside as they tried to see.

Emilia tugged the long selection that was meant for both Paulina and herself, flinging it over her shoulder and parading around the table. Paulina ran behind, grabbing at the ends to keep the cloth from dragging on the floor.

"Is there really enough of my red cloth to make a dress?" Marta worried, holding the length in front of her. No one had time to answer.

"You make me dizzy with all that rushing around," Lisa called over the hubbub, as she dropped down onto a stool. "Go get the patterns, someone, and let us see how they look against the materials. Bring the cloths back and put them on the table," she ordered. She smoothed them straight, and smiled gently as she touched a fold in the lovely gray length that was hers. A delicate small design had been worked into its firm weave, and was a special delight to her. She thanked the weaver, silently, once more.

The first pattern selected was the twins'. She placed it on their material as she pulled closer to her.

"Your yellow and blue plaid will make up beautifully. See?" The girls leaned over to see for themselves. They discussed it happily, then in a group took it to the window, pattern and cloth, to see the combination better.

"Mine, look at mine," Marta pleaded.

"Your red is so pretty," Maria said, "and of course there is plenty of material." Marta sighed with satisfaction and would place neither pattern nor material back on the table when they returned from the window a second time.

Reverently Maria drew the brown cloth to her, studying the pattern with the others as it lay against the soft material. At the window she held it up against her and bent over to see the ripple and sheen of the cloth, the pattern pressed upside down on her chest so she could study it also.

Lisa remembered there was one more cloth to look at.

"Where is the bright blue one for Carl?"

"Ack! Here it is," Paulina answered. "It slid down onto the floor."

"Dust it off right away," Lisa exclaimed, and reached for the Buster Brown pattern. "Oh, this is really going to be beautiful on the boy. I am using the pattern for both Carl and Johan, you know. Johan, don't look so worried. I have already taken Pappa's old suit apart. It will be cut and made first, I promise you."

"Are you going to make all these dresses and the boys' suits, Mamma?" Maria asked.

"That would be too much for me since I don't have a sewing machine. I will make Johan's, but all the rest we will take to Astrid Lindberg, the seamstress. She will make them up to fit us all perfectly. We will go there the first full day you are home again, Maria, and let her do the measuring."

The cloth was carefully folded and put away in the round-topped trunk. It was Johan who summed up what they were all feeling. "Soon we go to Pappa," he said.

*

Rain or shine, Johan now went with Marta each day, to keep the pastor's cows out of the wheat and rye fields. Too anxious to wait for them to come home and be sent to the village for mail, or until the twins came through the village on their way from Berta's farm, Lisa walked to the store herself. She asked the farmer's wife, working in the chickenyard, to listen for the telephone central. Jenny was eager to do it. Fascinated by the central, she had come to sit and watch the calls put through each time she was close enough to hear it ring. Lisa had let her handle a call on some days. At this time of day, she told her, there was small likelihood that any calls would come through. She promised to hurry.

Carl ran ahead or trailed behind. She carried the youngest on her hip, whenever the child became too weary to walk, and set her down when she became too weary to carry her.

The storekeeper handed her the envelope. It was hard to believe that the letter was really there.

"It's good living when money comes from America." The store keeper commented. Both he and his wife worked at being friendly, ever since Pappa's letters had started to come from America. She knew it was the bank drafts inside the letters that warmed their hearts in her direction. They could not guess how much Oscar sent, nor did they know how carefully she husbanded it, spending as little as possible here at the store, or anywhere else.

"It's a long time since your husband sent one, isn't it?" his wife came to inquire, wiping flour from her hands. The odor of her baking filled the store. Her eyes were on the letter in Lisa's hands.

"All I hope is that he has been well," she answered, the thick envelope like a touch of Oscar's hand in hers.

At that moment she saw Linnea Carlsson who stood in a darker section of the store, her eyes sad as she too looked at the letter Lisa held. An American widow also, it had been almost two years since she had heard from her husband.

Lisa went to ask her quietly, "Still nothing?"

"Nay," she answered, keeping her voice low. "If only I could know if he had died. Some around here go on saying he has married again, and made himself an American family over there. I can't believe it, nor will I let the children hear it."

"Oscar wrote to that town in Colorado, like I told you. Maybe I should ask him to try again."

"It's no use. Remember, he wrote the mine too. That letter was never answered either. I'm afraid Martin is dead. If only I could know for sure."

"I'll ask Oscar to try once more."

Linnea nodded her head, but with little hope, and left the store.

"Yaw, *Fru* Veldman, when is Oscar sending for you?"

This came from Beeda Gran, who still worked at being village gossip instead of raising her children. She rose up from a box against the wall where she had been sitting. Lisa wondered if there had ever been a time when she came to the village that Beeda had not been there. One winter day, when Emilia had been home with a sore throat, Lisa had taken the *spark* to ride its long runners to the store, to ask for mail and to buy salt herring. Beeda was there and had followed her into the bank, the only other building in the village. Like a well-wrapped mummy she had stood near the door of that small one-room, one-man bank. Pulling her wool kerchief back from one ear, she had strained to hear how much Oscar had sent in the letter Lisa had opened in the warmth of that building's roaring wood stove. Bank Director Lindbloom had slyly outwitted the gossip. He went to the open safe behind him, his back carefully hiding from Beeda what he took out of it. In a whisper he counted the monies as he cashed the bank draft that had been in that letter. With his head he directed Lisa which way to stand so that her back hid the denominations from Beeda, who sidled this way and that, tryng to see.

The memory was vivid as she answered Beeda this day.

"He'll send for us when he's ready."

She hurried outdoors. After a quick glance at the envelope, held up against the sun, she tore the end of it off. Halfway down the first page, reading as she walked the dusty road, she realized no bank draft was among the many sheets of the letter. She took them out, looked back into the envelope, then folded and reinserted the letter.

"Come, Mamma wants to hurry," she called, and reached for the youngest's hand. She told Carl, "Run ahead," and looked back. Sure enough, Beeda was out there watching; both the storekeeper and his wife, were at the window. They did not need to know there was no bank draft this time.

As if Bank Director Lindbloom would be disappointed, as she was, that she had no reason to turn in at that small wooden building so far from the store and nestled up against the forest behind it, she hurried past. Not until a good part of the forest was between her and the bank did she look for a hummock to sit on beneath a large pine. Beeda would not wander this far, she hoped. There she took the letter out again and began to read in earnest.

He was fine, so was Elvira. That she had already read. She skimmed rapidly to find a reference to the bank draft. Ah, here it was, at the bottom of the second page.

"It will be a while before I can send another draft. I have had such toothaches I have had to go to a dentist to have four upper teeth pulled."

She clucked in sympathy. The youngest, who had settled next to her, clucked in imitation. Lisa smiled down at her. Carl picked up mud chunks from the road and threw them, with little accuracy, at a farm wagon that stood abandoned temporarily in the field across the road.

Lisa returned to the letter.

"I did not sleep for many nights trying to avoid that expense," she read. "I put Hoffman's Drops in the aching teeth, but it didn't help. The pain was terrible, my face swollen on both sides."

She moaned and raised a hand to her own cheek. Hoffman's Drops. She wondered if she should ask him to send her some for the children's toothaches. Nay, she told herself as she watched the youngest go join her brother throwing bits of mud. It had not helped Oscar. She would go on using snuff, the only time tobacco was allowed into the house. Packed around, and in, the aching tooth, it always brought relief.

She returned to the letter.

"In my sorrow over Alli's death in my last letter, I think I forgot to tell you that some weeks before that Elvira sent you the items you asked for, to use on the girls' new dresses. You know better than I do what they were. They should be there long since, I think."

She looked at the envelope to see when it had been mailed and realized it had taken more than a month to reach her. The package he wrote about had still not come.

She turned back to continue reading.

"I wish I could say I am sending for you, but it will be necessary to borrow again before I can do that. I agree with you it would be better not to go further into debt, but there seems no other way. You'll be happy to know that I finished repaying your brother a week ago. Every payday I continue to give Ulf something on my debt to him. But, no matter how careful I am with the rest of it, the money to send you does not add up. Yet, I bought the items you asked for, although you told me to wait. It helped me feel that I would be seeing all of you soon. I am longing so for you, and for the children. It is already a year and a half.

"So, Lisa, I want to go to Herr Nyqvist, who has a food store here on the main street near where I live. He makes loans too. I keep in mind what you have said so often, that Maria, Emilia and Paulina can help pay for all your tickets to America when they find work here. That way I can tell Nyqvist the loan will be paid off quickly. Let me know that you agree."

Again Mamma turned back to the first page to look at the date of his writing. "He must be waiting for an answer by this time. He doesn't know his letter was delayed. I must write to him this very evening. Carl!" she called, "watch the little one. Don't let her run so close to the ditch."

She read on.

"Talk of Germany and her growing arsenal of armaments continues to be a large subject of talk here, as I have written you in the past. My only doubt is what direction the guns will point. The big Chicago newspaper I read, at the boardinghouse every day, is full of conflicting reports. I can read them myself now, the English-Swedish dictionary a wonderful help. Well worth the cost. Although the newspaper has excellent reports, from many parts of the world, it is what is between their lines, that is, what they do not say, that gives me understanding of what is happening. There is another paper a man here gets, once a week, written for the working man. With that to help me I become convinced Armageddon is ahead. The Molochs of War prepare to sacrifice their children once again. The fires are lit, there is no turning back for them. We must get you to America soon."

She sat nodding, her face strained, absorbed in his words. The children came running, Carl calling, "Pastor! Here comes Pastor."

Peter Rudolfsson came riding up on his bicycle, stoping in front of her.

"Good day, *Fru* Veldman," he greeted her, and added, "I see you have a letter from Oscar. May I hear the news from him?"

"Good day, Pastor," she answered, and got up to shake his hand. "It is good to see you, especially right this minute. Let me read you what Oscar wrote even before Germany went to war. I'd like to hear what you think of his conclusion."

She read him the paragraph she had just finished, then stood waiting, intent on his answer.

"I know Oscar's beliefs," he began, "but Armageddon?" He shook his head, his face very serious. "I thought this small war on the continent would soon be over. Germany's entrance into it changes the whole picture. I have just heard, *Fru* Veldman, that Germany has blocked the Gulf of Bothnia with mines."

"Mines?"

"Floating explosives. They will keep the Russian ships from getting out to sea. If a ship touches one of those it will be blown up an sunk."

"How terrible! What evil man does to man." The regarded each other, their faces equally troubled. "But what about Finnish ships? How will they get past those...mines."

"They won't," Pastor Rudolfsson hesitated, then tapped the letter in Lisa's hand with a forefinger, to say, "It might be a long time before you get another letter from Oscar."

"You mean boats crossing the Atlantic will not be able to sail up here to Finland?"

He nodded, and to avoid her stricken eyes looked down at Carl who knelt in the road to twirl a foot pedal of the bicycle with great interest. The youngest squatted near her brother, her short corn-colored braid pointing skyward, as she watched the pedal spin.

"But Finland needs to get her own ships out to sea," Lisa exclaimed, "and what about the goods she needs to receive?"

"If the blockade lasts very long all of Finland will suffer. If it is at all possible you should take the children and leave now for America."

Lisa shook her head. "Berta says the same thing, Pastor. But there isn't the money yet. Oscar has to borrow, he says. I'm sure he will find a way to get the money to us. He has to."

"Hold on to that. If anyone can, Oscar will. But I suggest you send your next letter to him through his family in Sweden. That way he will be sure to get it."

"Ah, boats still can go from here to Sweden, I see. If only we could leave now. Oscar will be quick to think of sending his letters via

over her.

"You can wear mine sometimes, and I'll wear yours," she promised.

Paulina's long dark braid slipped from her back to hang down in front of her. It swung as she shook her head hard from side to side, but she made no other answer to her sister's offer.

Marta, who had new shoes but not a new coat, looked at her with sympathy. Lisa had told her, before they left for Narpes, that her old coat, the one the Palmers had sent with her years before, would have to do. The worn leggings could be used to lengthen the hem and sleeves this time.

"All of you," Lisa said, "put your old shoes back on. I'll help the youngest."

Johan refused. He said nothing but would not sit down nor remove his new boots. He backed away as Maria tried to make him take the old ones she picked up and held toward him.

"Johan," Lisa called, "take them." Still he backed away. She dropped the youngest's foot and looked at him sternly. He scowled with unhappiness and determination. She relented.

"Let him be. I don't think he can remember ever buying a new pair of boots. He's always had Alli's old ones."

Johan, a big grin on his face, came to stand next to Lisa, his eyes on the shining toes of his boots.

Carl had removed his new boots where he sat on the floor but decided he had to be like his brother. But Lisa quickly had the old ones on before he had time to resist.

"Here," she told him, "go ask the shopkeeper to wrap your new boots in paper. You can carry the package yourself, all the way home."

"The graveyard next," Lisa told the driver, when everyone was back in the wagon. "Don't sit on the coats or the hats," she cautioned the children as she climbed up to the seat. The coats and hats had been purchased first and carried out to the wagon. Lying in bright colors against the straw of the wagon bed, they had been in the keeping of the driver. He had sat on the back of the wagon, visiting with a town friend, as they took turns spitting tobacco juice into the ruts of the muddy street.

Emilia had made a great show when she carried her new coat out to the wagon. She flung it from arm to arm, with her new hat square on top of her head and her neck stretched uncomfortably high as she spoke loudly, with a pretended indifference to be heard up and down the street.

"These will have to do until I get to America. Then, of course, I'll have to get new ones."

Lisa tried to hide her smile as Paulina laughed an appreciative, "Nyeh, nyeh, nyeh," at her sister's swaggering. "Hush such nonsense," Lisa scolded, only to burst out into open laughter as Maria joined in the play-acting with an exaggerated whisper.

"Let's go stand in front of that restaurant and pick our teeth. Everybody will think we ate in there."

As the wagon made its way to the churchyard they became silent, the only words spoken warnings not to get their dusty feet against any of the new clothes.

In silence they saw that Alli's grave was green with wild grasses. Lisa took a clump of lily-of-the-valley roots from a paper out of her knitted bag. She told Maria to dig a hole for them in the middle of the small mound. From the pump nearby Emilia and Paulina brought a pail of water. They poured it carefully over the few pointed green leaves protruding from the roots that Marta had covered with the fresh earth. Maria took the two younger ones in search of wild flowers to make sure they did not take ones decorating other graves. Johan stood admiring his boots.

They clustered at the foot of the grave when their work was finished. Lisa prayed aloud and was joined in "Amen" by all the children.

"Alli is at rest," she told them, "but we will see her on Judgement Day. We can be grateful we had her with us for almost eight years."

Maria said, "In the New Kingdom we will all be together again."

Lisa nodded and wiped her eyes. "Don't cry, Marta," she told the girl who had come to hide her face against her, "Alli is in God's hands along with her two brothers. She is not alone. We must not sorrow anymore."

The quiet among them lasted as the wagon made its way through the town into the country. Lisa took the newspaper she had brought out of her knitted bag and began to read news of the war to the driver. Quietly at first the children talked about their new clothes.

"I've got to see my new shoes again," Marta said, and tore the paper open.

"Me too," the others said and followed suit.

Paulina placed her new hat in front of her like the others had done with their shoes.

"Put it on," Marta suggested.

"Yaw," Emilia agreed immediately, "let's all of us put our coats and hats on."

At that Lisa turned around. "Sit still. Leave them where they are," she said. "Here, open this and pass the food to everybody. She handed them a large cloth, tied by its four corners, that she lifted from under the driver's seat. In a short time everyone, including the driver, was eating open-faced *knäckebröd* sandwiches with either cheese, pickled herring, or sliced beets on them. She lifted the tin milk container back to the girls. They took turns drinking from it, laughing as bumps in the road made the milk splash up into their faces, or dribble down over their chins. One yellow mug had been brought along for the younger ones to drink out of. Lunch finished, they began to sing. Lisa, and later even the driver, joined in. The driver's voice made the girls giggle. It quavered in uncertain tones from one note to another, and sometimes was so drawn out they had to wait for him to catch up.

Maria beckoned her sisters to come close. In a whisper only they could hear, over the rapid clop of the horse's hoofs, she wondered, "Do you suppose it's because of all that tobacco packed against his few teeth the sounds come out like that?" The girls rolled on the straw with laughter.

Johan had heard. He left off gazing at his boots to look at the driver. He opened his mouth to ask him. Paulina clapped a hand over it quickly and shouted, "Look, we're home."

*

The fire caught in the few twigs Lisa fed the banked ashes.

A sound at the door startled her, brought her erect, and twisted her around to look at it.

"What makes the door rattle?" Maria asked, raising her sleepy head from the sofa bed where she had slept with Lisa.

The sound came again, somewhat louder.

"Who around here knocks before coming in?" Lisa asked, then went to open the inside door. When she reached the outer one she hesitated, set one foot against it and pulled it just wide enough to see who was there. If they tried to push it open further her foot would stop it.

Maria heard murmurs, an exclamation from Lisa, then the shuffling of feet into the vestibule.

Lisa came back in, her head turned to look at whoever it was she had allowed in. "Stay there for a moment," she said, then to Maria, "get up. Put your dress on over your nightgown. There are people here who need help."

She blew out the kerosene lamp she had lighted only a moment before she started the fire, then went to the window and looked out toward the barn. It was dark.

"All right, come in," she said. The door swung wide.

Three people entered. Maria could make out a man and two women. They stood close together just inside the room.

"I blew out the light because the farmer will soon be out in the barn," Lisa told them. "Come sit at the table while I build up the fire. Maria, take their coats."

The man spoke. "Not yet. We are cold. It rained some during the night as we walked here."

Lisa said nothing further until she had the fire going briskly, the wood the children had gathered in the forest thrust generously into it. She set the kettle close to the blaze, then faced the three who sat silent on one of the benches.

"It was before my man went to America that other people came to us for part of a night. Do you run for the same reason?"

Again the man spoke. "Yaw, we were being taken to Siberia when we escaped. These two," he indicated the women with his hand, "are guilty of teaching people, somewhere out in the forests of the north, to read. The wrong things, according to the civil servants of the Tzar. As for me, I preached that no Finn should offer to join the Tzar's army."

"You are God's people," Lisa said, and smiled at them. The two women had untied their scarves and were wiping their faces with them. In the dim light she could see only that they both had dark hair, and that one had a broad flat face and was square of body, while the other was slim, her face small with pointed chin, eyes lost in the shadow of her deep eye sockets. The man was big, the light brown of his mustache and short beard hiding most of his face. His lighter colored hair fitted his big head like a cap. All three were young. The two women turned to their male companion. He spoke rapidly in Finnish. When he stoped the women smiled at her, their bodies relaxing, showing their weariness.

"They speak no Swedish?" Lisa asked.

"Like me, they are Finnish," the man answered.

"You speak Swedish, not Swede-Finn, and with little accent."

"I worked in Sweden for many years."

"I'll have oatmeal cooked soon. Maria, set out the milk and sugar along with some bowls for them."

"If we could just have a cup of coffee now," the man suggested, "and sleep for a while on the floor. We are all too tired to eat."

"On the floor! I should say not! Maria, go wake the others. Tell them to dress and have one of them help you carry the two young ones in here and put them in my bed. Try not to wake them." She turned back to the man. "I'm sorry, but I don't have any coffee. Let me fix you hot water and milk, with a lump or two of sugar. It will warm you at least."

As Lisa poured hot water and pushed milk and sugar across the table toward the two women, the man explained what she had said. Excited, the two women talked to each other, then indicated to Lisa, with hands raised appreciatively over the steaming mugs, that hot water and milk were fine. Then, pointing over their shoulders, they also told her with vigorous nods accompanying their gestures that the floor was good enough for them. She understood, and in turn shook her head, and pointed first to the closed bedroom door, then at the windows of the room.

They nodded with understanding.

"Are your clothes wet?" she asked.

The man reached to feel his trouser leg. "Somewhat," he admitted, "but I think the women's skirts may be more wet than my pants."

"Tell them I will dry their clothes while they sleep."

The seven children came out of the bedroom. Maria carried the sleeping youngest, Paulina the awakened Carl. They laid the two on Lisa's bed and covered them, urging Carl to go back to sleep. He would not. He sat up and looked at the people at the table. Johan, Marta, and Emilia went to stand near the fire away from the strangers.

"You are not to stare," Lisa told them quietly. "Can't you say good day to our visitors?"

Mechanically they said, "good day," but continued to stare.

"Did you all use the chamber pot?" Lisa asked, her back to the visitors. The children nodded. "Emilia, go take it out, then, and empty it, and put it back in the bedroom."

Head bent low Emilia went to do it, returned swiftly and placed the pot once again behind the bedroom door.

Later, after the three visitors had gone to bed, Lisa was about to hang the skirts and petticoats on lines near the fire, when she heard horses pounding over the wet land.

"Quick!" she told the girls, "help me pull the trunk away from the wall."

Together they strained with her, and she gathered up the wet clothes and dropped them behind the trunk. "Now, push with me." The trunk was back in place, no clothing showing above, or on either side of it, when there was a sharp pounding on the door. The dark form of a horse, with rider, blotted out the light of morning from one window.

Lisa put a finger over her mouth and looked at each of the children in front of her. She whispered, the finger now pointing at them. "You have seen no one, understand?" They all nodded, their faces pale and strained.

Johan asked, "Is it a Cossack?"

"Hush," Lisa told him, and went out. The children crowded into the windows on each side of the door, only Paulina going with her.

"Have you seen two women and a man come by here?" the Cossack on the horse asked, the butt of his whip still pointing toward the door. His caracal fur hat sat at a jaunty slant on his head, his mustache wide and drooping. Black eyes moved, from Lisa to Paulina, in hard searching jabs. The horse skirted back and forth, his hoofs churning up the damp dirt in front of the steps.

"We just got up," Lisa answered him. The Cossack pulled the reins of the horse and brought it to a snorting standstill.

"We're searching the farm," he said, indicating the buildings behind him with a jerk of the whip over his shoulder. Lisa saw that four other Cossacks, their horses standing with reins dropped, were entering one barn after the other, even the chicken yard.

"Did you ask farmer Albertsson?" she asked.

"They're asking. Don't worry. We'll find them," the rider answered.

At that moment Carl came and pushed between Lisa and Paulina. The Cossack looked down.

"You, there, have you seen two women and a man this morning?" He held three fingers out toward Carl.

Lisa held her breath. Paulina stiffened, and tried to pull the boy backwards by grasping the back of his nightshirt. But Carl pulled forward. He nodded. One finger raised he pointed at Lisa, than at Paulina, and finally at the Cossack.

"One, two, three," he counted, and held three fingers up in return.

The Cossack lifted his head and exploded with laughter. Before Lisa could protest he leaned down from the horse, lifted Carl by one arm and settled him in front of him in the saddle. With a quick move of his heel he set the horse into a sudden run, then slowed him to canter in a circle around the grassy plot between the house and the chicken barn. Lisa stepped down onto the ground and called, "He'll catch cold. He isn't dressed."

Carl in his white nightshirt, eyes big and staring, body stiff with fright at first, was like a small gold-capped cloud against the dark uniform of the Cossack. His curls bounced, catching in the two rows of decorations, like black and white cigars, that angled across the Cossack's chest. The horse was brought to a plunging standstill in front of Lisa. With a movement so swift she had no time to anticipate it, the Cossack handed her the laughing child. She staggered forward with his weight to bump against the horse, its strong sweaty smell thick in her nostrils as she wrapped the boy tightly to her with both arms.

"He'll never forget that," the Cossack said, his young face gay with a wide grin. Then becoming serious, "I see you have telephone lines here. If you see those people, call the sheriff in Narpes. Right away. Good day."

After a touch to his cap with his whip and an appreciative glance at dark-eyed, dark-haired Paulina, he sent out a whistle so shrill that Carl put his hands to his ears. Without any noticeable instruction the horse was put into an immediate gallop and the Cossack rode away bent low in the saddle. The other Cossacks mounted on the run, and waving their caps at the three who had retreated to the steps, yelled as they went flashing by, their black capes streaming in the wind. Mud was kicked high into the air from the hooves of the horses, some of it slapping against the wood of the house, bits of it sticking against the window glass where the other children pressed their faces to see.

Paulina ran out into the grass when the last horse had thundered past. "Beautiful!" she exclaimed. "Aren't they beautiful? I've never seen anything as beautiful."

Emilia ran out of the house and yelled at her, "Cossacks beautiful? Are you crazy?"

"The horses, silly," Paulina answered, never taking her eyes from them. "Oh, did you see that? They jumped the ditch without slowing down at all! They're gone!"

"Thank you, dear and good God," Lisa murmured, and went back into the house still carrying Carl.

The door of the bedroom opened slightly. Lisa went to it and told the man what had happened. He closed the door. When the children rushed in chattering about the horseman, she silenced them.

"Not now, we must be quiet. Tonight, when these people are safely on their way, we can talk. You go to school, but not a word to anyone about this. Johan, if anyone asks you just give your usual shrug that you do so often. Will you remember?" He nodded. "Show me," Lisa suggested. He lifted his shoulders almost up to his ears then dropped them.

"That's good. Do that whenever anyone asks you if you have seen any strangers. Emilia, you are going to have to be late for school. I want you to go to Berta's. I don't have food enough to feed these people. They need something more than oatmeal to give them strength. Tell her, and no one else but her, they are here. Ask her to bring what food she can. Don't run, but hurry."

"What will I tell the schoolmaster when I come in late?" Emilia asked.

"That you had a queasy stomach and waited to make sure it would be all right. It has happened before to you, so he will understand."

"But, Mamma, that's a . . ."

"It is not a lie when people's lives depend on what you say. You did have a touch of unease to your stomach when that Cossack was here . . . didn't you?"

"Na. . . yaw," Emilia grinned, then hurried to leave. The others left for school soon after.

With Carl and the youngest dressed and eating their oatmeal, Lisa sat down to a cup of hot water. She had just finished it when Berta walked in, a large sack under her arm. Before Lisa could ask how she got there so quickly, Berta told her.

"I was halfway here with the food when I met Emilia. She'll not be late for school." Then with a nod toward the bedroom door, she asked, "They sleep?"

"Yaw, and there I will keep them all day until they leave."

"Good."

There was no need for Lisa to ask Berta anything. Whoever had sent the fugitives to her had also contacted Berta, she realized. Could it have been Pastor Rudolfsson, she wondered? It could have been anyone, for Swedish-Finns and Finland's Finns were united in their feeling against the Tzar.

Berta was busy lifting the food out of the sack and placing it on the table. Potatoes. Lisa's mouth watered. For over a week there had been no potatoes in this house. Beets, a head of cabbage. Onions. And still Berta reached deep into the bag. She brought up something wrapped in a white cloth, and with a quick toss spread it open on the table. Lisa leaned over to look.

"Pork!" she exclaimed, forgetting to speak quietly. With a glance at the bedroom door, she lowered her voice and said it again, looking at

Berta with accusation. As Berta was about to respond, Lisa lifted her hand and shook her head.

"It's all right. They eat it, I'm sure. I'll cook it. But, you brought so much," she complained, as she lifted some of the meat and held it up toward her friend.

Berta took it from her, placed it back on the table, then stepped closer. "Dear Lisa," she began, "do you expect to keep your children well on just oatmeal and *Knäkebröd?* Ask your God if he expects you to starve them rather than have them eat some of the 'sinful' flesh of pigs, which I have in plenty."

Anger, doubt, and indecision replaced each other in swift procession on Lisa's face as she backed away. Her eyes were steady on Berta's.

"Don't be a fool, dear friend," Berta begged. "Remember, in hunger David took the shewbread from the priest's alter to feed those who were with him, and himself. Read it when you have time. It is in Saint Mathew's."

"Oscar would never..."

"Oscar isn't here, Lisa. You are."

"Nay," Lisa said quickly, then again, but this time more softly, one hand worrying her lips. "I...you say...but..." She went closer to look at the meat. Suddenly she picked up a portion of it, wrapped it in the white cloth and went to place it in the cupboard. "I'll think about it," she said, as she took what she had left on the table to the big iron kettle standing to one side of the hearth. Her back to Berta she said, "If I do, I would not be able to tell the children what they are eating."

"You will tell them," Berta answered. "They know you speak the truth to them."

Lisa swung around, but Berta was on her way out. She followed her, but when she got to the door saw that Berta was getting something more out of the wagon.

"I brought some good fire wood," she announced as she came in with short cuts of logs piled up in one arm, the other hand carrying a small *firkin.*

"Berta!" Lisa exclaimed.

As Berta placed the logs quietly into the woodbox after setting the *firkin* on the table, she said, "Since you don't seem to be buying any from Albertsson anymore, I decided the children need a rest for at least one day from scouring the forest for fallen branches."

"Nothing escapes you, does it?" Lisa said, looking with love at her friend.

"Water hot in the kettle?" Berta asked, ignoring the question. Lisa nodded. Berta went back to the *firkin*. From it she lifted a brown paper sack, then went to the ledge on the hood of the fireplace and took down the coffee grinder. "I'll go outside and grind the beans while you measure out the water in the pot."

"You brought coffee too," Lisa marveled.

"Hot water and milk I can face once, or even twice, but coffee puts good Swede-Finn iron in my blood." She went out, grinning.

Somewhere between laughing and crying, Lisa poured hot water into the copper coffee pot and set it close to the fire. When Berta came to hand her the small wooden drawer out of the coffee grinder, Lisa measured the grains and stood drawing the delicious smell deep into her lungs. As soon as the coffee boiled she withdrew it from the fire, found her mug and stood holding it, waiting for the steeping to be done. Berta waited next to her. After the first swallow of the hot black brew, her eyes closed in appreciation. Lisa smiled at her friend, then drank deeply again. When she finished, she poured another half a mug for herself and offered to pour more for Berta, who shook her head. Before drinking again, Lisa said, "Berta, today I accept what you bring, and I thank you deeply for myself and my children, as well as for the people in there. But you must not take me and my family as your responsibility."

Berta heard the pride.

"You don't hestitate to ask for food for others, Lisa, but you never ask anything for yourself," she answered. "If you need my help it is only as far away as that telephone central board."

"I know, Berta, I never forget it."

They drank, watching the fire.

"No word?"

"Hmm! I would have sent your telephone jumping off its hook should I have had another letter," Lisa said, with a dry laugh. "That one letter I got from Oscar, that came through Sweden, said he needed to keep what money he had in case the Swedish government wanted him to send them some to get us out of Finland. His petition to them, asking that they return us to Sweden because of the war danger here, apparently hasn't been heard yet. At least I haven't heard anything more."

"Mmm," Berta murmured, then said, "you know, it might be better for you to stay right here in Finland until the war ends. That boat on its way to Sweden, last week, got blown up, by a mine that got torn loose in the big storm. My two young people are here, thank heavens, from their summer in Stockholm, and back at school in Åbo.

"If the papers come, we will go. It is not my decision, but Oscar's, with God's help."

Suddenly Lisa set her mug down on the hearth, her mouth working, her eyes wet. She turned to Berta, clutched her arms and laid her head on her shoulder, her face turned away from Berta's. Too startled to set her coffee down, Berta placed her free hand on Lisa's head and pressed it closer to her. Gasps of agony came from Lisa's open mouth, diminishing in intensity as she swallowed them, until she stood quietly, her breathing short and loud, until that too became silent.

She pushed herself away.

"It has been too much for you. These people here, and you so alone with your children," Berta soothed. "They should have sent them somewhere else."

"Perhaps," Lisa said, "but whoever decided no doubt thought a small house with many children would not be the place to look. It is over," she finished, and avoided looking at Berta by reaching for her coffee and encircling the mug with both hands, as if in search of warmth to end the shaking that threatened to engulf her. She raised the mug to her lips, but could not drink for drawing in shuddering gasps of air.

"You are a brave woman, Lisa," Berta told her. "It is no wonder this last event made you break down for a few moments."

"It was my loneliness for Oscar," Lisa declared, when she could answer, "your friendship, and thinking of those wonderful people sleeping in there. I'm all right now. Oscar used to say I was like a big water barrel keeping everything inside until suddenly I spilled over like an ocean." She could not bring herself to tell Berta her biggest trouble.

"If that was an ocean spilling, Carl's chip of wood he calls a boat, is a steamship," Berta answered. "Thank you for letting me be the place to spill it."

She went to pick up the bag she had carried the food in, and pushed the small *firkin* on the table toward Lisa.

"Here are eggs," she explained, "for them in there, and enough so each of you can have one also."

Overcome, Lisa could only shake her head and look her thanks.

"Give them in there," Berta continued, nodding her head at the bedroom door, "my wishes for their safe arrival in Sweden." She lifted a hand in a quick gesture of farewell and left.

*

"You can talk about it all you want now," Lisa told the children as she lit the kerosene lamp and replaced its chimney. For perhaps five or ten minutes all of them had been sitting quietly in the room, lighted only by the sputtering flames on the hearth. "They must be well on their way and they haven't seen anyone, or they would have turned back."

There was a collective intake of air into young lungs. The girls had been careful to take shallow breaths in order to listen. The sound of the visitors' feet taking them away from the house, and the silence that followed, had become like an extra part of the room exclusively the possession of this family.

"Should we?" Maria asked in an exaggerated whisper. "Maybe somebody could be listening."

"No one is listening," Lisa answered, "but if it makes you feel any better why don't you all go out to the toilet now, then make a circle of the house. You'll sleep better for it."

The four girls and Johan crowded out through the door, leaving Carl and the youngest behind. Lisa urged them out also and followed with the lamp, telling herself it was to make sure they had their turn in the toilet.

It was past nine o'clock and still the talk went on about the day's happening. In imitation of his morning adventure, Carl had worn himself out by galloping around and around the table where the others sat. The youngest tried to ape him, but her coordination was not up to his stepping. She contented herself by running behind him, stumbling often.

"Circle the rocking chair for a while," Emilia suggested, when his galloping had lasted too long. Without a break in his stride he altered course, the youngest deserting him to climb up into Lisa's lap. At that Lisa got up and put both of them to bed.

When they were all back in the house, Paulina said, "Mamma, you never told us before about that other time."

"I know," Lisa answered. "Pappa brought people to the house when you were all asleep. He thought it best that way. Then if anyone asked, you could say honestly you had not seen anyone."

"We wouldn't have told," Emilia said.

"He knew that, but he wanted to spare you the need to tell what was not true. He was right."

"Did the Cossacks come then too?" Johan asked.

"Nay. This is the first time I've ever seen Cossacks since I came back to Finland."

"Me too," the boy told her, as if he had seen Cossacks before. His eyes were big with the memory of the morning scene. "I'm glad I didn't have to ride on one of those horses."

Paulina interrupted the laughter, choking off her own "Nyeh, nyeh, nyeh," with "I'm happy about what we did for those people today. I felt so good when I helped carry the hot food into the bedroom to them... Pork is delicious, Mamma."

"Sinfully so," Maria added, and defended her statement with, "I can't help it if it is," when Emilia and Marta looked at her with curled lips.

"You ate it when you were little, didn't you, Mamma?" Emilia asked.

"All the time. My mamma, your *mormor,* had many wonderful ways to fix it."

"God didn't strike her down, did he?" Marta asked.

"She did not believe as we do, child. He does not punish the unenlightened."

The girls exchanged glances. Maria seemed to have been chosen to ask her something more.

"Will he punish you for letting us have some, and us for eating it?"

"Perhaps God is trying me as he did Job, but if there is an atonement to make I will make it. We will pray and live our lives by His word the best we can."

"I'm not going to eat any more of it," Emilia declared, pounding her fist on the table, so like an action of Oscar's that Lisa smiled.

"You'll eat it, all of you, and stay strong so you can be of help to me," she said. "To bed now, but first let me say one thing more. We have talked all we are going to about today's happening. Your lips are not to open again about it after tonight. Not to others, not to me, not even among yourselves."

"If pappa was here," Johan boasted, his chin pushed out in belligerence, "he'd make those Cossacks stay away from us."

"Johan, the Cossacks do what the Tzar says, not what anyone else tells them. Pappa would say what I am saying now. Do you understand you are not to talk about them?"

The boy nodded, slightly crestfallen, but appeased as Lisa reached out to him and stroked his hair back from his forehead.

"You all understand now that we don't talk about it? If we don't, then we can't let something slip when someone else is within hearing. Yaw?"

Everybody nodded.

"This is our secret, and Berta's," she added. "I want you to keep it that way."

Serious, they all agreed. They knew they had been given a special trust.

"By the way," Lisa continued, as they got up to go to bed. She went to the cupboard and from it took the small *firken* of Berta's and held it so they would come and look into it. Eight eggs nestled against the straw it held. "Berta's gift to you," she said, as they gasped in surprise.

"But I saw you cook the eggs she brought," Johan said. "I even saw the people put two each in their pockets."

"You're not to talk about them!" Emilia shouted, giving him a push.

"It's all right tonight, Emilia," Lisa reminded her. "I did cook eggs for them to take, besides potatoes in their skins. But Berta brought enough so all of us can each have one. You'll have to thank Berta when next you see her."

"We will," they shouted, and went off to bed arguing which was the most delicious way to have an egg cooked. They reached no agreement, not even how long it had been since they had seen an egg.

It was Emilia's turn to sleep with Lisa. When the girl was settled in the sofa bed, Lisa went to the central and called Berta.

"You are home?" she asked, when Berta answered. "I need to walk. I want to see you... Nay, don't do that. I want to walk."

The call disconnected, she went to bend over Emilia. "I'm going to Berta's, you heard me tell her. I'm sure the Cossacks will not be back this way so you need not worry. If the central rings I hope you hear it, so Maria won't have to come running out of the bedroom."

"I'll hear it," the girl answered, and snuggled further under the covers. "Tell Berta I'm going to have mine hard-boiled."

Lisa smiled, put on her shawl and went out. She was soon too warm as she strode the damp ruts of the road stiffening in the early cold of beginning autumn. Gusts of wind pounced on her, made her breathe deeply, and helped to clear her mind, giving her courage to tell Berta what worried her so terribly.

"No one threw golden apples to delay you," Berta commented, as Lisa stepped in the door. She got up out of the armchair she was sitting in, the cat in her lap jumping out to stretch and yawn in front of her. She lifted the book in her hand waving it as she explained. "Greek mythology. I've been reading about Atalanta, and how a young man outwitted her."

"What a pity," Lisa responded, and walked over to the fire to warm her hands in its blaze, and without giving herself time to think, and thereby hesitate, said, "I need help to outwit Albertsson."

"Albertsson? I'm here. I'm ready," Berta answered, without asking anything further. She reached into the hearth to pick up the coffee pot and filled two cups already set out on a table near her chair.

As Lisa accepted one of the cups she turned her back to the fire and gazed around the room.

"I'm sure Oscar thinks of your place often, Berta, and wishes he could run over and borrow some more books. Even in the home I worked in, in Sweden, there weren't this many. Every wall is full of shelves. You don't have a space left to put any more."

"I'll build more if need be. In the vestibule if nowhere else, but there is still room for books in my bedroom. Have a *hjortron*-filled pastie. I don't bake often but when I do I make enough to last me awhile. Here, put more berries on it to freshen it up." She held a cut glass bowl toward Lisa, a large silver spoon in the mound of orange-red cloudberries drenched in sugar.

"*Hjortron!* What a treat. The children haven't found many this year."

"I'm afraid this is the last I will find. It is late for them now."

Lisa helped herself and bit into the pastie, and declared the crust was delicate and most tasteful. "Delicious," she complimented. "You are a fine baker." As she sat down in a chair near the one Berta had been sitting in she teased, "They are almost as good as mine."

"Never," Berta said in return, with a big smile, "you are the best baker in the land. Your blueberry *piirakka* is...mmm...heaven in itself."

"You have to thank the Karelian Finns for that. It is their dish and recipe." But her pleased smile denied her faint protest.

"Albertsson," Berta said, picking up her coffee and coming to stand in front of Lisa, saucer in one hand, the other holding the cup. "How or why are we to outwit him."

Lisa set her coffee and pastie down, laced her hands together, and looked up at her friend.

"In a few days I must pay rent in order to stay there. I can't do it. I don't have the money. What's more, I don't want to stay there."

Berta settled on the edge of her chair, in front of Lisa, their knees almost touching. "I've told you I'll be glad to give you money."

"Not give, loan me money if that is what I have come for," Lisa corrected her, "but that isn't why I'm here."

"What then? However I can help, I am happy to do it."

"When you live so close to other people you learn things about them they'd rather not have you know, and which you'd rather not know yourself. Something happened between Albertsson and us that I'm not going to tell you. It would anger you too much. But, if there is any way you can help me find another place to live, I would be eternally grateful. I have one more payment coming from the telephone company, and if I could find a place where rent would be very cheap, I could probably manage until Oscar's next bank draft."

Berta heard her out, realized she had used the word 'us' instead of 'me', and knew that somehow the children were involved in whatever had happened with Albertsson.

"You needn't tell me, of course, but how would your moving to another place outwit Albertsson?" she asked. "Did he do something when he was drunk?"

"He did," Lisa answered, her hands clenched in her lap. "I faced him with it when he was almost sober. He's never forgiven me for that. He can't pretend with me that he doesn't remember what he does when he's drunk. He still manages to terrorize Jenny so she doesn't ever face him with the results of his drunken acts. Not even that he crippled his own son. He knows that I know about that too. The boy was in bed for days after it happened, and Jenny too afraid to call the doctor."

Berta nodded. Everybody knew about that terrible incident.

Lisa hesitated, wiping her face with a cloth from her pocket. She gulped coffee. Berta waited.

"He knows it can't be long before I won't have enough money to pay him," Lisa went on. "He's waiting, won't hesitate to throw us out. I can't let that happen again to the children... Do you know of any place? You get around all over and would know if there is a place for us."

"I might," Berta began, "but the one I have in mind is probably too small. Only one room, with a shed entrance that can't be heated."

"It wouldn't matter how small it is. Where is it? Whose is it?" In her eagerness Lisa leaned forward and grasped one of Berta's knees.

"Mine," Berta answered, and got up. "I'll take you there and you can judge for yourself."

"Now?" Lisa asked. "Where is it?"

"Not far, but too far to walk. Have another cup of coffee while I hitch up the horse." Without waiting for Lisa to say anything more she put on her knit cap and her jacket and went out. "Have another pastie," she suggested before she closed the door.

Lisa sat staring at the fire, tension easing out of her, until at last she got up, filled her cup and took another pastie. As the pungent sweet taste of the berries filled her mouth she remembered Maria's remark, that pork was sinfully delicious. Anything that tasted as good as this, she smiled, must also be sinful. She swallowed with eyes closed in appreciation, listened for Berta's return and took another one.

Beside Berta on the high seat of the wagon ten minutes later, Lisa saw the glory of the risen moon. It lay in pale wash over the long wide fields of grain that stood ripe and heavy for harvest on each side of the narrow lane. The night had become a friendly place to be in, the wind an accompaniment for their two voices, the swish of the grain stalks a memory of the sound of the sea.

"I lease this land to a farmer," Berta explained. "Maybe you know him? Henning Holgersson."

"Nay, although I've heard his name."

"He'll be mowing here soon, but that won't bother you if you decide to move to this place. Be sure, Lisa, if it is too small say so. I can look elsewhere."

They rode in silence until Berta asked, "How did it go with the children and the pork?"

Lisa gave her a quick look then looked straight ahead, a smile lifting the corners of her mouth. "They gorged, but only after I assured them it was neither Nasse, nor one of her offspring."

Berta roared, her head lifted to the sky. The horse increased its pace thinking the sound was directive to hurry. Berta pulled him up.

"They ate so much," Lisa continued, "after they put the sin of it behind them, that I was afraid they would get sick. Especially Emilia, who has a sensitive stomach, and Johan, who does not like to eat fat. How I wish he would. He remains so thin."

"What about you. Did you eat it?"

Lisa gave Berta a sly glance in the moonlight. "Oscar isn't here. I am," she answered.

Berta whooped, lifted the whip from its socket and twirled it overhead until the long end made a wild whirring sound. The horse was startled into a run. This time Berta let it go. Lisa hung on with both hands, laughing as happily as Berta. The wagon clattered over the rough lane and was brought to a halt next to a small cabin.

They sat looking at it.

"People lived in it long ago," Berta remarked, and added, "it might not be good enough for you."

Without answering Lisa got down. In the moonlight the cabin loomed big and black, but she could see it was built of gray peeled logs in the manner of ancient builders, and was indeed small. Berta came with two lanterns she took from under the wagon seat and lit the candles in them. She handed one to Lisa, went to the cabin and lifted down the huge key that hung beside the door, and unlocked it. Inside the shed a door to the left led into the one room. Both doors screeched with disuse as they were pushed open, their long hand-hammered hinges rusty but still holding the doors securely in place. Lisa held her lantern high and gazed around.

"It looks sound, no broken windows. The floor feels solid. Smells of mice," she commented.

"Some knots must have fallen out of the logs, leaving holes in them for the mice to get through. I'll have Olof plug them before you come."

"Oh, look at that!" Lisa exclaimed, as she saw the fireplace to the right of the doorway. "Did they stand on their heads to cook in the old days?" she asked, and went to look closer at the hearth that came no higher than the middle of her legs.

"It is impossible for you to live here," Berta insisted. "After all there are eight for you to cook for."

Lisa made no answer.

She stepped the width of the room and thought the children's three beds would fit at the furthest end, but with no space between them. In the candlelight she walked the length and placed her sofa-bed against the wall. The table would have to be uncomfortably close to the fireplace, and at night pushed out of the way so her bed could open. Yaw, it would work. The trunk could stand under the table. She would not have it out in that cold damp shed. The new clothes, still unworn, would mould. Was there something more? The rocking chair. There would be no room for that. It would have to be returned to Sigurd. Much as the children would miss it they could do without it. As for herself, she no longer needed it for sitting with a new baby to rock.

At this thought she quailed. The lantern held high above her head, she stared unseeing into the gloom. Her ears told her Berta spoke, her mind recognized only that she could bear another child. America could mean she would be pregnant again. Every month she was reminded of that. She felt as if she had spoken, as she had done beneath the windmill.

She lowered her lantern so swiftly the candle was snuffed out.

"Here, let me relight it," Berta said, "I was saying, let me look for another place for you. You can't possibly fit into this one room."

"It is fine. I want it. How much will you charge?"

"Charge, Lisa! This has been standing here perhaps more than a hundred years without much use to anyone. I don't want any money for it."

"How much? I will not move here unless I pay. I might have to ask you to wait for it, if Oscar's money doesn't come soon, but pay for it I will sooner or later."

"All right, all right," Berta responded, lifting both hands in exasperation as she handed the lighted lantern back, and shook hers into a quivering light. "We will talk of that on our way back. Let's go out and see the toilet. I know the pump works and the water is good, for Holgerson uses it. I'll have Olof clean up in here and fix whatever needs to be done. When do you want to move here?"

"This coming Saturday when the children can help. That will be almost a week before Albertsson will be wanting his rent. I have to inform the telephone company too. Maybe Jenny would like to have it in the farmhouse, she enjoys it so much. I'll miss that money, but there is no other way. It's never been enough to pay the rent each month, but it always helped. Pray with me, Berta, that Oscar sends that money, or that the papers arrive soon."

"I do," Berta answered abruptly.

After a quick visit to inspect the toilet house, they agreed it was in good repair. A scrubbing was all it needed. They went to the well. They took turns pumping, and filled their cupped hands to taste the icy water that flowed clear and cold in the moonlight.

Berta locked the door to the shed again, and hung up the key. They went back to the wagon.

"I'll help you move," she told Lisa, as she flicked the reins and the horse strained to roll the wagon forward.

"You have enough to do," Lisa answered. "I'm going to call Emile Makela to come move us. He can use his big wagon with two horses. He can do it in one trip. I know he will be willing, and can wait for pay until I have the money. He's a good friend too. I can reach him by telephone. He recently got one."

"If you need my help don't hesitate."

"My dear friend, this is help enough. My heartfelt thanks."

"I'll take you home."

"Not at all, I will walk when we get back to the road." But Berta would not listen. They compromised. She took her halfway home before turning back.

"Sleep well this night," Berta said, as they shook hands after Lisa climbed down from the wagon.

"You too," she answered, looking up at Berta's silhouette against the light sky, "and may our three friends also find refuge and sleep in safety all this night."

"Amen," Berta responded, and clucked the horse into a sharp turn to point the wagon back toward the pig farm.

*

The weather turned warm again after the move to the old cabin. Lisa's only regret was that it was too far to visit Katarina, or for her to come. Besides, Katarina was ailing. But otherwise there was more company, at first, than in any of the other places they had lived. Harvesting the grain had begun a few days before their move. Two families, parents and children, came with scythes and began mowing. Slowly sheaves took the place of waving grain, first close to the cabin, then off into the furthest corner of the fields.

The pump became a gathering place. Here Lisa visited. Sometimes she took a scythe and worked at mowing, to give a woman a rest. The remembered rhythm of the strokes was quickly reborn. The strong feel of the wooden handles was good to her hands, the heat of the sun a soothing lotion to the pleasant tiredness in her back. She stopped now and then to listen to the far-off call of the cuckoo, and waved to her two young ones who played with others too young to help in the fields. When the mowing was finished the long rows of sheaves became her only company.

Loneliness was hers again. Up earlier than ever to get the children on their way to school, because they had much further to walk, the days became long before they returned.

One day Berta came with a load of wood. Together they stacked it in the shed.

"I will pay for this when the money comes," Lisa told her as she invited her in to have hot water and milk.

"I brought some coffee beans with me," Berta said, and in quick apology added, "you must let me indulge my own tase when I am here."

"All right, but I will not use it except when you come to visit."

"Stubborn!" Berta scolded.

They sat on the stoop in front of the shed drinking the coffee. Berta set her emptied mug down on the ground.

"I will be gone for some weeks, Lisa. First to Hälsingborg on business, then to visit my children. They grow away from me, as they should, but when I see you with yours I begin to think I'm doing wrong in letting them go so soon. I miss them. But, if I'm to see them at all, I must go to them."

Lisa consoled her friend. "Perhaps if I had money enough to send mine off to school, and summers elsewhere, I would do it too."

"Mmmm, perhaps."

"I'm thinking I might have to take the three oldest out of school, if it's possible to find work for them."

"Lisa, don't do that," Berta pleaded, and got up swiftly. Her legs, in their polished Russian boots and dark pants, were like two strong pillars between Lisa and the gold stubble left in the grain fields. "Borrow from me, if you have to, but keep them in school."

Lisa waved a hand next to her ear to silence Berta.

"I won't do it easily, I assure you. There aren't many hiring, what with the lack of work the blockade is causing, and besides that, everyone knows we are soon to leave for Sweden. They wouldn't want to take on help that won't be staying."

"Wait until I'm back?"

"I will do what I have to ," Lisa answered, and held out her hand for help to stand up. "What is Hälsingborg like? It would have been good to see Finland's capital city before we left the country. It must be a splendid big town."

"It is. The Finns can be proud of their capital they call Helsinki. What I'm curious about, this time that I go there, is to see what the blockade had done to it. With boats idle in the harbors, lumbermills closed, lumber stacked high in the yards, Hälsingborg must be severly affected. Wish you could come see it with me."

"How I would enjoy that. Impossible, but kind of you to say it. Send me a letter and tell me what is happening there. It would be good to hear from you."

"A letter, even if it isn't Oscar's," Berta teased, but kindly, a sympathetic hand on Lisa's shoulder.

"Ack, who knows? There may be one before you come back. We might even be on our way. But, tell me, what is the news of the war?"

"The Russians have given the Austrians a drubbing, and the Germans have been stopped, at least temporarily, at the River Marne in France."

"Can we hope it will be over soon then?"

"I doubt it. The Allies grow, yet Germany seems determined to swallow every country between it and the ocean."

Lisa picked up the empty coffee mug on the ground as she shook her head in despair. "War, the disease of the rulers. They send the young to kill the young. I thank God every night that Finland and Sweden are not in it, and pray that it will end soon."

"Let us hope so," Berta agreed. "I didn't have an easy moment while my two were on their way here on the Baltic. There could be more loose mines floating out there. Can't tell you how relieved I'll be when you and yours are safely across."

"Yaw," Lisa said, her longing for that day plainly visible.

"Well, then, I must go. You'll be all right here?"

"We're all right. Don't worry. Just write me a letter."

"I'll do it." Berta smiled and went off in the wagon.

Rains began, and the cold came.More and more the three beds, fitted so snugly at the end of the room, became the playground for the younger ones. The older ones sought that space and comfort also to study their schoolwork. Like visiting sheep, they sat hunched under the fur skins as they read or wrote. When their hands became too cold to write they teamed up to play clap hands. Facing each other, legs folded under them, knees touching, they began by slapping both hands down on their knees, then together, then crisscrossing and slapping first the right, then the left hand of their partner with their own right and left hands. They continued through the game until their hands were stinging with warmth.

Maria and Emilia were the best. Their hands would fly so fast, Lisa remarked more than once that she could not see them. Paulina's laughter would throw her rhythm off, and she soon would miss, collapsing in a welter of nyeh, nyeh, nyehs. Marta was learning swiftly to keep up, but Johan was impossible.

"Go turn handsprings," Emilia told him when he tried. He was apt to do this, anywhere, a new art he had learned from a friend at school. He knew better than to try on the beds, with Lisa right there.

Lisa worked in the narrow space between the table and the low fireplace, face flushed from stoooping to see and stir what food she had to cook.

Late one afternoon the children came running, shouting in a way that made Lisa put her knitting down and hurry to the door. She could make out their call, "No letter." That call, day after day, was a bitter disappointment she had trained herself not to show. But this time there was something more. An urgency in their lengthened shouting.

"What is it?" she called, from the open shed door, "Maria, what is it you're all saying?"

Panting, Maria told her. "The storekeeper...said...he won't sell us anything more...unless we pay for it when we get it."

"What did he say, exactly, or was it his wife who said it?" she asked.

"They both did," they all exclaimed.

"Ya so," she said, went in and sat down.

The children followed her. She tried to smile at them, but didn't quite manage. Hands on her knees she studied the floor, then pushed herself up to go to the hearth and stir the last of the rice she had cooked for supper.

"Where will we go to buy food, Mamma?" Maria asked.

"Get your bowls," she told everyone, and lifted the pot to put it on two flat pieces of wood she had placed on the end of the table. Without looking at the anxious faces she ladled out the rice and handed the bowls back without speaking. When she sat down to her own supper, she said, "I'll go see them tonight, Maria. I'll use the bicycle."

"The bicycle?" Maria said in surprise. "Can you ride a bicycle?"

"I've never seen you ride it," Johan told her, looking in vain for *knäckebröd*. Although it had been days since there had been any, he still looked.

"I can ride," Lisa told them. "I used to ride with Pappa in Sweden before any of you were born. I think I can do it again."

When the rice was eaten she asked Maria to take the bicycle out from the shed. The children crowded outdoors to watch her leave.

"It's so wet, and the lane so narrow, maybe you should walk the bicycle until you get to the big road," Paulina suggested.

"I'll manage," Lisa answered, still standing with one leg on each side of the bicycle. When she got her right foot firmly on the pedal she pushed down hard and sat quickly on the seat. The bicycle wobbled from side to side. Lisa twisted the handlebars rapidly to keep it upright. Johan and Emilia stumbled against each other with laughter. Marta ran after her yelling, "Don't fall, don't fall!" Maria ran alongside, hands ready to catch her if she did. Paulina, holding the youngest by the hand, turned on her twin and brother and shamed them into silence. Lisa applied more strength into her pedaling. The bicycle straightened out and sped down one rut on the lane. They all cheered.

"She didn't wave," Marta complained

"She couldn't. She'd have landed on her back in the stubble if she had," Emilia said with scorn.

"Ya so, *Fru* Veldman," the storekeeper greeted Lisa when, hot and spattered with mud on legs and shirt, she walked into the store. There was an uneasy welcome on his face. "It's a long time since we've seen you. You ride bicycle? It's several kilometers from Holgersson's grain fields here."

"So it is," Lisa answered, and asked, "you're not going to let us have any more credit?"

The welcome on his face was erased as if by lightning.

"How can you guarantee I will ever get paid for it?" he asked, and stepped back behind the counter as if she would accost him physically.

"You know Oscar will send me the money."

"All I know is that boats get sunk between here and Sweden. Besides, he hasn't sent you a letter for too long. Nay, *Fru* Veldman, there are plenty here now who buy without paying me. But they do not mean to run off to Sweden if they can."

His wife came rushing out from the back room before Lisa could respond.

"Off to Narpes she can go to buy shoes, hats, coats with her American money, but here she buys nothing except piddling amounts of food, with not a hard coin to ring on the counter. Where is the American money for us? Go home and come back when you can pay us. Eat those fancy clothes and see if we care."

From *Fru* Svensson's angry eyes to his cold ones, Lisa looked at the couple in turn as she swallowed words of defense. Her face felt still with the effort to do it. In as normal a voice as she could, she said, "Beeda Gran has indeed been busy. Will you give me flour and sugar in return for the bicycle?"

"Nay," the storekeeper said without hesitation.

"Wait," his wife contradicted him. "Our Emma is old enough, by spring, to have a bicycle. I'm willing. If the war goes on there won't be bicycles to buy. You know that, Tomas. How much flour and sugar?"

"All I can carry. Three kinds of flour for *palt,*" Lisa laid the sack she had brought on the counter.

"*Palt?* You have blood?" the wife asked.

"We don't eat blood. I make it without."

"Hmph, some more of that Swede's religion. Get it for her, Tomas."

Refusing to be drawn into further talk Lisa went over to the flour bins and waited. As each kind was ladled into separate small sacks she weighed them with her eyes, judging how much she could carry. The same with the sugar, shaking her head when the storekeeper asked if what she wanted was a cone of it.

While the two new owners of the bicycle went to wheel it in, Lisa slung the sack on her back. It was heavy. She arranged her shawl over it with difficulty, afraid that it might rain before she reached home.

"It's Mamma, she's home," someone shouted when she stumbled against the shed door, too tired to try to find the latch. All but the youngest were still up, worn with worry and waiting.

"Here, let me take the sack," someone offered, and the burden was lifted, making her stagger. Someone else led her to the bench nearest the fire. Other hands removed her muddy shoes. A pan of warm water was set on the table, the towel and soap laid alongside.

"Just let me sit," she gasped, slowly straightening her back, then easing it down into a restful curve again. "Make coffee," she said, "Berta won't mind."

When its aroma reached her she found the strength to stand to wash her hands and face. She asked for the comb, and when it came took the pins out and unwound her hair. Paulina would not let her comb it herself. Gently, Emilia standing alongside and hissing through her teeth when a snarl had to be combed out, Paulina brought order to the tangled wet hair.

After the first swallow of coffee Lisa breathed deeply, then told them, "We shall have *palt* to eat," and waved her hand at the sack that lay forgotten at the end of the table, where someone had lifted it.

"Hurrah!" the girls shouted, and together descended on the sack to pull out the bags of flour and sugar. Sleepy-eyed Johan came to lean against Lisa with a big smile.

"I'll go put the bicycle away," Maria was inspired to offer.

"Wait," Lisa called to her. "The bicycle bought the food. I walked back, that's why I took so long."

All movement stopped in the room. Then, silently, the girls took the bags of flour and sugar and placed them in the cupboard. They understood. Maria came back from the door.

"Tomorrow," Lisa said, "the two little ones and I will go to Ivarsson's farm and see if we can get butter to go with the *palt*. Now, let's everybody get to bed."

But the next day at Ivarsson's farm she was denied the butter, at first.

"I will pay for it before I leave for Sweden," she reasoned with *Fru* Ivarsson.

"My man says, nay." The round, dimpled face of that farmer's wife was cross, her full red lips pulled inward to tighten the resolve of denying this rebel from the church any help. Her heavy arms made themselves too busy slamming covers on pots that stood bubbling on the hearth. The smell of beets, and of meat cooking, made Lisa's mouth water. *Fru* Ivarsson went on, bent over to look into a pot. "It's hard times we have in Finland with ships standing still, and too many coming here to buy without money."

She glanced up angrily and saw Carl and the youngest peering from behind Lisa's skirts. Lisa turned to leave.

"Here, then," *Fru* Ivarsson said, and slapped a large pat of butter, she scooped out of the wooden butter *firken* with a wooden spatula, onto a piece of paper she took from on top the wood box. Without wrapping it she shoved it down the table toward Lisa.

"I will pay for it, you can be sure," Lisa told her, and folded the paper carefully around the yellow mound.

"Ack, forget it," *Fru* Iversson answered and looked once again at the children.

"I will pay," Lisa told her once more as she closed the door.

Homeward bound she took her time, let the children stray into the woods to find interesting twigs, and to see if they could scare up a moose, something Johan had once told Carl he could do. Their excitement was just as large when all he managed to scare was a squirrel. Too engrossed in her own thoughts, she paid small attention to their excited chatter. It had been a mistake to go to Ivarssons' although it was the closest farm to the cabin. Ivar Ivarsson was a rigid supporter of the church. He would not take kindly to helping anyone he considered infidel. Next time she would try Abelssons' whose farm was a greater distance, but who were lesser believers, and also knew of Oscar's support for Finland's independence.

The joy of *palt* with butter lasted for many days, but began to pall when the big dumplings cooked in salt water were the constant food at each meal. Sliced and reheated, and served with lingonberries picked the previous summer, helped somewhat to make it seem a different dish. Talk about herring, meatballs, rice pudding, but mostly potatoes, became the main conversation at mealtime.

Lisa took the beautiful china dish out of the trunk where it was stored and went with the two young ones to Abelssons'. She came back smiling with meat and potatoes, but also with the dish. They had told her she could come back for more and pay when she could.

That supper Paulina said, with her mouth full, "I don't want to swallow, it tastes so good."

"I wish I had my mouth right here," Maria said, pointing with her wooden spoon at her stomach, "then I could just empty the whole pot of potatoes from my plate right into it. I wouldn't have to chew so much, but feel full and good right away."

Lisa ate and gave the children second helpings. Soon she would have to send word to Katarina for help if that money did not come. Katarina was not well, the change in her monthly bleeding draining her of strength. She spent much time in bed, something strange for that strong woman. Her eyes weeped, the skin around them raw and red from constant wiping with as soft a cloth as she could find. Lisa had walked the there two different Saturdays when the children were home, but had returned each time so worn and tired she had to give up going. How she yearned to be of help to her sister who had done so much for her. But it was too far for the two young ones to walk, and Sigurd's horse had other duties.

To ask for help at the pig-farm was impossible. Berta did not know that Olaf Davidsson, who was in charge while she was gone, was not a friend to the Veldmans. He kept it quiet around Berta, but he and his wife had been ugly to Oscar, one time, when he had visited them with his Bible. Not that they were such church goers, but they had yelled at him, "You, Veldman, have no business acting like a superior Swede coming around trying to teach us the right and wrong of the world and the Word." Thanks be, Olaf had been kind to the twins when they worked at the farm, but only just.

Nay, she would have the girls send word through Eva, Katarina's youngest, in school. What worried her was that Katarina might get up out of her sick bed and come that long hard distance. It might do her harm sitting on that rattling wagon if Sigurd pushed his old horse into the journey. Yaw, come they would, she was certain, even though the blockade was beginning to affect their supplies too, she knew.

Dear God, help us. Where is your letter, Osacar?

A few afternoons later the children shouted, "It's come! It's come!" as they raced toward the cabin. Lisa ran out to meet them, the big stirring spoon still in her hand, her other hand reaching for the envelope she knew one of them must be carrying.

"It's from the King of Sweden," Emilia shouted, "not from Pappa."

"The King?" Lisa exclaimed, her eyes searching among them for the envelope. "You nean...yaw! Our papers! To go to Sweden. Who has the letter?"

"The storekeeper said he couldn't let us take it. You have to go sign for it."

"He said what? Oh, of course. I understand. All right. I'll go right off. Go in and eat. I'll hurry back. Oh my, to think it has come.

Hurry, hurry, I must go right away."

Talking, giving orders, hearing questions but unable to take the time to answer them, she pushed the children out of her way, found her shawl and was on the lane walking swiftly when she realized she had not said goodbye. She turned and waved happily to the seven who stood in front of the cabin. They raise their hands and waved wildy, shouting, "Sweden, we are going to Sweden! Hurry Mamma!"

Johann turned a cartwheel, almost successfully, in front of them. Carl, rump in the air, head on the ground tried to imitate.

*

Fru Veldman!"

Lisa lifted her head in surprise as she walked rapidly into the village the next day. It was Saturday, the children all at home. There were many places she had to go this day to get ready to leave for Sweden. The first stop had been Albertssons' farmhouse kitchen where the telephone central had been installed. Now she was enroute to Katarina's to tell her the news. To have the storekeeper call to her with smiles and a friendly voice seemed a dream that fitted the happiness of this day. Mail from Sweden's King seemed to have changed the man's attitude.

"Two letters from Sweden. From your husband's people," he called. She ran. He hurried back into the store but came to meet her halfway as she flew through the open door.

"Thanks, thanks!" she said, and laughed with him as she took the envelopes from his outstretched hand. "Excuse me, I must go to the window to read them."

She ripped one open, not bothering to decide which one would be first. Oscar's unopened letter was inside. Opened, she read it hungrily. Almost immediately she turned to tell the storekeeper and his wife, who had joined him, "My letters haven't been getting through. He says he hasn't received one in a long time."

Together they all shook their heads, clucking their tongues sorrowfully. She went back to reading.

'This is the second letter I am writing, to give you exact directions for your trip to Sweden. I sent the first one two weeks ago.'

She glanced at the other envelope but returned to reading.

'I do this to make sure one of them will reach you and help explain what the government papers will say. The Swedish Consulat in Chicago told me the papers will be sent to you along with tickets for the train in Finland, and for the boat to Sweden. When you get to Gavle, in Sweden, you must go to an office there. The address will be in the papers you get. There they will have railroad tickets waiting for you for the trip north, home. Write my brothers and one of them will meet you at the station.'

'I am not sending you money to Finland for fear it might not get there. It is safer to send it to Sweden so that it doesn't travel across the Baltic where another loose mine could send it to the bottom. How terrible it was to read about that in the papers here. How I worry about your getting across that sea. I will not breathe until I hear you are safe in Sweden. It is a torture to live through this, for you also. But we must put our trust in God. I know you will sell everything but the clothes you all need, so will have money for food on the trip.'

She nodded. Yaw, the sale was already arranged. One telephone call she had made at the farm was to Emile Makela. He, in turn, had called her back while she waited, to tell her his friend had agreed to come on Wednesday next to hold the auction. The guilt that had grown so large as day by day the children's, "No letter," call had greeted her ears, began to lessen. It had not helped that silently she scolded herself. Buying the clothes so soon had been a sinful foolishness. Telling herself she could not have known the letters would actually come to a stop had not eased her conscience. With a sigh of relief she read on.

Someone set a chair behind her, touching the backs of her knees with it to make her aware of it. Automatically she sat and tore the second letter open without looking to see who was being so kind.

The second letter held the same information, but had earlier news not repeated in the one she had just read. It was long, like a visit with Oscar, and eased the feelings of neglect, hurt, and some of the loneliness. It would take several readings to absorb all the pleasure it held for her. She tucked both letters into her pocket and stood up.

The storekeeper, his wife, and now Beeda Gran too, stood watching her. Where Beeda had come from, and when, Lisa had no idea. They all had smiles for her.

"Oscar is well," she told the trio, "and sends greetings to everyone he knows. Beeda, it is good you are here. Next Wednesday I am selling everything at auction at our place. Tell people. On Wednesday evening we take the night train to Rauma on our way to Sweden." She spoke to the storekeeper. "I'll have money to pay what we owe then. Here, take this envelope, it has Oscar's *mor's* address on it. If any more mail comes, send it there. I'll leave extra money in case you need it for that."

Accompanied by all three talking to her at once, she left the store, both the storekeeper and his wife assuring her they would take care of everything. She smiled to herself. The mail from the King, and Oscar's letters, had put friendship back into the world. She knew they came to see if she turned toward the bank, but she took the road before it that led to Katarina. Beeda scurried off somewhere, no doubt eager to spread the news of the auction, as well as the information that, at last, the Veldman family were leaving for Sweden, if not to America. It gave Lisa no concern that Beeda might twist the news for lack of hearing what was in the papers or the letters. The news of the auction would get around and that was all that mattered today.

The soft puffs of clouds in the blue sky, the dark green boughs of the familiar pine and spruce forests, the bare fields, all took on a nostalgic beauty as she walked toward the Olofssons' farm. This was the land of her birth. These were the scenes that were as much a part of her as her own children. the years spent away from here, in Sweden, seemed not to have been, as she looked with eyes that soon would never see them again. As though she gathered them like flowers, she raised her hands and with fingers slightly bent, swept the views together between her palms. She stood to look, to listen, to pull deep into her lungs the sun-enriched smell of trees and earth. To hold in her memory their every essence. She loved the land, yet yearned to leave it. Here she had been betrayed by terrible hardship, outgrowth of dishonesty, bigotry, and religious intolerance. That these were dictated by greed, by old hates for ancient conquerors, and firm belief in the established church, made them no less hard to take.

But the trees, the sky, the land, and the view there off over the Baltic beyond the long meadow holding the two windmills, were hers to take with her. To treasure with memories of childhood pranks, of escapades of youth, and of a moment of searing realization, the night she became an American widow.

With a quick rejection of that memory she hurried on. The hips of wild roses on bushes along the road, that someone had failed to gather, caught her eye. She picked a few and stored them in her pocket. How often she had cooked rose-hip soup from just such ones and served the delicious dessert to her family, not only to augment their poor fare. She wondered if there were wild rosebushes in Waukegan, along that brick paved street Oscar had described.

Alone on the road for the many kilometers she walked, she often took one or the other of the letters from her pocket to read again, before going on. Not until she saw the window of Katarina's *stuga* did the coming separation become real. She ran up the slight rise of the road to the house, burst in, and standing just inside the door looked across the room at Katarina.

Her sister stood at one end of the table pounding a wooden potato masher into a large pot in front of her. It was very warm in the room in spite of its size. The *kakelugn* was fired up for heat, and the cooking fire on the hearth was at full blaze.

"Lisa," Katarina said, the motion of her hand arrested. She wiped them on her apron, left the table and took a few steps toward her sister, but then stopped suddenly. "You have come to tell me you are leaving. you have had word."

The joy that had carried her to within sight of Katarina's house-ebbed even further as Lisa watched sadness age Katarina's face and heard the unhappiness of her voice. She went to her.

"Both from the Swedish government and from Oscar. Let me read you his letters, but first how are you? You look better than when I was here last."

Katarina nodded, and waved Lisa toward a chair before she went to set the coffe pot near the flames.

"I don't think I have any blood left in me," she said, "I flowed so hard last week. But it must be over now. I am cold all the time, but I don't flow anymore. It would be a relief if I never did again."

"So that is the way it goes?" Lisa wondered. "I hope it is over for you. But your eyes, let me see your eyes." She went to examine them in the light of the fire. "You don't wipe them as much, do you?"

"Ack, that has nothing to do with the other, I'm sure. Next time we get to Narpes I'll try to see a doctor about them. Maybe glasses would help. But that is enough about me. I am all right, just need time to warm up and get back to work. Let's hear Oscar's letters. What riches, two of them."

"They are alike in some spots, but I'll read them to you."

"You go straight to America?"

"To Sweden. For how long I don't know."

"Well, that's some comfort, even if it is false. You will be that close for a while at least. Here, sit. Drink coffee while you read."

Hands clasped together, arms on the table around her coffee cup, Katarina leaned forward and listened intently. The coffee in her cup grew cold.

"When?" she asked, the single word short and hopeless.

"Wednesday. First thing that morning we will have an auction to sell our things. We take the evening train in Narpes to Rauma. That is where the papers told me I had to go to take the boat."

Katarina pushed the coffee cup away, the coffee slopping into the saucer. "It is too soon," she cried. "Come here to us for a few days first. We have had too little time together. We won't ever see each other again."

Her words had become a whisper. With one hand she grasped Lisa's nearest wrist, and with the other she wiped her eyes rapidly with the cloth she took from behind the band of her apron. Lisa placed a hand on top of her sister's.

"We can't, Katarina. The papers from Sweden tell me I must go there to get a boat right away. We can't get there by Wednesday morning when the next boat leaves, but we can make it by Friday when there are two boats leaving. That means we must leave on Wednesday, so that on Thursday I can make sure of passage. So, you see, there is no time to come here."

"I can't live with that. Oh, Lisa, why did you marry that Swede?"

"Katarina! You saying such a thing! You know Oscar, you know what a fine man he is. Don't let me leave hearing those words from you."

"Forgive me, Lisa. It is only because I am losing you. Of course I admire Oscar, but it is because of him this is happening."

"Don't you blame him. If you do, you are against honesty, against truth. His honesty did him injury, I know that, but would you have us both be dishonest? Have him crawl to that Mangnusson?"

"Nay, nay, nay," Katarina placated, shaking her head at the anger in Lisa's voice. "I give you that you are right. Oscar is a man in a wrong world. What if the same kind of thing happens over there? What will you do then?"

"How can I know?" It is a big country, bigger than all of Scandinavia plus most of Europe, I guess. We will be all right."

"How can I let you go?" Katarina cried, and raised her hands to cup Lisa's face.

"If only you and Sigurd would come to America too," Lisa cried in return, pressed Katarina's hands tighter.

"America! Never. What makes you say that?" Katarina moved away to look at her sister with astonishment.

"I only this moment thought of it," Lisa admitted, "because it is just as hard for me to leave you. In Sweden I could always think that somehow we would see each other again. And we did. But, America.

It is so far. Seldom does anyone come here from that country. I know of only one, someone Oscar told me about. Oh, Katarina, I would go with joy if I knew you were coming someday too."

"And I could look with some happiness to the future if you could tell me you will all try to come back when times are better. Does Osacar never talk of such a possibility?"

"Nay, he never has."

"This is where you should be. This is your land."

"Not any longer. These are not my people any more."

"Aiy, yaiy, yaiy," Katarina murmured. "Have you been that hurt? You leave many good friends here."

"That is true, and they I will always remember. It is as hard to leave them as it is to leave you, almost."

Katarina got up. "Sigurd should be in soon for coffee. I had better heat it up again."

"Wait. I hope he doesn't come too soon. I have somthing else I need to talk to you about, I am very troubled."

Katarina sat down again.

Lisa placed both hands, one on top of the other over her coffee cup, as though preventing Katarina from pouring more into it. "You see," she began, looking down at her hands, "I can still have a child. It worries me so much." She sat silent. Katarina said nothing either, but sat waiting. "I long to be with Oscar, but I crawl up into a hard knot inside myself at the thought of another birth. How can I avoid becoming pregnant?"

"Have you told him your feelings?" Katarina asked severely.

"Oh, I have. The night before he left. He understood then, and it was why I could be sure when he left that I was not with child. But there is no way I can avoid him when I get there. I wouldn't want to. I love him dearly and want him as much as he wants me." Lisa's face was flushed at speaking of such feelings, even to her sister.

"But you must deny him, and yourself."

"Nay!"

"Anything else is sin to you, isn't it?"

Lisa nodded.

"Have you written to him these feelings?"

"I keep wondering if I should. It would make him unhappy. He looks forward so to my getting there, and I know, Katarina, I know so sure in my heart, he has never gone to another woman."

"That I believe," Katarina agreed. "He lives by what he preaches. If only he interpreted the Bible to..." She hesitated, then pounding a knee with one fist she continued, "if only the Bible read that the twelfth child and all the ones following, should be birthed by the husband, he would get busy doing it, and you would have no more birthing to worry about after that." She returned her sister's startled stare, Lisa's mouth wide opened in surprise. Suddenly they were both laughing, uncontrollably.

"Can't you see it?" Lisa asked, getting up to go grasp Katarina by one shoulder and lean over her. They filled the big room with their laughter, leaning against each other. When the laughing was about to stop they started in again, as wildly as before.

"It would...come...right out...through...the..." Lisa gasped.

"Of course," Katarina agreed, and held one finger out straight in front of her.

"Oh, oh, oh," Lisa moaned her hands on her stomach. "If Oscar or Sigurd should hear or see us."

"Maybe that is where our mistake is," Katarina sobered enough to respond, as she wiped her eyes again. "Women need to talk more about these things. Together, and with their husbands. I can't give you any other advice than what I have. Oscar wouldn't appreciate it if I did, I'm afaird."

"I suppose so." Lisa got a sly look as she said, "But now you don't have to worry, do you? You don't have to threaten Sigurd with sleeping in the barn anymore, right?"

"Ack!" Katarina scoffed, and got up to push the kettle of rutabaga back and forth on the hearth as though she was not sure where it should stand. "We are too old for such things, Sigurd and I."

"You are only two years older than I am, and I still have those feelings. I'm sure you have them too, but you just won't let yourself know it. Think of Sigurd."

"Hush! I don't want to talk about it." Katarina gave the kettle a final push, then turned to Lisa. "I have something for you." Her cloth at her eyes, she walked to a cupboard at the end of the big room. She came back to hold between her outspread hands their Mamma's Sunday shawl. "I want you to have it now. Whenever you see it or wear it I want you to remember our mamma had twelve children. Don't you do the same. Eleven is more than enough."

The black taffeta rustled. The intricately tied fringe of black jet beads reflected pinpoints of light as they swayed in front of Lisa.

She took it and with a cry stood up and clasped her sister to her. Each of them murmured words undefinable to the ear but expressing their love for each other.

Lisa visited long before starting back home. Reread the letters for Sigurd, and was assured that the horse would be able to bring them to the auction.

"And to the train?"

"We will come early in the day," Katarina said, "and say goodbye then. I could not face coming to the train and crying like a fool in front of everybody."

"All right, but what of ours do you want to keep? After all most of it came from your barn."

"Sell it all, even Mamma's trunk. You need the money to get you in comfort to Sweden."

"We'll bring the rocking chair to sell too. It sits out there in the barn," Sigurd said.

"And the cradle," Katarina added, the two women exchanging a long look.

"Thank you. How terrible it is to be leaving you." As Katarina threatened to begin crying, Lisa stood up hurriedly, and said, "I must get back to the children. Thank you again for Mamma's shawl. I will treasure it always."

It was early dark before she reached the cabin, to find Berta Lund's wagon and horse beside it. Berta herself was telling the children stories of her trip to Hälsingborg.

"How grateful I am that you are back," Lisa rejoiced, as they shook hands warmly. "Thank you for the letter. We all enjoyed it."

"The girls have told me the news," Berta said. "I'm happy for you, but sad for myself. Don't like losing you."

"It is hard for me too. You are a dear and special friend."

"I'm thankful I got back in time and to be back in trousers. You know, Lisa, there is talk in Hälsingborg that all boats between Sweden and Finland will be stopped because of the mines. Much as I wish you could stay here longer, I urge you to hurry."

"We hurry more than we like. Wednesday as soon as the sale is over we go to the train. Pastor Rudolffson will take us. Sigurd was willing but Katarina said she could not face saying goodbye in public. Nor can I."

"I will come to the train with you."

"Please not. Let us say goodbye here. It will be easier for me."

"As you wish. But I will come Wednesday morning to help."

"Thank you, Berta. Carl, what is that you are eating?" Lisa demanded, as she noticed his cheeks puffed out on each side of his mouth, red spittle leaking out of the corners.

He tried to answer but was unable to. Instead he pointed with one pudgy finger at a large paper bag on the table.

"It's candy," several of the children said, but with difficulty, around sweets in their own mouths.

Marta dipped her hand into the bag and brought out a fistful of small candies and held them out on her palm toward Lisa. Some were wrapped in white paper with colorful pictures of fruit on them. Others were unwrapped pillows of white and red striped peppermints.

"*Tant* Berta brought them from Hälsingborg for us," she explained, successfully shifting the candies in her mouth to her cheek.

It explained why the children had been so quiet since she got home. They all were as guilty of greed as Carl. The youngest too, held a candy in her mouth, eyes closed in bliss, fingers of her small fist glued together by the sweet drooling of her mouth. It was the child's first taste of candy. Lisa could not scold. She knew their hunger, their rare opportunity for sweets, and never in such abundance.

"Did you say thank you?" she asked. All heads nodded. She unwrapped a candy for herself, then exclaimed, "Carl, that's enough," as he held his hand out to Marta begging for more.

Berta stayed and talked of Hälsingborg, and her visit with her two students. Then listened to Oscar's letters, and talked about the coming trip. When she left all the children, except the youngest, went with her. She would take them to say goodbye to Nasse and bring them back.

" Look at that," Lisa said, early Wednesday morning as she and the girls carried some of their furniture out onto the grass in front of the cabin, "here comes Beeda Gran. First one, and I can tell from the way she walks she has something special to spread in gossip."

"Good day," Beeda called when she was within yelling distance. Lisa waited until she was close by to answer.

"Good day, and what brings you so early in the morning?"

"Have you heard? I think you haven't."

"Well, even if I don't ask you will tell me. What is it?"

Hunched over but with her head lifted to peer intently upward, Beeda came so close her unpleasant morning breath puffed into Lisa's face.

"Farmer Albertsson is dead," she said, and stepped back to watch Lisa's reaction.

"Albertsson! Albertsson dead? That can't be! I was there just last Saturday. He was in good health then."

"Didn't help any," Beeda said. "The horse did it."

"Did what?" Paulina asked, the girls all gathered around with stunned faces.

"Yaw, what about the horse?" Lisa echoed.

"Trampled him, it did. Into a mush."

"Ah! Ah! What is this you are saying? Beeda! You are making this up!" Lisa clasped her hands in front of her and shook them under Beeda's nose. "It isn't true, is it?"

"Why should I lie? I never do," Beeda responded. "The horse was loose somehow in the barn. Albertsson was drunk and did something bad to it, I guess, and the horse kicked him into Valhalla."

There were many horrified exclamations from the group in front of Beeda. Some of the girls covered their faces with their hands, Lisa turned in a circle as if this way she could get away from Beeda's words. Paulina stumbled toward the cabin, her arm over her eyes, sobs shaking her shoulders. Emilia stood grim faced, and stared at Beeda, her throat working as if she was going to be sick. When Lisa could talk again she asked, "When did this happen?"

"Last night. I guess the crippled boy did it."

"Did what?"

"Left the horse loose on purpose."

Lisa gasped, then lunged forward to grasp Beeda by both shoulders and shook her. "Don't you ever say that again. Not ever. What are you trying to do? Hurt that boy more than he is? Stop it, and right now."

Beeda shrugged her hands off, glared back with a surly face, and said, "I'm not the only one saying it."

Lisa walked awy rubbing her mouth. She saw Paulina leaning on the cabin, crying. She went to her.

"It is hard to hear of such a death," she told her, "but Albertsson can't feel anything any more, Paulina."

Wiping her nose and eyes on a forearm, Paulina pushed away from the cabin, and answered. "It isn't Albertsson, it is the horse. What will they do to it?"

Beeda right behind Lisa said, "Shoot it, I guess."

Again Paulina wept, but shouted, "It wasn't the horse's fault! he never hurt Albertsson. Albertsson always hurt him."

"Paulina," Lisa said, and pushed Beeda away, telling her, "I don't want to hear another word out of you. Not one. Paulina, there is nothing we can do about the horse. I doubt they will shoot it. His boys need it for the farm. The horse won't be beaten anymore, thank God. Come, we have work to do. Go wash your face at the pump."

Beeda went to sit by the side of the lane, the girls and Lisa returned to carrying out their belongings. They spoke, but quietly and seldom. As people began arriving the news was confirmed. Although there was discussion about it everybody seemed to accept it had been inevitable. No one expressed anger at the horse.

The sale went quickly for there were many people. Even those who had been critical or unfriendly. But not Mangnusson. Nor Alfred Ohlin, although Hilda, his wife, was there. Lisa exchanged a sly, but sad smile with Berta when she saw that Hilda bought the cradle. The kettle of hot water had perhaps changed Alfred's romantic pursuits, and with as many children as they already had, another cradle was probably needed. It was with mixed feelings Lisa heard Hilda tell another woman, "It is for my eldest. She is expecting her first on this winter."

Emile Makela, with his pretty round-faced wife, were there and two of her Finnish friends. She chattered happily in Finnish with them as they each bought on thing after the other. One of her friends spoke some Swede-Finn to help the transactions.

The Qvists came, both showing the effects of liquor. Many small broken veins on cheeks and nose gave them false ruddy complexion. They carried an odor that brought the sawmill, and their too close proximity, vividly back to Lisa. When she saw that they bought the scrub brush, she asked, "For Dagmar?"

"That one!" Fru Qvist ranted. "She took off and lives in Vasa, can you beat that?"

Lisa hid her approval, and asked, "She is working there?"

"She works, although she went there talking about going to school. It is your Elvira put that in her head. How about her? She talked school, school, school all the time. Is she going to one in America?"

"Nay, I'm sorry to say she must work and earn her own living. Oscar writes, and Elvira does too, that she is learning American rapidly. The *herr* of the house, where she works,is a professor in a college. but, tell me, how are your two other boys?" She looked out into the field where the youngest Qvist ran in games with Johan and the many other children who had come to the sale with their parents.

"Ack, they started here with us, but who knows where they ran off to. Up to some devilry no doubt. Good riddance."

"How goes it with you?" Lisa asked Qvist himself.

"Bad. Bad days," he muttered. "It's too quiet, too quiet, I tell you. The sawmill stands there making no noise. Too quiet. It's not right. No one there but Mangnusson most days."

Lisa looked around at the people. Many of the men present, she realized, were there because the sawmill no longer could operate. The distant war had reached its long fingers through the blockade to affect these lives, too.

Beds, table, benches, stools, the sheepskin covers, the copper and iron pots and pans all sold rapidly. Lisa kept nothing but the yellow mugs with their black and white checked striped, and the three legged copper coffee pot. She could not imagine making coffee in any other pot. The wooden spoons, too, of course. The *puukko* Oscar had refused to take with him, she slipped into the knitted bag where she would carry a few necessary items on the trip. To Lisa's joy Berta bought the trunk. She felt as if it was still in the family. It was with equal joy to see the Rudolfssons buy the rocking chair.

The auctioineer was a cheerful man. He mixed Finnish and Swedish with happy indiscrimination. Rolled long hard Finnish "r's" as he held different objects up to encourage bidding. he made everyone laugh, and took liberties with the women, calling them sweet names, chucking the under the chin, and generally behaving like a clown. Even the men enjoyed him, especially when he made off color remarks when selling the chamber pot, and the cradle.

At the height of the auction the Olofssons left. Lisa rode with Katarina down the lane, the children alongside with Sigurd and the Olofssons' young. Here Lisa presented Katarina with the china dish, Eva a blouse she had sewed out of the yellow and green remnants from the twins' dresses. To Sigurd she gave Oscar's hammer, a tool he had treasured and almost taken with him to America. She had nothing to give the boys but her farewell hugs and good wishes. They said goodbye quickly, their hands lingering on each other, the children hugging them all, even the horse. Paulina ran to pick a few wisps of straw from the field to feed the surprised animal.

When the auction was over, the people gone, and with only Berta and the auctioneer left, Lisa counted the money. She sighed with relief.

"Girls," she called, "come here. Two of you will go and pay what we owe. Maria, you for one. Choose someone to go with you." She decided on Paulina. "You'll have to hurry to get to every place you have to go. But you have time before Pastor Rudolfsson comes back to take us to the railroad station. Walk, don't run."

"I'll take the girls," The auctioneer offered. "My buggy is light, my horse swift."

"Would you? How kind. Thank you," Lisa said. "Here, Maria, you hold on to the money. When you get back I will pay you," she told the auctioneer.

"No hurry," he said, and rushed the two laughing girls to the buggy by grasping each one by an arm.

Two hours later the girls returned without the auctioneer.

"How is it you come alone?" Lisa demanded. She and Berta hurried to meet them as they came running with stricken faces.

"He wouldn't come down the lane. He made us get off after he took his pay," they said, interrupting each other. Maria placed what was left of the money in Lisa's outstretched hand. With Berta, Lisa bent over the coins.

"Is this all of it?" she asked in horror.

Both girls nodded. Paulina explained, "He took what he said you had promised to pay him, and then something more for taking us around to Albertssons' to pay for the telephone calls, to the other farms, and to the store."

"I didn't promise him any certain amount! He said he would discuss that when the sale was over. He offered to take you around! Didn't say he wanted pay for it. Berta, do you hear?"

"What a thief! I blame myself for not taking the girls myself instead of letting him do it. When I see him again...Ack, whatever I do won't help now. It's done and there's no way to catch him. Don't feel it's your fault, girls. Lisa, don't," she called, as Lisa walked around the money cupped between her two hands. She shook them up and down and looked at the sky in despair.

Berta went to stop her, took her hands by the wrists, and told her, "I'll loan you the money, I have plenty right here. You know I won't miss or need it. This is a loan you must not, cannot, say nay to. We are friends, Lisa."

Lisa focused on Berta's face. "God in his wisdom gace you to us. I will take it, gladly."

"And not pay it back until you are firmly settled in America. Promise?"

"God be with you always, Berta. I can do no other. That includes the other monies I owe you for the cabin, the wood, and I don't know what all this minute. Girls, help me open the yellow basket."

"Open the basket?" Emilia protested, echoed by the others. "Why?"

"Never mind. I want it opened."

Berta gave a hand. Lisa bent to dig down below the top items to bring up the copper coffee pot. She handed it to Berta.

"I want you to have this. We have had such wonderful visits around this pot. It will make me feel I am here with you when I think of you pouring coffee from it."

About to protest, Berta took the pot. Lisa needed to make the gift. The round polished copper belly was lost between Berta's large strong hands as she cradled it, the three iron legs curved to point in different directions. One leg was worn to a needlepoint from the many firings in hot coals while coffee reheated. The long rubbed wooden handle, and the curved copper spout, jutted from between her fingers.

"You will be here with me, I promise you," Berta said, and looked down at the pot, too moved to say more.

The family was ready to leave in their new clothes, the old outer garments they had been wearing during the sale taken off and packed in the suitcase Berta had gone to Narpes to buy for them the day before. Johan in his black Buster Brown suit, Carl in the bright blue duplicate of it, and the youngest in her red top, leggings, coat, with a bonnet of the same knit and color, stood in a circle within a circle as everyone admired them and each other. If there had not been excitement before it was at high pitch now, for wearing the new clothes for the first time gave truth to what all the preparation had been leading to.

Johan's call, "here comes the pastor," put the final touch of excitement into the group. Returned from delivering the chair and his wife home, Rudolfsson was ready to take them to the train station.

"Thank you, Berta, thank you more than I can say," Lisa began when everything was on board the wagon. A confusion of goodbyes began, the children crowding around Berta who tried to embrace them all at one time. Suddenly she stepped away from them and enveloped Lisa in a hug, kissed her on both cheeks and held her again, before turning away swiftly. Lisa wiped her own eyes, and had to do it several times before she could call, "Everybody, once more to the toilet before we leave."

The two wagons moved to the main road. The green knitted bag in Lisa's lap bulged with cheese, two large round loaves of bread, and a firkin of butter, its wooden lid firmly attached by a wooden peg on a short string pushed through a hole in one of the extended slats of its side. A large package of sausages from Berta lay deep in the bottom of the bag also.

"Goodbye, dear friends, goodbye!" Berta called, when the pastor clucked to his horse. The last Lisa saw of her, she stood again behind the seat of her wagon, legs braced in their high Russian boots. She turned to wave.

The train ride to Rauma sped by. Lisa spent her time counting children, counting baggage, counting money as she made sure there was enough for everything she had to do. At the hotel there were four to a bed and not much sleep, but Johan made them laugh when, after climbing to the second story, he commented, "So high," when he went to look out of the window. Carl, with Johan at the window, bounced with excitement as he pointed a small fat finger at one of two Cossack horsemen patrolling the main street.

"The man!" he cried. He was eager to get down and go for another ride.

The next morning the first ride in an automobile removed all fatigue and annoyance, and the driver added his own youthful zest to the ride by squeezing the rubber horn to scare people out of the way as he drove the family down to the dock. And then an adventure beyond any they had imagined ended their last hours on Finnish soil. As they stepped out of the taxi two Cossacks stepped out of the door of a small restaurant and stopped right in front of them, barring their way.

"Look here," said one of them in halting Swedish, "who are these people?"

The family stopped where they were, even Lisa afraid to open her mouth.

"Where do you go?" the second one asked. "You have papers?"

"We go to Pappa," Johan answered proudly. Lisa put a hand on his shoulder and tightened it.

"We go to one of the boats there," she explained, indicating the smaller of the two boats. She lifted her purse to find her papers, but the Cossack ignored her to laugh and point to Carl.

"Look at him. Friendly little soul, and with a stomach as round as a banker's". He paid no attention to the papers Lisa offered him. Instead he bent down and lifted the boy up. "Where did you get such a bright blue suit?" he asked, and pushed the matching cap further back on Carl's head. "Shouldn't hide those yellow curls," he teased, as Carl reached to pull the cap back into place.

"And this little red bird could be my baby sister at home," the other cried, paying no more attention to Lisa's papers than the first one. He swooped the youngest up to jiggle her in his arms. "What is your name, little red bird?"

But the child reached out to Lisa, tears forming and mouth open to cry.

"All these young people are yours?" asked the first Cossack, indicating the group with a quick look.

Lisa nodded, quietly putting her papers deep in her purse.

"You're not Finns?"

"Nay."

"I could hear that. Have you had your supper?"

"Nay," Lisa answered. "We carry supper with us."

"Sausages, I bet," the second Cossack said. "I say, Igor, let's feed these two little ones, and their folks. Those big girls are too pretty to go to Sweden with just sausages in their stomachs. Come. Come into the restaurant, my dear *fru*. We can recommend their food...and drink."

Without waiting for Lisa to agree, they turned and went into the restaurant, with the youngest screaming and holding out her hands to Lisa. She could do nothing but follow.

The suitcase set down, she hurried to take the child, shushing her cries and soothing her. Dish after dish was ordered by the Cossacks, and placed on the big table they had commandeered for the family. After some hesitation the girls ate, following Lisa's example. Carl waited for no one. He grasped a foreign object, a metal fork, and stabbed meat and potatoes without being told. The Cossacks laughed at him, and encouraged him to eat more. Soon the girls were laughing with the young men, teaching them new words in Swedish, receiving a few in Kazak in return as well as Russian. Lisa saw the growing awareness her girls had for young men, Maria and Emilia especially. Paulina sat quiet, saying little, until she created a minor explosion.

"You have horses?" she asked.

"Do you hear that, Gregor?" Igor shouted, and slapped the table with a hard fist. "What's a Cossack without a horse? If there was time we'd put on a show for you. Ride like you've never seen men ride."

"Maybe there's time," Gregor shouted, half rising.

"Nay," Lisa hurried to say, waving the young man back down into his chair. "We must eat and go right away."

Johan, she noticed, ate slowly, his eyes on Igor who had a mustache so like Oscar's. She hoped he would not be too disappointed when they got to Sweden. No matter how many times he had been told Pappa would not be there to meet them, he refused to believe. It was his need for Oscar that made him so stubborn, Lisa knew.

Marta alone was completely at ease with fork and knife. She talked constantly as she ate, her interest not in the young men, but just to be talking. It surprised Lisa that not once, since they knew they were leaving for Sweden, had she mentioned the Palmers. Could she have forgotten them?

When the meal was over the Cossacks insisted on accompanying them, after paying for the meal and stuffing the last slice of bread into Carl's coat pocket. One carried the suitcase, and between them they carried the basket, Carl was in one young man's arms and the youngest in the other's. They came on board too, to make sure the family was given good cabins and plenty of blankets, although Lisa explained she had learned they were to be the only passengers on the trip. When the Cossacks finally said goodbye the older children went up on deck to watch the waterfront scene. They came running back down.

"Mamma, the bigger boat alongside is going to Sweden too...! And one of the sailors on it told us we should come go with them. Can we, Mamma? They leave in a few minutes and will get there ever so much sooner...And he said a big storm is coming, and it would be better for us to be on their boat."

Breathlessly they waited for her answer.

"We stay here," Lisa answered. "It is arranged, and that is that. This is a strong boat. I told you, I sailed on this boat when I went to Sweden. We stay on it."

Reluctantly, the girls and Johan went back on deck, to return shortly when the bigger boat had gone. Some hours later their own boat put out to sea.

Rain and wind had started again, and the sea was alive with growing swells and white-topped waves. A flash of lightning followed by a clap of thunder seemed to order it into more violent upheaval. It became hard to stand up. At first it was fun for the children to stagger back and forth, clinging to whatever they could. But soon they turned pale, and complained of dizziness, and were eager to climb into their bunks.

Lisa took the four young ones into her own cabin. She tried to help them as they became seasick but found it impossible to stand up without gripping the bunks with both hands. It was all she could do to stay on her feet. She crawled into the bunk with the youngest and Carl to keep them from rolling around and yelled to the others, "Cram pillows between your legs so you will be steadier on your bunks!"

Claps of thunder pounded her ears and yellow lightning ripped the blackness apart. On land she had always sought a dark corner in which to hide at such times, or the comfort of Oscar's arms. Now she found a kind of release she could not explain to herself. Here was proof she could face anything alone. She wanted to yell, "There is more to me!" but the children might hear and think her crazy. She buried her shouting inside her.

The storm seemed endless but through some alchemy of God and weather she slept and wakened to the calm of a ship in port. Not once had she doubted, she remembered afterwards. Not once did she think the little boat might sink.

Sweden

"Is she there?" someone called.

"Yaw," came a whisper not far from Lisa's ear. The voice lifted to call hoarsely. "She's still sleeping."

Lisa stirred, and lifted a hand to a bruise on the side of her head. The boat was still, tied up to the dock in Gavle.

"That you, Maria?" she asked. Quickly awake, she swung her legs up and over the guardrail. A quick look showed her the little ones still slept. She turned to Maria. "How do you feel? And the others?" she asked, as she bent over Marta, then Johan. They both slept, but with evidence of sickness on their faces and in their hair. She shivered.

"We were terribly sick during the night," Maria said. "Emilia worst of all. But we feel fine now."

Emilia and Paulina came to stand in the doorway.

"Wasn't it too bad that we lost that good dinner?" Emilia asked.

Paulina commented, "The best one we've had in a long time too."

"I think we all ate too much," Lisa suggested. Let's get out of this messy room and into a clean one. Get your clothes and we'll go dress and wash up."

When the twins had washed and dressed, replacing from a bundle the things that had become soiled, she sent them to ask for the suitcase that had been stored along with the yellow basket in the hold. She would have to wear her new gray dress to go to the office in Gavle where she was to pick up the railroad tickets.

"When the others wake you will have to help them wash," she told the older girls. "Ask for more water so you can rinse out things and their hair. I'll go to the ticket office now, so I can get right back and then we can get the early train north. One of your *farbrors* will be waiting."

The three went with her up on deck, forgetting their chatter about the storm as they gazed at the town of Gavle.

"Look, there's a house right in the middle of the street!" Maria exclaimed.

"What a funny thing," Paulina added. "It's got so many windows."

"That isn't a house," Lisa said, "that's a streetcar. Do you see the iron rails in the road? It rides on those on wheels."

"Ooh," the girls marveled.

"We've read about streetcars," Emilia said in disgust, "we should have known."

"Well, I'm taking the streetcar to that office," Lisa told them. "I should be back in an hour. When I come back we will go have breakfast together. Better get below so if the others are awake they won't be frightened at finding all of us gone."

"We'll go as soon as we see you get on that streetcar," Maria promised.

They stood waving, shouting, "Hurry back," as she stepped on board. The girls looked lonely standing at the rail of the boat watching until the car had traveled so far she could no longer see them.

Lisa found the office. A gangly clerk, his hair wetted and combed back so hard it seemed to pull his eyebrows upward and set his ears out into large pink wings, stretched out a bored hand from where he sat for Lisa's papers. He did not wait for her to explain before he was up and away, studying the top paper as he went to a door in the left wall behind him. It was a long time before he returned to seat himself, rearrange the cuffs of his sleeves importantly, then address himself to the papers piled in stacks on his small desk, often banging them with a stamp.

Lisa continued to stand, her eyes expectantly on the door he had closed behind him. She shifted from leg to leg as time passed. The door opened and a man holding some papers went directly across to the wall opposite and through another door. He did not look at her. She did not know if the papers were hers or not. She waited. Slowly she looked around and saw there was a bench against the wall. She turned toward it hesitantly.

"I'll go sit," she said.

The clerk glanced up, nodded shortly, but said nothing.

The clock on the wall ticked on. An hour passed. At last she got up and demanded, as an older man came from an inner office, "Why does it take so long for tickets that have already been ordered and paid for to be delivered?"

"What's this?" the older man demanded. "How long have you been here?"

"Since you opened. I have seven children waiting for breakfast at the waterfront, and we have to catch the train to Nyland."

"Get those tickets", the man yelled at the now red-eared clerk. In moments they were in Lisa's hands.

"You came from Rauma last night?" the man asked.

"Yes"

"You are fortunate to be here." He opened the door for Lisa as she hurried back to the street car. It came at last. All the way she leaned forward in her seat as though that would help make it run faster. The children stood clustered on the deck, looking so forlorn a lump formed in her throat. It was Marta who saw her first.

"Mamma, Mamma!" she screeched, and bolted down the gangplank, the others streaming after her, some of them crying. They gathered around her, touched her, held her, saying they thought she had died.

"We thought the streetcar had gone off the other end of those rails," Maria told her, her chin quivering, the howling youngest in her arms. She lifted the hem of the child's knitted coat and wiped her eyes with it. Lisa took the child and bent down to Carl, to let him put his arms around her neck. His snuffles were loud in her ear.

Johan encircled her neck, too making it hard for her to get up. "I heard the train," he wept, "and thought you had gone off to Pappa."

"I wouldn't go without you, Johan. You should have known that. Pappa is waiting for us in America, don't forget."

"Have you eaten?" she asked, as soon as she could stand up. They all shook their heads. The captain, who had come up on deck, called to her. "We offered them food and drink, but they wouldn't come below, or even eat when Cook brought milk and sandwiches up. No one, except the youngest boy and the little girl. The rest of them said they wouldn't be able to swallow."

"How foolish of you," Lisa scolded the older girls, as she led the way back to their cabins. "We will hurry and get to a restaurant before the next train leaves. We have a few hours before the late afternoon train."

With thanks to the captain for his concern over her children, they left the boat. Lisa ordered food generously when they found a small restaurant. Cheerfulness had been completely restored by the time they boarded and found seats for the journey north.

*

Paulina said it first as the train chugged north.

"I hope *farmor* has lots of potatoes cooked when we get there."

"And piled this high for me," Johan added, a hand raised to the level of his eyes.

Marta dreamed out loud. "All peeled and with clumps of butter to eat with them."

Lisa could not resist joining in. "Nay, cooked in their skins. That's when they tasted the best. It would be wonderful if she had anchovies too." Thinking of the good salt taste she wiped a hand across her mouth.

The train pulled into the station in the dark of the October evening. People came to meet those who got off. Lisa searched for the familiar face of either one of Oscar's brothers, but did not see them, nor anyone she knew.

"We'll stand right here," she said. "Let *farbror* Johan, or Evert, find us. Paulina, what are you doing?"

Emilia answered for her twin who stood crowded against the yellow basket and was tugging the bundles to settle them on and around her feet.

"She's hiding her *pjäxor* again like she did in Narpes and Gavle. Doesn't want anyone to see she doesn't have real shoes like the rest of us," Emilia informed her.

About to reprimand the girl Lisa remained silent. Standing here in this town, where it had happened, she remembered her own haste to hide, from *Fru* Palmer's critical gaze, her own worn shoes on that holiday visit almost five years ago. Trapped by the warmth of the beautiful tile stove, she had held her feet out to it for one revealing moment. Those same shoes, carefully mended by Oscar before he left for America, were the same ones she wore this day. In Finland, as in Sweden, she had worn them only when she walked any distance from home. Oscar's old darned stockings, a triple pair in the cold winter, had continued to be her everyday wear at home. Nay, it was not hard to understand Paulina's feelings.

The platform cleared. They were left standing alone. No wagon or horse waited, other than one for hire, the driver watching them in expectation.

"Can it be my letter didn't reach *farmor* in time? Do you suppose they met the morning train, then gave up? Surely they wouldn't do that."

Maria suggested, "Maybe they're just late."

"Should I run down the main street and see if they're coming?" Emilia asked. "I remember where to go look for the street *farbror* Evert would be coming on."

"Wait, I hear horses."

A carriage with two seats, and pulled by two matched, high stepping horses, came around a corner and up to the platform. A man jumped down hardly waiting to bring the horses to a halt.

"Marta!" he called. "Is it you? *Fru* Veldman! You are really here? Thank the Lord!"

"It's *farbror* Palmer!" Marta shouted, and flew to meet him. She was gathered up into his arms, her feet lifted high off the station platform as he hugged her.

"You're alive! You weren't on that other boat," he exclaimed, as he set her down to come shake hands with Lisa, and to touch each of the others assuring himself they were real.

"What about another boat?" Lisa asked.

"You haven't heard? Another boat left Rauma last night and it went down in the storm."

"Nay!" Lisa gasped. With sudden realization she knew the headline she had seen in the government office, and the remark made by the last man who had interviewed her so kindly. "You are fortunate to be here," had been references to that boat. The tragedy had been on the Baltic, not the ocean.

"How awful! Terrible!" the girls cried.

With a stricken face Maria told *Herr* Palmer, "It's the one the sailors wanted us to go on, but Mamma said nay. Remember?" she demanded of the others. Sorrowfully, they nodded.

"It was the storm?" Lisa asked.

"Nay, a mine," *Herr* Palmer answered. "The boat telegraphed before it sank. The papers today say they don't think anyone could have survived in the storm. Late today it has been announced by both governments, Sweden and Finland, that shipping on the Baltic is to cease until all mines have been removed from the sea."

"That won't be until the end of the war," Lisa said, "and there's no sign of that yet."

"Nay, it grows bigger every day. But *farmor* Veldman thinks you were on that boat. She received a cable from your husband in America telling her about it?"

"From Oscar? That isn't possible! How could he know so soon about it?"

The cable said it had been reported in the American newspapers that the *Tammarfors* had sunk with all people on board."

"Aiy, yaiy yaiy! And he thought we were on it. How he must be weeping. I must cable him immediately." She strode without further word toward the station office. Maria, carrying the youngest, hurried after her.

"Come, all of you," Herr Palmer said to the others, "we'll get the luggage into the carriage while we wait. Come on, give a hand."

Before Lisa reached the carriage, as she came rushing back, she called, "*Farmor* too must be weeping. Let us hurry." She climbed up without noticing *Herr* Palmer's hand extended to help her. She snatched the youngest from Maria's arms and ordered the panting girl to hurry up and get in.

To Paulina's question, "Does Pappa know we're alive now?" she answered a quick, "He will in a few hours. When we get to *farmor's* we will get on our knees and give thanks to God."

Herr Palmer swung up into the seat, touched the horses with the whip, and encouraged them into a fast trot. He talked into the silence of the family.

"I met this morning's train too. Yesterday I happened to meet Evert as he came to town from Solefteä. That's how I knew you were coming. But this morning he wasn't here to meet the train. I drove out to your *farmor's* house to find out why. It was then I learned of the boat sinking. I mourned all day, but this evening I could not rest until I decided to meet this train too." He took Marta's hand and held it tightly. "Thank God, the news was wrong."

"For us," Lisa agreed, "but think of those who were lost. And their grieving families. We will pray for them tonight."

She turned to count noses for the first time since getting into the carriage. "Johan, don't look so sad. Be happy like Pappa will be when he knows you are here and safe at his Mamma's *stuga.*"

Herr Palmer clucked the horses into a faster trot.

"Here, Marta, you can drive two horses now that you are so grown up, can't you?" He offered her the reins. Marta shook her head but with one hand took hold of the ends that dangled from his hands. He smiled down at her and clucked to the horses once more.

The carriage rolled rapidly through familiar roads in the moonlight. The older girls began to point out places they remembered from trips into town years ago. By the time they came to the small village where their *farmor* lived, their spirits were high, their voices vying with each other to be heard over the whip of the wind the speed of the two horses created.

Lisa did not silence them as they neared the unpainted weathered *stuga* with its fresh white trim around the windows, although their shouts, and the clatter of the horses, brought people out from other *stugas,* and into other windows.

"*Farmor,* we're here...*farmor*!...Look, *farmor,* we weren't on that other boat! Here we are!" The joy of being alive, of being back, filled their voices.

The carriage came to a stop on the short rutted lane in front of the *stuga.* The door was jerked open and Evert stepped out. He shouted, and with a wilk waving of his arms that startled the horses into frightened stamping, called over his shoulder.

"*Mor,* they're really here! Come see for yourself. Come!" he yelled, then leaped down off the stoop to hurry to the carriage. "Are you here all of you? Everyone?"

"All eight of us," Emilia yelled in midair, skirts flying as she leaped down to the ground, adding, "we weren't on the *Tammarfors.*"

Evert reached up to help Lisa down. They grasped each other, both of them crying, the youngest in her arms squeezed between them.

"We came on a different boat," she managed to say, then released him to let him lift Carl down. Evert tried to count heads as the other leaped down and ran past.

Farmor stood in the doorway, her wrinkled face wet, eyes swollen and red. Her gray dress, with its up and down stripes, small colored apron with crocheted edge, were so familiar it set the world right again. It was as if only yesterday they had left her standing just so, wiping her eyes after their last visit before leaving for Finland. The only mark of difference was her hair. It was grayer and gave evidence that this day she had not had the will to slick it back tight with a fine comb, or to replait her short braid and fasten it into the usual hard knot on top of her head.

The girls flung themselves at her. She staggered back into the *stuga* surrounded by them, and sat down on a chair. She hid her face in her hands, murmuring, "Dear God, thank you, thank you." She tried to gather all her granddaughters to her at once. When Lisa came in, with the youngest, she stretched her arms out between them to take the small girl.

"This is Ketty?" she asked. "The one whose name sounds like flower bouquet?"

"This is Ketty," Lisa answered, and went to give her the child before she sank onto her knees in front of the old woman. Without being told the others did the same. Evert stopped inside the door. Johan, attached by both hands to his free arm, stood smiling up at him. Still carrying Carl, Evert raised his voice to lead the family in giving thanks to the Lord.

"Amen," was a shout as the girls jumped up to be first to tell *farmor* the whole story. Lisa's words were drowned out, although she got up to bend close to the older woman, their two right hands joined in a long warm clasp. Around them the children laughed, cried, went to hug Evert, then dashed back to hug *farmor* again. In their rush, back and forth, they hugged each other by mistake. Everything was blotted out, especially for the two women, until Marta asked a question.

"*Farmor,* are there enough potatoes so *farbror* Palmer can have some too?"

Lisa gasped, wiped her eyes with the heel of her hands, and hurried to the door. *Herr* Palmer had turned the horses and the carriage to face homeward, but sat waiting.

"Forgive me," she called. "You must come in and be with us in our happiness. Please come in."

Without hesitation he tethered the horses and came in.

Lisa realized she had not inquired after *Fru* Palmer. She did so now.

"She is in Stockholm," *Herr* Palmer answered. "She is fine, thank you."

"Potatoes?" *farmor* was saying. "I have not potatoes cooked. I didn't think you would be here. One of you, lift the trapdoor and go down and get some. Take plenty," she added, as the three older girls pulled a rag rug back from the trapdoor in the floor. As *farmor* got up to welcome the guest, the girls argued who should go down into the root cellar. Emilia settled it by seating herself in the opening, then jumped down, without using the short ladder attached to one end. In moments she was handing up potatoes by two and threes to her sisters.

"There's a lot of them here," she shouted upward.

"Foolish child," *farmor* went to scold, and got a wooden bucket to hand down to her. "Fill this, don't hand them up a few at a time. You are many mouths."

The potatoes washed they were transferred from kettle to kettle to find that none of them were big enough to hold them all.

"Go to the summer house," *farmor* told the girls, "and get the biggest kettle out there."

There was no need for her to tell the girls where that small building was. They dashed out the door, all three of them, to circle past the carriage, across the lane, and into the ancient log building where *farmor* did her wash and baked her knäckebröd, in the summer. They took the large kettle to the pump and half filled it with water. Two of them carried it between them, sloshing water on their skirts in their hurry to get back in the start the potatoes cooking.

"You must have heard Mamma talking on the train, *farmor*," Johan said later, his mouth full of potatoes and butter. "You have anchovies."

Everyone laughed. Lisa studied the boy. He had made no fuss at not finding Oscar here. Evert had softened the blow, she believed. Evert, who was so much like Oscar. Even now the boy crowded next to his *farbror*, who drank coffee, while the family gorged on potatoes and fish. Beside the boy's plate rested Oscar's cable from America. He had not let it out of his sight, even since *farmor* had let him have it, once everyone had seen it.

Herr Palmer, drinking coffee also, was seated on the edge of one of the alcove beds since all benches, chairs, and stools were in use to seat the family at the long table.

"May I ask, *Fru* Velman," he said, addressing Lisa, when the meal ended, "if you would let me take Marta home with me?" As Lisa stiffened he hurried to add, "For a day or so, perhaps? You are so many here. Surely you can spare her for that long?"

"That we can," *farmor* answered, from near the hearth before Lisa could speak. "You were kind to bring them all here, so should have the girl in thanks. Do you want to go, Marta?"

"Yaw, *farmor*, yaw," Marta answered, a quick glance around at her sisters, her head lifted in self-importance.

Lisa caught herself about to contradict *farmor*. The question had rightly been hers to answer, but she knew it was too late to say otherwise. Angry, she reminded herself that it was not like *farmor* to interfere. In the past, even in the matter of religion, though it had been an overwhelming tragedy to the old woman that her eldest son had left the church, she had never interfered. Oscar had told Lisa, even before they were married, how his *mor* had argued. Vehemently at first, even crying out to her dead husband to look down and speak to his boy who rebelled against, what he called, the dictates of the church. Worn out with anger, after months of argument that turned eventually into pleading, she had become silent, never to speak of it again. Nay, almost never, Lisa corrected herself. Only at the birth of each of her son's children, when she had always come to help, she had pleaded again. Each time, with obvious small hope, Lisa remembered, she had asked that the new child be taken to be baptized. Almost always the answer went against her. Silent, she would leave, shaking her head to hurry home to pray for another newborn who would have to make it through life on earth without a proper union with Christ for life in the hereafter.

Could it be that, now because Oscar was not here, *farmor* would take a different stand? Was she planning to order their life? She pushed the thought away. If so, she would show the old woman different.

Guilt edged into her mind. How could she be plotting, even for an unspoken moment, against Oscar's *mor* who had taken them in so willingly? She turned hastily to Herr Palmer.

"Marta must start school here with the others," she told him. To Marta she said, "You're to be back tomorrow night. I want you to start school together."

Marta found her coat. Herr Palmer came to take it, and held it for her to put it on, as if she was a lady. Lisa saw that he recognized the coat. Did he also notice its many alterations? Faded almost to grey, the bright blue bands at the ends of the sleeves, along the seams, and at the bottom of the coat, revealed where she had enlarged and lengthened the garment. The quality of the material was still good, although she saw that the coat fitted the girl snugly again.

Marta hesitated in the door, blocking the way for Herr Palmer. It was evident her desire to leave had lessened. Her sisters roamed the room discovering the pictures *farmor* had on her walls. Marta remembered them, for they had been the first pictures she had ever seen on any walls, her own home innocent of such sinful things. There were the pictures of Sweden's king and queen, of *farfar,* Pappa's pappa, in his reserve naval uniform. But she remembered especially the picture her sisters were now pointing and laughing at. They had kept the memory alive for her, for they had spoken of it often in Finland. Without walking over to it she knew it was a newspaper picture of three women drinking coffee. They sat looking into the room and their eyes followed where anyone went. *Farmor* had put it right there, her sisters had claimed many times, so that if anyone of them tried to get an extra lump of sugar from the corner cupboard drawer right next to it, those women would see. She wanted to laugh with her sisters, but instead she felt like crying. They did not notice she was leaving.

Lisa saw her hesitation. It was good for the child to go. She was learning she would miss her family, especially her sisters. Lisa told her they would all miss her, and walked out to help her up into the carriage.

"She is to have nothing more than her sisters have, Herr Palmer," she said quietly to the man, as he sat down and picked up the reins.

"I understand," he answered, his face reflecting her seriousness.

They nodded to each other. Lisa patted Marta's knee and the carriage rolled off. Until it disappeared around a curve Lisa watched it, her head shaking as she wondered how this visit would affect the child. Perhaps she should have faced *farmor* immediately and said, nay.

Back in the stuga she went about arranging with *farmor* where everyone would sleep. The girls in the main room, three together behind the colorful handwoven wool curtains that hid the two alcove beds. One for them to use, the other one *farmor's*. The next night, with Marta added to their number, they would have to begin taking turns to sleep with *farmor*, they were told, a different girl each night. Lisa and the two youngest were given the one bed in the small and only bedroom. Johan could sprawl alone on a borrowed cot alongside.

Sunday evening, when Marta returned, Lisa saw that, perhaps, she had worried needlessly. Marta ran from sister to sister, and to her brothers, not at all filled with talk of her visit, but eager to hear what had happened while she was gone. Lisa had to remind her to say goodbye to *farbror* Palmer, which she did with hugs and kisses, but turned back immediately to her sisters. Emilia was the only one who teased.

"What? No dolls?" she asked.

"Of course not," Marta replied, hands on hips. "Dolls are a sin." Lisa relaxed.

Marta took her turn along with the others as the weeks and months passed to sleep with *farmor*. Fitted tightly together, the girls were sometimes too warm in the bed but whispered that sleeping with *farmor* was dangerous. She took too much room, and the many pillows she thrust around her threatened to smother them by morning. They tried to barter with each other to trade off, but Lisa and *farmor* defeated them, remembering too well who had slept with her last.

On the afternoon of the first day that the children came home from school, Lisa and *farmor* had a contest of wills that settled their way of life for the time they lived together. Maria innocently started it.

"We told the teacher we would not be allowed to learn the catechism," she reported proudly.

Emilia, spit flying in her eagerness to report also, told Lisa loudly, how definitely they had stated their parents' position.

"We said our Pappa is against our learning it, because it's not from the Bible, but church teachings."

"What's this? What do you say?" *farmor* demanded, leaving the hearth, where she had been stirring brown beans, to go bend over the girls. "Of course you are to learn the catechism." About to say more she heard Lisa gasp. She whirled around, the spoon in her hand dripping onto the rag rug below.

Lisa had dropped the articles she had been sorting from the yellow basket and was striding across the room, speaking even before she reached *farmor*.

"Don't tell my girls such a thing. You know their Pappa is against it, and so am I." She wrenched the spoon from the older women's hand and went to slap it back into the beans. *Farmor* stalked right behind her to pull the kettle away from the fire and took the spoon out, to hold it like a staff giving her authority in her own home. Eyes angry, mouth set in determination, she faced Lisa.

"My own grandchildren, living with me in my house, are not to know their catechism? I say they will." She pushed the kettle back into the fire and stirred wildly.

It took some moments for Lisa to control her anger. "*Mor* Veldman," she said, using that title in an attempt to appease the older women, "have you forgotten your son's belief? Would you have me go against him, because he isn't here?"

"Against God, that's what it is. Against God!" Some of the beans hissed over into the fire from the rapid stirring.

Lisa raised her voice angrily and stepped so close to *farmor* she was shouting almost directly into her ear. "I will not have you say such a thing to me. I will not!"

About to say more, she noticed the children. Their faces were frightened. Maria came as if to plead they stop their argument. Lisa spoke to her.

"You've all been wanting to see the neighbors. You can go now. Take Carl and the youngest along too." She watched them put on their coats and dress the younger ones for the outdoors. Not until the doors closed behind them did she turn back to *farmor.*

"*Mor,* kind *mor,*" she pleaded, calming herself with the words, "come sit and let us talk more quietly."

Instead *farmor's* stiff back bent just enough so she could look deep into the kettle, adding vinegar and brown sugar with unnecessary concentration. The sharp set of her jaw gave Lisa small hope. She persisted.

"You know we worship God as much as you do. We live a Christian life. We raised our children in our belief as you did in yours. Perhaps we will be more successful."

At this *farmor* began to stir. Fully erect she faced Lisa, her hand a tight fist on the long shaft of the wooden spoon resting motionless on the bottom of the bubbling kettle. She seemed to gather heat from it as she hurled rebuttal into Lisa's face.

"What about Elvira off there in America? She does nothing but dance, you tell me. No time to be with Oscar, not even to read the Bible with him. Is this evidence that your children will continue to think as you do? Nay, Lisa, it is the church, the church alone who must give guidance to the young."

The possible truth of some of what *farmor* said startled Lisa, but she recovered quickly as anger heated her own response.

"Elvira has a Bible, bought with her own money. She reads it, I'm sure, and gets her guidance there. She doesn't have to go to church to understand the word of God. We have given her the intelligence to understand for herself."

Now both the spoon and the beans were forgotten. The two women moved back and forth in front of the hearth, interrupted, yelled, lifted their fingers in emphasis under one another's noses, in turn and simultaneously. They followed each other into various parts of the room, *farmor* spilling out all that she had not allowed herself to say the many years her daughter-in-law had lived in Sweden. Lisa retaliated, using the same reasoning Oscar had spelled out to her about his discussion with his *mor* regarding his belief. She quoted the Bible. *Farmor* quoted her minister. The two women seldom heard each other out. All of a sudden their voices stopped, as with one accord they raced to the hearth. The smell of scorched beans joined their hands for a moment as together they drew the hot kettle away from the coals.

Farmr did not take time to mourn the beans. Hands on her hips she faced Lisa again.

"At least Oscar got his firm foundation in God's work in church. That's where these children will go and every Sunday they are here."

"Never!" Lisa cried, and drew a deep breath for fresh battle. Suddenly she had no heart for it. Instead she knew she must tell *mor* Veldman what she had resolved the old women need never know. The words came out ragged, and grew in pain as she continued. "You would ask me to take them to church, the church that refused my dead child entry through the gate? For them to listen to sermons given by someone, perhaps like that minister who made us wait an hour in the hot sun alongside Alli's coffin outside the church yard? Nay, *mor* Veldman, if ever I planned to let them see inside a church I would want myself dead first now."

Farmor's face had gone from anger to dismay. She sagged, her tall frame seeming to fold in on itself. "What is it you are telling me? You wrote nothing of this in your letters."

With several shuddering breaths Lisa calmed the cries that ached to be shouted out loud. She pulled her lips tight, took *farmor* by the arm, led her to a bench, and sat down with her.

The story of Alli's funeral came out. Sometimes in anger, sometimes in joint moans with the older woman. When the telling ended they cried, one woman's tears as many as the other's.

Farmor spoke, almost whispering. "That man...that minister...he couldn't have been God's...he must have been...possessed by Satan!" The last was said in a loud quick burst of words.

Lisa did not answer. She sat slack, her head tilted back, her eyes closed, open hands resting palms down on her knees.

"That congregation," *farmor* continued, "don't they know he...is possessed?"

Without moving or opening her eyes Lisa told her, "Katarina knows," and said no more. *Farmor* sat silent.

At last she said softly, "I miss Alli so much."

Lisa nodded.

"She was the prettiest."

Again Lisa nodded, but after a slight hesitation.

"Hair like curled sunshine. Eyes the blue of the Baltic." Lisa nodded after each statement.

"Could sing like a nightingale."

Lisa opened her eyes and turned to look at *farmor*. "You remember that?"

Farmor nodded. "Even when she was so small." She lifted a hand not far above her knee to show the height of the girl. Together the women smiled.

"We should not quarrel, *mor,*" Lisa said, and touched the other woman. "We worship the same god."

"Yaw, you are right. But it is hard, Lisa."

"I know, I know. But you understand how I feel now?"

Farmor rocked back and forth slightly as she answered, "I do. I will keep silent from now on."

"Nay, *mor,* let us talk, but in harmony with each other, so we can know how we believe. Can't we do that?"

"It is wiser we leave it alone, Lisa. You read the Bible with the children. I will listen, that's all."

It was strange, Lisa thought, she felt no happiness in victory. The old woman's feelings were torn, her concern for her grandchildren real. For a moment Lisa hesitated, then made an offer.

"*Mor,* I will let the children learn the catechism. It is little enough we can do for what you do for us. But, we will not go to church. On that I remain firm. Will you accept that?"

Silent, eyes first filled with surprise, then gratitude, *farmor's* smile said thank you more clearly than words.

Lisa smiled in return, but could not resist a final thrust. "It will not hurt them to memorize what man has written."

Farmor stood up abruptly, and said with a sharpness back in her voice, "Don't say anything more. We leave it right there."

She went to the hearth, removed the kettle from its edge where in their haste they had left it, took it to the table. "It's burned only in one spot," she announced. "I hear the children coming. They will enjoy a bowlful to warm themselves up."

"Good," Lisa agreed, and went to the door to greet the children with a smile, and told them what *farmor* had cooked for them.

*

A letter arrived from America, written the same day Oscar had received Lisa's cable. *Farmor* sast close to the blazing hearth cutting rags for next year's rug weaving. The youngest, in her lap, fought sleep as she watched the big scissors open and close in front of her. On a stool next to them Lisa read the letter aloud, the family gathered to listen. Oscar told of his agony when he thought they were all lost in the angry waters of the Baltic Sea. Lisa's voice dropped, almost vanished, then stopped altogether. Mist in her eyes made seeing difficult. She looked around at her daughters and selected Paulina.

"Here," she said, "you read it. Your handwriting is so much like his."

Paulina had to clear her throat and blow her nose before she could begin from where Lisa's finger pointed. When the honking of other noses stopped, she read:

'So I weep now instead for your safe arrival at my *mor's,* and give thanks to God without end. Dear *mor,* my heart is full of thankfulness that you take in my children, and my wife. Surely God will make your life a happy one to the end of your days in reward. My many thanks speed over the distance that separates us.'

Farmor spoke, her voice gruff. "Ya so? He knows my only happiness would be his return, to have you all right here in Sweden."

Lisa made no comment. Paulina continued.

'Lisa, I fear for you to cross the Atlantic. The despair I had when I thought you had all been lost returns like a knife to torture me. If I thought the war was ending I would say, stay in Sweden until it ends. But instead I think the sooner you can come the better. If it is to be Armageddon, we would be together here in this big country. I am sure you feel as I do. Our separation must end. My loneliness is an ache every minute of the day and night.

'Since Swedish boats are blocked by mines you will have to take the train to Norway. Neutral Norwegian ships are not bothered by the German U-boats that hunt from under the water for enemy shipping. This eases my worry.

'The storekeeper money-lender says he will not be able to let me have a loan until December or early January. There are many who borrow from him. I must take my turn. I suggest you write, now, to make sure of passage for March. That will give me time to get the money to you by February at the latest. Use what is enclosed here to make a payment to hold the passage. I will send more for your own use, and to give to my *mor.*'

The wind strained against the windows in gusts of sleet and snow, and made America seem impossibly far away. The tone of the letter changed as he dreamed of their arrival only months away.

'I can hardly wait to take you all to a beautiful park that sits high on a bluff above Lake Michigan." Paulira stumbed prounouncing the name of the lake.

'Foss Park has beautiful trees, areas where there are many swings and slides that children play on. A place for a game called baseball not at all like soccer, nor as interesting to watch. The older girls will like the large open pavilion where people dance, an orchestra there to play waltzes, but other music too that hurts my ear. I see Elvira there every Sunday I go. Some of the dances have movements that make me ashamed to watch, but nothing I say stops her from being first out on the floor with that same young man I told you about, to trot around in the new dance steps. I watch as little as possible. Perhaps you will have more influence with her when you come. For you, Lisa, there are lovely areas of grass, much like that glade we loved so much in Sweden. Here families spread their blankets and hold their picnics. I can hardly wait to taste the thin pancakes you will make and fill with thick lingon preserve for our own picnics. Yaw, it is possible to buy lingon here at the market my friend the money lender owns. I see he has big barrels of it.'

Farmor interrupted. "What kind of country is that where lingon has to be bought?"

"I guess it doesn't grow in the woods where Pappa is," Maria answered, then urged Paulina to read on.

There were many more pages. As Paulina finished each page Lisa took it and smoothed it onto the others on her knee. It seemed to her Oscar's happiness had kept him writing through the whole night. The girls interrupted each other anticipating the fun in store for them. They wished March was already here. *Farmor* mumbled under her breath.

"Frosting, frosting," she said. "What will it really be like?" she asked, but no one heard.

On the last page Pappa told them he now had false upper teeth. He hoped Lisa would think him handsome, not like a grinning horse. At this the girls had to stagger around in their laughter patting each other on the back. Even Paulina's "Nyeh, nyeh, nyeh," was too uncontrolled for the reading to continue.

"Ack!" Lisa protested, a flush on her cheeks, "why does he say such a silly thing? He knows I always thought him handsome."

Paulina managed to return to the letter. "He has six American words this time. Says they mean, 'let us pray for peace.' "

"Let me see," Emilia demanded, and grabbed for the page. Paulina waved it high overhead and held her sister away with her other hand as she tried to see and pronounce the words herself.

"You'll tear it! Give it to me," Lisa ordered. She settled the last page on top of the others on her knee. Her thoughts were not on the American words, but on a few that had occurred earlier. Throughout the entire reading they had sounded in her mind like bells of hope...'stay in Sweden until the war ends.' A hope, guilty in its birth, had been born.

The twins leaned on her to hang their heads over that final page, vying in loud contest to pronounce the foreign words. They did not stop her thoughts.

Her youngest, over there on *farmor's* lap, had been born just before her thirty-ninth birthday. If only that child could be her last one. Already Lisa was aware of signs. The years of regularity in her monthly bleeding had changed. A year, perhaps two, would be enough and she would be sure it was impossible for her to become pregnant again. Too many, she had heard and knew about, had become mothers once more at that change in their lives.

A shudder shook her as she realized what in essence she was doing. Wishing the war to continue for her sake, planning to desert Oscar who needed her, keeping the children away from their pappa. Her eyes followed *farmor* as the old woman got up to settle the sleeping child on one of the beds behind the wool curtains. She heard the soft, reassuring sounds she made to keep the child from awakening. Nay, she must crush the hope. It would not be fair to *Mor* Veldman either. Already the potatoes she had stored for her whole winter's use were almost gone, as well as the salt herring, the cereals. The inroads on the *knäkebröd* in the ceiling was frightening. And yet...

Over the noise of the children, who compared at the tops of their voices which promises in the letter were the best, she asked, "*Mor* Veldman, should I write and pay part of the passage as Oscar suggests?"

Farmor straightened with effort as she untangled herself from the bed curtains. "You'll do as he says, of course," she answered, and turned to the child again.

Lisa nodded as if in agreement, but silently struggled with indecision. She slipped the letter into her apron pocket, where the bank draft rested. As *farmor* returned to her chair Lisa said, "I wonder what Oscar does look like with those teeth. He had good ones when we were first married."

Johan came to poke her arm. He too had been thinking of what Pappa had written. "Pappa has teeth," he said, as if challenging Lisa to deny this.

"Of course, Johan. New ones that he can take out and put back in, any time he likes."

The boy shook his head but kept his doubting eyes on her. He huffed an uncertain laugh then lifted a hand to grasp one of his own teeth between thumb and forefinger. He wiggled it. He let go.

"When my teeth come out I can't put them back in again," he protested, and pointed to the large gap down below where two teeth had once been.

"You'll grow new ones," Lisa explained. "Pappa is too old to grow new teeth."

Farmor told Johan, "Your pappa's teeth were bad and hurt him. Maybe someday I can buy new ones too, and will be able to chew again. That would be wonderful," she sighed.

Maria grasped Johan's shoulder and swooped around to stand in front of him.

"That's exactly what I'm going to do when I get to America," she told him. "Buy teeth that I can take out and slip back in when I want to look pretty." She swept her hands gracefully over her mouth then held them out, fingers curved, as if she had something in each one. Johan stretched to see if indeed her teeth rested in them.

"I don't care about teeth," Paulina declared, "I'm going to ask Pappa to take me to the zoo he wrote about. Just think how it will be to see a lion."

Marta and Emilia outshouted each other announcing what their first wants would be. Marta, to have as many dresses as there were days in the week. Emilia, to get to that park and swing out over that big inland sea. Her face glowed as she imagined the sensation of swinging high over water. She denied with loud cries those of Maria and Paulina, who insisted that now she was too old for swings.

"Never," she declared, and went to tickle Carl on his fat stomach as she made him a promise of her own. "You can sit on the seat and I'll stand and pump you high up into the sky."

Shrieking, Carl bent double to protect himself against the wiggling fingers, and ran to burrow his laughing face in Lisa's lap. Lisa pulled gently on his curls and told him he would be old enough to swing by himself when they got there.

It was late before discussion of Oscar's letter died down. Paulina, Emilia, and Marta undressed and climbed into bed together to whisper further wants behind the privacy of the bed curtains. Maria settled in *farmor's* bed, the youngest was carried into the bedroom. Just before she slept, Maria lifted her head above the mound that was *farmor,* and her many pillows, to call, loud enough to penetrate the drawn curtains of both beds, "Just think, they'd never ache!"

Lisa sat alone in the main room, paper, pen, and ink on the table in front of her. She went to add a small log to the fire, paused at the bed holding the three girls, to hush them. She pulled the bed curtains tighter to seal out the light of the dangling electric bulb, and the cold that by morning would have the room in its hard grip. Again seated at the table she picked up the pen, but sat staring into the furthest corner of the room.

The whispering behind her stopped. The putter of *farmor's* snoring began. A loud snap in the fire behind her sent a coal skittering. She turned and saw that it had stopped on the edge of the hearth so did nothing about it. Elbows on the table, chin in her hands, she wondered if she could tell Oscar what she knew she must. The decision had come to her, fullblown and inescapable, as soon as she had tucked the letter into her pocket. But, how could she tell him? Nay, let it wait. The next letter would be soon enough, she told herself. She pushed her fingers through her hair until they became entangled on top her head. It reminded her of Oscar's habit of ruffling his hair until it stood in uncombed disorder. Immediately, she picked up the pen and began to write. She knew she could not put it off.

'Oscar,' she began, 'my loneliness is as yours, although I am fortunate to have the children with me. I regret Elvira is not with you more often. Hard as it is to accept, I know she wants to be with her own friends. We both have to understand that. What is harder for me is that she writes so seldom. I hope the young man you speak of is a good man, even though you have said he does not embrace our belief. So few do. Do not judge him too soon. He might see the TRUTH. Perhaps they do not intend more than friendship? How I wish I were there right now to see him for myself. Tell her again to write me.'

The pen remained motionless over the paper for a long time. She knew that if what she wrote now sounded wrong to her own ears, she would not be able to write it over again. Hesitantly the pen began to move across the page.

'Oscar, I must tell you something that troubles me greatly. It may give you despair once more. I feel I cannot come to you if it means I must have another child. I write these words while I have the courage to do so. It is still possible for me to become pregnant. I know this for certain, and I cannot face it. I must say it as simply as that. Can you understand? You must. Can you help me? Give me hope that it will not happen?

'When I think of the night you left me in Finland, and that I add this plea to your worries, I feel small and mean. Undeserving of God's Plan. Will the Lord punish me for what I ask of you? I cannot help it.

'I will write to make the reservations for passage on a Norwegian boat, but when the time comes to leave I will have to answer to myself if I will use it. Forgive me.

'I send you my love and all my thoughts on this winter night. Snow has drifted over the windows enclosing us here in this tight *stuga* still warm from the day's fire. All the others sleep. They send you their love. Your *mor,* also.

"How I wish you were here and that we could talk until the night became old. I go to bed relieved that I have written you my feelings, although I carry a terrible burden of guilt. Goodnight, dear Oscar. I want you as much as you want me, but I will not have another child.'

As she got ready for bed, removing only her dress and one petticoat before slipping her nightdress over her head, she bent to study what she had written. Hair brushed and braided, she sat to reread it more thoroughly. Quickly she picked up the envelope, inserted the letter and sealed it, rubbing the flap far longer than necessary before addressing it. The string overhead pulled to put out the light; she made her way in the dark to the bedroom, lifted the sprawled youngest further over to make room, and checked Carl at the foot of the bed to assure herself the fur blanket covered him. A quick thought passed through her mind as she plumped the pillow before laying her head on it. Perhaps Katarina's hand had been on the pen along with her own. And Berta Lund's. A smile faded slowly as she slipped into sleep.

*

The winter became a time of waiting for Lisa. busy as she was relieving *farmor* of the added work that a houseful of children brought, the days were made of creeping hours.

Farmor sensed her unease, saw the unguarded moments spent staring into space, and noticed how silent she had become.

"You should get out, Lisa," she said one day. "Leave the two young ones with me and go see your old neighbors back at the sawmill. Most of them are still there, I hear."

"Thank you, *Mor* Veldman. I'd like to do that, if I could go on a day when the others are home from school."

"Just go, and don't worry about us three. Take them some coffee. I know they are always short of it."

"But, *Mor* Veldman, should you do that? Your pension is so small, and I have so little to add to it. We eat you out of house and home."

"Take it. When we run out, we run out. We'll be English and drink tea." Lisa resisted no further.

When the older children were off to school in the dark of the winter morning, she got ready. At the last minute she decided to take the youngest with her. In gray twilight of mid-morning she brought *farmor's spark* up to the entrance, took the sheepskin fur from her bed and spread it over the seat of the sled. A big pillow gave softness to the seat and the back of the sled for the three-year-old girl. Dresed in red knitted bonnet, coat, leggings, and mittens the child was engulfed by the double thickness of fur as Lisa tucked it tightly around her. Only a small space to see was left open.

Carl stood inside the doorway with *farmor* to wave goodbye. Lisa called, "You help *farmor* like you promised. She's depending on you." He nodded. the door was already closing against the cold as Lisa grasped the high handle above the back of the seat, pushed the *spark* into speed at a run, then jumped onto the long runners behind it. With a kick from one leg, then the other, she maintained and increased the speed as the sled hissed up and down over the snow covered hillocks.

Exhilarated by the movement, the freedom of the white landscape, and even in the tug of her skirt and wool underskirts as the wind whipped them around, she forgot her worry. Cold flew up against her legs as she bent to the right or the left to steer the sled. her skirts dipped into the snow to stir up a small cloud to trail after her. Once she stopped to rewind her knitted scarf. When she checked the youngest, the child smiled at her, looked out into the snowy world and cried, "Ride! Ride!"

As eager to be in motion again as the girl, she slapped her mittened hands together, then kicked the sled speedily over the frozen waters of a small inlet of the sea. Sooner than she thought it possible she arrived, bringing the sled to a halt to look once more on the old sawmill. The remembered piercing song of the saws again sent it snarls and whines out into the woodland setting of the *stugas*. There it was, third from the right, her home for most of the years of her marriage. There was the pump, the pivot of her household work. She saw no change.

She had told herself that it would seem she had come home. Instead she found herself rejoicing that she was no longer a part of this sawmill community. Grateful that none of the men, working in the mill, were either Oscar or his brother, Evert. Old memories crowded her mind. She felt she had arrived at a decision, but could not say what it was. The small world in front of her took its rightful place, just a long stopover on the way to the New Kingdom. The New Kingdom of the Lord. America? Nay, not America. Surely that was not an earthly kingdom, she told herself quickly.

Riding the long runners, she kicked the *spark* down the small incline of the snowy road, over one of the paths past the pump, and up to the *stuga* next to one that had been hers.

Greta Swanson welcomed her with open arms and a screech that announced across the clearing that others should come see who was there. They came, the women with their new young in tow, shawls hastily thrown on and clutched to their breasts with red hands lifted from morning work. The gift coffee quickly added its good aroma. Sweet bakings were taken down from the highest shelf. Women made journeys back to their *stugas* for more baked delicacies, in honor of the visitor and her child. The youngest was admired, and given ride-a-cock-horse rides on many an upraised foot. Questions about Finland, Oscar, Elvira, and the other children were asked endlessly.

"And Marta?" one of them dared to voice at last. "The one left behind so long to become a rich man's child. What of her?"

Lisa heard the echoes of the censure she had faced when Marta had been sent to live with the Palmers'. Even now some of the women's lips tightened, their faces hardened. But, in the tone of the speaker she heard envy too.

"She is thick and fat," she answered, "as a child should be. Marta is a good member of the family. Worked herding cows to help us these past years. Even drove a manure wagon when her sister was sick. She is one of us and is ready to go to America."

The women exchanged glances then, as if in apology, lifted their voices higher, and smiled more widly to ask about America. Some spoke of it in envy, others with pity bordering on fear. She might get lost in that big country, like others they knew about. Never heard of again back here in their homeland.

The noon whistle blew sending the women to scatter like shrieking birds. They gathered up their young, crowded out the door, and rushed homeward to get hot food on the table for their sawmill husbands. Gus Swanson came in to welcome Lisa with a warm handshake. While washing his hands he gave her news of the men.

"Yaw, Bengson, he's off in America somewhere, I guess you know. Minnesota. Oscar hasn't bumped into him?"

"Nay, no fear of that," Lisa answered. "Minnesota is far from Illinois, I understand. Bengson can stay where he is and do his dirty work firing for the bosses up there. But Olafsson, he stays on?"

"Yaw," Gus told her. "He is a good manager, that one. It hurt him to fire Oscar. This I know. That's why he made Bengson do it."

"Oscar always spoke well of Olafsson all the years we were here. He was sorry he wasn't man enough to do that job himself."

"Yaw, yaw," Gus agreed, and began to ladle hot yellow pea soup into his mouth from the large bowl his wife set in front of him. He pointed his wooden spoon at Lisa, but turned to his wife. "Aren't you going to give her and the child some?"

"Give me time, give me time," his wife answered, and turned to Lisa. Eyes and face uncertain, she asked, "You'll eat it? It has ham in it."

'I'll eat it, and so will the child."

"You have changed," Greta Swanson commented, as she set a bowl of the fragrant soup in front of her old-time neighbor.

"Nay," Lisa answered. She settled the youngest in her lap. "I have learned that what the Lord provides in time of necessity is no sin. Your good soup will give me the strength to make my way back to *mor* Veldman's."

Gus drained the last of his soup by lifting the bowl. Coffee cup in his hand he stood up as he drank it. "Tell Oscar from me," he said, as he lifted his jacket off the wooden peg on the wall, "union work goes on again, here as well as in other places. Slowly, too damn slowly. It's going to take years before we get what we need."

"I'll tell him," Lisa assured him, but added, "Oscar knows. He reads a Swedish newspaper over there, printed in America. Also a newspaper written for the working man. He tells me he learns much from it, although it takes him some time to read it, because it is written in American."

"Ya, so? Oscar always was one for reading. A smart man, reading American already. I've heard of that Swedish paper. Would like to see a copy of it, that I would. Do you suppose Oscar could send me one?"

The blast of the sawmill sent him hurrying toward the door and out. Lisa set the child down on the floor and followed him. "I'll make sure you get one," she called, "and one of the working man's paper too. The schoolteacher could read some of it to you, I'm sure."

He nodded and waved as he tramped throught the snow toward the mill.

The dark shadow of the sawmill was being swallowed up by the gray of early afternoon when she said goodbye to Greta Swanson. The first kilometer, of the many back to *farmor's* was quickly traveled. Her thoughts were happy as she relived the reunion with the Swansons and the women. Her breath, vaporized in the cold, puffed out in an enlarged cloud as she laughed out loud. Running, riding, kicking the *spark* over the snow was joy itself. The cold advance of night began to put a crust on the snow. She grew tired, thought again of the question that tormented and lengthened her days. What would Oscar's answer be? On this small journey she had discovered there was only one place whe wanted to be. The certainty began when she first looked at the *stugas*. It flowered in her mind as she sat at the table with Gus, Greta and their children. A rush of memories of her own family sitting just so, in the familiar setting of the sawmill *stuga,* had made her realize it. To be with Oscar was what she wanted more than anything in the world. If only she could hurry the days. Unite the family at last. How she longed for Oscar. Felt hunger for his arms. Could almost feel the brush of his mustache on her cold lips. A rough involuntary sound burst from her mouth into the chill wind. She stopped the sled. How long would it be, she asked the darkened sky, before she would share a bed with him again. A bed where there would be only one world, the world of their feelings for each other. With a cry she sent the sled forward, and answered herself with, soon, let it be soon. And yet...

Home again the question of Oscar's answer was once more beating like a hammer within her head. What would it be?

Christmas arrived. *Farmor* kept the pact as did Lisa. The school children learned the catechism. Emilia did it in one night. While seated on a stool she recited it out loud, bumped her head against the wall to pound the words into memory.

Farmor complained. "Tomorrow you will remember only the pain in the back of your head, not the catechism."

But Emilia returned home the next day to tell *farmor,* "The schoolmaster had a hard time to believe it, but I recited the catechism without missing a word." *Farmor* placed an extra potato on Emilia's plate that night.

In the dark of Christmas morning *farmor* went to church, alone, carrying a lantern. The candle flame sent feeble rays of light out to sparkle in the snow. That evening she produced a kind of Christmas celebration with special foods, never consulting Lisa. There was *lute fisk,* with rich buttery white sauce dotted with white pepper. Potatoes cooked to mealy goodness, enought to fill the largest of stomachs, rice cooked in milk until creamy, with lingon berries cooked, sweetened, and strained into a clear ruby red sauce to pour generously over the rice. *Spritz* baked in shapes of rings, stars, moons, and squiggly lengths, just right for popping whole into eager mouths. Thin ginger crisps, enough so everyone could eat their fill, and more. They had all been baked when Lisa was out on errands, so they came as a surprise to her too.

When the supper dishes had been washed the old woman announced with an air of defiance, "We are going to make *knäk* tonight."

With shouts of anticipation the girls clustered around her, eager to do the cooking as well as eating. They hovered together over the carmelizing sugar in the smallest black kettle, and added water in careful measurement. In turn they tested the drops for hardness, dripped from *farmor's* only silver spoon into a sauce of cold water. Between times they buttered squares of paper, even the youngest given a pat to smear on one. The shine of grease around her mouth and on her nose, betrayed that her fingers were as often in her mouth as on the paper. Carl, too, was given a square but ate the butter immediately, to the great disgust of Johan. He scolded and told Carl, "You can't have any *knäk* when it's ready."

Carl howled. But Lisa assured him, from where she sat darning stockings. if he could butter at least one paper he would not be left out. Marta and Emilia put their coats on and dashed out to fill a tin tray with a mound of snow. Paulina and Maria hovered over the delicious smell coming from the pot.

"Are the papers twisted?" they yelled.

"They'r twisted, but wait. We have to set them in the snow," Emilia answered. The buttered squares had been made into miniature funnels, the lower ends turned up to seal them against leaking. They stood now, with *farmor's* help, in the snow, ready for the pouring of the candy. The hot syrup, dribbled from the smallest ladle, was watched by nine pairs of anxious eyes, Lisa set aside her darning to join in. As the hot liquid melted the snow around each funnel, many hands added fresh snow.

"Let the older ones do it," *farmor* cautioned. "You little ones will burn yourselves."

At last all the cornucopias were filled, the kettle empty. Maria carried the tray slowly, step by careful step, toward the door. Johan rushed ahead to fling first the inner door open, then the outer one. The others crowded behind Maria, until Lisa called, "Only Maria to go outside, the rest of you stay inside."

"Put it in the snowdrift in front of the door," several voices advised Maria. She returned in triumph. Not one drop had spilled as she pressed the tray down into the snowbank. The cold hurried the hardening process of the candy, and soon everyone was sucking the pointed sweets. Lisa knew *farmor* had given the children a Cristmas gift. She neither said thank you, nor scolded. The two women exchanged knowing smiles, and let it go at that.

*

A snowstorm in mid-January threatened to bury *farmor's stuga* completely. It began on Friday, and continued into the pre-dawn hours of Monday. Snow covered the windows again, and was piled high in front of the door. With a shovel, pans, and mittened fingers the girls and Johan cleared a hole large enough so they could crawl up and out into the changed world. The summer house, they reported, was just a huge smooth curve in the light of the moon. The sky above was clear but more snow clouds hovered on the horizon.

"Nay, you had better stay home this day," *farmor* advised, as she went to put her head out and look around.

"We can't," cried Palina. "Today the schoolmaster is giving us tests in spelling and arithmetic."

"Are you sure you can get through this deep snow?" Lisa asked.

"Of course," was her answer. The children were eager to be out in that exciting world.

"Take the *spark* then. Maybe Johan might have to ride in it," she told them.

"I can walk," he declared, "but I can kick the *spark* and let Marta ride in it."

"I can get through better than you can. I'm taller," his sister shouted at him.

"Quiet," Lisa scolded, "Go then, all of you. I'll have your sandwiches ready by the time you have your coats on."

The *stuga* was warm with the snow packed against it, but too dark. Before midday Lisa made her way around outside to each window and shoveled the snow away to let in wintry light. It began to snow again before she finished. Battered by the wind and driven snow, she made her way back toward the door. To her surprise she heard the children calling to her. It was too early for their return from school. She pulled her shawl back behind her ears in an effort to make out why they were calling as they struggled through the snow.

"Pappa's letter...brought...school."

Had she heard right? She ran. The pull of the snow made her fall. Laughing she got up and reached toward Maria, who held the letter out to her.

It was real. It was here. There was Oscar's handwriting, sightly blurred where snow had brushed against it.

"The postman left all the mail at the school for the children to take home," Maria explained.

Paulina added, "The schoolmaster closed the school. Said we all better get on home before the storm started up again."

Lisa nodded hardly hearing what they said. She pushed the shovel into a snowdrift, turned and slid down the long slant of snow into the *stuga*. The five children followed rapidly, one after the other, their whoops silenced only when they staggered through the vestibule to face a disapproving *farmor*.

"The little one sleeps," she scolded.

The envelope was thick. Lisa's hand shook as she picked up Oscar's *puukko* to slit it open. She withdrew the sheets of the letter, a bank draft, and saw that there was another smaller paper with her name in large print on its folded side. Immediately she knew what it was.

"Hang up your coats," she ordered the children, "I must see if the youngest woke up. I'll read you the letter as soon as I come back."

She hurried into the bedroom and closed the door firmly. Still in her shawl she unfolded the small paper and read, "I understand your worry. Believe me, I will see to it that you will not have to bear another child. I will take that sin upon my own shoulders."

Here was his answer. Clear and to the point, written for her eyes only. She stumbled forward against the bed where the child lay in deep sleep, and leaned her legs against it for support. Bent over she read the words again. She stifled a gasp. Her mind repeated endlessly, "I will take that sin upon my own shoulders."

What had she done to that good and religious man? Was she to push him into sin? Why, why, had the Lord so ordered things? She sat on the edge of the bed to reread once again, and felt a happiness begin, in spite of that final sentence. Soon she would be with Oscar. The family would be whole again. Whatever he meant to do she would take half the sin. This she would write him immediately.

"Mamma?" Johan whispered at the door, as he opened it a crack, "aren't you coming back yet?"

"Yaw, yaw, here I am," she smiled at him, and went out of the bedroom, her shawl falling unnoticed off her shoulders onto the floor.

The small piece of paper was in her apron pocket. The letter was filled with advice and directions for the travel to Norway, over the Atlantic, and through the United States. A schoolbook was opened on the table and once again fingers traced, on its small world map, the journey that would begin in March. North to Solleftëa, where they would change train to travel west, through Sweden into Norway. When they reached that country's shore, at Trondheim, they would transfer to a coast mail boat to travel south to Bergen. There the big ocean going steamship would be waiting. All that needed to be done now was for Lisa to get the rest of the money to the steamship company. As the children turned the pages to a map of the United States and began plotting their train trip to Chicago, Lisa studied the bank draft.

She handed it to *farmor*. "Can you imagine how much he had to borrow," she said with a shake of her head. "Some of it is for you, you know."

"If that is so," *farmor* answered, "I want you to take it and go to Härnosänd with Paulina and buy yourselves each a good pair of shoes at *Herr* Palmer's shoe shop."

"What! Nay, *Mor* Veldman. We will do no such thing. Your money is for you. Oscar spells that out right in this letter."

"So, it is my money. I can do with it what I want. If you don't take it and go I will go with Paulina and buy you a pair too. Just hope they will fit when I bring them back."

Paulina came to stand shyly in front of Lisa. "I can have new shoes?" she asked, and without waiting for an answer went to *farmor*. "Thank you, *farmor,* thank you. I would like that so much."

"Hooray!" shouted Emilia. "Get some just like mine, Paulina. They're real good."

Lisa could not deny *farmor* after that. She thanked her and went to stir up the coals in the fireplace and set the copper coffee pot near the red embers. When the loan had been paid back, she told herself, she would make sure bank drafts would be sent to Oscar's *mor* as long as she lived. The girls could help send their *farmor* money.

The trip to Härnosänd was made on a sunny day. Along with the new shoes came a can of shoe polish sent by Herr Palmer. Elbows flew as the Finland shoes of the others were polished to a new gloss, in preparation for the departure to America. More than that, Lisa had bought a coat. Pink cheeked with the excitement of this first new coat since she married, she paraded for the family and swept them curtsies in her happiness.

"Nay, but can you believe this?" Lisa inquired out loud of herself, some days later, as she happened to glance out a front window.

"What do you say?" *farmor* asked, looking up from the salt herring roe she was getting ready to fry.

"Come see!" Lisa urged, one hand beckoning the old woman while she still looked out the window. "It's *Herr* Palmer, and his *fru!*"

"*Fru* Palmer? Here?" *Farmor* hurried to peer over Lisa's shoulder. "She has come all the way here to say goodbye? But Marta isn't home and won't be for more than an hour."

"I think there is more to this than to say goodbye." Lisa said, with a quick nod of her head. She went to open the doors to welcome the visitor.

"*Valkömmen, valdömmen,*" Lisa greeted them, and shook their hands. She introduced *Fru* Palmer to *farmor* and urged them to let her have their coats. It was warm in the house. As she placed the garments on *farmor's* bed she ran a hand over the soft fine fabric of *Fru* Palmer's coat. It was heavy, had a quilted lining. She could see the colorful silk that covered it. A beautiful coat, but with no more style than her own new purchase, she consoled herself.

Farmor had whisked away the herring roe and now prepared fresh coffee. She brought out her finest coffee cups, and the recent bakings, while Lisa settled the visitors in chairs where they would be comfortable, and then sat talking small talk with them.

Yaw, Marta was doing very well in school. It was too bad the children would have to leave before the end of the term. The voices slowed and died. Then *Herr* Palmer spoke.

"Marta, let her stay with us. Let her grow up here. We will educate her, care for her. When she is grown she can join you in America." There was a desperate question in his voice. *Fru* Palmer said nothing.

"We would have her talk English, so when she comes to visit you in America, she will speak it as well as your other children. Listen to me, we feel she is ours almost as much as yours. Don't we, Sabina?"

There was only a slow belated nod from his wife.

"Nay. She is *our* daughter," Lisa answered, and set her cup down hard. "We will do for her as we do for the others, and raise her in our own faith." She looked directly at *Fru* Palmer as she spoke. That fine *fru* was carefully smoothing a crease out of her fashionable skirt and looked up neither at Lisa nor her husband.

Herr Palmer sat back. He studied his clasped hands pressed tightly together on his knees. It was plain he felt deep disappointment, yet she could see he had expected that answer and, perhaps, respected her for it. He looked up.

"Do I dare ask, *Fru* Veldman, if you would consider letting me take her for at least a day before you go?"

Lisa nodded, already sorry she had spoken so abruptly. She noticed he pleaded for himself, saying "me", not "us". He pressed further.

"The coat Marta wears is the one we sent with her to Finland. It is to small and badly faded. Would you let us buy her a new one? A last gift?"

Lisa glanced at *farmor,* sitting motionless with her knitting needles poised.

"Only a coat, nothing more," she answered, and saw *farmor's* needles resume rapid movement. "Marta will thank you, as I do, *Herr* Palmer," she said with a smile, and saw *farmor* nodding agreement over her clicking needles.

"Did you see?" Lisa demanded of *farmor,* when the guests were gone. "She never wanted the child. I'm positive. No wonder Marta never spoke of her in all the time we were in Finland." She shook her head and mourned anew that her child had spent so long a time in *Fru* Palmer's company. "That one!" she exclaimed, the tone of her voice summing up her opinion of the woman. "Palmer, now, there is a good man," she announced.

Farmor agreed, and over the frying roe discussed the visit and their guests endlessly with her daughter-in-law.

The day to leave for America arrived, cold, snowing and with a blustery wind. *Farbror* Evert and *Herr* Palmer came with horse-drawn sleds to take them, their bundles, the suitcase, and the yellow basket to the nearest train station, Arlansbrö. The yellow basket was heavy with sausages and *knäkebröd,* their food for the trip until they would board the steamship in Bergen.

"Goodbye, *farmor!*"

"Goodbye, *farbror* Palmer! I love my coat!" This last was from Marta, aglow in a new bright blue coat, the collar a wide cape that lifted up to be tied, as it was now, into a warm hood.

To America

Farmor stood on the platform, one hand exposed and red with cold at her throat, as she clutched her dark woolen shawl. In the strong wind her long striped skirt billowed in front, to either side, sometimes up in back, but she did not notice. Dry-eyes, blinking only when snow whipped into her face past the protective edges of the shawl, she searched the train windows.

The doors were closed, frost on the windows making it hard for the children to find clear spots so they could see and wave to the two left standing on the platform. Behind them Evert settled Carl on a seat, lifted bundles up on racks and searched for a place to put the yellow basket out of the way. He had insisted on going with them as far as Solleftëa, even though *farbror* Johan and his family, Evert's family too, would meet them there to say goodbye. They could help them transfer to the train that would take them to Norway, but *farmor* had sided with him, unwilling to let Lisa start off on this long journey without a member of the family along. It meant she would have to drive Evert's horse and sleigh home, and return to meet him on the afternoon train, but she was willing. Evert could tell her then that they were safely on their way, as he dropped her off at her own empty *stuga,* before he headed home to Sollefteå again.

"Goodbye, *farmor,*" Maria mouthed softly against the cold glass. With exaggerated movements of her lips, she added, "We'll come back someday." Since early morning she had wanted to give *farmor* this reassurance, but knew she would have wept uncontrollably if *farmor* had answered, as she knew she would, "Nay, I'll be gone by then."

The train whistled and began to move. The calls became loud, frantic. Foreheads bumped and noses squashed against the frosty windows. The Arlansbrö small yellow railroad station seemed to move past the train. The two figures were close together on the platform. Herr Palmer waved both hands in their fur-lined gloves. Suddenly the shawl of the old woman flew upward, in an erratic dance of farewell of its own, as she released her hold to wave. Quickly *Herr* Palmer gathered the wind-whipped garment and wrapped it around her again. They were lost to sight. Lisa, holding the youngest, stood watching the name Arlansbrö beneath the peak of the station, disappear in a thick rush of snowflakes. Amazed at herself, her last thought was of the long icicles hanging from the sign. They should be knocked down before they fell hurting someone. She turned swiftly, placed the youngest down next to Carl, and began sorting out where everyone was, and where they should sit.

*

As the train wound westward through the Norwegian mountains, Lisa wanted neither to look back nor ahead. She made the children and their eating of the sausages *farmor* had packed first in importance, fussing over them. She did not mingle with the other passengers, also bound, most of them, for the boat to America.

A group of Lap men in their blue and red costumes came on board at one stop and briefly distracted her. She could see they admired her for her many children. A moment of anger flooded her. For this, she thought? For six, for seven, for eight that I could not help, did not choose? For this I am admired? Just before they got off they scattered paper-covered candies in the children's laps, much to the relief of sausage weary mouths. Lisa gave them a final glare. There won't be a twelfth, that I'd like you to know, she snorted inside herself.

At Trondjehm it was another night of four in a bed, an almost midnight rise to catch the coastal boat to Bergen. Although it was not really rough many people were sick, but luckily none of Lisa's party. The four younger ones continued their interrupted sleep on the many bundles while the three eldest went out from the comparative warmth of the main salon to stand in the shelter of an overhang and sing songs to the snowcapped mountains. The young sailors were appreciative of the singing but the bitter cold brought the girls in, and stinging rain welcome them to Bergen.

Paper work finally completed, they were taken by tender out to the massive liner, "Stavanngerfjord", where at last Lisa could relax. Wearily she sagged down onto one of the lower bunks.

"Go explore the boat," she told the older girls. "You look like excitement is going to burst your skins if you don't. I must sleep, and alone. Take the two young ones with you, but watch them carefully."

Exhausted, she slept, but not so deeply she did not know that now and then her children quietly opened the door of the cabin to make sure she was there. When the thrum of the engines sent their message through the ship, she awakened. Stretching comfortably, she looked about her at the neat bunks, the play of winter sunshine throught he large port hole. The washbasin promised cleanliness to her and the three younger ones. She would have to get up and see if the girls' cabin next door was exactly the same. She placed a hand flat against the wall next to her. It felt solid, the throb of the engine like a heart beat against her palm. For the first time since leaving *farmor's* she felt secure. This colossus of a ship, like a Norwegian city sent out onto the waters, would face no dangers. No storm would be great enough to disturb it, its neutrality a guarantee for safe passage. Seated on the edge of the bunk, she clasped her hands and gave thanks for having reached this far on their journey, and prayed for safe passage to New York. She removed the pins from her hair, found brush and comb, and freshened herself.

The children, tumbling down the stairs from the deck, met her halfway up.

"We're on our way!" they shouted.

"Do we have to stop somewhere else before we get to America?" Johan wanted to know, worry large on his face.

"Where could we stop?" Emilia asked in disgust. "There's only water between Norway and America."

Paulina corrected her. "There's Iceland, and Greenland. But we aren't going there, Johan. We won't stop until America."

"Hurrah!" he shouted. "Pappa will be there." Without waiting for possible contradiction he ran up the stairway shouting, "To Pappa! To Pappa!"

Carl, doing his best to run up the stair behind his brother, loudly echoed him. The youngest enchanted by their shouts took up the words. Step by difficult step upward, she cried, "To Pappa! To Pappa!" until the laughter of her elders, behind her, made her laugh too.

Norway disappeared as they stood watching at the rail, longer than many of the others, who were driven in by the cold. A bell within the ship sounded.

"That's for us to come eat," Maria explained. "We found that out while you were sleeping, Mamma."

"I'll show you where our dining room is," Emilia offered, and hurried first through the door leading inside.

"I can show the way," both Maria and Johan insisted, as they crowded ahead too.

Johan stopped suddenly, his mouth turned down in distaste. "Are we going to have to eat more sausage?" he asked.

Lisa laughed. "I don't think so, Johan, but if that's what it is we will eat it."

The girls quietly exchanged looks of horror at the thought, but kept silent.

Long tables, already well filled with passengers ran the length of the large dining room of the second class. Every head turned to watch Lisa and her seven troop in and find a place where they could sit together. Printed menus lay on the table. The older girls read one together. The Norwegian writing was only slightly different from Swedish. They vied with each other to read it out loud.

"Cabbage soup! My favorite!"

"Not only soup, but more!"

"Meatballs!""and potatoes!"

"Pickled beets, besides!"

"*Limpa*!" This they all shouted together. Lisa had to hush them. Seldom had the Veldman table been able to afford the wonderful delicious soft rye bread.

"Butter. Coffee. Milk—and buttermilk too!"

"What is this?" the girls puzzled. The final item was written in American. Paulina read a note in Norwegian that followed the item. "A common American dessert," and spelled it aloud. "A-P-P-L-E P-I-E," then pronounced it. "Ep-pleh pee-eh." There was silence. She asked, "What is it?" No one knew.

The first course was set down in large serving dishes in the middle of the table. Lisa could not remember her children being so silent at a meal. They ate without looking up, reached for more, and sat smiling, licking their lips until the strange dessert was brought in on separate plates and put in front of each person.

"It's good."

"Tasty."

"I hope Pappa knows about ep-pleh pee-eh."

"It must cost very much," Paulina said, suddenly worried. "Do you have enough money, Mamma, to pay for such meals all the way?"

Maria explained with impatience, "They are paid for already, Paulina."

"Haven't I told you that the tickets pay for everything?" Lisa asked in surprise. "Bed and meals are paid for until we get off in America. I thought I had made that clear. Nay, Carl, no more *limpa.* you have had enough. All right, Maria, give him one more slice but not so much butter. No crying, Carl."

The boat was luxury to Lisa. No meals to prepare, no dishes to wash. Coffee in mid-morning, mid-afternoon, and before going to bed. Wonderful Norwegian bakings to dip and eat with the coffee. Meals that filled and fattened the children, and so varied that she made mental note to cook some of the dishes should fortune be theirs in America. Under the click of her flashing needles many new pairs of stockings grew for Oscar, as she visited with the many immigrants on board. There was time to reread Elvira's last letter at leisure. It had arrived only days before they left Sweden. In it she told Lisa she was marrying her young man, Leander Olsson. The marriage would wait until Lisa was there. It was a long letter. The hurt of too infrequent, too short notes of the past was removed. There was a letter from Oscar to reread also. He had written that the lad was a good man, in his opinion. A union man. Lisa was content.

The days were clear, the large ship plowing through gentle waters until the third day. A strange quiet brought Lisa's head up from her knitting and silenced everyone in the lounge. the engine had stopped. The propellers no longer sent their vibrations through the ship.

A man came bursting in from the deck. "A German boat is out there! A submarine chaser. It's made us stop!"

What more he had to say was lost in the noise of the people rushing up out of their chairs to the deck, shouting questions, Lisa among them.

The railing was thick with milling people, many arms points to the German boat, voices loud with fright. Some crying. Lisa searched for Maria trying to locate her children. They came running toward her, the four older ones shouting something.

"What? Maria, you," she indicated, and picked up the youngest to hush her whimpers.

"A man back there," Maria reported, with hardly enough breath to say it, "said we were all going to be blow up and sent down to the bottom of the sea!"

"Are we?" Marta cried, holding tight to Lisa's knitting bag.

"He said they are going to torpedo us!" Emilia shouted, her small mouth grim.

Paulina, dark eyes wide, said, "We are not at war. Can they do that?"

Johan stared at Lisa, his whole body asking the same question.

"Nay," Lisa answered, making her voice calm. "God is not going to let that happen. We will go watch. You will see."

A small boat was being rowed from the submarine chaser to the ocean liner, two officers standing amidship. There was an unnatural silence among the people at the rail as the officers mounted the stairway that had been lowered alongside almost into the water. Every head turned to watch their meeting with the captain. They spoke together for a few moments before the captain turned and led them into the ship. Two words, "contraband goods," heard by those who were closest, were passed from mouth to mouth in hushed and frightened tones as talk began again among the passengers.

"Yaw," Lisa said, when the words reached her, "they will find no such thing on this boat. We will be on our way again, soon." She saw that her children believed her. It was enough. They leaned, with new interest, to look down on the sailors who sat in the small boat far below, their oars at rest. The submarine chaser lifted on the swells of the ocean like a bristling promise of evil.

"I'll be in the lounge until the officers come back," Lisa called to Maria. She saw the girls nod as they lifted Carl and the youngest to see better. Several women joined Lisa. They sat knitting, talking of the horrors of war, and tried to reassure each other they were in no danger. Their ears strained for any change in the sounds out on the deck. Time passed and more people came in out of the cold.

Lisa looked up to gasp. She saw three of her young walking behind the captain and the German officers as they strode past the lounge door. Emilia was first, her stomach stuck out to adopt the silhouette of the largest officer. She aped his walk with large solid strides. Her mouth was pulled down to imitate his large drooping mustache. Paulina, a hand over her mouth to smother her "nyehs," walked behind her. Marta, grinning broadly was last. Lisa frowned and shook her head fiercely.

The girls did no more than grin in return and hurried on behind the three men.

Among everyone in the lounge Lisa hurried out to the deck. By the time she reached it the three girls had disappeared in the crowd. The captain was nowhere in sight. In a short time the engine throbbed into life. Men cheered. As the German officers reached their boat, the *Stavengerfjord* moved forward. It built up speed. With silent, intense concentration the passengers watched the submarine chaser head in another direction.

"Hurrah! Hurrah! Hurrah!" everyone yelled, Lisa more lustily than any other, unashamed of her tears of relief.

That evening the dance orchestra played so loud and lively the sound penetrated down to the Veldman's two cabins. Celebration vibrated through the ship. Lisa felt it and was unable to resist.

"We will go up tonight after the young ones sleep. You can go too, Marta." Stunned, the girls hurried into their own cabin. Lisa knew they wanted to fuss with clothes and hair. On previous nights the three older girls had been allowed to go watch the dancing for a while, but she knew they had done so from the doorway. They never entered, never encouraged the glances of men who looked their way--most often at Maria in hopes of a partner. Men outnumbered the women. Young or old, any willing woman or girl, was danced into happy exhaustion.

Lisa called the girls. They arrived at the door to the lounge in a group, but Lisa swept right on in, found chairs against a wall and settled down to watch in comfort. Several people came to welcome her.

"You and the girls have come to dance?" a woman asked.

"Nay," Lisa answered. "not me, but when a schottische starts I think my girls can dance it with each other."

That they did, Emilia with vigor, Maria with grace, and both with such excellence it denied that their *stuga* had been the only place they had ever swept through the precise and graceful steps. Paulina and Marta tried too. But Marta too new at it, and Paulina's reluctant attempts, had them stumbling nearby and laughing so hard they staggered back in defeat.

The next dance was a waltz. Maria and Emilia stood in front of Lisa, mopping their perspiring faces when two men arrived and asked them to dance. The girls loked with entreaty at Lisa. She nodded. Away they went, forgetting after the first steps, to look back at her with large smiles of thanks. When the dance ended Maria asked, "Are you going to tell Pappa?" Emilia and Paulina crowded close to hear her answer.

"In time, in time," she said, and added, "here come three men.

Paulina, you get out there too."

Lisa made it known she would not dance. Yet she was continually asked, especially by one tall burly man. He came at the beginning of almost every dance, his eyes admiring, a friendly smile of his lips as he made a bow before her. He made her feel young, beautiful, desired. With a start she brought her thoughts up sharp. She realized, suddenly, she was responding to him. How could that be? Did he remind her of Oscar? Her eyes sought him out among the dancers. Nay. But his hand, there, flat against the back of the woman with whom he was dancing. It was like Oscar's. Big, fingers thickened by work. They would be capable of gentleness in love.

She jerked erect at the thought. That she should sit her thinking like that! She, mamma of those three almost full grown girls out there dancing. What was happening to her? Was it because she had been alone so long?

Alone? She was not alone. Oscar was always with her. Why had it taken so long to recognize that? She had seen Oscar in Berta Lund, she realized. The same independence of thought and action, and in their reverence for books and learning. And in Pastor Rudolfsson. Like Oscar he worked for a New Kingdom, the pastor placing his in heaven, Oscar's here on God's own green earth. She had seen it in the good Finnish three who had come in the night, giving themselves without reservation for their cause. Perhaps in Sigurd too, there had been much of Oscar, although few could equal Sigurd's gentleness. But, his total belief in the preaching of the church was solid, like Oscar's dedication to his interpretation of the Bible as set forth by their own small sect, Ephraim's Messengers.

In Katarina? Nay. Unlike her, Oscar would never pay the price of a bed unwarmed by bodily love, his mate lying right alongside.

Nay, she had not been alone.

The burly man was coming towad her, the next dance started. She yearned suddenly to go below, to lie in the bunk and pull the protection of Oscar around her like a soft cover. As she shook her head once again, to the man's invitation, she was grateful to him. Because of him she had seen so clearly that Oscar was with her. And she saw herself too. Not only mamma and wife, but a woman, admired, perhaps coveted, but appreciated for herself.

The dancing came to an end. Lisa gathered the excited, happy girls. Emilia delayed them. She stood lifting first one foot up behind her then the other, examining their soles.

"What are you doing?" her twin demanded.

"Got to see if my shoes are worn out like Elvira's. Remember? In her first letter she said she wore them out dancing."

"Ack, see that you don't," Lisa advised, but laughed as heartily as the others.

The ship plowed serenly toward the American shore. It was March 31, Carl's birthday, and the day they were to land. A snowstorm raged across the choppy sea, making it impossible to pull into port. The ship had to anchor off shore. In the dining room, birthday wishes were showered on the small boy. Sweets had been dug from bundles in many cabins and presented to him. The birthday song had been sung, most of the diners coming to stand at their table to sing it. The words of the song wished him to live to a hundred years.

"Only ninety-five years more", Maria told Carl.

America

Sometime during the night the storm died, the ship hoistedan-chored, steamed into port and docked. The deep quiet and lack of motion wakened Lisa. She struggled into her dress and went to tell her four girls sleeping in the next cabin, "We are there!"

The hallway had become noisy with people hurrying up on deck to see America for the first time. Lisa joined them, stopping only to get her shawl, her coat carefully put away until they would land in America.

Sun, shining on snow, almost blinded her when they first stepped out onto the deck. The shed roof alongside supported pillows of snow as deep as any that had fallen on *farmor's stuga*. Off to the left the dark rise of tall buildings, under a clear blue sky, were jagged imitations of Norway's snow-crowned mountains. Sounds from the city, muted, hard to put a name to, filled the air. Closer were the calls of men, in a language that told her nothing. She looked down from the rail and saw stevedores were already unloading the ship.

Nightmares are supposed to happen in sleep, but the weary day spent getting through immigration was a waking one. But at last the dome-shaped building was left behind and once again they were transported to a boat that took them to the appropriate train shed indicated by the number and color of the tag hanging around Lisa's neck. As she settled her family on straw seats that looked worn and dirty, she wanted then and there to judge and condemn the new land. Finding a rag, she cleared enough grime from a window so that they could look out as the train started and see America. It was not impressive. The buildings were dark with soot.

Lisa was tired to the marrow of her bones. But the children were reviving.

"We're off to Pappa," Maria leaned to tell Johan, who nodded wisely.

"To Pappa, to Pappa," the youngest echoed next to Lisa and clapped her hands. Carl, beside the youngest sat in bliss. His fist clutched the remains of something called a doughnut. His mouth was full of it, his eyes closed as he chewed.

The train gathered speed and chugged westward. Evening was already lighting the lamps of the buildings, the coming night graying the streets. Tired immigrants, both in back and front of Lisa, settled themselves to sleep. She did the same, pushing the yellow basket in between the seats and under the window to arrange the two youngest for sleep, their heads pillowed against bundles on the seat, their legs mingling on the basket. Johan, and the four across the aisle, were soon sleeping also. It had been a taxing day.

In spite of the discomfort of the seat that seemed too straight for any back and hard as a block of wood to sit on, Lisa slept.

In early morning she was the first person up to go use the toilet room. A glance out the window surprised her. The train had taken them from winter into spring. There was no snow. Green growth pushed up through wet, rich looking soil. The coach seemed warmer too, as if spring had entered, but not enough to refresh the stale air created by the many sleeping people.

When her family had awakened and had been to the toilet room, she opened one of the boxes of food they had bought for the trip. Johan expressed it for all of them.

"Sausages! Nay, not sausages!"

There was silence as everyone leaned over to see.

"Ugh!" Emilia uttered, and grasped her nose between two fingers to emphasize her disgust.

"That will do," Lisa scholded. "Sausage is good food no matter how often it has to be eaten. There is bread too. Goodness, look how white it is."

Oscar's *puukko* was produced, the protective leather and fur sheath removed, and with quick cuts she gave each of them a piece of sausage.

"We will have to drink water," she said, and lifted the lid of the basket and fished out a mug. The girls went to the water bottle at one end of the coach.

As the sun rose the coach warmed further. By midmorning it was hot. The windows would not open, no matter how hard some of the men tugged at them. One woman made the remark to Lisa, "May be if they washed them they might open. Disgraceful how dirty they are. Now, back home..."

"Back home," Lisa interrupted, "we don't have such a big country, nor so many peole coming into it. Maybe some of us could get work washing and cleaning this coach."

The other woman considered what Lisa had said. Her chin trembling she confided, "I long for the good clean trains of home."

Lisa nodded, but turned her head away to hide her own suddenly moist eyes. The train was speeding through a small town. All at once the girls were shouting, standing up to point out the window.

"Look! Look! There's a little girl who has wheels on her shoes! Mamma! Come see! Quick! Oh, look, there's a boy ahead of her. He has wheels too!"

Before Lisa could get up and over to their window the girl and boy were left behind. Among the children in the coach the excitement was catching. Those who had not seen this remarkable thing came running to ask excited questions. It was true, the Weldman girls reported many times, those two children had been riding swiftly on shoes with wheels, on some kind of hard pathway.

Marta pushed her way out from the cluster of children "Mamma, I want a pair of shoes just like that when we get to where we are going to live," she said.

"You want. You want," Lisa answered with severity. "Remember, Marta, what you want and what we can get for you, or any of us, may not be what we would *like* to have. It will be things we need. Shoes with wheels will not be the first thing anyone in this family will get. Go sit and look out the window."

The train rushed on. Now and then it stopped in what was larger towns. Sometimes people got off, but no many. Underway again, after such a stop, there was new excitement in the coach. A man in a white coat with a huge wicker basket on his arm came from the coach ahead. He called something as he displayed the basket from one seat across to the other. Heads craned. Word was passed back that he had fruit and candies to sell. The children's eyes pleaded.

"You may each choose one thing," Lisa told her family. They chose oranges, each one wrapped in a thin orange paper twisted into a small tassel to keep it around the fruit. They smelled them, hefted the firm roundness between both hands, admired the dimpled skin of sunshine color, once they had removed and folded the thin pretty paper for keeping. Marta announced she had oranges many times at Palmers. The others paid her no attention. They had received oranges in that same house; that long ago Twelfth Night celebration, but had not tasted the fruit since then. They relished the delay in savoring the sweet and juice-filled fruit. It would be that much better if they waited, they agreed.

Lisa's thought raced ahead as she shifted on the hard seat. Would Oscar get the telegram? Would he know for sure where the station was in that big town of Chicago? Would Elvira be there? How would Oscar be? She pushed the next thought away but it persisted. Could he hold to his promise?

The note, "I will take that sin upon my own shoulders," lay in the deepest part of her purse. Without wanting to, she remembered their wedding night. He had been as innocent of sexual experience as herself. The suddenness, the pain, her outcries followed by tears, he had regretted all the years of their marriage, she suspected, yet he had never been able to say so. It was almost two and a half years since he had left for America. Would he be able to do whatever he had planned, to make sure she would not conceive? She shivered, and looked around as though others knew her thoughts.

To busy herself she took both young ones to the toilet. On her way back down the aisle with them she stopped short of her seat. It was not just for him to say. It was for both of them. Yaw, she would see to it. She remembered Berta. Women had their own strength, she thought. This decision was hers to make.

*

"Chicago. Chicago. Chicago." The conductor came through the coach as the train rolled to a stop under a long roof that turned the dark night even darker. He said the name in many different tones as he worked his way past the passengers who were already up in the aisles, their bundles in hand, their suitcases and baskets blocking the way. Lisa bent to see out the windows. She found no one but railroad men pulling huge empty baggage wagons by their long heavy handles. Where was Oscar?

The door at each end clanged open. The exodus began. Once on the platform people headed toward light up beyond the engine that puffed and steamed. Lisa and her seven followed along. No one came to meet them. As they neared the light they saw glass doors and behind it a throng of people. Lisa searched faces, but saw no one who looked like Oscar. How would she find him if he wasn't there? In her anxiety she forgot that he had spelled out in his last letter exactly how to get to Waukegan, should some unforeseen reason keep him from getting to Chicago. He had assured her he would be there, never fear.

But she feared. The line of people slowed as the first ones opened the door and entered the huge waiting area. By the time Lisa and her children got there many were embracing relatives, voices exclaiming in happiness, others shrieking as they located someone of their own.

"Is Pappa here?" Johan asked, too short to see beyond the first line of people. Lisa, about to answer stopped for a hand grasped her shoulder. She turned, and before she could recognize who it was, felt herself enclosed in a strong embrace. There had not been time to set the suitcase down.

"Lisa! Lisa! You are here. My love, my life, you are here. Lisa." Oscar's voice, his mouth on hers. His mustache, so clipped and trimmed, prickled against her lips. She dropped the suitcase. The warmth of his greeting pulled her two worlds together and she felt whole. They separated, but with eyes for no one but each other.

"It's Pappa! It's Pappa! Pappa! Pappa!" The children clamored, Johan in the lead. They pulled at his hands, his arms, stood and smiled unable to get to him past Lisa. He stroked her face. Kissed her again, then looked at the children.

"It can't be," he exclaimed. "These cannot be mine, they are too grown up. This is really you, Maria? Emilia? Paulina? How fine you all look. Where is Marta? Here you are." One by one he embraced them, then stooped, hands on his knees, the better to see the two young ones. He laughed loudly as Carl stooped also, to take the same position, a wide smile returning his. He ruffled the boy's hair, then turned to the youngest. "And this must be Ketty, who is no longer a baby, I see, but a young lady, I think," he pulled both of them to him.

Lisa said, "Oscar, Johan is right next to you."

"Johan," he exclaimed, and was almost knocked back off his heels as the boy pushed past the other two to lock his arms around Oscar's neck. He squeezed so hard he ground his teeth together.

Oscar said, "Step back, let me see you."

Johan remained where he was, and sobbed, "You stayed away so long."

Laughing Oscar agreed. "That I did. You and I shall give thanks to God that I caught up with you, Johan. Now, let me look at you." Solemnly he examined the boy, shook his hand, and told him as soon as he got a little fat on his bones he would certainly be the second man in the family. Johan listened, wiping his eyes with his sleeves.

"You haven't noticed who is standing behind you," Oscar said to Lisa, before he picked up the youngest, and settled her in his arms.

"Elvira!" Lisa exclaimed, only seconds before the girls did. Renewed hugs, greetings, questions, and exclaimations made a new cluster of the Veldmans.

"I didn't know you," Lisa admitted. "It's that you look...so... American," she continued, examining her eldest from head to foot. Elvira. No longer a girl, but a woman. One with a mind of her own, for pressed against the high crown of her hat rested four light blue velvet flowers. Roses, possibly. Blue roses? Ack, the girl...woman ...stated her independence with the hat. If only we two are not lost to each other. I will have to be content with that. The other girls were being loud in their praise of their sister's clothes, eyes big as they looked at her hat.

"You all look as American as anybody else here," Elvira returned, and turned one sister after another around for a better look at their clothes.

"Thanks to the patterns you sent," Maria laughed.

With a frown Lisa asked, "But how can you walk in such a tight skirt? Tighter than the one you left Finland in."

Elvira flushed, gave a self-conscious laugh with a quick look at Oscar. "I can kick, see?" She made a small movement of one leg through a slit in the side of her skirt.

Oscar frowned, but before Lisa could say anything, demanded, "Don't I look the most American of all?"

All eyes turned to him. He had been holding his hat in one hand while he embraced them, but when he had stooped to greet the young ones he had put it on hurriedly. It sat far back, his hair pushed forward onto his forehead. His curls thinner, darker, reflected Carl's thick golden ones.

Johan insisted, "You look like Pappa."

"He's right," Maria said, the others agreeing. "But you have such white teeth."

He laughed, with a glance at Lisa. "You like them?" Everyone nodded. Lisa the hardest.

Oscar looked around at his family again with a satisfied smile. "You all have new hats, I see. Lisa, yours is beautiful. What is that shiny cloth that goes so fancily around it?"

"Satin, Oscar. I'm glad you like it."

"I do, but, I still have my same old hat," he told her, as he slapped the crown with a light touch of his fingers. "Here they call it a derby. What do you say, Lisa. Do I look American?"

She shook her head. "Nay, you look the same, except you are too thin. Those clothes, the same ones you left Finland in, fit you much too loose. I'll have to take them in."

"See?" he asked no one in particular, "already she begins to take care of me. But enough of this. Come, we have another train to catch. Not a long trip this time. I'll carry the suitcase and Ketty. Lisa, you are not to carry anything. You have done enough of it these past weeks, I'm sure."

So have the girls," Lisa answered, and told Elvira, "come, you and I will carry the basket. Twins, take the bundles along with Maria, Johan seems to be attached permanently to Pappa's sleeve. Marta, take Carl by the hand."

Oscar set out, led the way across the huge station waiting room, but turned often to make sure the whole family was with him.

The youngest's face became a beacon for them to follow through the crowds as she looked back over his shoulder. Once she called to Lisa, her arms straining against Oscar as she studied his face. "Who is this man?" she asked.

"Pappa, of course," the girls answered, laughing. "Didn't you hear us all say it? Didn't you tell everybody on the boat you were going to Pappa? Pappa is carrying you."

She turned back to look at him again.

A boy, Johan's age, went past, a bundle of papers under one arm, the other holding a copy up in the air. He yelled something, many times.

"What is that little boy doing here at this time of night?" Lisa asked, and added, "what is he shouting?"

Oscar stopped to switch the youngest to his other shoulder and the suitcase to his other hand. "He yells a headline to help sell his papers.

Wilson's hope of ending the war has had a setback." Lisa saw his pride in being able to translate the boy's words. "The armies of destruction march on to Armageddon," he went on, "America will be in it soon, you will see. That is their plan. Thank God you are here."

But suddenly the war, even Armageddon, was not frightening to Lisa. She was no longer an American widow. Oscar's solid presence, a half step ahead of her, gave her peace. Her family surrounded her, all of it. All there was to be.

Or was it? She glanced at Elvira who, despit her narrow skirt, kept pace easily. Yaw, the girl was in love. Was to be married. There would be children. Grandchildren. American grandchildren.

The family would continue.